The

POSTCARD

from

ITALY

BOOKS BY ANGELA PETCH

The Tuscan Secret
A Tuscan Memory
The Tuscan Girl
The Tuscan House

ANGELA PETCH

The
POSTCARD
from
ITALY

bookouture

Published by Bookouture in 2022

An imprint of Storyfire Ltd.
Carmelite House
50 Victoria Embankment
London EC4Y 0DZ

www.bookouture.com

ISBN: 978-1-80019-963-7
eBook ISBN: 978-1-80019-962-0

To Uncle Billy: Sergeant William Francis Beary, RAF 1584477
and Daddy: Major Kenneth Richard Peter Sutor

You fought on the beaches
You fought on the landing grounds
You never surrendered

'Memory is the treasury and guardian of all things.' Cicero

CHAPTER 1

MARCH 1945

BILLY'S STORY

My eyes are open. I bring my hands to my face. They're bound in rags and when I pull at them, the pain is so bad, I call out. My head drums and thumps and I'm nauseous.

'He's awake.'

I hear the voice of an old man before I hear his shuffling feet. He kneels to peer at me, one tooth in his mouth like a dirty brown tombstone, eyes lit with joy.

'So, you decided to wake up, *figlio mio*. My grandson has come back to us at last.' He moves to the other side of the room and pulls open a door to the outside. 'Roberto is awake,' he calls, before returning to my side.

'I prayed and prayed to see this day,' he says, bending so close that I can smell onions on his breath. He sobs, tears running down the lines of his weathered face, splashing onto mine.

'Hush, Nonno,' a younger voice says.

Now there is a boy at his side. The pair speak in an Italian different from the way I know. I understand most of what they say but they pronounce words with a strange inflexion, some I've never heard.

'Roberto has come back to us,' the old man says over and over and the boy shushes him, speaking gently. 'Nonno, *calmati!* Sit over there while I tend to him. Stir the soup for me. *Stai buono.* Calm down.'

I watch as the old man hobbles to the fire, glancing at me as he moves, as if to make sure I am still there. Then he throws a couple of sticks on the glowing ashes. Flames dance about the stone walls of this unusual, conical-shaped space, crudely whitewashed, disappearing to a blackened hole above where I lie.

'Where am I?' I say, struggling to sit. But the room spins, nausea rises again and I slump down, closing my eyes to stop the swimming in my head.

I feel a cloth, damp and soothing on my face, and my eyes flicker open to see the boy's look of concern. 'You still have a fever. Lie still.'

I give in and let my mind drift away to the crackle of flames, my body growing heavier as I sink down, down, down to the oblivion of sleep.

It is dark in the room when I wake again. The fire, where the boy and the old man sit opposite each other, hisses gentle heat. They talk in hushed voices and the old man puffs on a long pipe, the scent of strong tobacco wafting to my nostrils. I need a fag and I lean on my elbows to feel in my pockets but I am naked beneath the covers and my hands are still wrapped up.

The boy moves quickly to my side. He's older than I first thought. Maybe fifteen or sixteen, his skin olive brown, his eyes great pools of brown and black.

'How do you feel?'

'Where am I?'

My head is full of mist as I look around me. I need something to still my nerves.

'I could do with a smoke,' I say, my voice sounding croaky to my ears.

He frowns and moves to a niche in the wall. 'We found this in the pocket of your trousers,' he says, holding up a crumpled package. 'And a packet of matches. Nonno thinks they were *americano* cigarettes. But I'm sorry. He took a liking to them and now they're finished.' He holds the packets near my face and I read the brand names: Woodbines. Swan Vesta.

I shrug my shoulders. 'I don't think they are mine,' I say. I really have no idea.

The old man offers me his pipe. 'You liked to puff on this when you were a boy, Roberto.'

He places it gently in my mouth and I splutter when the vile fumes seep down my throat and I shake my head.

'Nonno, leave him in peace.'

When I have finished coughing, I ask again. 'Where am I?'

'Nonno found you on the beach,' the boy tells me.

'You fell from the sky with your long white wings,' the old man says. 'Our Roberto has returned to us like a guardian angel.'

The boy shakes his head, almost imperceptibly, and takes his grandfather back to the settle by the fire.

'Nonno Domenico thinks you are my brother,' he tells me when he comes back to where I lie. 'But Roberto is dead. Nonno's mind...' he says, lowering his voice to a half-whisper, '... his mind is somewhere else.'

'I don't think my name is Roberto.'

'What is your name?'

I open my mouth to answer but my mind is blank.

'I don't know. I really don't.'

He bites his lip. 'You don't know? Or you don't want to say? Signore, we won't harm you. You're safe here.'

I shake my head again. The dizziness returns and I lie back. 'I truly do not know what my name is.'

'You have been with us for five nights now. You must be hungry. Maybe after you've eaten, you'll remember.'

I watch him as he moves about the kitchen area. He ladles liquid into an earthenware bowl from a black pot that sits in the ashes. He sprinkles herbs from a jar and the smell of fennel is strong like aniseed. Then he slices a thick piece of dark bread, holding the loaf to his chest the way I have seen it done before. Where I have seen it and who cut the bread this way, I cannot fathom.

Setting the bowl by my side, he helps me sit up and I breathe in his scent of sea and herbs as he arranges a pillow behind my back. My head is dizzy but I force myself to focus on the wall opposite where curtains cover two archways and then he begins to spoon warm broth into my mouth. It is good and I could eat more but the bowl is soon empty.

'I think you should wait to see if that settles in your stomach, signore,' the boy says, 'before you have more. You've been very sick. Nonno helped me sponge you down.'

I am moved that these strangers have cared for me like a baby, sheltering me in their simple home.

'I am sorry,' I say.

'Don't be. How could we leave you to die?'

The old man hands me a pair of patched trousers and a shirt, the collar and cuffs frayed. 'Anto washed these for you, Roberto. We knew you would return one day.' He smiles his one-toothed grin at me again and I nod my head.

'*Grazie*,' I reply, adding 'Nonno' as an afterthought to my thank you, and I am rewarded with a shy smile from the boy, whose name I've now learned is Anto.

. . .

I don't know for how long I sleep. As he removes the bindings from my hands, Anto tells me that I have been drifting in and out of consciousness for more than twenty-four hours. He nods his head, seemingly satisfied, and tells me that everything is healing well, that fresh air will do the rest but I must keep the bandage on my head.

'And you must keep your hands clean, signore.'

I look at my hands, turning them this way and that. The skin is inflamed and as I try to flex my fingers, they feel taut.

'The saltwater helped their healing,' he says.

I cannot remember how my hands came to be burnt and I continue to stare at them, hoping for a clue, but nothing comes.

'Come,' he says, helping me to my feet. 'It's time for you to sit outside.'

I feel wobbly but he steadies me. He is at least a head shorter than me, his frame slight and wiry and I worry about leaning on him but he encourages me on. Outside, the dazzling sunlight makes me squint. The cluster of buildings where I have been sheltered is built of stone, a rather temporary kind of dwelling it seems to me, with three conical roofs topped with stone embellishments. As far as I can tell, there is no mortar bonding the stones, as of drystone walls. We are surrounded by dozens of olive trees and other trees in blossom that I do not recognise, their flowers pink and white against a clear blue sky. Chickens scratch about the scrubby grass but most of the rust-red earth around the buildings is freshly dug and tilled. Tethered to a fruit tree is a goat, secured with a long chain.

Anto leads me to a stone bench next to the door and tells me to soak up the morning sun. Nonno is bent double like a hairpin, weeding a patch of ground about twenty metres from the building, and he looks up at me and waves. '*Buongiorno*, Roberto. *Dormito bene?* Did you sleep well?'

I wave back and assure him that I slept like a baby. And I did. I am like an infant: fed, clothed and washed. But it feels wrong and I want to know why I am here. I can't let these good people care for me like this. When Anto starts to wield an axe to chop a pile of firewood, I insist on helping, but my head swims after hewing three logs and I have to return to my bench.

I think he understands my frustration as I watch him work, perspiration stains spreading over his shirt. He wipes his face with a kerchief and comes over.

'You must be patient,' he says, as he drinks from a water bottle bound with woven wicker. Then he wipes the neck and offers it to me.

I shake my head. 'Thank you. I'm not thirsty. What work have I done? I don't deserve water. I am useless.'

'When you're stronger, you can help us.'

'I can't stay here long. I need to know who I am. Where I come from.'

'It's not a good time to go wandering about on your own. I heard in the market square that the war is almost over. But there is confusion everywhere. They're hunting for deserters and people are taking revenge for what has happened over these past years. You're a stranger here. The way you talk... you're not *pugliese*, I'm sure—'

I interrupt. 'War? What war?'

He frowns, incredulity on his face. 'The war. Against the *tedeschi*. Surely you know that there's a war going on and we've been fighting the Germans for two years now? How could you not know? Everybody knows...' Then he breaks off. '*Mi scusate,* signore... your memory. I didn't mean to upset you. But... the uniform you were wearing...'

'What uniform?' I ask. I put my head in my hands, frustration, anger, despair bubbling up in me like a shaken bottle of beer and I realise I do not have the faintest idea of how or why I landed up in this place.

'If I can find where Nonno Domenico hid your belongings, then maybe that'll help you,' Anto says, coming to stand near

me, blotting out the sun, so that when I look up at him, I read in
his eyes how earnest he is. He turns to look at his grandfather,
who is singing as he works, bending to tug at weeds as he makes
his way down rows of seedlings. 'But Nonno told me nobody
must find your uniform. He's frightened you'll put on your
wings and fly away.' He smiles at me and shrugs his skinny
shoulders. 'What can I do, signore? His mind is fragile...'

I look up and see his anxiety.

'I'm sorry. I have lumbered you with more trouble. But, tell
me, how did your grandfather find me? And what are these
belongings you talk about?'

'He appeared from the beach, carrying you on his shoulders,
signore. I wasn't down there when he discovered you. He'd
been tending his fishing nets and he told me he looked up to see
you fall from the sky, with long wings trailing behind you.'

I shake my head. 'I can't remember. Everything in my head
is a blank.'

He looks at me curiously. 'I don't believe you are a *tedesco*.
You speak fluent Italian. You're one of us, I'm sure.'

The only fact I can verify from his statement is that I speak
roughly the same language as my two rescuers. 'I suppose I am,'
I say. 'But... I feel so strange, I think I should see a doctor. I need
to get back to normal.'

I hear his intake of breath and see the way his shoulders
hunch up.

'Apart from the market once a month,' he says, 'we don't
venture anywhere. It's too... dangerous. And... I've been asked
more than once why I haven't enlisted—' He breaks off and I
can tell he is terrified so I don't insist.

'But surely you're too young to be a soldier?'

'Yes. But I've lost my documents, signore. So, I can't prove
it... Nonno and I – we try not to go too far these days. We keep
to ourselves, but I'll see if I can find where he concealed your
things. One thing I'm certain of, signore. Although you speak

Italian like an Italian – you're not from Puglia. Are you from Rome, perhaps?'

I shake my head. '*Non lo so*. I do not know.'

An idea comes to me. 'Do you have paper I can write on?'

'I've an old copy book of Roberto's, *si*.'

'I will keep notes. Writing down what I do from now on might help me remember what I have done before.'

He shrugs his shoulders. 'It can do no harm.'

While the boy is gone, I attempt to gather my scattered thoughts from the cotton wool of my brain. How can I not have known that a war is waging? What part have I played in it? Has a battle injury caused me to be the miserable wretch I am reduced to? Which side am I on? I speak Italian but I think in English. These things of mine that the old man has hidden... if I can find them, maybe I can find answers to who I am. The thoughts tangle further until I can't think logically.

I shake my head in an attempt to knock back sense to my addled brain but it only serves to make the pain return. Sinking back against the wall, I stare at the blue sky before closing my eyes. I can't stay in this place forever. But if I am to leave, I need to grow stronger first.

CHAPTER 2

MARCH, 1945

FRIDAY, MARCH 30, 1945.

And so when the boy brings me his tattered notebook, and after I ask him what day it is, I begin to jot down events, starting from today's date that Anto shows me on a calendar hanging by the hearth. I want to record where I have landed up, how hard Nonno Domenico works, how strong he is for an old man of eighty-two, as he keeps proudly telling me. And he surely is, to have carried me on his shoulders. His stories are repetitive, but I do not mind as it helps reinforce some kind of recent past. All these happenings are incidental, seemingly unimportant but they give me a framework. What happened before these days is a blank sheet of history. Will writing it all down help claw back my memory? And what is hiding in the darkest recesses of my mind?

SATURDAY, MARCH 31, 1945.

I draw a picture of the *trulli* where these two good souls live, for that is what these strange buildings are called. Anto explains they are temporary constructions because in the past, peasants working on the land had to dismantle them quickly to avoid paying landlords when the tax collectors were around.

SUNDAY, APRIL 1, 1945.

I roll up my sleeves and help Domenico repair a smaller *trullo* that sits beyond the ones where we live. Anto covers my hands with a clean layer of rags again and warns me not to overdo it, as the skin will not heal properly.

WEDNESDAY, APRIL 4, 1945.

Inside the small *trullo*, Domenico keeps string and tools for his fishing nets, a long-handled hoe, a rake and a sharp-ended spade. Strings of onions hang from the walls as well as bundles of sweet-smelling thyme and pungent sprigs of fennel flowers, their seeds beginning to dry. Anto uses this herb a lot and we share a small bottle of fennel liqueur after supper and he tells me it is his eighteenth birthday. I am surprised, because he looks younger, his skin smooth and free of facial hair.

FRIDAY, APRIL 6, 1945.

I venture away from the *trulli* for the first time and walk with the old man to the beach down a steep path lined with aromatic plants. I inhale their pleasant scent as we brush past and the old man cuts straggly branches and tells me we will collect them on our return. '*Rosmarino*,' he tells me as I hurry to keep up. 'Very good with baked fish. We always eat fish on a Friday.' His mind is feeble, unlike his body, and I appreciate that more as he tells me how this is the route he carried me from the sea. He seems to grow less rattle-brained as we approach the ocean, his conversation more lucid.

'My heart swelled with happiness at finding you again, Roberto, and you were as light as a feather when I carried you up this path.'

Anto and I have decided my name from now on is to be Roberto. It keeps Domenico happy and it is less complicated. I am no nearer to learning who I really am and Anto suggests we will tell anybody who snoops that I am his brother, invalided from the war because of a brain injury. I am still weak, wobbly on my feet and plagued with headaches but as the days pass, I grow a little stronger and I hope my mind will eventually heal too.

'You are the same stature as Roberto,' he says. 'And your hair is dark too. Your brown eyes are flecked with green, but his were dark as chestnuts.' His own eyes are sad as he speaks. 'But you will have to act a bit soft, *tonto*, if anybody starts to talk to you. And I shall tell them you have lost your memory.'

'That won't be difficult,' I respond, my mouth pulled into a rueful smile. In the last couple of days, I have begun to wonder if I am as weak as my mind. Am I a coward? Fleeing from a war I do not want to fight?

The beach is a calming place, the shore a mixture of flat, bluish cobbles and silver-grey sand. In the sheer rock face that we descend, there is a deep cave above the waterline where Domenico keeps a boat, and crates for carrying fish. At the edge of the bay on the left-hand side, a strange wooden construction sits on stilts in the sea, looking for all the world like a huge insect with gangly legs. I wander over to investigate. There are steps leading to a platform holding a small shed, its door gaping on broken hinges. Two long poles with shreds of net protrude over the sea's surface and a mess of wires and ropes tangled like torn cobwebs.

'Our poor old *trabucco*,' the old man says. 'You can help me repair it and then we can fish from up there and we won't have to use my boat and fight the storms.' He sits on an upturned bucket, bent over a small fishing net and I sit nearby and watch. The action of his gnarly hands threading string through to mend the holes is mesmerising. Despite days of rest, I am weary and soon my eyes begin to droop and I lean back against a rock in the gentle sun and doze.

A gull screeches somewhere and I am on a different beach, the temperature cooler, children's voices squealing as the sea rolls and splashes to the edge of the stone-strewn shore. My young legs are bare but I am wearing a jumper, the wool scratchy against my bare skin. I am filling a metal pail with sand, hunkered to pat it with a small wooden spade, my father's hands, hairs dark on his fingers, arranging shells around the edge of a sandcastle. 'We will buy a *gelato* soon, but it won't be like Pappy's,' a woman's voice says and I turn to look up at her. She is beautiful, her fair hair swept back from her face in a colourful scarf. Her face is like the statue I see at church and I scamper to snuggle into my mother's arms.

A bony finger prods my shoulder and I am torn from my dream as Domenico tells me it is time to take out the boat. 'The blue fish are ready for us,' he says, pointing at the mended net and telling me to load it into the boat and to help him push the vessel into the shallows. The tide has come almost to the edge of the cave, scouring the shore with shells and pebbles. Rolling up my patched trousers, I push the boat deeper into the water and then climb in, falling clumsily against the seat.

'Eee, Roberto, careful, boy! Have you forgotten how to handle a boat?'

I make a mental note to myself that whatever life I had before, it was most likely not working on the sea. After a futile attempt at rowing, Domenico spits out a filthy oath and takes the oars.

'Keep busy and watch for fish,' he orders, annoyance in his voice.

How on earth am I supposed to look for fish above water? I

scan the horizon and then I spy a shadow near the surface, broken by the occasional leap of silver. I point excitedly towards distant rocks. 'Over there!' I shout.

The old man shakes his head. 'We must wait until they come further towards us. Eee, *ragazzo*, where have you been to forget all this? Those rocks are dangerous.'

Shading my eyes to peer towards the headland, I see that what I first perceived to be the slender stem of a tree is the mast of a sunken boat. If Domenico had listened to me, we would have torn a hole in our hull to join it.

Suddenly the water around us is a ripple of rolling silver. The old man yells at me to help him as he casts his net. I feel its pull as many fish tug to escape.

'*Basta, basta,*' Domenico shouts above the slap of waves against the boat. 'We have enough. Leave the rest for another day. Today the ocean has been generous.'

When we beach, I jump into the shallows and use all my strength to push the boat to shore. Domenico shakes his head and laughs. 'Wait for the water to help bring it in. *Porca miseria*, boy! Do you not remember a bloody thing?'

It might be the right moment to tell him I am not his Roberto. That, as far as my fractured memory can tell me, I have never fished before and I am trying my damned best to help him today. But something tells me it would be cruel as well as pointless, and so I apologise.

'It's been too long, Nonno. I am sorry.'

He nods his head. 'Yes. Far too long. Years in prison in an African desert where there is no sea. I can understand why you are rusty. But we will soon get you back to old times. Don't you worry, Roberto.'

Have I been in Africa? I have no idea. Once again, I rack my poor brain to conjure up a past that is lost to me. The old man falls silent. He is puffing on his pipe again and this time I take up his offer to share and he tells me he will hunt out another pipe to use. I must have been a smoker in my former life because this time as I drag the nicotine deep into my lungs, the sensation is good. It relaxes me.

With the boat safely anchored, Domenico sorts his catch. I recognise sardines and mackerel, their colours iridescent as they flap in the sunlight. But there are larger blue fish with wide mouths and sharp teeth that he calls *palamita* that I have never seen before.

'We shall have a feast tonight. Anto will cook these over the fire on skewers of rosemary.' He presses a finger to his cheek and makes a circular motion, moving his fist, and I recognise the gesture: an appreciation of good food.

I reach into the haul to discard a couple of sea urchins, their black spines spiky like tiny hedgehogs, and he slaps at my hand. 'Have you forgotten that too? I used to have to stop you and Anto bickering for these. Eee!' There and then he pulls out his knife and carefully cuts them open. From his pocket he produces a lemon and cuts that too, before squeezing juice over the yellow creatures inside and then he swallows one raw. I copy him. The taste is not unpleasant and, I am sure, new to me. Feeling that some kind of progress has been made today with my memory, I nod my head and tell the old man that it's good. I like it. But my pleasure is due to the realisation that I am discovering more about myself. I am sure of what I have never done before. And in that sense, I am owning a snatch of my former self.

'The rest we take back for Anto. These *ricci* are a favourite,' Domenico says.

I carry the net and crate for him and we return up the steep path, the sun beginning to drop to the sea, where the waters absorb its colour. And then I hear a sound. A sound that rings bells. The sound of aircraft high above, the drone of its engines familiar. Placing my burdens down, I gaze up, shading my eyes with my right hand as three planes, glinting like the silver fish we have caught today, pass overhead.

'Liberators,' I say, without thinking twice.

'*Inglesi*,' the old man adds.

And, without a shadow of a doubt, I know that both facts are spot on.

CHAPTER 3

When we are back from the sea, Anto's words bubble out as he pulls me to one side and tells me in a half-whisper that he has worked out where Nonno has concealed his treasures. Perhaps I should have searched for them myself, but there has not been a right moment. The boy or the old man are always nearby. My heart leaps and I ask Anto if I can see them right now, but he shakes his head.

'We will have to wait for the right time to look. I don't want to upset him. And Nonno has a temper. *Mamma mia*, what a temper he has when he is riled! I believe he has hidden your things because he is afraid you might leave us once you see them.'

'You talk about my things but I have no idea what they are, Anto. Tell me where they are...'

He gestures to me to be quiet as the old man approaches up the path, carrying a stick on his shoulder with a net containing fish.

I almost wish Anto had not mentioned his find at all, as my curiosity is now piqued. Nonno's hidden treasures might reveal more about myself. My real self, for I am living a curious existence at the moment, disguised as somebody else. But despite my impatience, I know I must wait. Anto knows his grandfather's ways best and I shall respect his advice. To distract my thoughts, I help out by breaking sticks for the cooking fire.

We sit for a while outside after a wonderful fish meal. As the day fades, Nonno puts away the hens. They follow him as he walks slowly towards their coop, and he bribes them to enter with his dish of fish skins and bones, scattering bits around their cage as they squawk and squabble.

'A fox has been seen roundabouts,' Anto says. 'And a neighbour lost her chickens last week to two men on the run. She thinks they were *tedeschi* runaways refusing to fight any longer. Now that they know they won't win this war, they're desperate. They ordered her to prepare a meal and one of them pointed a gun while she rolled out the pasta.'

'Remind me how long this war has been going on,' I say.

'Too long. First, we were on the side of the *tedeschi* but since 1943, and with Il Duce no longer in power, we have been on the side of the *inglesi* and *americani* – the *alleati*. They say fighting will end soon, but I'll only believe it when all the bells in Puglia ring out.'

He looks at me, a frown puckering his thin face. 'Do you remember *nothing* about all this?'

'Nothing.'

'Your mind doesn't want you to know. Something very bad must have happened.'

My head begins to ache and once again, dizziness returns. Suddenly, I am exhausted.

'Forgive me, Anto. I need to sleep.'

Nonno has given up his bed for me, despite my protests, and that night as I settle down on his old metal cot that creaks with every movement, I try to imagine the possessions that he has secreted away. Maybe tonight I might dream of who I was and, in the morning, my old self will have returned.

SATURDAY, APRIL 7, 1945.

After a good sleep, I am still Roberto. I go outside to fetch water from the well to sluice myself. Anto is already there, gutting the remainder of the fish we caught yesterday. He works quickly, swatting at flies trying to feed off the catch.

'I'll make you coffee but I have to preserve these first before they turn bad,' he says.

'Can I help?'

He laughs, his teeth white against olive skin, sunlight glinting at a crucifix on a chain round his neck.

'With those damaged hands, you'll be more hindrance than help, signore.'

'Am I not Roberto this morning?'

'It sounds strange on my tongue. Go and help Nonno in his vegetable patch if you want some work and later, when the time is right, I shall show you where your things are hidden.'

Domenico is busy tying wayward tomato shoots to sticks. I watch as he pinches between the slender stems and when I try to help, he slaps at my hand and tells me I have pinched out a flower.

'They must have stuffed that head of yours with so much soldier nonsense that there's no room now for daily things that matter,' he says, a look of disgust on his face.

'Here,' he says, shoving a metal bucket into my hands. 'Gather stones instead. Surely you can manage that, *figlio*?' And then he leans up to ruffle my hair, the back of my head still bandaged from the wound taking so long to heal. '*Povero* Roberto,' he says, 'some of your poor brain must have fallen from your head when you fell down to us.'

For one hour I work hard by his side and soon I have collected half a dozen buckets of limestones, big and small, which Domenico directs me to add to a huge pile in the corner of the olive grove.

For our midday meal, Anto has prepared a tasty fish soup he calls *ciambotto*. To various shellfish he's added potatoes, aubergines and tomatoes. Domenico slurps at the shells, sucking out the contents and Anto smiles at his enjoyment, topping up his tumbler of strong red wine several times, which the old man knocks back, belching loudly when he has finished. He is like a child, uninhibited, seemingly without a care in the world.

I help Anto clear away the dirty plates and then as soon as Domenico has settled himself down for his siesta, the boy wipes his hands on a cloth and gestures to follow him outside.

'We must be quick,' he says as I follow him under the olive trees to the little *trullo* where Domenico stores his tools. 'He doesn't usually sleep for more than one hour. But I made sure to give him extra wine today.'

'I noticed.'

At the back of the *trullo*, he pushes crates and a wooden barrel to one side and points to the earthen floor, the colour of the soil darker than elsewhere.

'We should dig here,' he says, taking the long-handled, sharp-edged *pala* from where it leans against the wall.

I take it from him and begin to dig, my heart hammering not so much from the effort, more because I am anxious – and at the same time, curious as to what we shall find. The earth is soft, recently worked. At about twenty-five centimetres down, my spade reveals a metal ring.

'*Eccola!*' Anto says. 'I knew it. Here it is!'

We work together and he uses a small bucket to scoop out soil until we can pull up a wooden box, about 65 by 35 centimetres, two hands deep. There is a circular metal ring at the top to pull it open.

'It's the box Nonno packed to take to America but at the last minute he refused to board the ship,' he tells me. 'He was so in love with Nonna that he ran away instead and they married very young. They lied about their age to the priest. Nonno stores all his treasures in here.'

He opens the lid and pulls out metres of creamy-white silk.

'Your angel wings,' he says.

Domenico's wings are a parachute. He described me as falling from the sky like an angel. So, if this parachute truly belonged to me, then I must have jumped from an aircraft. I take the material from Anto, marvelling at the silk running through my fingers, willing my mind to recall if Nonno's angel was really me. Before I have a chance to examine the rest of the contents of the box, the old man rushes through the open door into the *trullo*.

'*Vigliacchi*! Miserable cowards – what are you doing with my things?' he hollers, picking up the spade from where it leans against the wall. He raises it above his head, his face contorted with rage and Anto screams at the top of his voice.

'Nonno, stop! You'll kill him.'

The old man is strong but he is old and I wrench the tool from his hands and fling it outside while he continues his rant.

'I knew you were up to no good. Plying me with extra wine. You have no right to meddle with my things—' He steps towards me and I raise both my hands in surrender, attempting to placate him.

'You are right, Nonno,' I say in as calm a voice as I can muster and I hand the parachute back. It has unravelled and he pulls it to himself, trying to fold the slippery material, which keeps unfurling and tangling round his bandy legs. I move to help him but he pushes me away. 'I should have burned your wings, Roberto,' he says. 'You have to stay here with us.' He begins to sob. 'Too many of our loved ones have disappeared. Stay here, stay here.'

He lets me pull him into my arms. His head reaches my chest and I let him cry, his bony shoulders heaving.

'Nonno. Let me brew you a good strong cup of chicory

coffee,' Anto says. 'We'll put some fennel liqueur in too. *Vieni*, Nonno. Come,' he says, bending to speak to his grandfather where he clings to me. 'Pack the wings away. We promise we won't go near them again. We promise, don't we, Roberto?'

After the old man has stuffed the parachute into his wooden case, muttering all the while, we walk slowly back to the larger *trullo*, the old man between us. He drinks his coffee and then he falls fast asleep, no doubt exhausted from his emotional outburst. We leave him to rest and we step quietly outside.

The sun is hot and we sit beneath a fig tree, its branches trailing almost to the ground, creating a canopy of shade.

'I'm sorry, signore,' Anto says. 'He's getting worse. If you'd met him even six months ago, you wouldn't recognise him as he is now. I guess he's worn out with sadness. I hoped once we returned to Mattinata, he would be more at peace with the world.'

It is the first time he has spoken to me of his past. Maybe it is because he is more at ease with me now. As each day passes, I witness his many acts of kindness with his sick grandfather. And with me, he is patient too. He is a caring and sensitive lad, wary of pushing me to deal with my own past. A past I cannot recall. A past that teases me.

'Where did you come from?' I blurt out, breaking the silence that has fallen between us.

He sighs. 'I was born here but when I was very young, we moved to the city of Foggia with my parents, my brother Roberto as well as Nonno and Nonna. We all lived together in a new house near the station. My father had a job at one of the big new factories where they make paper from straw. He did well and became a foreman. Not bad for a man who had always worked as a fisherman. Every August without fail, when the factory closed, we came here for a month. I looked forward to that time so much. Life here is simpler but my parents wanted Roberto to have a good education in Foggia and here there is only a primary school. Everything was fine until the outbreak of this war…'

He breaks off and I wait for him to continue, pleased that he can trust me with his story. He is struggling with tears and clenches his hands, his knuckles white as he bites his lips and tries to compose himself.

'Nonna died first. She'd been ill for a long time. Then, Roberto enlisted. We received a telegraph to tell us he had died in Africa. After that my parents were killed in a traffic accident. A Jeep, driven by a crazy soldier. He knocked them down as they crossed the road by the cathedral.'

He unclenches his fists and looks into the distance. 'So, then there was only Nonno and myself. Foggia was in ruins; there wasn't much left for the planes to flatten and we came here. Nonno had always wanted to return to the place where he was born. Until we left for Foggia, he'd fished every day of his life. I don't know how many times he's told me that in these last months. Since we've been back here, he's calmer. It's the best place for him.'

'I am sorry, Anto. You have been through too much.'

He shrugs and runs his hands through his spiky hair. 'There are many people worse off.' He stands and hitches up his baggy trousers, pulling the string tighter in the loops that keeps them from falling below his skinny ankles. 'Nonno is all I have left. I have to look after him, signore. There's nobody else.'

'Let me help you. After all you have done for me, it is only right. And I understand better now why it is best that you continue to call me Roberto,' I say. 'For the sake of Domenico, I will continue to be your brother. I think you are right not to upset him with the fear I might disappear.'

'You're very kind. But, your own memory…' he says. 'You're very young. Not like Nonno, whose memory will soon disappear completely. I've seen it with so many old people. If your memory comes back, then you won't want to stay here. There'll be a family waiting for you somewhere, I'm sure.'

'Let's take it day by day. I'll stay as long as I can.'

As soon as I utter those words, I know it will not be hard for me to remain here. I'm admitting to myself that these two souls are the only ones who know me right now. The person I have become. I should hate to leave. It would be like jumping into a fire and I am not ready yet.

'I must admit it would help if you kept an eye on him. I can't be with him all the time and he does tend to wander off.'

'Of course. It's the least I can do to pay my way. But I will recompense you as soon as I can.'

He waves his hands to stop me and then hesitates before asking me if I would mind sleeping at night in Nonno's *trullo* store instead of sharing with them. 'There's not enough room for three in here,' he says. 'We can find you bedding to use and I'll explain that you've longed to sleep on your own after years of being with soldiers.'

'That could work,' I say. 'Of course I don't mind.' I want to add that the old man's snores often keep me awake and it will be a relief to have a sleep-filled night, but it sounds ungrateful and so I don't mention it.

Anto helps me clear a space to sleep in the small *trullo* store and I carry Nonno's treasure box to put beside his bed in the larger building. My fingers burn to rummage through the rest of the contents stored under the parachute, desperate to see if I can learn more about myself. There might be more clues. But I decide to wait. There will be a better opportunity, I am certain.

That evening, Nonno is subdued. He sits on his box, staring into the fire, watching Anto preparing a meal of fish and polenta. Anto sings as he works, his voice high and clear, not yet broken, like the voice of a chorister. He urges his grandfather to join in. '*Dai.* Go on, sing with me, Nonno. Roberto loves it when you sing the old tunes, don't you, Roberto?' he says, winking at me.

But Nonno remains silent and before darkness falls, I bid them both goodnight and make my way to the little *trullo*. Before turning in on my makeshift bed of straw, I smoke the pipe that Nonno has unearthed for me. It will have to do for the moment but it would be good to get hold of cigarettes. Leaning against the stony wall, I jot down the day's events in my note-book. Inside the *trullo*, I lie down and pull a worn blanket over my shoulders. Outside, the sound of the sea sucking at the shore helps me drift to sleep.

That night, I have a series of dreams, as clear as pictures in a comic book.

CHAPTER 4

APRIL, 1945

SUNDAY, APRIL 8, 1945.

A girl with blonde hair and scarlet lips hums as we dance to the latest Glenn Miller tune. We kiss and I inhale her perfume, the faces of my friends around me dancing in a blur of colour as we all jive and jitterbug to the band.

I walk her home and as we slip and slide over compacted snow, she hangs on, pulling me behind the bins as we say our long goodnight. The snow is cold through my thin soles but she's warm under her dress and she lets me do more than I've done before. Her name escapes me but my dream is full of her mouth and soft curves. In the mess of moonlight her face is blue, her lips a gash of red and I am cold as ice as she floats away.

I am in a tightly enclosed space, perishing cold, icicles forming on my nose as I am shaken around, my head scrunched against a low roof, my feet glued to the floor in heavy, fur-lined boots, and outside this confined space the world is full of lights which scratch a black sky. Vomit is in my mouth and I swallow it down as I am turned, turned, turned and plummeted earthwards, screaming for my mother as I fall...

. . .

I feel a hand, gentle against my forehead and I struggle to open my eyes. My body is drenched in sweat and I shiver, my teeth chattering.

'You had a nightmare,' Anto tells me. 'And your fever has returned. I think you have a touch of malaria,' he says as he dips a cloth into a basin of cold water and squeezes out excess liquid before dabbing my face. 'We heard you shouting.'

I am shaking. My dream was very real and it takes me a few seconds to register where I am: in Nonno's little *trullo*, onions hanging from the stone wall next to my straw bed. Daylight pours in through the door and I steady my breathing.

'You were shouting in a language that wasn't Italian,' Anto tells me.

'Pass me my notebook,' I ask and when he hands it to me, I write down what I dreamt, racking my fevered brain for a name, my hands shaking. I have to pin my past, bring it back to life with my stub of pencil. My instincts tell me that these dreams are more than hallucinations caused by fever: they are a part of me. I try to recall as much as I can before the memory of them slips away with the day, and I scribble words frantically, without punctuation.

'What are you writing, Roberto?'

'I'm trying to make sense. There was music, dancing, somewhere very, very cold in my nightmare.' I read out the words I've written and hold them up for Anto to see.

He shakes his head. 'I can't read that.'

'Dancing, Glenn Miller, freezing, snow,' I read out.

'Those aren't Italian words,' he says.

'I know.'

'What languages do you speak – besides your Italian?'

'*Inglese*,' I tell him. And when I follow that with, 'English', the word slips easily from my tongue, for the first time since I've been here.

'So, Roberto's wings – the parachute – you came from an English plane, or maybe American. They speak the same language, I think,' Anto summarises. 'You are either *inglese* or *americano* but you speak good Italian.'

'I think you are probably right.'

It's a relief to know this one, key thing about myself. It feels right too. *I am English.*

'There are many *inglesi, americani* and *canadesi* planes in the valleys round Foggia. When you feel stronger, you could visit one of those bases. Somebody might know who you are. But it isn't safe at the moment.'

He repeats what Nonno has pleaded. 'Stay here with us. Stay until you are stronger.'

I have little energy to protest. 'One day I will repay you for your kindness,' I say. I am really shivering now despite the sunlight creeping through the door. I cannot stop my shakes and my teeth bang against each other.

'You need medicine,' he says. 'Mamma used to make us eat grapefruit and lemons each morning to keep malaria at bay. She added cinnamon, which I don't have. But I can find the fruit for you as well as different herbs.'

He stands up. 'Stay there, Roberto. Rest. Nonno will bring you another blanket. I'll be back soon.'

He returns with a concoction of green liquid. '*Assenzio,*' he says, 'wormwood,' as I pull a face at the bitter tea. 'Drink it all up and then try to sleep.'

Sometime later, he returns and tells me to sit up. He helps me drink a sour citric mixture of grapefruit and lemon.

'I can find more of this fruit after dark,' he says. 'My neighbour won't miss a lemon or two from his land. Now is not the time to go into town to buy more from the market.'

I am too weak to argue, powerless and feeble. When I have finished drinking, I lie down again and sleep the sleep of the dead.

I am floating by the light of the moon. I have pushed up through layers of clouds and below me I see what resemble flies crawling over a large white tablecloth. My eyes are sore and watering. I am freezing, my hands have no feeling and I long to rest, to crawl beneath warm covers and sink into blessed sleep. But there is no respite from the white glare. Suddenly one of the flies in the distance approaches, its body huge, silver and menacing. Flashes of fire burst around me. There is nowhere to hide. I am rescued by an enveloping cloud and I pillow myself into softness and find precious moments of peace.

WEDNESDAY, APRIL 18, 1945.

Anto tells me I slept on and off for several days until my fever broke. Nonno comes to help me wash, sponging my body down, talking to me all the while as if I am his little Roberto. I am still weak and it takes another ten days until I start to feel stronger. Each day, I mark off the date in the tatty notebook and every day I have to drink disgusting concoctions that Anto prepares for me and he insists that as soon as possible, he will get hold of proper medicine. 'There is no quinine to be had at the moment, but I can find you Atabrine.'

'I have no money to pay for it,' I say.

'Please do not worry, Roberto. You will pay us back when you can.'

In my weakened state, the generosity of these people brings me to tears and I marvel at the gentle kindness of this boy, who seems older than his years.

THURSDAY, MAY 3, 1945.

I lose track of time. There is no radio, no newspaper to tell me what day it is as they pass by. If it were not for the jottings in my notebook, I would have no idea of the date. I begin to wonder if this is even correct. This place is isolated. Since arriving here, I have not seen another person besides Anto and his grandfather. We are far from any road, our *trulli* hidden amongst hectares of olive trees that stretch far and wide to the sea. Today I wake early to the call of the cockerel. For the first time in many days, the dizziness has gone and when I stand up and stretch my stiff body, I feel almost normal. I emerge from Nonno's *trullo* to a new morning. There is a slight wisp of mist caught in the trees. The sun is a hazy ball in the sky. There is nobody about in the yard and no smoke curling from the larger *trullo*, but the chickens have been let out and they cluck and scavenge beneath the trees.

I call out to Anto and Domenico but there is no reply. A tumbler of fresh goat's milk and a corner of bread sit on the table inside the main *trullo*. I am hungry and wolf it down. Feeling strong, I take the axe and manage to chop half a dozen logs. The day is already warm and I am soon dripping with sweat. The idea of plunging into the ocean tempts me and I make my way down the footpath I last trod with the old man. The sea in the distance is turquoise-blue broken by white frothy breakers and I cannot wait to dive in to cleanse myself.

I am the only person on the beach and I strip off and dive, the water warm as a bath. Turning onto my back, I float for a while in the salty water, my legs and arms spreadeagled as I watch two gulls soar above, feathers on their bellies reflecting the aquamarine sea. Then, turning on my stomach, I change pace and slice the water with my arms as I crawl past Nonno's fishing platform and out towards a rocky outcrop on the far left of the cove.

As I draw near, I spy a grotto, impossible to see from the shore. A figure stands on a flat rock at the entrance, poised above the lacy breakers and I tread water as I watch a woman execute a perfect dive, slicing the surface with hardly a splash. She is naked, her hair short like a boy's but she is definitely female, with her pert breasts and the gentle curve of her hips. To my utter surprise, I realise she is unmistakably the boy who calls himself Anto. I sink beneath the surface immediately and swim back towards shore underwater until I can hold my breath no longer, hoping desperately she has not realised I have watched her like a voyeur.

My limbs are wet and I am fatigued after days of fever and it takes me longer than I want as I struggle to pull my shirt and trousers on my wet body. As I struggle back up the path, my mind is full with a single question: why does Anto disguise herself as a young man?

CHAPTER 5

ENGLAND, PRESENT DAY

Her father's painting was in the shadows where it always hung in its corner: the image of an old Italian farmhouse mysterious, melancholy, echoing her own unsettled feelings. It was not the best place to display it and Susannah Ferguson removed it to carry it round the living room until she was happy with a new position. Light poured onto the opposite wall through a large window that gave out onto the courtyard of her terrace house. It was crying out for the painting and she wondered why she hadn't thought of it before.

As she'd unhooked it, something fluttered to the carpet. The old postcard her father had talked about – a black-and-white photo of the Italian farmhouse he'd painted.

Once in its new place, she stepped back to gaze at the work in oils created by her father at evening class. He'd had very few possessions and she was delighted he had left it to her. He'd told her he had no idea where in Italy the old house was and had simply used the postcard for inspiration. His mother, her grandma Elsie, had apparently given it to him when he was a boy. 'One day, I'll track the place down,' he'd told Susannah.

She'd laughed. 'Good luck with that, Daddy. You'll be going round in circles with that quest.'

'I'll enjoy that. Round and round in Italy. Not a bad project for the future.'

He'd begun to cough and she'd waited at his side until he'd stopped, trying not to notice how thin and old he'd become as she straightened the bedclothes, filling his glass on the bedside table with fresh water. Her daddy, once so strong, who'd carried her on his shoulders when they'd walked along the stony Hastings beaches when she was tired and grizzly, was a shell of his strong self. But he was still her daddy with his glimpses of humour and his cheeky grin that always cheered her up.

She missed him so much. Her gaze moved to the ugly plastic urn on the mantelpiece containing his ashes. 'Scatter me where you think best,' he'd told her when she'd reluctantly listened to him planning his funeral arrangements. 'Best to sort it now,' he'd said when she'd protested. 'I don't want to leave a mess.'

Typical Daddy. Thoughtful to the last.

Next to the chimney breast, the dolls' house he'd made took up far too much space. It would be more sensible to build bookshelves there really, she thought. Maybe she should be ruthless and declutter by selling it in her shop. It was nothing fancy and probably wouldn't fetch much, made by Daddy from an old packing case and rather heavy. But it held a special place in her heart. The roof was painted bright red, and all the chunky furniture had been carved by her father. As a child, she'd spent hours inventing stories about the family that lived in the house but she doubted whether she would ever have children herself to pass it on to. At thirty-eight, her biological clock was ticking away and there was no man on the horizon. And there was no way she would bring a child into the world unless she was truly, madly, deeply in love with the father. Maybe she watched too many romantic films, but that was her dream.

Although her dad had always loved her so much, her own childhood hadn't been the best. She didn't want the same for a baby of her own. How often had she heard Grandma Elsie nag her father – her shrill voice going on and on like a needle stuck in an old LP. 'You ruin that child, Frank.'

Susannah swore she'd ask for those words to be chiselled on her grandmother's tombstone once she passed away. At ninety-seven, Elsie was now living in Mountview Care Home and Susannah pitied her long-suffering care assistants. Susannah knew what a difficult woman she was to her cost, having looked after her for three long years before a care home had recently become inevitable. Her dormer bungalow was empty now but soon she and her sister, Sybil, would have to clear it of a lifetime of possessions. 'Only things,' Sybil, had muttered when they'd made a preliminary recce of what should go to the house clearance company. 'And grotty things at that.' Although there was little love lost between Susannah and her grandmother, she couldn't help thinking it was sad to have to clear her bits and bobs while she was still alive and that she would never live in her own home again. But the care fees were steep and needs must.

Elsie had always been on the warpath, always needing something or someone to pick on. They'd come to live with Grandma Elsie and Grandpa Cedric when Susannah's mother had died giving birth to her.

'You were such a big baby, and you took so long to arrive,' Grandma Elsie told her repeatedly, so that Susannah came to believe that it was her fault Mummy had died. It didn't help when her older sister started to pick up signals from Elsie. 'If it hadn't been for you, Susannah, Mummy would still be here,' Sybil had said, on more than one occasion.

Daddy had always stood up for her. And that was another cause of resentment.

'Daddy's girl. You're Daddy's girl,' Sybil would taunt, if

Susannah fell over and ran to him rather than Grandma Elsie, who would only tell her it was a little scratch and not to be a crybaby.

Her daddy picked up Gran's favouritism for Sybil and let Susannah help him in his garden shed. It was his bolthole where he worked on old pieces of furniture bought at jumble sales and country auctions, slowly bringing them back to life. She remembered one particular cream-painted dresser: it had taken him months to strip, carefully scraping away layers of paint with a little knife while he listened to Radio 4 on his transistor. When every flake of paint was gone, he'd rubbed beeswax into the wood to bring out the grain.

'Never use that new-fangled spray polish, Susi. It does the furniture no good. Full of silicone that doesn't allow the wood to breathe.' Only once had he talked about Grandma's cruel comments. 'Don't mind too much what she says, Susi darling. She can be spiteful, I know, but *I* love you. Never forget that.'

He'd put his rough fingers under her chin and kissed the top of her head. Susannah knew he loved her without him having to spell it out. She sat with him in his shed, on a stack of old encyclopaedias as she watched him at work or pored over the stories in the volumes. The hut was cosy, warmed by an old cylindrical paraffin lamp that cast patterns of diamond lights on the walls. Daddy wore his tweed jacket with its leather elbow patches and smelled of pipe tobacco and bonfires. Sometimes he gave her simple jobs. She applied polish to silverware and buffed up Edwardian teapots so that she could see her face in them – distorted, like in the mirrors at the funfair that came every year to park on the prom. Daddy could never go anywhere without rescuing an old piece of furniture other people had given up on. He'd returned from a walk on the clifftops on West Hill once, carrying a Victorian balloon-back chair with slight woodworm dumped under a hedge. Over the years, he'd rescued several items from skips, destined for the municipal dump.

'Woodworm is no big problem. It's treatable. A good polish and a new cover and I'll find a home for this old chair,' he said, stroking the wood with his calloused fingers, as if it were a living thing.

She'd inherited his bug: a love of old things. She'd owned Cobwebs, her bric-a-brac shop along the High Street in Hastings Old Town, since she'd turned thirty, after giving up a stressful investment banking job in the city. It was her own sanctuary, as the shed had been for Frank: a place to be herself after years of reluctantly commuting up and down to London, caught on a treadmill which had eventually led to a mini breakdown.

Frank had passed away almost six months ago and his loss had left Susannah bruised. They'd spent so much time together in his last years. They'd pooled resources and shared a house along Oxford Terrace. He'd helped her man the shop when she was busy on a house clearance, or when she had to travel to source paint and upholstering materials, and he was always keen to attend auctions with her. They'd sit near the front, their box of sandwiches and sausage rolls between them, and he was usually right when it came to guessing what would go for a song and what was a clever reproduction. 'The feet aren't right,' he'd say, running his fingers down the legs of a Victorian dressing table. 'Somebody's patched this up. Badly.'

He wasn't keen on the painted, shabby chic look, but as she pointed out, fashions and tastes changed. 'Nobody wants huge pieces of brown furniture anymore, Daddy. It's gloomy and houses are smaller.'

'Such a shame to cover up the grain of the wood, pet.'

This, when she'd painted a 1920s bookcase with chalk paint, distressing it afterwards with streaks of gold paint.

'This would have been thrown away otherwise, Daddy, or sold for nothing and shipped to America. I can sell it now. You watch, it will go in no time.'

On the following morning in Cobwebs, memories of him kept her company. She switched on the kettle in the galley kitchen for elevenses and automatically pulled down two mugs from their hooks, before shaking her head and reminding herself for the thousandth time that Daddy was not here. She couldn't bring herself to throw away his mug, the glaze on the willow pattern chipped and faded, and as she hung it back on its hook, it swayed back and forth as if waving at her. It had been a quiet morning so far, summer rain lashing against the windows, keeping customers away, and she switched on the radio for company. Strong filtered coffee at her side, she settled down to write more price labels in her neat italic script. *Life is a dance,* she wrote, adding the price to attach to a black sequined pre-war dress found in a battered leather suitcase under a bed in a recent house sale. She hung the dress on a mannequin in the display window, next to an ornate three-piece table-top mirror, its price label bearing the words: *Here's looking at you, kid.*

Her customers told her they liked these touches and she enjoyed coming across lines and scribbling them in her note-book for future items. A tapestry clutch bag attached to one hand and a fan with a carved bone handle to the other completed the mannequin's costume and she stood back to see what was missing from the display.

The bell pinged as the door to the shop opened.

'Morning! Only me. It's awful out there. Have you got the kettle on?'

Susannah's face broke into a smile and she went to hug her friend. 'Hi, Maureen. Lovely to see you. Coffee or tea? The water's still hot.'

'Any Earl Grey left?'

'Think so.'

She left her friend, hands on hips surveying the window display, while she prepared tea. When she returned, Maureen had added a few finishing touches and arranged a pile of sheet music next to a wind-up gramophone player that had been languishing for weeks on top of a wardrobe.

'Got a decanter and glasses?' Maureen asked. 'We can turn this window into more of a story. Make it look like a romantic rendezvous.'

'You're a genius. How come I didn't think of that myself?'

'Must be the artist in me.'

By day Maureen taught at the high school. Frank had attended Maureen's weekly evening adult art classes, where he had worked on the painting of the old farmhouse, and had introduced her to Susannah. 'You'll like her, Susi,' her father had said. 'She's full of life. If I were ten years younger...'

Maureen had managed to winkle out a talent that Frank never knew he possessed. Susannah had even sold some of his watercolours of the Downs and Romney Marsh. There were still a couple hanging amidst the Wedgwood plates and antique mirrors on the shop walls and Susannah was tempted to keep them herself, but her little house was already too cluttered with items she had fallen in love with.

'How's business?' Maureen asked from where she perched on a green velvet chaise longue that was draped with an antique Chinese wedding shawl.

'Very quiet. This wet July doesn't help. There are very few holidaymakers about and everyone's being careful with their money after last year. The sort of things I sell aren't exactly life's basics.'

'I disagree – what you sell cheers people up. And we all need that now.'

'To tell the truth, Maureen, it's not only July that's been as dead as a dodo. The shop is losing money and I've had to take out a loan to tide me over.' A tear trickled down Susannah's cheek as she spoke and she wiped it away angrily.

Maureen produced a tissue from her handbag and came to sit beside Susannah. 'You're missing your daddy, aren't you?

Come here, sweetheart.' She opened her arms and Susannah sank into her hug.

'I'm being ridiculous,' she said, her voice muffled by Maureen's Fair Isle sweater. 'I should be over it by now, but, yes,' – she pulled away, dabbing at her eyes and blowing into the tissue that Maureen had handed her – 'yes... I really, really miss him.'

'There's nothing ridiculous about having loved somebody special and losing them.'

'But it's been six months now. It's weird, but at the time I didn't cry. But now it's as if I can't bottle up my sadness anymore. I'm thinking about Daddy all the time – everywhere there are reminders of him: here in the shop, at home... I almost made him a cup of tea today, for goodness' sake... we'd have shared a problem over a cuppa and he'd come up with solutions. I wish he were here, Maureen. He'd know exactly what to do about the shop...' Another tear slid down her cheek. 'I mean, I miss him for him – not because of offering help about the poor sales...'

'I know exactly what you mean, dear girlie. I miss him too, you know, and I haven't got all the reminders around me.' Maureen handed Susannah another tissue. 'Maybe you need a break. Stress catches up in the end. You look exhausted and you've lost weight. Why don't you let me look after Cobwebs while you get away and spoil yourself? When was the last time you had a holiday?'

'Three or four years ago. Maybe more. I honestly can't remember.'

'You definitely need a break. What you did for your father, the way you looked after him, on top of years of caring for your impossible grandmother. You're exhausted.'

'I looked after Daddy because I loved him.'

'I know. But now it's time to look after yourself. You're lonely too. When was the last time you dated anybody?'

'I've given up on men.'

Maureen laughed. 'Don't talk nonsense. I should think you need a jolly good seeing to. A tumble between the sheets. Do you the world of good.'

Susannah spluttered. 'Honestly, Maureen, you're a one and only. So, I go to the doctor and ask if I can have a prescription for a man? I don't think so. Not after the humungous dating cock-ups I've had recently. No puns intended.'

Maureen laughed.

'I seem to remember you going out a few times with a married man who said he was single. With a wife expecting twins?'

'Yes! And don't get me started on internet dating. I might be lonely, but I'm not desperate. I'd rather snuggle up to a hot water bottle than go on any dating apps again.'

Maureen laughed and went to fill the kettle. 'How old are you? You'll be knitting bedsocks next. But there's truth in what you say. A man is not always the solution, you're right. But you're still young. Don't hide yourself away, Susi.'

Susannah had bottled her feelings up for too long and it was a relief to talk. 'You're such a lovely lady, Maureen. Thanks for listening.'

'That's what friends are for, my darling. And – if I'm honest – whilst we're being frank and earnest, so to speak, I brought up my looking after Cobwebs because there's something I've been wanting to talk to you about for a while now.'

It sounded ominous to Susannah. She picked up a vintage hand mirror to peer at her face and wipe smudged mascara from under her eyes. 'Put me out of my agony then.'

'I'd love to invest in Cobwebs,' Maureen announced. 'I can see ways to add to the business.' She paused to gauge Susannah's reaction.

There was a split second before she replied, while

Susannah replaced the mirror on a Victorian side table. 'But what about your teaching job?'

'Oh, Susi. Where to start? Basically, I'm sick of it and I've decided to retire anyhow. Everything in education has changed so much since I first qualified. There are umpteen bits of paper to fill in for assessments and predicated grades, targets to write, hoops to jump through. So much of my spare time is spent painting scenery for school shows. I'd like more time to paint for myself and... if this doesn't sound as if I'm telling you how to do your job...'

'It probably will, Maureen.' Susannah laughed. 'But you know I love you and I'm always prepared to learn.'

Part of her was finding the idea of sharing the shop hard but she could see the sense of it too. One of Daddy's wise sayings rang in her ears: 'A little bit of help is worth a lot of pity.' Maureen's suggestion was presenting itself as a lifeline and she listened carefully to what her friend had to say.

'I think you could do more with your shop. Continue along the theme you've started – I love the way you create little narratives for what you sell. But be bolder, Susi, more dramatic with your displays. And you could expand and use the courtyard at the back for a summer café. Plant it up, dress the tables with priced chinaware and trinkets that customers could buy after a full-on afternoon tea experience. What do you think?'

'I like it. But...' Susannah sighed, thinking that Maureen's idea of a café was great and wondering why she had not thought of it herself. 'I know I'm going to sound like a wet blanket, but I don't have the energy at the moment.' She pushed back a lock of her dark curly hair as she spoke.

'Exactly, Susi. Like I said, you need a holiday. Somewhere completely new. In the sun. And while you're away, I can experiment with Cobwebs.'

Susannah looked up in alarm.

Maureen laughed at her expression. 'Don't worry! I won't

do anything drastic. Simply move stuff about. Maybe canvass customers about the café idea. There are more than sufficient chippies along the beach. I'm picturing old-fashioned afternoon tea served in vintage cups; cakes and dainty sandwiches without crusts arranged on stands; tasteful music in the background. It would be a novelty. You've got the makings of a little gold mine. What do you say?'

'Can I think about it, Maureen? In principle, it's a great idea.'

'Wonderful!' Maureen rose to her feet. 'Now, I prescribe our favourite walk along Beachy Head, followed by a cream tea. Strictly for research purposes,' Maureen said, with a wink. 'Let's start right away to build you up again.'

Susannah hugged her friend. 'Thank you so much. I feel instantly better for offloading. You're a real treasure, you know.'

'Anything to oblige the lovely daughter of the lovely Frank.'

'Anything?' Susannah laughed. 'Does that mean you are up for coming to help me with Elsie's bungalow too? I've been putting it off and Sybil has been on my case. Now that Elsie's in Mountview, the place needs selling and before the house is cleared next week, I need to take a last look.'

'Of course. You know I like a good old rummage. I'll turn the sign to CLOSED; we'll go after our outing.'

CHAPTER 6

The two women stopped for a breather near Beachy Head at the edge of its sheer chalk cliffs. A wreath of flowers lay on the grass, the blooms wilted, and Susannah shivered at the loss of life. The benches by the monument were free and Susannah read aloud the moving sign beneath an etching on granite of a RAF fighter bomber: '"They fought in the skies above the enemy and paid the terrible price that war demands."'

Looking out over the expanse of blue sea, the white sails of a boat in the distance like a child's drawing, she said, 'It's hard to comprehend war in such an idyllic setting.'

'The lanes of Sussex were chock-a-block with tanks and servicemen, especially in 1944 when invasion was expected. One of the soldiers was a Canadian beau of my mother,' Maureen said. 'I don't think she could find a man to match up to him; that's why she never married.'

'Oh, of course. I'd forgotten. I remember you telling me about that. How she always carried the badge from his cap in her purse. How romantic.'

'Sadly, he didn't make it past the beach at Normandy, but I can't imagine Mother being able to stay married for long. She was too feisty and independent. After she left Father, she did an excellent job as a single parent, bringing me up. There weren't many spare men to go around at the end of the war and I think her heart had been stolen by her Canadian chappie, anyway. Father never matched up to him.

'Here you go, my dear,' her friend said, producing a bar of chocolate. 'I reckon we've earned this. I've come to the conclusion I'm too independent to settle with anybody. Just like Mum. That's probably why Douglas left me for a more biddable woman. I prefer being on my own now. Got the whole bed to myself. I can eat what I want, when I want, especially now my two are off my hands.'

They munched on the chocolate in silence, watching a flight of terns pass above, Susannah reaching for her binoculars and then passing them to Maureen.

'Thank you for this afternoon, Maureen. You don't know how much you have helped.'

'Sharing is caring, my dear.' Maureen stood up. 'Now to investigate the tea room down on the beach, and then lead me to Elsie's home.'

Over tea, talk about Cobwebs was not discussed. Instead, Maureen brought up the subject of boyfriends with Susannah again.

'Are you seeing anyone these days?'

Susannah stared at her over her mug of tea. 'I told you, I've sort of given up on that front.'

'But you're too young. Don't waste these years and turn into a lonely woman set in her ways. It's easily done, you know.'

'That's what Daddy used to say.'

'He asked me to keep an eye on you, actually.'

Typical Daddy.

'I guessed as much. I'm fine, honestly I am.'

'What about Jonathan from the bookshop? Didn't he take you out for dinner once or twice last year?'

Susannah set her mug down. 'Goodness, Maureen. Are you spying on me?'

'I spent a lot of time with your father, as you know. He filled me in.'

'Jonathan is a lovely man, but I think he's too much in love with his dusty old history volumes to want a woman in his life. He's purely a friend. Always there to help me lift heavy stuff into the shop. And I pass on any books I feel might be of interest to him. But that is all there is to our relationship.'

'Are you sure you don't want to try out another dating app?'

Susannah laughed out loud. 'No way! It was traumatising and I don't want to even go there, Maureen.'

Susannah squirmed as she thought back to the last evening she'd tried to pursue any sort of romantic interest. With the shop, and looking after her dad, it just hadn't seemed worth investing any time or energy on any more strange dates with strange men.

After Susannah parked her van outside Elsie's drab home, they trod down the path, lined with straggly rose bushes in need of a good pruning. An elderly neighbour peeped from behind net curtains festooning her bay window and Susannah waved.

She pushed against a pile of mail on the mat and sorted the rubbish from brown envelopes to pop in the post for her sister to deal with. The proceeds from the sale of the bungalow would help towards paying for Gran's care in the home. It wasn't cheap, almost £1,000 a week, but it was the only practical solution for Elsie. Susannah found it hard to call her Gran. In her mind, a grandmother should be somebody warm and cuddly, who always had time for her grandchildren; someone to lovingly show you how to bake, sew, dress up with you and act soft – like the grandmothers of her friends who seemed easier to confide in than parents. Elsie had never been like that with her.

Whatever was left over after the sale would go to Sybil. Susannah hadn't been surprised to learn of this; Gran had never hidden her preference for her older sister.

'Nice,' Maureen said with sarcasm, wrinkling her nose as she took in swirly, sludge-green patterned carpets and floral polyester curtains.

'Gran thought it was the bee's knees when she moved in. She chose all the furnishings herself after Grandpa Cedric died. I dread to think what happened to the beautiful antiques she got rid of from the house in Lower Park Road.'

'That's now a highly desirable address. Lots of Londoners snapped up the Edwardian houses, especially during the pandemic when they wanted out of the city and were hunting for places with office space. Goodness, Susannah, do you really think there's anything here saleable for the shop?'

Maureen stood with her hands on her hips as she gazed round. There was an abundance of orange in the décor, from the geometrically patterned rug before the gas fire to the cushions in their brown and orange crocheted covers. She moved to an MDF sideboard to switch on a lava lamp and laughed as the bubbles of liquid started to move. 'God! It's like looking at the contents of somebody's stomach after a heavy meal,' she said. 'Who would want this in their living room?'

'I'm sure the house clearance bloke will know where to sell it. Stuff from the seventies and eighties is beginning to be fashionable, but it's not my bag, as you know.'

'Shall I forage upstairs and you start down here?' Maureen asked.

Susannah began with the contents of the pale green Formica cupboards in the narrow kitchen. No dainty tea sets or silver spoons within, but scratched Pyrex dishes and plastic-handled cutlery. The only item that appealed in the musty space was a cheeky cuckoo clock she knew would sell. In a bottom drawer of the units, she found a set of embroidered cotton tea cloths and serviettes and put these to one side too.

'This any good, Susi?' Maureen called and Susannah climbed the stairs to join her.

In the back bedroom, a 1930s dressing table with carving on the oval mirror and drawer fronts was almost obscured by a pile of luridly coloured towels and candy-striped polyester sheets.

Susannah bent to examine the wood. 'Oak. I could chalk paint this. It's pretty enough.'

There was nothing else inside the bungalow but outside Susannah picked up a couple of turn-of-the-century stone gnomes, one holding a fishing rod, the other sitting on a toad-stool. Then between them, they manhandled the dressing table down the stairs and wrapped it in old blankets before lifting it into the boot. The cuckoo clock and gnomes were treated with the same care.

'You'll rue the day you chose to have that clock in Cobwebs,' Maureen said.

'You might be right. I bet you it sells quickly though, and if it doesn't, we'll incorporate it in a scene in the shop window with the gnomes, and create a vintage winter wonderland before Christmas. Come on, let's get out of this place. It's damp and deeply unbeautiful. And, although Elsie is not my favourite woman in the world, I'm feeling sad the way her life has panned out.'

'I agree,' Maureen said. 'This place is pretty soulless. But are you sure there's nothing you'd like to keep for yourself? A reminder?'

The look that Susannah gave her said it all. She didn't turn back to the bungalow as she locked the door and made her way to the car.

CHAPTER 7

As it was the start of the school holidays, Maureen popped into Cobwebs frequently in the following days to keep Susannah company. With her friend manning front of shop, Susannah was able to make a start in her work room on the backlog of items to restore. As she'd predicted, the cuckoo clock sold almost immediately. 'I *have* to buy this for my annoying brother-in-law,' a woman had told her. 'It's his fortieth and we've been asked not to give serious gifts. He's a bit cuckoo, anyway.' She had laughed at the description on the price label hanging from the clock: *Living in cloud cuckoo land*.

Susannah listened to Radio 6 as she sandpapered her grand-mother's dressing table, being careful not to scratch the mirror. The oak was in good condition, without a sign of worm, so it didn't need treating, although sometimes little holes added to the antique look. Occasionally she used crackled glaze for the same reason. Having finished rubbing down the top with its two sets of miniature drawers, she pulled out the main drawers. The bottom drawer was stuck and she tugged on it until it released. On its base, a brown envelope had once been securely attached with several strips of yellowing Sellotape, but they gave way easily as she pulled on them.

Inside this envelope was another envelope containing a thin sheet of paper and a postcard, the black-and-white photos on the front divided into four sections: a beach scene showing strange rock formations, a cathedral, a street of tiny conical white buildings and a farmhouse. It felt strangely familiar. Had she seen it before?

She pulled her magnifying glass out and squinted at the name on the board above the farmhouse door. The script was blurred and some of the letters were indecipherable, but she could make out a couple of words: *della orre*. Could it be the same farmhouse from her father's painting? She remembered his words – a joke at the time. 'One day, I'll track the place down.'

The word *Puglia* was stamped across the bottom of the card in old-fashioned, curling script. With mounting curiosity, she examined the front. It was addressed to her grandmother's former house in Hastings and the stamp was Italian. On the back were a couple of handwritten lines:

January 1, 1947
    In my dreams I imagine the day when we shall be reunited. Until then, I hope my letters fill the gap. All my best love xx

With mounting curiosity, she unfolded the flimsy paper. The handwriting was faded but easy to read, written in rounded capital letters. Her heart beating faster, she read the contents, feeling like an interloper but at the same time eager to understand why the letter and postcard had been hidden away:

I write this by the fire after a busy day of work. Despite today's feast there is no let-up in the amount to do on the land. You'd be surprised how cold it is here in the winter. Chestnuts are roasting in the ashes. How I wish you were here to share them.

I wonder if your Christmas was good and if there was turkey. Living here by the sea, I had a fish feast. Delicious!

Before the meal, I started whittling the cricket bat. For some time now I'd had my eyes on a clump of willow growing along a stream that trickles to the beach. The wood is tough and light – it will be perfect. I wonder if children here will be interested at all in my favourite sport? It is completely unknown here...

My heart will never feel complete without you at my side. For today, all my kisses are sent across the sea to you. One day we shall be together.

There was no signature, the final line being a row of tidy *X*s and at the bottom of the page, there was a crude pencil drawing of a cricket bat, stumps and ball.

Susannah sat back on her heels, her mind brimming with questions. Who had written these things to her grandmother and why were the card and letter hidden away? From the shop she heard Maureen say a cheery goodbye to customers. The doorbell pinged as they left and Maureen called out, 'Yippee! We've got rid of that humungous wardrobe at last.'

Maureen popped her head round the door to the workshop. 'What's up, Susi? You look as if you've seen a ghost.'

'I think I have, Maureen. These were hidden under the drawer.' She held up the postcard and letter and Maureen took them.

When she'd finished reading, her friend shook her head. 'Oh, my goodness. How strange!'

'I'd love to know who sent these to her,' Susannah said, replacing the card in the envelope. 'Unfortunately, I don't think I'm going to get a lot out of Grandma Elsie. Sybil is always warning me not to upset her.'

'But goodness, Susi, I can see why you'd want to find out more. Why did she hide them? Were they from a Latin lover, do you think? Oh, naughty Elsie! How delicious.'

Susannah pulled a face. 'I pity anybody who fell in love with the old battleaxe. Poor Grandpa Cedric was bossed about every day. Sometimes I think he pretended he was deaf, you know. I'm sure he wasn't, though. He had to watch Formula One with the sound turned down really low on the telly, but he always knew what was going on.'

Maureen laughed. 'Shall I put the kettle on, Susi, or shall we go to the pub? You look as if you could do with something stiffer than tea.'

'Dad used to keep a hip flask in the kitchen containing his medicinal brandy, as he called it. Let's stay here. I want to mull this over.'

'Right. Sit there and I'll do the honours.'

'The flask is on the top shelf. Thanks, Maureen. You're a star.'

As they sipped their medicinal drinks, they discussed the finds.

'When are you going to confront Elsie?' Maureen asked.

Susannah bit her lip. 'Although I want to know more about it, I do feel like an intruder. Maybe I should hand the envelope back to her.'

'But would she know what you're talking about anyway, Susi? Isn't her head lost in another world?'

'She has her moments. Sometimes she can be lucid, especially about the past. It's the fact these messages were hidden away that's got me hooked. They obviously weren't meant to be found.'

'It's so intriguing. Like an Agatha Christie mystery.'

'Who knows why she hid them? As you know, she gave Dad a similar postcard without a message on the back when he was a teenager and that's what inspired him to do the painting he left me.'

'Yes, he worked really hard on that in class. He told me he'd always liked the look of the house.'

'I found it the other day; it slipped out from the back of the frame when I moved the painting. I wonder if the same person sent it.'

'I should imagine so. Fancy old Elsie having a secret Italian lover.'

'We don't know that, Maureen. But I now want to know more. I'd like to ask her who sent the card and letter, rather than guessing. But it's a bit delicate.'

'There's nothing delicate about Elsie. You're too nice. She's always been such a cow to you.'

Susannah paused for a few moments. 'You're right. All I wanted was for her to be the loving mother figure I never had but it didn't happen. There were so many horrid instances of how mean she could be. I'll never forget one Christmas; she bought Sybil a beautiful brand-new dress from M&S. I was so jealous, because Grandma Elsie gave *me* a party frock she'd picked up from a jumble sale and I hated it. I wouldn't have minded, but it was so embarrassing to be forced to wear it – it even had holes and rips in. The row it caused when I refused to go to the party! She locked me in my room and told me to stay there all afternoon to "mend my ways". She always used to say that. Grandpa Cedric got into trouble later by unlocking my door and taking me to the cinema to see *The Jungle Book* while Gran and Sybil were out. He wasn't such a bad old stick but he never stood up to her, really. Nobody dared, except Daddy sometimes. I think he was grateful to have help from her after Mum died and, anyway, he wasn't there to witness how awful she could be. When he got home after work, she was always sweetness and light.'

'Horrible woman. *She* should have been locked up. Poor you.'

'I could spout off loads of other examples... but I'm not a little girl anymore and that's all in the past. And now she's locked up with dementia...' She looked at the note in her hand again and sighed. 'I'll visit the home and see if I can get anything out of her.'

Susannah pushed the envelope into her tapestry carpet bag and as she snapped it shut, Maureen teased her. 'I hope you've got your magnifying glass in your Miss Marple bag.'

'But of course. What else?' Maureen had always teased her about her bag, but Susannah found it useful for carrying items that she came across for the shop. She'd even once managed to hold a whole set of dainty French porcelain coffee cups and pots in its depths. The bag itself was a flea market find. The days of resentment over jumble sales were long gone now since she'd unearthed so many brilliant pieces – although she always checked for holes beyond mending in vintage clothes.

Susannah shut up shop earlier than usual, the dressing table discovery occupying her mind so much she couldn't concentrate properly on anything. It was a mild evening and back home, she sat for a while in her courtyard patio, an Angela Marsons thriller on her lap. Usually, she could escape into the intrigue but tonight she couldn't concentrate. She'd read the same page over and over, until she snapped the thriller shut and sat back. She listened to the sounds of the Old Town settling for the night, saxophone music from the pub at the end of the street ebbing and flowing, and she thought back to Maureen's sugges-tion. Did she want to give up a share in Cobwebs? It was true that her antique-cum-junk shop had taken a battering during the pandemic, as had countless other small businesses. It might be good to try out Maureen's offer for a trial period and see how they worked together, see if their combined efforts and ideas could revive funds. It was not that she didn't trust her friend. On the contrary. It was more whether or not she wanted to relinquish her independence after years of being at the beck and call of others. And it was true that she felt exhausted, as Maureen had pointed out. Somehow, she had kept battling on, like you did when you lived alone and had nobody to chat about the day or to bounce ideas back and forth. Her attempts at dating had put her off but she was lonely. Lonelier than she had ever felt in her life.

As darkness fell, the air turned unseasonably chilly and she moved into the living room, closing the windows behind her. Her father's painting of the Italian farmhouse was now more prominent in its new position on the wall and she stood in front of it for a while.

'What should I do, Daddy?' Susannah whispered, as she ran her fingers over the canvas. It needed glass inserting into the frame, before the colours faded with sunlight. 'Shall I talk to Elsie and get started on your quest? *Round and round in Italy.*'

The idea of a long holiday certainly appealed. She could just about afford it if she spent wisely. The postcard she had found had been sent from a place called Puglia…

On a whim, she fired up her laptop and scrolled through holiday adverts for August. Rome was expensive. Tuscany too, although the hilltop towns and the lines of cypress trees like exclamation marks dotting the countryside looked magical. But she had no wish to stay on her own in a villa in the middle of nowhere and none of the city apartments in her price range appealed. Further south attracted her. An initial search showed that regions like Apulia and Abruzzo were less expensive.

Checking the postcard heading again, she confirmed it had been sent from Puglia and when she worked out that Apulia was the English way of saying Puglia, that decided her. A quick scroll through Booking.com made her even more interested. The region looked beautiful, with its sea views, olive groves and baroque buildings. Yawning, she decided to sleep on it. 'Things always look better in the morning,' Daddy used to say.

CHAPTER 8

Mountview Care Home had a pleasant enough lookout over Hastings' rooftops, and if you craned your neck and leant through an open window, you could just about spot the sea on the horizon. Susannah was buzzed in via sliding doors and the assistant on the front desk pointed to numbers of a code, partly concealed within patterns of daisies, stuck to the top of the lift door for when she needed to let herself out after her visit.

'Be careful, Miss Ferguson, not to let any of the guests out when you get to the door of Rosemary Ward. There are always a couple of folk hovering, wanting to walk away.'

The home was clean and bright, false flowers arranged around ledges along the corridors, but fragrance-diffusers didn't mask a faint whiff of urine. Elsie was in a corner of the communal sitting room hugging a large white teddy bear and staring at a television showing a repeat instalment of *Antiques Roadshow*.

Susannah sat down next to her and Elsie looked up briefly. 'That's where Cedric normally sits. He's coming to fetch me to take me for a drive. After he's cut the lawn. He'll be tired and want to sit there. You'd better move.'

Elsie turned her back slightly on her granddaughter and Susannah's heart sank.

'Hello, Elsie,' she said. 'It's Susannah.'

The response was pursed lips and a frown on the old lady's forehead.

Susannah persisted. Maybe if she called Elsie Gran, the old lady might pay her more attention. 'I'm thinking of going for a holiday in Italy, Gran. Where Dad always wanted to visit. It's supposed to be really beautiful.'

'What does he want to go there for? Waste of money. It's perfectly fine here in Hastings.'

Susannah decided not to remind her that Frank and Cedric were both gone. At the introductory talk the home had given to Susannah and her sister when they'd delivered Elsie, they'd been advised not to try and correct relatives when they were confused. 'Most of our guests remember the past far better than something that happened five minutes ago. It will only upset them if you try and set them right about recent events.'

'Dad painted a picture of Italy, didn't he, Gran?'

'I've asked Frank again and again to paint me a picture of the fishing huts, but I'm still waiting.'

'I wonder who sent him that old postcard of Italy, Gran. Can you remember? The one he copied for his painting...'

Elsie turned to Susannah, the frown still there. 'I wasn't going to give it to Billy at first,' she said. 'But there was no harm in it, was there?' She grasped Susannah's wrist, her bony fingers like claws.

Elsie was obviously confused, mixing up names from the past. 'No, Gran. No harm at all. Daddy loved it. That's why he painted his picture. The postcard inspired him. You did the right thing.'

'Your daddy was better off where he was. No good would have come living with macaroni, you know. Always disappearing off for days in his airyplane.'

Elsie's wispy eyebrows knotted together in a frown and her nails dug into Susannah's flesh.

'They say a change is as good as a rest, but the change wouldn't have worked...'

'What do you mean, Gran? Were you thinking of moving?'

'What?' The old lady turned to her and shook her head. 'We were never going to move. Never. What are you talking about?'

'About the postcards, Gran. And the note.'

'I should have thrown it away.'

Elsie released her grip and turned to watch the television, the moment gone. 'What a load of old junk they're trying to flog to poor unsuspecting people,' the old lady said. 'They belong on a bonfire. Like the stuff in your shop, young Susannah. Why can't you sell nice clean modern stuff that's shiny and useful? And your hair is still awful, young lady. I keep telling you to dye it the colour of Sybil's. You'd look far better blonde.'

To some people, an elderly relative's cruel words would be a heart-breaking side effect of dementia. But the things Elsie was saying were more or less what Susannah had been used to hearing her whole life. She grasped at this chink of lucidity. 'Can you remember, Gran, where the postcards came from? And if there were any more notes?'

'They came in the post, of course, you stupid girl. In the post. Frank was only little. I kept the card for him until he was older.'

The old lady started to rock backwards and forwards, her raised voice showing her distress. 'Maybe I shouldn't have. But I was worried, you see. Frank was my only baby. I wanted the best for us.'

'Is everything all right, my love?' A middle-aged care assistant in a tight pink overall approached and bent down to Elsie.

'Tell this nasty girl to go away,' Elsie shouted, still rocking backwards and forwards, pointing at Susannah.

The woman smiled apologetically. 'It might be best to leave her to calm down now. I'm so sorry, my dear. She's having one of her bad days.'

She helped Elsie out of the chair and supported her under the arm, speaking gently all the while as she coaxed her from the sitting room. 'Shall we go and have a lie-down, Mrs Ferguson, my love? And I'll bring a nice cup of tea and digestive biscuits to you in your own room. You like dunking digestives, don't you?'

Elsie tottered away, holding fast to the care assistant's arm and Susannah watched in dismay as a stain spread on the back of the old lady's baggy trousers as she shuffled off.

As Susannah walked away from the home, she was full of admiration for the caring staff who worked there, whilst hoping fervently that she would not have to end her days in such a place. *Better to swim out to sea and sink beneath the waves.* If she had to select a final place, maybe swimming out into an Italian sea would be top of her list.

Why had Elsie grown so agitated at the mention of the cards and notes? What secrets did she keep locked in her befuddled mind? What did she mean about keeping the cards until Frank was older? Susannah wondered if it was too late, if the old lady's disease was now too advanced for her to make any sense. Still, she'd had to ask her grandmother. She didn't regret that, but she did regret not being able to make head nor tail of what she had said. And what had macaroni got to do with anything?

'I hear that you upset Gran.' Sybil's voice was loud and accusatory on the phone and Susannah switched to speaker to avoid her ears ringing.

'What did you say to her? The home told me it was best to postpone my visit until tomorrow because she's agitated. But I *always* go on a Tuesday. I can't go tomorrow. Honestly, Susannah, why do you always rub Gran up the wrong way and upset everything?'

'I obviously didn't mean to,' Susannah replied, bristling. 'You know what she's like with me – always has been.'

'Were you talking about Dad? She still thinks he's going to come and visit her one of these days.'

'I only asked about the postcard she gave him. You know the one of the farmhouse? But that set her off.'

'Why on earth did you ask about that?'

'Because I found a similar written postcard when I was at the bungalow. I was curious.'

'And did she give you any answers?'

'No.'

'And it's highly unlikely she ever will. I would throw them in the bin if I were you. They're not addressed to you, are they?'

'No, Sybil.' Susannah could hear herself sounding like a monosyllabic teenager. But it was impossible not to when speaking to her sister.

'Don't you feel embarrassed about poking your nose into other people's affairs? Where was this postcard anyway?'

'In Elsie's dressing table,' Susannah mumbled. She didn't feel like telling her bossy sister she had found it taped beneath the dressing table drawers. It would only compound her sister's criticism of her snooping.

'Throw the postcards away, Susannah. They're nothing to do with you. And leave Grandma alone. She doesn't need any more hassle from you.'

That decided Susannah. Her curiosity further piqued by her bossy sister, a couple of days later she popped into the home again. This time she would try to be gentler. It wouldn't do to upset her again. Her grandmother had never been kindness itself, but two wrongs didn't make a right.

Susannah perched herself on the plastic-covered armchair at the side of Elsie's bed, the postcards and note in her bag, waiting for her grandmother to open her eyes. But there was nothing doing with Elsie. The staff had warned her straight away she was very sleepy.

'You're welcome to sit with her for a while, but she's had a difficult couple of days. We've had to alter her medication because of a water infection, so don't expect much interaction.'

The room was spotlessly clean, painted in a cheerful yellow emulsion. Photos of Grandfather Cedric in silver frames and one of Sybil and her twin sons were arranged on the window ledge, but none of herself, she noted. Susannah picked up a smaller frame with a rather blurred image of her father from about twenty years earlier, his fair hair free of grey. He was laughing and Susannah remembered why. She had been standing behind her grandmother pulling faces to make her father smile.

'I know what you're doing behind my back, Susannah,' Elsie had said and Susannah had replied, 'Yes, I know, Gran. You've told me since the year dot that you've eyes in the back of your head.'

Dear old Daddy. She missed him so much. What she would give to have him by her side investigating what she had found. They'd always enjoyed identifying the age of the stock in the shop and Susannah was sure that her love of research was born of the board games Frank had introduced his daughters to at a very young age. It might have been a way of keeping them away from television on winter evenings, but he made them such fun. Scrabble, Monopoly but especially Cluedo were her favourites. Professor Plum became his nickname in the shop when they were trying to pin down the exact age of a hallmarked silver tea set or a brooch.

After a quarter of an hour of listening to Elsie's wheezy breathing and waiting pointlessly for her to waken, Susannah gave up, feeling hugely frustrated. She would have to find out about the mysterious messages on her own.

That evening she hunted for a place to stay in Apulia. With the postcard at the side of her laptop, she scrolled through hundreds of hotels and guest houses on offer. Modern blocks with views of the sea and endless rows of sun umbrellas lining the beach did not appeal. City hotels would be busy and stifling at this time of year. She narrowed her search to country locations and just as she was about to give up, there it was!

Picking up the black-and-white postcard again, she squinted at the writing above the door of the old farmhouse. Eureka! The letters matched like a missing part of a puzzle: *ella ore* fitted in to the name of the place she'd just found, Masseria della Torre. The building was not the same as her father's painting – perhaps it was a common name in that area, but at least she had made a start. When she tried to book a room, a message came up telling her there were no vacancies, so she found somewhere else for the first night and resolved to drive to Masseria della Torre to see if arriving in person might secure a room.

She phoned Maureen to firm up details about looking after Cobwebs.

'Well done, Miss Marple,' her friend said. 'I'd love to be a fly on the wall and see you sleuthing about over there but don't you worry one bit about the shop. Book a flight ASAP – and get away. Like I said, you deserve it!'

As Susannah packed, she slipped both postcards and the note into a clean envelope and wrapped her lucky shell ornament into a sheet of kitchen towel and tucked it down the side of her case. Made of a misshapen oyster shell that shone pearly and cream, it had the tiniest piece of sea glass for an eye. It was one of her most treasured possessions and she'd owned it since she was tiny, her own special charm. Her daddy had told her an elderly man had given it to her in the park one day. Whether for exams, job interviews, long journeys or whenever she was feeling insecure, the shell went with her. This trip would be no exception. She needed all the luck she could muster.

One whole month in Italy stretched ahead of her. She couldn't wait.

CHAPTER 9

ITALY, PRESENT DAY

Susannah was in love. With Puglia. Not Apulia. She preferred the Italian name, and there'd been a moment yesterday when she'd stood on a boulder by the sea, thrown her arms wide and shouted, 'Puglia, Puglia, Puglia,' causing an elderly man to wobble on his bike and shake his head at the mad tourist with wild, fly-away dark curls.

Now, she leant back in her chair, in the shade of an umbrella outside a bar, waiting for breakfast coffee and sweet, creamy *pasticiotto* to be brought by a very handsome waiter. He looked like a film star. The people were generally so beautiful here with their tanned skin and shining black hair, the clichéd images of fat mommas with hordes of children clinging to a Vespa a thing of 1950s black-and-white movies. Everybody from children to elderly looked attractive, healthy and stylish.

The baroque city of Lecce, which she was presently exploring, was a maze of incredible corners that ran through her head like a slideshow. This morning, she'd slipped out early from the *pensione* where she was staying, to visit the city centre before it grew too hot. It was hard to imagine anywhere else matching up to these first days and she was almost tempted to stay here. But she had a mystery to solve for Professor Plum. Elsie hadn't been able to help, so she would crack on alone. *If only Daddy could be by my side to help.* Susannah couldn't dwell on that thought. He wasn't here and that was that. *Doing this for you, Daddy. Wish me luck.*

She had developed a crick in her neck from gazing up at the ornate balconies, supported by intricate stone carvings of buxom, naked-breasted ladies, nymphs and fantastical, mythological creatures. Every corner she turned had some new delight: a fountain shaped like a dolphin tinkling with water drops that sparkled and sang in the sunshine, palm trees planted in a row of old wine barrels, a black-and-white cat balanced precariously on the railings of a balcony filled with plumbago plants, oleanders, bougainvillea and succulents that hung down walls of pale pink, sun-washed *palazzi*. Peaches and pomegranates were piled in pyramids, as if from a still life painting, outside a greengrocer with garlands of fresh grapes and figs draped around the door.

Last night the *pensione* owner had told her about her dancer daughter who was starring in a free concert, *La notte della taranta*, in the Roman amphitheatre in the centre. 'Free ticket for you. Front row. I give you cushion for hard chair,' the signora had told her. 'Is a *concerto* for the *tarantella*,' she'd explained.

After that spectacular evening, she yearned to learn Italian, to join in with folk songs sung from the heart by those men and women on stage. She wanted to copy the complicated *tarantella*, the dance of the spider, and arch her body into artistic shapes. She wanted to play the drums and tambourines with the same passion of these people, the heavy echoes reverberating around the piazza, beating deep inside her very being. The shapes of the dancers in their dramatic black-and-white costumes had been projected as shadows onto the side of the church, the orchestra's notes drifting intoxicatingly into the night air, and at the end of the evening, tears streamed down Susannah's face. A woman sitting next to her had nodded in sympathy when she'd seen her silently crying. She'd said something, touching a fist to her heart. When Susannah had replied, 'I can't speak Italian,' the woman had answered in English, 'No words necessary.' She'd handed her a programme and pointed at a line printed along the bottom of the page in both Italian and English. 'THE HIGHEST FORM OF BLISS IS LIVING WITH A CERTAIN DEGREE OF FOLLY.' ERASMUS. Susannah smiled, taking it as a message: that she needed to come out of herself, sink in to her holiday in Puglia, go with the flow, be a bit crazy and to stop thinking too much. *Run a few risks for a change. Open your mind. Stop worrying about the shop. Maureen will have everything under control.*

In the morning, she posted a card to Maureen. *Magical. You'd love it here. I might never come back,* she wrote.

The day after the concert, Susannah drove along the coast towards the hotel, full of renewed energy and thoughts of her father, of the postcards, and of the beautiful farmhouse painting. Taking a break in a small town, Monte Sant'Angelo, she took in the higgledy-piggledy scattering of dwellings that tumbled down the mountainside. Through gaps in the narrow streets, some not wide enough for the smallest of cars to pass through, were glimpses of the azure-jade sea.

I should write a guidebook to southern bars, Susannah thought, as she waited for lunch on the terrace of a wine bar called Mo Vini. Traditional local dishes were a feature of the menu and she'd pointed to the top choice. The owner had worked in Manchester for a while, his English accent an attractive mix of northern English and Italian. He'd explained that the broad beans in the dish were grown only in one place: in the fields of a village a few miles from town. 'It's a simple dish poor people have prepared for hundreds of years,' he told her. 'Pork cheeks, tomatoes, plenty of fennel and these special beans, cooked slowly overnight in a pot resting in ashes.'

The taste, when the food came, was one hundred times better than his description. All along the country lanes of this part of Puglia she'd seen the wild fennel he spoke of growing tall.

These new sights and flavours were a tonic and slowly but surely she began to unwind. Susannah had already taken hundreds of photos on her phone. She'd lingered in one particular street where tiny shops brimmed with local products: round loaves as big as bicycle wheels, piles of truffles and dried mushrooms, packets of snacks called *taralli*, flavoured with fennel, bunches of wild thyme arranged like bouquets, the aroma intoxicating, far stronger than any thyme she'd used back home. Home seemed miles away and she realised that although she'd sent her postcard, she'd not had time to think of how Maureen was coping with Cobwebs. She resolved to phone her as soon as she had a signal.

'Where are you staying?' the friendly waiter asked when he topped up her wine.

'I'm not sure yet,' she said. 'But I'm hoping to find a vacant room in a place called Masseria della Torre.'

'Not bad. But emphasise those vowels.' He repeated the three words and she copied him and he applauded. *'Brava!'*

'I think I know it,' he continued. 'A small hotel that's often closed. A typical fortified farmhouse. That's what *masseria* means. You might be lucky, but if not, come back to me and I'm sure I could sort something for you. Masseria della Torre. Repeat, signorina.'

His smile was infectious and she laughed as she tried her best with the pronunciation, wondering if all Italian males were given chatting-up lessons at their mother's knee. 'I'll soon be fluent,' she said.

'The best way to learn is to have a go, without worrying about mistakes. If you like, I can give you lessons.' He held out his hand. 'I'm Giacomo. That's James in English. But you can call me Jack if you like. That's what they called me when I worked in Manchester.'

'Susannah.'

'An Italian name,' he said.

'But written with an h.'

A group of four entered the bar and he excused himself. She watched as he pulled chairs back for the women, his smile charming and welcoming. For a while, she listened to him, not understanding a single word of the Italian, thinking to herself it sounded like music, wondering how old he was. His dark hair was cut well, beginning to salt and pepper a little at the temples and his tailored white shirt fit snugly on his trim body, but she reckoned he was younger than her. *Cradle snatching, Susi*, she thought as she sipped her second glass. *What the heck. Enjoy yourself. He's only helping you with Italian.*

When she paid her bill half an hour later, the place was buzzing. He gave brief directions and stapled his card to the receipt. 'Call me. I'd love to meet with you again. And if you want an Italian lesson, I'm your man.'

'If I'm free, I'll ring. *Grazie*,' she attempted, wondering if she wasn't sounding standoffish. He was definitely flirting with her. *I'm your man...* what was all that about?

His grin was wide as he nodded his head in approval and inside she realised she was smiling too. Maureen had told her she should have fun in Italy. She might well take up her advice.

CHAPTER 10

PUGLIA, 1945

THURSDAY, MAY 3, 1945.

Nonno Domenico is working in his vegetable garden when I return from the beach, reeling from my new knowledge about Anto and how he – no, she! – hid her identity. What does Nonno Domenico know? Does he see Anto as his grandson, or granddaughter?

An old sun hat is pulled down on his head. He's singing. I catch the words *figlia mia*, my daughter, but the rest is dialect and I don't understand. He looks up to me and shouts cheerily, 'Find your accordion, Roberto, and this evening when the sun goes down, we can make music like the old times.'

'It's broken,' I reply. I'm sure I have never held an accordion, let alone played one.

The situation grows more bizarre by the day: this pretence; the loss of who I am. I have to decide what to do. If I were to set out on the road, I might ask a passer-by the way to Foggia and find the airfields that Anto has mentioned. But I am uncertain, wary. Anto has mentioned more than once about the present danger: how young men are picked up and taken away for being deserters. There is a war going on, apparently. Who is fighting whom? I have no idea, but Anto and Nonno Domenico say I speak Italian well. But I speak English too. Are we enemies? If not, who is my foe? I need to find out more. I have no wish to be taken for a deserter and executed. I am safe here at the moment. My hope is that, as each day passes, my memory, stuck fast like a fly in amber, will come back to me.

I pick up a bucket and resume my task of collecting stones, my thoughts whirring. The stones seem to grow overnight and push themselves to the surface like weeds. Domenico nods approval as I start. 'We will soon have enough to build a pigsty and then we can go to market and buy a piglet to fatten up for new year. You love *porchetta*, don't you, Roberto?'

'Even more than sea urchins,' I reply as I tip another pail-load onto the growing pile.

Not long afterwards, Anto returns from the beach and half an hour later, we sit to share a simple meal. '*Focaccia pugliese*,' she announces. A kind of cooked sandwich of olives, soft onions and tomatoes is placed before us on the table. It is a delicious meld of flavours and as I watch how Anto moves, everything slips into place: her small hands, her skills in the kitchen, her delicate frame and the soft, smooth skin on her face devoid of hair, the fact that she was so eager to have me sleep in the little *trullo*, which would give her more privacy – all these factors make me ask myself how come I did not realise earlier that Anto is a woman. Burning with questions, I sneak looks at her while she goes about her tasks. I cannot rid my mind of her diving into the sea: naked, her curves, her breasts, the triangle of hair between her thighs. I am living in a fantasy world. Nothing is real: Domenico is in a world of his own, Anto is in disguise and I do not know which world I belong to.

During the day, I help with odd jobs around the place, trying to distract my thoughts. There are no more stones to collect for the time being, but I help Anto mend a fence. She holds a stake fast while I hammer in nails to bend into staples to secure the wire. The nails are rusty. I prised them from an old door. Everything about this property is make-do. Cracked windows are held together with tape, hinges are rusting or snapped off, paint is blistered on woodwork, Nonno's tools are patched together with lengths of wire and string.

'When we arrived here, the place was ramshackle,' Anto tells me as I tut when another rusty nail snaps. 'In the past, we only managed to come for one month each year and many items of furniture have disappeared. With all the evacuees from the cities, we are fortunate that nobody decided to move in and claim it as their own, but...' She gestures to the land. 'It is a poor piece of ground. We have done what we can in the months we've been here. You are a great help to us, signore. You truly arrived from nowhere like an angel, as Nonno continues to remind us.'

And so, another reason not to leave presents itself. As I wind the wire through the home-made staples, I am distracted by the tiny curls of hair on the back of her neck as she bends to hold the post secure. As her hair parts, I see the lighter skin the sun has not touched. Soft and tender. If I were to leave now, her life would turn more difficult with the decline of her grandfather's health. And I do not like to think how vulnerable she will be, left completely alone.

We eat the rest of the fish in the evening and Domenico remarks that tomorrow I must help him fish again. 'Although Anto is a better fisherman than you have become, Roberto,' he says, his face a grimace.

Anto winks at me and I smile.

The night is balmy and after Nonno has taken himself off to his bed, Anto and I sit outside. Fireflies flit in and out of prickly pear plants that form a border around the perimeter of the land. The way they light up flicks on something else in my brain, but

I cannot pinpoint the memory and anyway I am distracted by the person sitting near me.

'I love this time of year,' Anto says. 'The cool of early mornings and evenings. Before long, the heat will become too much to bear. Do you think you come from somewhere hot, Roberto?'

I sigh. 'I want to answer you in a different way but... I truly don't know, Anto.'

'Something will happen to spark your memories and then they will return in a whoosh of fire,' she says, 'like from the mouths of fire eaters who used to come to *carnevale* in Foggia before the war.'

'I hope so.'

'But the life you are living at the moment, here with us, is it so very bad?' she asks.

My reply is instant. 'Of course not. But you must understand why I need to know who I really am. I know nothing of my history. I am living in a void.'

There is a long silence while I wrestle with my thoughts.

'Can I ask you something?' I eventually blurt out.

'What do you want to ask me?'

'Why you dress as a boy?'

I watch her face. Her mouth forms an 'o' and when she looks at me, I read fear in her eyes. She jumps up from the stone seat where she's sitting and backs away.

'What are you talking about?'

Her voice is angry but I don't regret my bluntness. Selfish as it might seem, I need to grasp hold of some reality. I hope she will tell me the truth.

'I'm not going to hurt you, Anto,' I say. 'But, if I am to remain here with you and Domenico, I need to understand.'

Her silence is filled with the vibration of cicadas, magnified in the still night.

'How did you know?' she asks.

'I saw you swimming today.'

She swears then, a filthy, unladylike oath and I smile, hoping she will not see my expression in the dull light.

'I thought I had got away with it,' she says. 'The reasons are... complicated.'

'You can trust me and I am not going anywhere soon, as far as I can tell. I won't be telling a soul.'

Another spell of silence falls and then she begins to talk. But she doesn't return to sit near me. Instead, she crouches on the ground facing me, clasping her knees, a safe distance between the two of us.

'My name is Antonella, but since I was very small, the name Anto stuck. I couldn't pronounce my full name properly and all my family know me as Anto.' She adds quietly, 'Knew me...

'I was pleased when Nonno asked if we could leave Foggia and return here to Mattinata. I had to get away. It was increasingly more difficult to look after him in the city. He'd taken to wandering off and each time, it took me ages to track him down. He was bewildered by the ruined streets; it was easy for him to get lost in the mess of bombed houses, and the illness in his mind grew worse with each day. But that wasn't the only reason for wanting to come here.'

She gulps and glances over at me. 'It became too dangerous. Someone wanted to do me great harm.'

CHAPTER 11

FOGGIA, DECEMBER 1943

ANTONELLA'S STORY

'Has the old man wandered off again, Antonella?'

Sixteen-year-old Antonella jumped when she heard his voice. Salvatore Zuccaroli was leaning, one foot propped against the outside wall of the *osteria*, the buttons on his police jacket undone. As he talked, a cigarette hanging from his mouth waggled up and down, matching his greasy gaze that slid up and down her body.

'Would you like me to help?' he asked.

'You have helped me – more than enough, Salvatore.'

The last time she'd allowed him to help search for Nonno, he had grabbed her as they stepped inside the ruins of their home. If Nonno had not moved out of the shadows when he did, she knew what would have happened next. Salvatore had wandering hands and one thing on his mind.

'Oh, there you are, Nonno. I've been looking for you for over an hour,' she'd said, hurrying over to him. Wearing no jacket over his threadbare shirt, he was shivering in the winter air.

'They're not here, Anto,' he'd repeated. 'Where are they all gone?' It was a question he repeated dozens of times each day.

She'd wrapped her shawl around Nonno's shoulders and guided him gently across the fallen stones. Their old house was dangerous, uninhabitable since the bomb raid by the *alleati* back in spring that had flattened half the city. It didn't seem to matter whose side the people of Foggia were on. The *tedeschi* had moved out in October 1943 and by that time Italy had changed sides and was with the *alleati*, but bombs still continued to rain down on the city. Foggia was a hard place to grub for a living.

'This isn't our house anymore,' she'd told her grandfather. She'd stopped telling him that Mamma and Babbo were dead, and her brother Roberto too. It only made him more agitated. 'Let's go back to Zia Giulia's house. She'll have a portion of delicious minestrone in the pot to warm us up.'

Salvatore had dawdled after them as they made their way back to Aunt Giulia's house. Antonella couldn't shake him off with Nonno walking so slowly. She could feel the man's hot breath on the back of her neck but she couldn't hurry her grandfather as he shuffled along. Her aunt's place had been straining at the seams even before she and Nonno had moved in. Six children and an invalid husband to care for were now stretched to ten. But where else could they go? Many of the ruins were used by families who had nowhere else. Corners of buildings held shelters patched together from scavenged timber, old sacks pinned at broken windows, women cooking over fires in the street, fed with sticks of broken furniture. There were rats everywhere; the *tedeschi* had dynamited the sewers as a parting gift before retreating from Foggia and piles of excrement drew flies and a stench that lingered in the nostrils. Once the *alleati* liberated Foggia, they'd promised to repair the town and there were rumours their doctors were going to start vaccinating civilians soon. People were dying from malaria, cholera and typhus as well as air raids. There had been no other option but to move in with Aunt Giulia.

Reluctantly, she'd found a job through Salvatore. They'd been at the same elementary school, and she hadn't liked him then either. A bully and a sneak, he'd picked on the younger ones and even now he seemed to think Antonella owed him more than a spoken thank you for helping her with Nonno. He was always turning up when least wanted, like a scuttling cockroach pouncing to devour smaller insects. Antonella was working as a result of his recommendation, delivering parcels of food to shopkeepers and one or two private houses. Salvatore had given her strict instructions not to tell a soul about what she was doing. She knew that some of the parcels contained stolen rations destined for the *inglesi*, hijacked from their lorries and trains.

Last year she had been involved with a group of women who had congregated outside the *questura*, protesting about heavy action by the police.

'*Vogliamo il pane – vogliamo sfarinare,*' they had chanted. 'We want bread – we want to make flour.'

The final straw for the women had been when the police commander impounded maize flour that a queue of women had carried in their baskets, waiting patiently by the town ovens to bake into bread. Rationing had reduced the daily bread ration and flour to 150 grams per head and the milling of cereals was forbidden. Several mills had been closed to prevent clandestine grinding and hunger and anger had driven the women to protest. Antonella had joined in with her aunt, linking arms with a line of women as they advanced across the piazza and when gunshots rang out, she and Aunt Giulia had run down a side road. Salvatore had pursued them and grabbed hold of Antonella, pinning her against a door.

'*Addhu sta bai, bedda?* Where are you going, pretty one?' he asked, in the dialect they'd both spoken since they were tiny.

When she struggled and told him to go to hell – 'Fàtt' sci ingùlo' – he pushed her closer to the door and she felt him grow excited as she wriggled.

'Get off me, Salvo.'

'I will, but I could oh so easily arrest you and take you back to the police station with me – for joining in with a riot.'

She wanted to spit in his face but she willed herself to stay calm. Aunt Giulia was hovering nearby, concern on her face, gesturing to her mouth to warn Antonella to watch what she said.

He loosened his grip. 'You can go, my lovely Antonella Saponaro. But I shall be keeping a careful eye on you, *signorina bedda*. Remember that you owe me now.'

She and her aunt had hurried away, turning every now and again to make sure that Salvatore was not following. Back at her aunt's house, she couldn't stop shivering. She knew it would not be long before Salvatore came knocking.

And so, ten days later, when he turned up and pushed a perambulator through her aunt's entrance and into the hall, she was drawn into his plans, powerless to avoid.

'Keep a very careful guard of this,' he'd told her, pointing at the large iron-framed contraption. It was odd to see a man with a perambulator. 'If you lose it, then you not only lose your job but I shall report you for being part of the women's revolt.'

In return for knocking at the back door of half a dozen designated grocer shops in the city, and handing over a parcel of goods from under a pile of blankets in the pram, she was paid by Salvatore with small food parcels, which she handed straight away to her aunt. They always made sure to wait until evening and to close the shutters, before opening these packages. A lump of cheese, a bag of salt, tins of ham stolen from trains transporting *inglesi* rations, flour or a cured sausage were like Christmas gifts. Cigarettes could be bartered – and that was a job entrusted to Antonella. 'The fewer people who know,

Antonella, the better,' her aunt had warned her, when she'd suggested her cousin Ernesto helped her. 'Don't get him started down that road,' her aunt had said, shaking her head at the idea. They both knew that what Antonella was doing was criminal. To exchange goods on the black market was punishable with prison or even the death penalty, but the alternative was to starve. From time to time, Antonella borrowed Giulia's baby son to push about in the perambulator to help disguise her activities and her aunt was happy enough to be free of one of her children for a couple of hours.

'You're young to be a mother,' was a comment she heard often enough and she would invent stories about how her husband had been killed and would never see his child, and then sympathy for her circumstances would divert their attention and out would pour their own woes.

Lies began to gush from her tongue like rainwater down drains as she continued her life of deceit. They had a roof over their heads, Nonno had his own bed in the warmth of the kitchen and they had food in their stomachs. But her luck was soon to run out.

'Tomorrow I need you to help with something else,' Salvatore told Antonella as she packed more contraband into the pram. Bottles of grappa and tobacco this time. Slim pickings for her. They would not fill her family's bellies.

'And what if I say no?' She already took so many risks for him.

He caught hold of her arm. 'You would be wise to not argue with me, Antonella. It will be the easiest thing in the world to drop your name as a prime suspect for the disappearance of certain merchandise.' His look was venomous and she stopped her comment that he was not so innocent himself. She knew her words counted for little.

At seven o'clock on the following evening, she turned up at Foggia Station as instructed. Salvatore was waiting.

'Undo the top buttons on that blouse,' he ordered. 'Take out those hairpins. You look like a Mother Superior.'

Antonella's long coffee-brown curls were one of her best features and Salvatore drew in breath as she undid the long plait coiled around her head.

'You're to keep the station guard busy when the next train draws in,' he told her.

'What are you talking about?'

'Get him excited. Divert his attention. Do whatever it takes to distract the young fool. There'll be plenty of flour and fresh vegetables for your family afterwards. Maybe a sack of rice too.'

The drought that the region of Foggia had suffered had caused greater hardship than ever that summer. Antonella couldn't remember the last time they had tasted fresh vegetables. Prices for everything were sky high and Foggia had seen many riots. *We want bread and work* was scrawled everywhere on the walls of the city. There was nowhere for its citizens to grow food in this devastated city and there was no water for irrigation. As long as Antonella wasn't expected to do more than flirt with the guard, she was prepared to obey Salvatore's orders in order to acquire food for her loved ones.

Supplies for the allies were shipped to Taranto and from there loaded onto trains. Lately, there had been a number of organised thefts from warehouses and extra guards had been placed on duty. It was a risky business but a lucrative one for black marketeers.

She'd attracted the attention of the young, pimply-faced guard by falling over on the platform, pretending she'd sprained her ankle, crying out with pain. He'd scooped her from where she lay and she'd asked him if there was anywhere quiet he could take her.

'I've come over all faint,' she said, enjoying being the actress, bringing her hand to her head, her blouse gaping, revealing a glimpse of breast.

'I need a glass of water and to rest for a bit... My, but you're strong. What's your name?' she asked, running her hand up and down his arm as he carried her, gazing up at him from beneath lowered eyelids. 'I bet your *fidanzata* loves that you're so *forte*.'

The guard blushed and told her his name was Pasquale and that he didn't have a girlfriend, and when Antonella stroked his cheek, it was as if she'd pressed a go-button. He couldn't keep his hands to himself and she let them wander for a bit, checking through the window of his little office to see the progress of Salvatore and his men. When the guard's fingers fumbled to undo the final buttons on her blouse, she gave a little moan of encouragement but slapped his eager fingers away from her breasts. 'Just one little kiss on the lips is permitted, Pasquale. I'm not that kind of girl,' she murmured, watching all the while over his head the half a dozen men unloading goods from the back of the train. When she saw that they were finished, she pushed the guard away.

'Don't you have to blow your whistle or something?'

His eyes widened in shock as he looked at his pocket watch. 'Don't go away, signorina. I'll be back.'

But as soon as he left the little room, she was out of the station and running away as fast as she could, stopping only to do up the buttons on her blouse, laughing at the stupidity of men who were governed so easily by their cocks instead of their brains.

Two days later, she heard the words she'd always dreaded. 'You are under arrest, signorina. Come with us.' Finally, her fears had come true as she knocked on the back door of the big fancy house in the centre of town that belonged to the owner of the paper factory. Instead of the usual maid opening up, a young *carabiniere* stepped forwards and slapped handcuffs round her wrists.

'I've been observing you for a while,' he said as she struggled to wriggle free. But it was impossible to escape and he shouted at her to keep still or else he'd slap her. 'You were seen at the station at the time a supply train was robbed. You are to come with me to the *questura* to answer questions.'

Fortunately, there was no baby cousin in the pram on this occasion. But the guard pulled back the covers to find bottles of grappa and brown paper parcels of sugar and rice that Salvatore had ordered her to deliver from the latest haul.

She spent an uncomfortable night in a cell with three other women. Two were prostitutes, dressed in skimpy clothes. The third was ill and lay on the stone ledge that took up one side of the wall.

'She's diabetic,' the older, chattier prostitute informed her. 'And she has no medicine and the *bastardi* won't get hold of any for her either.' She spat in the direction of the bucket in the corner that served as a latrine. 'Bloody hellhole, this place, run by bloody bastards.' She stretched out her hand to shake Antonella's, her fingernails bitten right down. 'Iole's me name,' she said, introducing herself. 'Welcome to the royal palace.'

'What they got you in here for?' the other woman asked. She was thin and her hair was scraped up in a greasy bun. Antonella couldn't help thinking that to pay to go with either of these two, a man would have to be truly desperate. But these were desperate times and that was after all why she herself had landed up in this cell. The thin woman's name was Sibilla, she'd told her with a lisp, an unfortunate name for someone with missing front teeth.

'Let's say I'm in here because of food deliveries,' Antonella said. 'Contraband. *Spaccio.*'

'Got any food hidden on you?' Iole cackled. 'I swear I'll die of hunger in here before my sentence is over. Even wondered what a juicy rat would taste like roasted.'

The place was grim but the two women were kind and they made a space for her on the floor to sleep beside them that night. It could have been worse.

'Who you working for?' Iole asked.

She was reluctant at first to tell them, but as she lay on the cold floor, the snores of the inmates in the next cell keeping her awake, she thought about the injustice of her situation. Salvatore was no doubt asleep in his comfortable bed with his pretty plump wife. He'd escaped punishment. Why should he get away with it? And so she told the two women about her black market activities.

'Not surprised,' Iole said, when she revealed that her boss was a *carabiniere*. 'I could tell a thing or two to the wives of some of the guards.' She delivered another expert spit towards the bucket. 'Good night, girl. Sweet dreams.'

After a sleepless night, watching cockroaches scuttle along the edges of the cell walls, Antonella made up her mind what she should do. In the morning, when they were brought a bowl of brown-coloured water that was supposed to pass as coffee, and a hunk of mouldy bread, she told the guard she wanted a message delivered to one of his colleagues. To goad him on, she had a bribe... She always carried a ten-lire note in her underwear, hidden in the elastic casing.

Aunt Giulia had advised her to do this. Anto had thought it a ridiculous waste of money at the time. But she'd kept it there for the sake of Nonno. She knew there might come a time when he would need a doctor. The money had been earned by selling a kilo and a half of pasta to the station restaurant, nicked from one of Salvatore's parcels. And those ten lire proved to be how she managed to get out of the cell.

As she spoke to the guard and told him he must tell Agent Zuccaroli to come to her, she dangled the banknote before him.

His greedy eyes lit up and he shoved his hand through the bars to take it but she snatched the note away. 'You only get this when I see Salvatore Zuccaroli standing before me.'

'Put in a good word for us too,' Iole said, a grin on her face when Anto sat down near them, her legs trembling, fingers crossed that her plan would work.

The next day, Salvatore's face appeared at the grille. 'What do you want, Antonella?' he hissed.

'I think you know what I want. Get me out of this place. And help my friends while you're at it.'

'If you're asking me to smuggle in a saw to cut through those bars,' he said, 'then you can think again.' He started to move away but she called him back.

She lowered her voice. 'You will have to use that brain of yours, and come up with another way of getting us out of here. Or else, I will be broadcasting to every guard and officer in here about your dealings on the black market.'

His face registered panic.

'I'm not bluffing, Salvatore. You owe me this time.'

Those ten lire had proved to be the best she'd spent in her life so far. That very same day she was released, her friends shuffling out of the cell after her. But, of course, life is never smooth and that was not the end of her ordeal.

'Watch your back,' Salvatore had hissed as he walked by her side from the prison entrance.

'I always do,' she answered with a boldness she did not feel, 'especially when *you're* around.'

The morning after, she was draping washing on Aunt Giulia's line when she was grabbed from behind, a hand clasped tightly over her mouth, preventing her from screaming. Salvatore dragged her into the ruins of a house on the next block. As hard as she struggled, the harder he fastened his grip. He tied a scarf around her mouth and hit her around the head with his fists, warning her not to try to escape or he would shoot her.

'Nobody gets the better of me, Antonella,' he snarled, hatred in his eyes as he delivered punches to her stomach. 'If you ever open your mouth to blab about me again, then I will stick a knife in your stomach, you stupid bitch.'

She doubled over, clutching her hands to her belly and to her horror, he ripped off her blouse and then she felt the full force of his belt whipping her bare back as she fell to her knees. When he had finished, he turned her round roughly. She brought her knee up to his groin and was punished with more blows to her face as he pushed her to the ground. She tried to kick against him, but it was no use. His full weight on top of her now, he forced her knees apart and there was nothing she could do to stop him.

She remembered later how she tried to tell him that it was her time of the month but she was gagged and her protests came out as nothing but desperate noises. It would have made no difference, anyway.

When she came to later on the hard stones, the air was cold on her bare breasts and she ached all over. Salvatore was gone. Tearing the gag from her mouth, she vomited into the rubble. Too traumatised to cry, sometime later, she crawled back to Aunt Giulia and collapsed on her kitchen floor.

Later that very night she and Nonno left Foggia for good. Aunt Giulia had shooed the children away from the kitchen as she bathed her niece in the zinc tub, whispering to her as if she were one of her little ones. 'Everything will be all right, Antonella *mia*, but you must go far away from here. He will be looking for you all the time now.'

Giulia dabbed the girl's swollen face with eucalyptus oil and placed cold compresses on her bruises. She cried out in anger when she saw Antonella's back, invoking Jesus, Mary and San Rocco, their patron saint, to care for her. Not once did

Antonella cry. Her aunt cut her long hair and dug out a spare pair of her teenaged son's trousers, and that night, in all outward appearances, Antonella became a boy.

Her body was bruised but Salvatore had not broken her spirit. Despite her terrible wounds, she knew she had to remain strong to take care of Nonno for the journey ahead. She insisted on bringing him with her. He was a burden on Aunt Giulia and the household, and they would be safer travelling together.

Giulia distributed food between two small sacks and gave them each a blanket to carry. Antonella's back was so sore from the beatings, she had to swivel the bag with its load round to her front as they embarked on their journey.

It took them the best part of five days to walk to Mattinata. Nonno was not strong, Antonella was a physical and emotional wreck and progress was slow. They kept to tracks and the edges of fields, never venturing along the main route, sheltering in derelict buildings during the night.

On the third evening, they slept in an abandoned barn on old hay, while the January wind whistled through the gaps and Nonno kept announcing that he could smell the sea. And he was right. All the rest of the way from Manfredonia, they made their way along the shore and over the rocks, Nonno nosing the salt tang like a sea dog sniffing his territory. Despite the winter air and despite Nonno telling his granddaughter that she would catch her death, when they came to the wide bay where the land rose up to meet the Gargano forests, Antonella stripped to her underclothes and threw herself into the sea. The saltwater stung her wounds like a penance and as her back smarted, she told herself that if ever Salvatore Zuccaroli was to lay a finger on her again, she would kill him with her bare hands.

CHAPTER 12

PUGLIA, 1945

THURSDAY, MAY 3, 1945.

The cacophony of cicadas decreases as Antonella ends her story. She tells it dispassionately even when she revisits the most brutal part – the only indication of her inner feelings is when she averts her eyes. At first, I say nothing. What can I say that does not sound trite? I feel shame that I am a man and deep anger that this brute Salvatore should believe it his right to treat a woman in such a cowardly, barbaric way. I want to tell Antonella that not all men are like him, but I am sure she has already formed her own opinions. It's easy for me, a man who has never been abused, to dish out platitudes of empty comfort. I can only hope that her mental scars will heal with time and that she comes across a man of kindness who will respect and love her. In the meantime, I hope in some small way to ease her pain.

Fireflies continue to flit through the vegetation and they remind me of lights I've seen at the edge of a large, open field somewhere – but the flash of recall extinguishes as fast as it flares. I start to rack my brain for further glimpses of my past but the girl's voice interrupts as she begins to talk again.

'That monster escaped punishment and wasn't thrown into a cell. It's the people he works with,' Antonella says. 'Many people in high places are involved in the black market. They look after their own.' She pauses, her eyes fiery. 'He must never find me again.'

Her dressing as a boy is an escape not only from Salvatore, but from all men, I think. The fact she has entrusted her story to me is a huge responsibility, one which I accept seriously. 'Thank you for telling me,' I say. 'I understand now.'

She yawns and rises from the ground where she's been crouching. 'To be honest, Roberto, *I* am the only person who can understand. But it has helped to talk. Nonno can't understand so I don't talk to him about what is going on in my head. Talking to you has lightened a load. *Buona notte.*'

Her goodnight wishes do not work, for I toss and turn that night, the whine of mosquitoes accompanying my black thoughts. Next morning, I am covered with bites, inflamed welts on every exposed part of my body.

FRIDAY, MAY 4, 1945.

At breakfast, Anto suggests we take a trip to Mattinata on the following day. 'If you exaggerate your head injury and keep quiet, we can go to town and look for medicine for your fevers. It's a fair walk, so we'll leave early,' she says as we dip dry bread into a cup of something she tells me is coffee, but to me tastes nothing like it.

'The home-made remedy I used on you last time will help soothe your malaria but it won't keep fevers at bay. And I need more flour, if there is any to be found. Today, you can help us with our salt. We're running out and we need it for curing our fish.'

It is a laborious task and renders little. Down at the beach, I help them carry a large metal pot and two rakes from Nonno's *trabucco* to a small salt pan they have created. The old man tuts as he examines the pot, pointing to its base, worn thin.

'*Porca Madonna,*' he swears. 'This will not last much longer. How to patch it, Roberto?'

'We can look tomorrow for a new one, Nonno,' Antonella says. 'If you catch extra fish this evening, we can sell those and add to our savings.'

The old man looks out to sea and nods. 'It will be overcast later before the rain. I shall try.'

Anto and Domenico instruct me how to reinforce the mud walls around the salt pan and close gaps to trap the seawater caught at high tide.

'It will evaporate in the sun, but it will take many more weeks before we can collect it,' Anto tells me. 'But salt is necessary to preserve our fish. It's impossible to buy now.'

Nonno takes himself off to try his luck with casting a rod from his *trabucco*, while I help Anto bundle up more driftwood to carry back to the *trullo* for the cooking stove.

The sun is high and before long, I am sweating like a pig. The sea beckons: flat, calm, inviting. The old man sits on the *trabucco*, his wide straw hat sheltering him from the strong rays, his legs dangling over the side of the platform, his body supported by thin rails behind which he sits with his rod.

'We've done all we can for now for the salt. There is nothing else to do, Roberto,' Anto says. She walks towards the sea, fully clothed in her patched trousers. With a smile, she turns and calls me to join her. I wade out and she warns me to avoid the rocks. 'They're full of urchins and the spines are difficult to remove. Start swimming as soon as you can.'

And then, with hardly a splash she is off, swimming with strong strokes towards the grotto and I follow, struggling to keep up. When we reach the flat rock where I watched her dive naked the other day, she hauls herself up with ease and, panting from the effort, I climb up to join her. The waves slap about our feet, the water sucks and echoes deep in the cave behind.

'This is my favourite place in the world,' she says, her voice raised above the noise of the ocean, her head on one side to release water from her ear. 'Nobody can find me here.'

She is relaxed. Her eyes smile. It's plain to see now, her wet clothes sticking to her shape like a second skin, that she is a woman and I feel like an intruder in her special space. I inch away to the other side of the rock.

'I'm sorry I saw you here the other day,' I shout above the sound of the sea. 'In your place where nobody can find you.'

She shrugs. 'Roberto and I used to come here every August holiday. He taught me to dive and hold my breath underwater. I don't mind you being here,' she says. 'One day, I'll show you another place where we used to hide.'

And in that moment I feel honour, as well as responsibility, that I am being accepted by this spirited girl.

'Race you back,' she calls. 'Nonno will be wondering where we've got to.' And in one smooth movement, she dives from the rock like a flying fish, and although I try my best, she beats me to shore. She laughs at me when I crawl onto the sand on all fours and collapse, panting to catch my breath like a beached whale.

Domenico has caught plenty of fish for our meal from his perch on the *trabucco*. I remember him saying they always eat fish on Fridays. But the sea is bountiful and every day is like a Friday. Anto grills large prawns over the embers of our drift-wood fire, their backs striped like tigers. She adds a handful of sardines and two sea bream from Domenico's catch. To round off this feast, she produces a small dish of a summer salad she'd left cooling in Domenico's cave. I'm sure I've eaten this some-where else.

'*Panzanella*,' she tells me. 'Made from hard bread soaked in vinegar, seasoned and flavoured with herbs, tomatoes and cucumbers.'

I need to know where I have tasted this before.

That night, I write more than usual in my notebook. Today has felt like a holiday. Almost perfect. If it were not for the hole in my memory, life would not be too bad. The inside of my head is like a kaleidoscope. A turn of the wrist, the tiny mirrors move and patterns fall apart.

SATURDAY, MAY 5, 1945.

We leave Domenico behind in the morning and set off to market. He has no wish to come along, tired after last night's fishing trip in the choppy sea when I helped him haul in another catch of goodly sized gilthead bream.

'But be sure to fetch me some more pipe tobacco if you can,' he commands us. For a few days now he has been smoking his own concoction – a mixture of herbs collected from ditches – and the smell is foul. It will be a welcome relief to get hold of proper tobacco and, if I'm lucky, cigarettes for myself.

'Then, we must fetch a good price for your fish, Nonno, if we are to buy a new salt pot as well as your baccy,' Anto says, kissing him goodbye before we set off down the dirt track to reach the provincial road. She's bound up my head with an old rag again and added a streak of fish blood for good measure to make my old injury look authentic. For a while, I lollop as I walk, acting soft, and she laughs. I realise it is only the second time I have heard her laugh. She balances the basket of fish on her head, but I insist on carrying it.

'*Grazie*, Roberto,' she says, as I lift it from a circlet of cloth she's arranged on the crown of her head. 'It's only women who carry loads this way, but as we draw nearer town, it's best I take it from you. It would look suspicious for you to carry a basket with your wounded head, so I shall carry it then. I'm a young boy, after all.' Her face lights up with a cheeky smile.

'So I see,' I reply.

'I often wish I'd been born a boy. A woman's life is hard.'

She stops and I turn to listen.

'I wanted to continue at school. But there was only money for my brother to study. I left without learning how to write much except my name, sufficient for signing a form. All those words you scribble in your notebook. Will... will you teach me how?'

It's clear it takes a lot for her to ask this of me.

'With pleasure,' I say. 'And we will start right now.' I talk to her about the lines she must learn to put on paper and point to a tall plant soaring above the scrubby vegetation in the ditch. 'That is the shape of the letter "I",' I say. A round stone on the track becomes my teaching aid for the letter 'O'. Putting down the basket of fish, I draw other vowels in the sandy track. 'Each day we will learn a few,' I say, excited at all I have to teach her. 'Until we have completed the alphabet. Then we will make words.'

She beams at me when I tell her that if there is any money left from today's shopping, we should buy her a notebook. And with that, a picture of a homely room shimmers in my head: a woman is reading in a cosy sitting room, the reflection of fire-light glinting on her glasses, her fair hair escaping from an untidy bun. There's a bookshelf to one side of the hearth and a young boy is bent over an exercise book on the rag rug at her feet. He is sounding out his letters. And as soon as it flashes in my brain, the mirage is gone and I stand stock-still and rub my head.

What am I doing, making plans to stay here with Anto and her grandfather? What about my life before?

'Is everything all right, Roberto?' she asks.

'A picture,' I say. 'Another picture from the past. It's like a lamp that flickers on and off to tease me for a few seconds.'

'I believe one day the lamp will stay on all the time.'

'So you have said before, Anto. I hope you're right. It's taunting me.' I pick up the basket and we continue on our way to town. Neither of us talks much after that.

Mattinata is an untidy straggle of stone houses, most of them whitewashed, many in ruins. Piles of rubble have been swept to the sides of the narrow streets. There are troughs planted with herbs and washing hangs down the sides of houses still standing. Fishing boats are moored at the sea's edge and as we join the main thoroughfare, we merge with other people. Antonella moves closer to me and lowers her gaze, her smile has gone as we enter a large market square. Draped from some windows are home-made banners and flags: the green, white and red of Italy, Stars and Stripes and a couple of Union Jacks. *Evviva gli alleati* is scrawled on the walls of a ruined building and I can make out the few remaining letters that shows this was once the town hall: *MUN...* the rest *ICIPIO*, blasted away. In the centre of the square, a young man sits at a table littered with empty bottles. He's playing a guitar and a cluster of people listen to him as he sings a lively tune. Some of the onlookers clap and a couple dances.

'*La tarantella,*' Antonella whispers to me and we watch the couple twirl faster and faster.

'But where is today's market?' I hear her ask two smiling spectators above the music.

'No market today,' one shouts and her friend chips in, holding high a bottle of greenish-yellow liqueur. 'We're too busy celebrating.'

'Celebrating?' Antonella asks.

'In which cave have you been hiding, *ragazzo*? The war is over. There'll be plenty of time for markets in the future, but it's not every day a war comes to an end.' One of the women pushes glasses into our hands and tops them up before making a toast to peace.

I want to ask questions but I keep to my promise of remaining mute and when another woman asks me how I hurt my head, I ignore her, look down at the ill-fitting shoes that Nonno has given me, my toes peeping out from where I have cut the ends away to give me room.

Antonella tells them how I was caught in a raid; that I haven't been the same since.

'You should take him to the hospital the *inglesi* have set up. My son had typhoid and they saved his life.'

'And can they help with malaria?' Antonella asks.

'*Certo.* They give out tablets and spray for your house too.'

'To put in a Flit gun,' the second woman explains, 'and spray the walls to kill the mosquito buggers and lice.'

At the other end of the piazza, there is a crash of breaking glass and men start to shout. A fight breaks out. More men spill from an *osteria*, a table is turned over and people scatter in all directions. The women tell us to come inside to escape the fray as other men and youths join in, hurling chairs and abuse. Peering through her kitchen window, I see a woman attempt to break up a brawl by throwing a pail of water over a couple of lads rolling on the floor, busy with their fists, their feet kicking each other.

'It's the *fascisti* receiving the bashing they deserve,' the owner of the house says. 'One war has ended, but another begins. When will they ever learn?'

With a blare of hooters, a couple of Jeeps career into the piazza, the screech of brakes as they skid to a halt dispersing the brawlers. I recognise the white belts and red berets of military police.

How do I know that? Some deep dark corner of my memory is still working.

I listen as they bark orders in a mixture of English and

pidgin Italian. They are joined by *carabinieri* who take over and, as quickly as trouble broke out, order is restored. A handful of men are handcuffed and taken away and Antonella thanks the woman of the house before we leave.

'The Jeeps were *inglesi*,' I mumble to Antonella as we walk away, stepping over the debris of scattered tables and chairs.

'*Sì*,' she agrees. 'And we will go now to their hospital and see if we can find medicine for you.'

All the while, she keeps her head down and sticks to me like a shadow, her fear palpable. But this town is a day's drive from Foggia and her attacker, Salvatore. Surely, she is safe here? I want to tell her that I am at her side to protect her. But how can I? A man with a mind of missing pieces?

Red crosses on the roof and flaps of a large tent indicate a field hospital. A queue stretches before us: a mixture of elderly women with young children and a dozen or so injured men like me, bandaged, leaning on crutches. Feeling a fraud, I want to tear the rags from my head but I resist. Today they are a disguise for Antonella. While we wait under the sun, a blue-eyed nurse, her face rosy from heat, distributes water. She is tall, her colouring different from the women in the queue. I hear a child pipe up, asking why the woman's hair is burnt orange like fire and his mother rebukes him, telling him to be quiet.

And when it is our turn and Antonella speaks slowly and explains that I need medicine because I am suffering from malaria, the middle-aged doctor tells me he wants to check my head wound too and when he stumbles over his Italian and I instinctively help him and answer in perfect English, he asks me quietly if I have perhaps been suffering from battle fatigue. I know this expression too well. It is another way of describing cowardice or absence without leave. Desertion. And I curse my stupidity. I promised to keep my big trap shut for Antonella and that promise has been broken.

'I really do not know, sir,' is my reply in English to this doctor.

'What is your name and rank?'

'I don't know that either, sir.'

And when I catch the look he gives me, I know he is suspicious.

CHAPTER 13

'We need to look into this further,' the doctor says, tapping a pencil on his notepad and he tells me a nurse will check my head wound while he fetches another doctor to help examine me. 'I won't be long, young man.'

But when he leaves, I get up from the couch where he's told me to sit. I indicate to the approaching nurse that I need to pee, and I brush past her. Outside, Antonella is waiting, sitting out of the sun under the tent awning.

'We have to leave. Fast. I'll explain later,' I tell her and, without asking the reason, she follows as I dash off.

We keep away from the main piazza and hurry through side streets, darting through alleys, up and down flights of stairs, past piles of stones that were once houses until we are at the town's edge. Antonella leads me across a field still planted with last year's closely packed maize, the browned leaves reaching above our heads, concealing our passing, rustling as we push past.

'Why didn't you want to stay to get help?' she asks, when we have put in enough distance. 'The *inglesi* could help mend your memory.'

'I was afraid I'd be arrested. The doctor thought I was a deserter. I need to find out more about myself first.'

I do not admit that I am afraid of what I might discover. And there is something else too. If I am not with Antonella, who will protect her? Nonno is an old man. I don't know what I truly want.

It takes longer to return to the *trullo* along the circuitous route that Antonella follows. We don't use the road but travel through grove after grove of olives. For a while we rest in the shade of these ancient trees, our backs against thick trunks, gnarled and contorted into swirls and knots.

'This tree could be as old as one thousand years,' she tells me, while we recover our breath.

I scratch the word 'olive' in the dust and she traces the outlines with her finger.

'We didn't get you a notebook,' I say.

'Or a new pot for the salt. Or tobacco. Nonno will be angry when I tell him we left the fish outside the hospital tent.'

She holds up a flat metal tin and I read the label – *Atabrine Malaria Tablets* – and the instructions to take one a day after a meal. 'At least we have these,' she says. 'A nurse gave them to me while you were inside the tent.'

The shadows of the trees are long across the track as we round the final bend leading to the *trulli*, pale pink in the falling sun.

'We're back, Nonno,' Antonella shouts, making her way straight to the well to pull a pail of water from its cool depths.

Never has water tasted so good as we drink deep to quench our thirst.

She calls him again, but there is no answer.

'I'll pick tomatoes and wild salad for supper,' she says. 'Perhaps he's fishing. Can you fetch him from the beach, Roberto? He'll have lost track of time without us here.'

As I tread down the coastal path, the sun spills gold on its slide to the sea and I stop to gaze, thinking to myself how this place has become a sanctuary. As I resume the steep descent to the shore, I wonder at the way gut instinct made me escape from the British field hospital today. Something had blocked me from accepting help. I hadn't liked the way the doctor intimated I was a deserter, but I also wonder if it's something to do with not wanting to leave Domenico and Anto, two people who have become dear to me.

The old man is still fishing from his *trabucco*, despite the late hour. I call to him but he ignores me. The evening breeze is blowing from the sea and so I shout louder.

I step along the gangplank to the fishing platform and as I approach him, he doesn't turn to greet me and my heart sinks.

I hunker down beside his body. His head is slumped on his chest as if he is dozing, and his trunk is supported by the wooden rails. I know immediately he is gone.

His body is surprisingly light as I carry him gently from the fishing platform to the cave where he stores his gear. His eyes are closed and I hope he passed away when he was in the middle of a happy dream of his wife. Antonella will be distraught and I feel vindicated at my decision to flee from the doctor. She will need me in these coming days. I return slowly up the track, planning how to tell her that she has lost all her family now.

There are no tears from Antonella. Instead, she falls silent as she continues her work about the kitchen. She rinses clean a pile of plants she has collected in her basket. She chops an onion and a carrot. From a dented bucket at the back door, she cuts a handful of parsley.

'Can I do anything, Antonella?' I ask. I can't imagine how lost she will be without him. I am sad and I only knew him for weeks, not a lifetime.

She shakes her head. 'Best call me Anto. Tonight, we'll eat the last of Nonno's catch. Tomorrow we'll say goodbye to him.'

That is about the sum of her words for the rest of the evening. She lays a third place where her grandfather would have sat and we eat our portions of fish soup in silence, his empty chair a sombre reminder that he is gone. Before I leave the *trullo*, I reach out to touch her arm to offer her comfort, but she shrinks away with a frantic shake of her head before taking up a piece of material which she begins to stitch.

I realise it is a length of silk that she must have cut from the parachute that the old man described as my wings. It is the first time I have seen her sew and for a while, I watch her slender fingers pushing the needle and thread back and forth through the cloth, thinking about time and tide. How they wait for no man. How it is highly possible that time might not bring back my memory. I leave Antonella sewing and retire to my lonely *trullo*, the loss of Nonno Domenico making me brood on the passing of time. He snatched me from death when he rescued me. I owe him. I'm not sure if I believe in prayers but I find myself vowing that I will protect his granddaughter for as long as I am around. A kind of peace descends on me, as if floating on clouds, and I sleep easy.

SUNDAY, MAY 6, 1945.

In the morning, Antonella calls me to a breakfast of coffee she has brewed from the roots of chicory. She adds goat's milk and we dunk dry bread into our bowls. She is very pale, bruised shadows under her eyes telling of her sorrow. But as she talks, she is matter-of-fact.

'We need to catch fish to sell. There's very little money left. I need flour to bake bread too. After we've said goodbye to Nonno, we will catch fish for market.'

I want to comfort her, to soften this brittle, controlled

façade, prompt her to talk about her grandfather and release her grief, but I can't reach her the way she is. And now is not the right time.

Only when we enter the cave and she sees Nonno where I left him lying on top of the fishing nets yesterday, does she falter. Her shoulders slump, she falls to her knees and a single tear falls down her cheek. She joins her hands and mumbles a prayer and I leave the cave to give her privacy.

I am gagging for a smoke but I've left Nonno's spare pipe in my *trullo*. Instead of nicotine, I breathe in the salty air and walk towards the end of the rickety *trabucco*, in sore need of repair. I promised last night to the old man that I would make myself useful and so this will be my first task to help Antonella. How long I stay depends on unknowns: if my memory returns, if Anto wants me around. While I wait for the answers, there is enough to do. The nets need repairing and I will ask her to show me how to use the old man's netting needles. It shouldn't be too complicated. The door to the hut is ajar, hanging on one hinge and I pull it open and step inside. Against one of the walls is a tangle of nets and I pull one of them up – it is surprisingly heavy. Only by laying it out on the beach will I be able to determine the extent of the damage, so I heave it on my shoulders and tread warily down the gangplank, stepping over the loose boards. It will keep me very busy, this repair work, but if I am to catch fish, I prefer to do so from the *trabucco* rather than drowning myself at sea in a boat I cannot control. On a flat stretch of sand, I begin to arrange the net, untangling years of neglect, and then Antonella approaches and, without a word exchanged, we work until the net is spread like an enormous cobweb over the shore.

'This will take weeks to mend,' Anto says, 'but your hands and mine will manage it together. I'll show you how.' Her cheeks are streaked with tears and she wipes them away with the backs of her hands and then kneels to inspect the condition of the net. Her courage reinforces my decision to stay. At least for a while. Although the war is over, its ripples still spread as people settle scores. We heard gunshots the other night and Anto dropped her cup on the kitchen floor, cutting her finger as she scraped up the pieces. I can't bear to think of her fending for herself in her isolated *trullo*.

After a while, when I see her tears have stopped, I ask, 'How does it all connect on the fishing platform? All these wires and pulleys?'

'Tomorrow we'll visit the *trabucco* in the next bay. If there's nobody there, you can see for yourself.' She pauses and sits back on her haunches. 'But now we will bury Nonno.'

'Don't you have to notify anybody? Tell your priest? The authorities?'

'Nobody else needs to know. I want it that way.' She picks at the pebbles on the sand, her head bowed. 'I don't need people prying. I thought you understood.' She looks up at me, her eyes boring into mine.

'If that's what you want, Antonella.'

'And please call me Anto.'

Like a hermit crab, she retreats again into her shell. What difference is it to me if we keep it simple and bury the old man in a place he loved? It makes sense. There must be thousands of others swallowed quietly into the land by this war.

'Where shall I dig?' I ask.

'There's a spot on the rise, at the end of the olive grove. Nonno often sat there in the evening smoking his pipe. There will be perfect.'

And so, shortly before sunset, we dig a hole together in the stony ground and say goodbye to Domenico. There is no tombstone to mark the place. Only we know that he lies there. I leave Antonella alone after we have covered up the fresh soil with stones, scattered haphazardly, as naturally as possible, so that nobody can tell what rests beneath. I leave her, sitting where

Nonno used to sit, and walk back to my *trullo*, leaving the door ajar. It is dark when I hear her footsteps approach but she walks straight past. It takes me a while to sleep, because I picture her in her own *trullo*, grieving alone for her grandfather. But I know she will not want me there with her.

CHAPTER 14

MONDAY, MAY 7, 1945.

In the morning, we walk to the opposite end of the beach from the grotto and I follow her as she clambers over rocks. Above us, olive trees and prickly pears grow to the furthest edges of the cliff and small pink flowers nod in the gentlest of breezes.

'We have to swim around this point to get to the next bay,' she calls and she dives away from the rocks into the white-tipped waves. I wonder if she would have stripped off her clothes if I had not been there. But the sun is hot today and we will soon dry.

As we round the outcrop, another small bay opens up where an intact *trabucco* sits at the edge of the sea.

'We need to check nobody is about before we swim ashore,' Antonella calls, treading water as she waits for me to catch up.

The bay is empty.

'I hoped as much,' she says. 'This belongs to the Rizzi boys, but they all left for war. And it's too much work for their elderly father. Who knows if they will ever return?'

On shore again, we squeeze out excess water from our

clothes and approach the structure, similar to Nonno's but somewhat larger and more intact. Again, the image of a huge insect springs to mind: a dragonfly perched at the edge of the water to catch its prey.

'When we were on holiday, Roberto and I used to help Nonno all the time. Maybe we were a nuisance when I think back, but he was always patient with us.'

She points to one of two long poles pointing horizontally over the sea. 'Roberto used to climb up and balance, and shout when he saw the fish approaching. And then Nonno and Babbo would race down the platform. I remember the spring of the boards under their bare feet as they hurried to take up positions to turn handles on the shaft to raise the net. The fish flapped like diamonds in the sunlight and I would lean over the side and shout out what we had caught. Most of the time it was red mullet. We call them *cefali* round here. And there were crabs, sometimes lobsters dragged from the bottom if the tide was out, plenty of sardines and mackerel, tuna, swordfish.' She smiles when she tells me how she yearned to find a mermaid. 'But I only ever found seahorses. You never knew what the sea would gift from one catch to the next. We have never gone hungry here, Roberto. Not like when we lived in the city.'

While she talks, I cast my eyes over the complicated arrangement of wires, and wade through the shallows to climb the ladder to the platform, trying to understand the mechanism that raises the net. I pull off my shirt and hang it to dry over a railing and Antonella does the same. She wears a vest underneath and I try not to look at the small swell of her breasts. When she walks to the end of the platform and stands gazing out to sea, I am horrified. The top of her neck and shoulders are horribly scarred with purple lines crisscrossing her back and I clench my fists in anger as I picture how she was whipped by the brutish *carabiniere* called Salvatore. As she turns and sees me staring, she reaches for her shirt.

'No, Antonella.' I walk towards her and she shrinks back. 'Please don't be afraid.'

She stays where she is as I tell her to leave off her shirt, that the sun will help heal her scars.

'He's made me ugly,' she whispers and I shake my head.

'Not ugly at all.' I'm longing to reach out and take this beautiful girl in my arms, offer her any comfort I can. But I know she is too fragile. I have earned her trust and I must keep it.

Instead, I turn away and continue to take note of the way the pulleys and wires at the end of the shorter poles support the weight of the wide lift net. There are stouter poles buried in the sand on the beach to which more wires are secured to hold the *trabucco* steady. It is a feat of engineering.

'I need to make a sketch of all this as soon as we get back,' I tell her. 'If we are to repair Nonno's *trabucco* properly, I have much to learn.'

Every day I stay with Antonella is a day my life here becomes more permanent. But where else would I go? Somehow my missing memories don't bother me anymore. Taking what each day brings is enough for the moment.

MONDAY, DECEMBER 31, 1945.

Life is easy; we work well together. There is little time to write in my book when we are busy, but tonight I want to mark the end of the year. We shared a festive meal earlier with wine and a dish of lentils that Antonella told me would bring wealth in the coming year. 'Grapes for good health,' she said and blushed when she served up pomegranates. 'These are supposed to bring fertility, but I eat them because I like them.'

If Antonella is not busy with the vegetable patch or working inside the *trullo*, she helps me. I concentrate on the *trabucco*: replacing rotten wood, carving new pulleys and threading lengths of wire from a coil I found in Nonno's store. When she is down on the beach, Anto sits near Nonno's cave and mends the net – the most crucial element that we removed from the *trabucco* and hauled ashore.

In the evenings, we share meal preparations. She shows me how to gut fish and clean crabs, and I learn local words for eel, sea bass and tuna: *capomazzo, arrannassa* and *tunnu*, all strange to me. All delicious. She prepares octopus one night and I watch with suspicion as she cuts up the slippery creature and adds fresh tomatoes, onions, oil and parsley. It cooks all night in a brown earthenware pot at the edge of the fire. A revelation, tender and succulent, and she promises to make the dish for me again.

We are comfortable with each other, talk when we want to. These days I hardly think what my past was like. I'm making new memories with Antonella. She chides me for not always calling her Anto, but to me she is a woman, not the young boy she thinks she can hide behind. The silences between us are not awkward. Anto sings as she goes about her chores and I sometimes join in. I love it when she wrinkles up her nose and laughter bubbles at my mistakes. Sometimes I sing the wrong words deliberately – simply to enjoy her infectious happiness. We laugh together and I forget why. It's like medicine and costs nothing. When our jobs are done, before we return to the *trullo* to eat, I help her collect shells and sea glass along the tide mark and strange, contorted lumps of driftwood that she crafts into sculptures to hang from olive trees, or props against huge tufa stones scattered in the groves. Sometimes of an evening, she continues to work on the parachute cloth and tells me she is sewing the story of Nonno and her family into embroidered pictures.

WEDNESDAY, APRIL 10, 1946.

After a mild winter the time has come to fish again from Nonno's *trabucco*. At the top of the path, Anto halts at the spot where we laid him to rest. She pulls a small cross from her pocket that she's made from a scrap of olive wood, to which she's fixed pieces of sea glass in blue, green and white patterns.

'This is for you, Nonno,' I hear her gently say. 'Watch over us and help us catch your fish. We miss you.'

She buries the cross beneath the soil above where he lies and smiles at me. '*Andiamo*, Roberto. Let's go.'

Together on the *trabucco* we turn the thick wooden staff to lower the lift net. It creaks as it moves and I remind myself to oil it before next time. As we work on the shaft, pushing on the handles, I think of an image I have seen of a donkey trudging round and round an oil press, his master goading him on to work harder.

'I hope we catch red snapper, and if we're lucky, swordfish,' Anto tells me, her voice breathy from the effort of turning. 'They fetch good prices at market.'

We sit at the end of the platform to wait for the fish to come. The sea is choppy today and a slight breeze ruffles the curls at the back of her neck, like down on a fledgling.

'If we catch enough, we should go to market tomorrow. We have hardly any money left,' she says, her legs swinging back and forth over the waves. 'Will you help me cut my hair before we leave?' she asks, tugging at the back of her head. 'I can manage the front bits but Nonno always did the back for me.'

'You're still worried that monster will find you?'

Silence.

'I'll be with you. There's no need to keep cutting your hair, Anto. I can look after you. Haven't I shown you over this past year?'

'What would be easier still is if you went alone to market, Roberto.'

I am about to tell her that she cannot hide forever when the screeching of gulls alerts her and she jumps up and points at the net. '*Eccoli.* There they are! Fish are coming. Quick, Roberto. Help me.'

And we run to turn the thick shaft again to raise the net. It wriggles with a mass of fish weaving under and over each other, water dripping as we pull the net towards us, sea birds swooping down to pinch what they can.

'For next time we need to find the sticks with hooks that Nonno used,' she shouts, 'to keep the birds away.'

It's a good catch – two swordfish, eels and plenty of fish I have never seen before but Anto reels off the names, exclaiming all the time, bending over the catch. I think how the scars on her olive-brown back will fade with the sun, but her mind will always be marked.

'I will make *zuppa di pesce* tonight. You will love it.'

CHAPTER 15

THURSDAY, APRIL 11, 1946.

We walk together to market. Anto was reluctant to come but I persuaded her with my ignorance. 'What price should I barter for?' I'd asked her while we ate our fish soup the night before. 'And where is the best position in the piazza?'

The box is heavy and the spring sun burns down already at this early hour. When we stop for five minutes to drink water, my mind is full of concern that the military police might still be around.

'If this is to be your main source of income, Anto, you will need transport. The fish will spoil along the way in the heat. How can you compete with fishermen who live in Mattinata and sell their catch fresh from their boats?'

'And with what shall I buy this transport?' she asks. 'Or do you think money grows on prickly pears?'

I ignore her sarcasm. 'What if we were to set up a small eating place? And specialise in serving meals fresh from the sea?' It's something I've been thinking of for a while. How to make ends meet if I am to stay? The thought of leaving is never at the front of my thoughts these days and not only because I made a vow to Nonno Domenico to watch over Antonella. There is more to it than that. I could only say goodbye if I knew I could say hello again. The idea of parting grows harder with each week that passes.

She snorts at my idea. 'And who would come to this fancy eating place? And how would they miraculously find us down our track?'

'From signs we could erect at the end of the track, by notices and by word of mouth. Start from small. I've eaten in restaurants that started from a simple market stall...' I stop.

I have indeed eaten in a restaurant that started off humbly, in the back room of somebody's home. I am certain of this. But where it was, I cannot recall and the memory in my head is gone as soon as it arrives. It's the first time in months that a glimpse of the past has surfaced. I'd forgotten what it feels like.

Anto is tugging at my arm. 'Roberto? What is it? Your face... you look as if you've seen a ghost.'

'Yes. I think I have. The past is a ghost...' I let out my breath in one long blow. I had not realised I was holding it in and I continue to walk.

'You said something about eating in a restaurant and then you turned strange,' she says, blocking my path.

I shake my head. 'Let's keep walking. Market will be over by the time we get to town.'

For the rest of our journey into Mattinata, I am inside my head, wondering about this crack in my memory. But nothing comes back to me.

When we arrive the best places are already taken by stall-holders busily setting up their stands. The only spots left are in full sun and hardly have we set down our boxes than bloated flies begin to cluster on the fish. Anto crouches over our wares, fanning Nonno's straw hat back and forth to shoo them away. A couple of cats approach and take up hopeful positions. As the piazza fills with shoppers, our pitiful haul is given little attention, despite Anto's offers of discount prices. At the end of the morning, we have sold less than a quarter of our catch. The fish begin to smell and we empty the box and leave them on the piazza cobbles for the cats.

As we start to leave, a woman who is packing up her fruit stall calls out. 'Oh, Antonella – it *is* you, isn't it? Domenico's granddaughter? I've been racking my brains all morning to place you. You're the spitting image of your mother, Cristina. And who is this fine young gentleman?'

Without hesitation, Anto replies, 'My husband. Roberto. Roberto Bruni.'

I swallow my astonishment as she says this and incline my head. '*Buongiorno*, signora.'

'I saw you had difficulty selling your fish this morning,' the woman says.

'It was a stupid idea to bring so much to market,' Anto says. 'I didn't think it through properly.'

The woman picks up a melon and a handful of apricots and hands them to Antonella. 'If it's work that you're looking for, they're asking for help at Masseria della Torre. Trying to keep the business going since the old man died. It's not too far from your place. You could do worse.'

'*Grazie*, signora. I'll think about it.'

'Well, don't be thinking too long. Now that the men are back from war, jobs are in short supply.'

As we trail home, I ask her why she introduced me as her husband. 'What was all that about? Am I no longer your brother?'

'She knew Roberto too well.'

'And is my name to remain Roberto?'

A shrug of her shoulders. 'It's a common enough name. There is more than one man with that name in Mattinata. It will do.'

'So, I am your husband now?' I laugh but as I play with the idea, I'm flattered.

Antonella's cheeks are pink when she looks at me but she doesn't answer my question and quickens her stride, dust flying up from her boots as she hurries ahead.

About five kilometres from the *trullo*, we pass another track leading to the sea and she points it out. 'That is the way to Masseria della Torre.'

'Then I shall try my luck tomorrow,' I say. 'Man cannot live by fish alone.'

'I won't come with you.'

I'm unsure whether I have offended her with my earlier reaction and I regret having opened my big trap to tease her. Does she not want to come because she is annoyed with me, or is she still afraid to venture out? I wish I could help her open up and banish her past, but I can tell I won't get far with that today and so I have to be content with her silence.

SATURDAY, APRIL 13, 1946.

I arrive, hot and sweaty, on this first morning at Masseria della Torre, a large, ramshackle building with a home-made restaurant sign hanging askew above its huge front door. A comely middle-aged woman opens up to my knocking, introduces herself as Signora Fortunata Pinto, and beckons me to follow her. In the kitchen, where pots bubble on an old stove, she looks me up and down, squeezes the muscles on my arms, tells me to turn round twice and then orders me to lift a heavy box of grain from a top shelf. I feel like a beast of burden prodded for its worth at market, but when she steps back and says, 'You'll do. But no messing with my daughters,' all that is forgotten in my delight at finding employment.

'We can offer you a meal on the three days you work here

and a bed in an outbuilding on late nights and five hundred lire a month.'

I don't argue, having no idea of going rates, grateful to bring in a little money to buy us the basics. After the first week, it is more than apparent that the most difficult aspect of this job is to avoid being alone with her buxom daughters, Eva and Maria.

Maria all but pins me against the kitchen wall on the second morning, her bosom straining at the seams of her cotton blouse as she invites me to the *festa del pesce* in the piazza in Mattinata the following month. 'There'll be dancing and fried fish and plenty of vino, Roberto,' she giggles. 'You can dance, can't you? I'll show you if you don't know how.' She winks at me. I can see fine whiskers and drops of sweat on her upper lip and manage to slip out from beneath her bosoms just as Eva comes in and starts to shout at her sister in the local dialect that is like a foreign language to me. I leave them screeching at each other, pick up a broom and hurry off to sweep clean the dining room.

The arrival of both these girls, being far from light on their feet, is never hard to hear and I am perfecting my vanishing acts. So far, so good. Anto thinks it is hilarious and looks forward in the evenings to my accounts of their pursuits. I'm not sure for whom their mother is saving them, but come hell or high water, it will not be me.

The *masseria* is a warren of rooms, a kind of farm fortress that Anto tells me is typical of this area, where the landowner lived in relative comfort, his workers on hand within the high walls. Entering wide doors, you step into a paved courtyard shaded by tall palm trees. Flights of chunky stone stairs lead to a walkway all around the top of a square perimeter above rooms that house stables, storage rooms and lodging for workers and their families. The signora has allotted me a compact room near the main entrance, large enough for a truckle bed with a straw mattress and I have already resolved to block the door latch with a chair on the nights I stay to keep out her predatory daughters. But so far, I have returned each night to my little *trullo*.

More than one half of this place is shut off; windows are broken where crows have flown in and nested in cavernous niches everywhere in the thick walls. I never know what I will come across: An old hay cart riddled with woodworm, as well as rickety furniture festooned with cobwebs, an armchair, its stuffing bursting out like innards, where mice have made their home. I wonder why this place is falling apart? With its enormous arches and huge limestone blocks it is an architectural wonder and could look splendid if restored. But the place needs money and an artistic eye and these farmhouses are two a penny, apparently. Who will salvage it? Apparently, it was used for a while by the Germans at the start of the war. Signora Pinto shed a tear when she explained how she has been left alone to cope, her husband and brothers all having perished in the war. In the meantime, she and her two daughters reign supreme in their neglected palace.

TUESDAY, AUGUST 6, 1946.

Time passes in routine. Mondays to Thursdays I work with Antonella on her patch of land in the early morning while the August sun permits. In the afternoons, we go to the beach to catch fish or rest in the cool of Domenico's cave. Having abandoned the idea of ever going to market, we sell our catches to Signora Pinto for the restaurant, and that adds to our income. She has loaned me the use of an ancient bike that I found in one of the storage rooms – rusty, its tyres punctured when I found it. But I've patched it up and use it to deliver the fish to her early in the morning on my days off.

I work at the *masseria* on Fridays, Saturdays and Sundays. There is a slow trickle of guests in the dining room at the weekends, mainly from Mattinata and Manfredonia. Signora Pinto and her daughters are excellent cooks and sometimes the guests linger afterwards to stay near the small pool that I have cleaned up, lounging on wooden daybeds that I painted white. I'm happy to do any odd jobs that Signora Pinto sets me but most of all, I enjoy waiting at table.

'You've done this before,' she tells me and I shrug my shoulders.

'I think you may be right,' I say. Certainly, I do not have to be told what to do; the work is instinctive. Is this another memory coming back? It's been so long now. Am I simply a shell of a person, my life before never to be known to me?

THURSDAY, AUGUST 15, 1946.

I work an extra day. *Ferragosto* is the biggest feast day of summer, when everybody uses the excuse of the feast of Mary's Assumption as a jolly. The signora emerges from her kitchen to where I am serving in the restaurant and plants two kisses on my cheeks. 'For the first time I truly feel it is the end of the war,' she says. 'Our first *ferragosto* celebrated in peace. Fetch the best wine for everybody, Roberto. Fetch it from the *cantina*.' She has already shown me the barrel of vintage wine in the cellar, put aside for her daughters' weddings. I siphon off a dozen bottles and hurry to the dining room.

Eva and Maria are busy setting a long table with places and I watch as a straggle of uniformed men enter and make their way over to the newly laid table. The men are boisterous and they speak in English, their shirtsleeves rolled up. They hang their blue-grey jackets over the backs of chairs and something moves in my brain, like the pushing against a door that has been stuck fast.

Signora Pinto introduces me. 'Roberto speaks *inglese*,' she tells the group. 'He will take your orders.'

And then, one of the men approaches. 'By Jove,' he says, 'it can't be.'

As I set the bottles on the sideboard, he grabs hold of my arm. 'Billy? What the blazes are you doing here?' He turns to his friends, who are looking at me suspiciously. 'Everyone, this is Billy. My arse-end Charlie on a number of ops.' He starts to pump my hand up and down. 'We all thought you'd gone for a Burton, old chap.'

I stare at him in bewilderment and then my head begins to thump. 'I don't know what you're talking about, sir,' I hear myself say in English.

But it's too late. Someone claims to know me. I think my old life has come calling.

CHAPTER 16

PRESENT DAY

The signpost indicating Masseria della Torre was partly covered by a swathe of brilliant orange trumpet vine and if it had not been for Giacomo's extra directions, Susannah would have missed the turning. She drove slowly down a dusty, potholed track that wound through an olive grove, and pulled up next to high walls smothered with purple bougainvillea and scarlet Russian vine. Two wooden doors set in an archway of a sombre building were closed. Her heart sank. *Not a good start*, Susannah thought as she pulled on a thick rope hanging down beside the door. A bell sounded from far within. Just as she was beginning to wonder if anybody would answer, bolts were pulled back and a man with a shock of white hair poked his head out. He looked as if he had woken from a deep sleep and he sounded irritated as he rattled off something.

She shrugged her shoulders and said, '*Non capisco.*' It was one of the first phrases she'd picked up in the brief time she'd been in Puglia. 'I don't understand.'

'Are you German?' he asked in English.

'English.'

'Not many English tourists come here.'

Susannah was surprised that any tourists at all came to this unwelcoming place. She followed him as he stepped over the threshold and out of the door, indicating to follow him. She took in his crumpled appearance from behind. He wore an old-fashioned silk paisley dressing gown that flapped over baggy cotton trousers and leather, slip-on sandals. Perhaps she had got him out of bed from his afternoon siesta.

When they rounded the corner of the building, she gasped. It was such a contrast from the drab façade. The place was different from her father's painting and despite the stunning view, she was disappointed. Maybe it was a waste of time to come here. But then she reminded herself she had the remainder of the month to do her detective work. She would enjoy the moment and with its spectacular setting, here was not such a bad springboard from which to carry out her investigations. The sea sparkled and glinted in the distance through sun-dappled leaves of lemon and olive trees. The owner led her to a table under the shade of a pergola heavy with ripening grapes, the fruit like purple jewels.

'Would you like a drink? Tea, maybe, or a glass of chilled sparkling wine?'

She'd tried tea already in Puglia but it was weak, the water lukewarm and the taste nothing like builder's tea she favoured back home. 'Wine would be wonderful. But first I should explain: I don't have a booking, but I need somewhere to stay for a couple of weeks and I found your place online and it seemed perfect but I couldn't book.'

He smiled and his craggy face transformed from grumpy to more-than-passably good looking. It was unfair, she thought. Italy had more than her fair share of beautiful people and in one day she had met two of the handsomest men she'd ever set eyes on. This guy and Giacomo at Mo Vini could both have stepped from catwalks.

'I have plenty of rooms. In fact, you can choose for yourself. But, first of all, relax! I'll fetch wine.'

While he was gone, a Dalmatian padded over the terracotta tiles, its claws clicking as he approached. He sat down nearby, crossed his front paws and stared at Susannah as if checking her over. He was long limbed, like his owner, and she couldn't help thinking the pedigree looked like a fashion accessory.

The man returned with a tray set with a bottle of Prosecco, droplets of moisture on the neck promising a refreshing drink, and two amber-coloured glasses engraved with intricate leaf patterns. *Antique Venetian*, Susannah assessed.

'Aren't you worried those will break?' she asked.

One languorous shrug of the shoulders, followed by, 'Life is too short, signorina, to worry about such things. I could have offered you a glass from IKEA, but I chose not to.' He popped the cork from the bubbly wine and poured it. 'Enjoy! You are my first customer in a long time. What shall I call you?'

She paused as she raised her glass, thinking it an odd way to ask her name.

'You can call me Susannah.'

'Welcome, Susi,' he said, raising his glass.

She wanted to correct him, tell him that only her father and her best of friends were allowed to abbreviate her name, but it felt prim and proper. He was a smooth-talker and very attractive.

'I wasn't expecting anybody to arrive today,' the man said. 'I was listening to music and... I nodded off, as you say.'

'Your English is brilliant.'

'I had an excellent teacher.' He looked away towards the sea and the silence was awkward.

'And what should I call *you*?' she asked, feeling it was time this man introduced himself if she was going to stay at his place, and pick his brains and ask him about the name that matched with her father's postcard. Although she hadn't yet viewed the rooms, she already liked it here. It was nothing to do with the excellent wine and the beautiful drinking glasses she could have sold for a bomb in Cobwebs, although that had been a pleasant start. She was intrigued by her host, his surroundings and the tempting finishing touches around her: cushions on the chairs covered in expensive linen, a mismatch of high-quality antique wrought-iron furniture and faded striped deckchairs under the pergola. After minutes, she felt strangely at home amongst these eclectic antiques. It was a place of restoral and beauty and she couldn't wait to explore further.

'My name is Mario,' he said. 'Mario Andreani.' He extended his hand and when she took it, his grip was firm.

'*Piacere,*' she said, thinking that this Italian word, pleasure, was infinitely more intimate than a standard English 'pleased to meet you'.

When he took her later through an entrance hall and out again into an inner courtyard, she stopped still, aware that he was talking to her about the house, but she wasn't taking in his words. Susannah had to hold on to the stone wall for a few seconds to steady her dizziness. She felt she knew this place.

CHAPTER 17

Mario took her arm as he showed her to her room off the main lounge, concern in his voice. 'Rest for a while, Susi. Southern heat is something that northern foreigners need to acclimatise to.'

'And wine in the afternoon,' she said, although it was not alcohol that had caused her head to spin, but the strangest of sensations that the house was weaving. 'I'll be fine in a minute,' she said. 'Thank you.' She couldn't explain to herself her reluctance to give her reason for being here to this man. Not yet. He was a stranger and she needed to steady herself and be sure her mind was not playing tricks, making her believe what she wanted to believe: that this could well be the same Masseria della Torre depicted on the postcard and her painting. There were most likely plenty of fortified farmhouses like this with the same name. How many Seaview Hotels were there in Hastings, after all? And so far, she had seen nothing tangible to link this *masseria* with her daddy's painting.

One of the windows in the bedroom was high in the walls and he showed her how to open it with a special rod to let in the sea breeze, pulling a gauzy curtain across to blot the sun's glare.

The other two offered views over the back of the hotel, a billowing canopy of olive trees like dozens of unfurled green umbrellas stretching to the sea.

'Your bathroom is through there if you want to freshen up,' he said, pointing to an alcove. 'Call if you need anything. Dinner is at eight.'

She sank onto the large double bed, its metal frame draped with antique lace, and ran her fingers over the Indian cotton sheets. She'd never stayed in a boutique hotel like this and, gazing around, she felt as if she'd somehow been dropped into a stage set. Next to a ceramic pot holding a branch from which three top hats hung at jaunty angles, an old pine chest was positioned with an elaborate ceiling candelabra leaning on its surface, acting as a table lamp. It was propped up by a pile of leatherbound books and she went to peer at the titles. Three were Italian but there was an old English copy of Dickens's *David Copperfield*. The chair by her bed was upholstered in thick black velvet, a clean white towelling robe draped over one gold-painted arm. In the bathroom, she splashed water on her face from a tall stone vase customised into a wash hand basin, a bar of olive soap resting in a marble container shaped like a woman's hand. Susannah looked at her reflection in the gold-framed mirror, wondering if she should pinch herself to wake up.

Feeling the need to hear Maureen's sensible voice to bring her down to earth and steady her emotions, she punched in her number on her mobile, hoping there'd be a signal through the thick walls. She was about to give up when her friend's familiar tones came through loud and clear. 'Can I call you back, darling? I have customers.'

It felt like a waste of precious time to sleep in the afternoon, so after hanging up her only summer dress in the wardrobe to let the creases drop out, and pinning her long curls into a top knot, she went to explore further, to dispel these weird feelings that the place was familiar in some way. In the lounge, a grand piano dominated. Several silver-framed photos were arranged on the lid and she bent to examine the largest. The famous tenor Pavarotti was seated between a much younger, dark-haired Mario and a beautiful woman. Rather than being in a hotel, Susannah felt as though she was in somebody's private lounge and she hurried from the room in case Mario should enter and think she was nosy.

Against one wall of the courtyard, beneath a stairway, an old cart rested on its shaft. She climbed stairs to a walkway with crenelated walls like the battlements of a castle and she recalled Giacomo's definition of the *masseria* as a fortified farm. The view extended far and wide, sunshine glinting off cars on the main road a couple of kilometres away. In the distance, the sea beckoned from the far side of olive groves. She'd learned olive oil was the main produce of Puglia and a deadly bacterium was eradicating many trees, especially near Lecce. These trees looked sound, thankfully. A garden with an infinity pool was set beneath the house and she decided to make her way there and read the book she'd bought at the airport. She'd chosen it because of the alluring cover more than anything else: a sun-filled scene with a woman staring over olive groves and sunflower fields. The coincidence was not lost on her.

She had the garden to herself. This too was laid out artisti-cally, with cacti planted in an old wooden wheelbarrow and, here and there, stumps of unusually shaped olive wood, old farm implements nailed to a stone wall and an area under the trees arranged with dining tables.

As she leant back in the rattan settee against jewel-coloured cushions, the rear of the old house made her immediately sit up. It couldn't be, could it? Was she jumping to conclusions because she wanted to?

But she was sure now. The feeling she'd had earlier returned, even more powerfully than before. She knew this place. The rear of the farmhouse was identical to the image her father had painted. The picture hanging on the wall of her house in Hastings, the same picture as on both postcards.

She dashed to her room to fetch the postcards, almost skidding on the gravel path in her haste to return to the pool to compare the view.

The back of the house was an exact match. With trembling fingers, she texted Maureen.

Can you talk now? Sending amazing photo. Look where I am!

Susannah snapped a photo of the building and sent it.
A text came winging back a few seconds later. *And? What?*

Staying in same house as Dad's painting!!! If poss can you go to my house and take photo of it?

It was easier to talk than to text. Susannah switched to phoning Maureen. 'I'm almost positive it's the same farmhouse – can't believe it. But I'll talk to the hotel owner later and find out more.'

'Bit of a coincidence if it is.'

'I know – it's not as if this is a particularly touristy area either. I was going to begin a search of the area but if this *is* the same place as in the painting, then this happy coincidence has fallen right into my lap. Grandma Elsie told Dad she couldn't remember who sent the postcards. But I might be nearer to finding out who did. God, Maureen, I wish Daddy was here with me right now.'

'I bet you do, my darling. But do it *for* him. Find out as much as you can and then when you come back, you *have* to grill Elsie. Perhaps the former owner of the place had his wicked way with her.'

'God, poor man if he did. Maureen, I don't think I'm ever

going to get any joy out of questioning her. In the meantime, *would* you mind going to my place and taking a photo of the painting? I should have done it myself before leaving. I might be wrong and letting my imagination run away with me.'

Susannah wandered over to the other side of the pool to capture a different angle of the farmhouse on her phone, her mounting excitement dampened with sadness that her lovely daddy wasn't beside her to see the subject of his painting in real life.

'Are you still there, Susi?' Maureen's voice came through the loudspeaker.

'Yes, sorry, Maureen. I'm just so flabbergasted. I can't stop taking pictures.'

'I was saying that of course I don't mind. I'll go to your house straight after I've finished at Cobwebs.'

'Sorry – I should have asked – how's it going?'

'Very well. I've sold that wind-up gramophone and the 1920s chest of drawers at the back of the shop. I spruced it up, dressed it with a beauty set and an old vanity case and hung up a vintage poster advertising journeys on the *Orient Express. Et voilà!*'

'Clever you. Thanks, Maureen. You're a gem.'

'I'm enjoying myself.'

'Good. Speak later. You'd love it here, by the way. I'll send more photos. There are heaps of curios dotted around the place.'

Susannah gazed at the back of the *masseria*, her heart thumping. What was the significance of this place? The messages from the card and letter writer had mentioned the sea and hard work but what had all that got to do with Grandma Elsie? Who had sent them to her? Somebody who had worked hard in this place near the sea? Gran had seemed to express regret about giving them to her son. Maybe Mario could shed light on the history of the *masseria*.

. . .

She was the only guest in the dining room and Mario asked if she minded him joining her.

'I've asked for something simple to be prepared by my cook. Do you like seafood?'

'Wonderful. But you'll have to tell me what I'm eating. At the market the other day, I didn't recognise half of the fish.'

They shared a starter of thin slices of grilled aubergines drizzled with extra virgin olive oil and parsley pesto. Mario told her the oil came from his own trees. There followed a typical regional pasta known as *troccoli* – a slightly thicker version of spaghetti – with a sauce of tender squid and home-grown tomatoes.

'This is so scrumptious,' she said, sitting back against her Louis XV-style dining chair as she finished the last forkful.

'You should mop up the sauce with some of our special bread from Altamura,' Mario said, leaning over to her plate and tearing a piece of bread to scrape up the juices. Then he brought it to her mouth, as a mother would to her child, or, Susannah thought, as a lover would to a lover.

She smiled, trying to imagine a semi-stranger doing this in England. 'I love the Italian passion for food.'

'We are a passionate people.' He poured more white wine into her glass. He looked smarter than this afternoon's crumpled appearance. Now he wore fashionably faded blue jeans and a crisp white shirt rolled up over bronzed arms, a couple of buttons undone to reveal the thin glint of a gold chain round his neck. Tonight, the table was laid with fine Murano glass goblets and she held hers up to the candle to examine the fine etchings.

'Your home is wonderful. I have a shop at home where I sell antiques, so I feel as if I'm in heaven here.'

He nodded. 'I'm pleased. They are mostly bits and pieces

picked up on my travels. But I've incorporated things found in outbuildings and inside the house when I bought it.'

'It's a treasure trove. And the way you've set everything out is so artistic. I'd love to explore it.'

'Certain rooms are closed to guests and... some areas are not safe either... structurally, the place is not sound in some places. It's best if you don't explore on your own.'

He raised his glass to her and smiled. 'But I'm pleased you like what we've done. *Grazie!*'

Her stomach fluttered as it hit her how attractive he was and she paused, not quite knowing how to open up to this man without sounding barmy. 'It's uncanny, but I feel I know your home already. Can I show you something?'

'You are sounding mysterious.'

'I know. It's a little crazy,' she said as she brought up the images Maureen had sent her before dinner. She passed her phone over. 'Could this be a painting of here?'

He pulled a pair of gold-rimmed spectacles from his shirt pocket to look at the photos.

'My place is typical of others in this area. A *masseria* is a fortified farmhouse found everywhere in the south of Italy. You'll have seen dozens in the countryside on your drive here. The landowner, in order to protect his tools, his produce and workers built these huge places to defend against thieves and the enemy. Most *masserie* date back to the fifteenth and sixteenth centuries when Spain ruled our region. The Spaniards were here for three hundred years.'

He used his fingers to enlarge a detail. 'It could well be mine,' he said and then he nodded. 'This *pinnacolo* – I don't know the word in English' – he pointed to an elaborate carving at the top of the domed roof in the painting – 'is the same as on my building, above what used to be the chapel. Each builder had his own trademark *pinnacolo*.' He handed it back to Susannah, 'But you have to understand this builder will have constructed more than one *masseria* in his time. Many are used for bed and breakfast or holiday homes nowadays.'

She took back the phone from his outstretched hand. 'It would be serendipity if I was staying in the very farmhouse that my father painted,' she said.

'Maybe he visited the area.'

'No. He never had the chance to visit Italy at all. He copied the farmhouse from a postcard sent to my grandmother.' She pulled the envelope with the two cards from her bag. 'Take a look!'

While Mario examined them, she continued. 'Daddy always wanted to tour Italy. That's partly why I'm here: to fulfil his wish. We lost him earlier this year.'

'I'm sorry for your loss, Susi.'

She believed his words. The way he said them didn't sound throwaway.

'I've never come across old postcards of my place; these are very interesting. They'd look good framed on my walls amongst the other souvenirs I found here and there.'

For a minute, Susannah thought he was going to keep the postcards and she had to stop herself from snatching them back.

'I love how you've incorporated your antiques and use them so they're not museum pieces. As I said, the interior decor is exquisite.'

'Thank you. But that was down to my American wife, Anita.'

She felt unaccountably disappointed after he'd uttered those words and told herself not to be ridiculous. Twenty-four hours ago she hadn't even known this man existed, so why should she feel a twinge of regret?

'In the beginning, it was our holiday home and we planned to fill it with our children. But children never arrived. We both had extremely busy working lives, travelling around the world. My wife was an opera singer and her health suffered from constantly being on the move. It deteriorated and she never recovered.'

'I'm so sorry,' Susannah said, feeling hypocritical as she said this, because there was no need to feel jealous of a dead woman.

'It happens, Susi, it happens.' He was quiet for a moment, fiddling with his fork.

Susannah remembered the photograph she'd spied on top of the grand piano of a younger Mario next to Pavarotti. The woman, if it was his wife, had been stunning, dressed in a long gown, her dark blonde hair swept up on her head. She made a mental note to have another look.

'We bought the *masseria* fifteen years ago. It was almost in ruins and I've been doing it up ever since. Opening it up to guests again will help pay the bills, but I can't be here all the time. I'm in the process of looking for a manager to help out while we're away.'

There was a thump on the ceiling and he stopped abruptly, running his hand through his hair and tutting. Then he pushed back his chair and stood up. 'My dog. Upstairs,' he said. 'I need to take him for his night walk. I'm sorry. Anyway, I'm keeping you up with my talk... Breakfast is served until nine thirty in the olive grove. Sleep well. *Sogni d'oro*, as we say.'

She didn't feel particularly tired. Maybe talking about his wife had upset him. She watched him hurry from the dining area. He was in good shape. Buff. As if he worked out regularly. With Italian food being so delicious, she would have to watch herself, otherwise none of her clothes would fit by the end of her stay.

On the way to her room, Susannah paused in the living room. On a vintage glass 1960s coffee table, a pile of yellowing manuscripts was furled up like petals of a rose, a candle in a crystal glass bowl keeping the papers secured. Mario's comment about including pieces that he had found in the building after purchase had made her wonder if there might be anything to help her dig deeper into the postcard story. Could the sender have been a former owner? Or a guest? Someone who worked here? She heard footsteps approaching and moved away to her room.

Susannah's dreams were indeed golden that night. She dreamt she was a princess sleeping in a room decorated with oversized ornate mirrors, chandeliers lit with hundreds of twinkling candles, and side tables laden with silver platters piled with pyramids of pomegranates. Beneath a teetering pile of mattresses on her double poster bed, a tiny golden morsel of squid dug painfully into her back, but a manservant with beautiful white hair entered the room from the window to massage away her pain, until dawn brought deep sleep as she lay in his arms.

There was no sign of Mario at breakfast, so any chance of asking more about the past owners would have to wait. Instead, a middle-aged Italian woman with a friendly smile, but who spoke no English, indicated a side table under the loggia where a variety of cheeses, fresh fruit, bread and juices were arranged on fine white porcelain. One waxy cheese was shaped like a cottage loaf, and the woman told her it was *cacciocavallo*. The peeled fruit was a pink magenta colour and full of tiny seeds. '*Fichi d'India*,' the woman explained, pointing to an oil painting of a prickly pear on the rough stone wall. The taste was insipid to Susannah and she selected a large juicy peach instead, followed by home-made rustic bread and slices of cheese, finishing off with a piece of buttery sponge cake.

'*Come si chiama, Lei?*' Susannah asked the woman's name, proud of herself when the woman obviously understood her scratchy Italian and replied with a beam on her face. '*Mi chiamo* Emma. My name is Emma.'

'*Grazie*. Wonderful breakfast.'

'*Prego,* signorina.'

It was satisfying to communicate simply in this beautiful language and Susannah hummed to herself as she returned to her room to change into a bikini.

After ten lengths in the pool, which she had all to herself, she phoned Giacomo from the wine bar. It seemed a waste not to take up his offer of the other day, when he'd helped her with Italian. She had just over a fortnight left of her holiday and she wanted to explore further afield rather than spend the day soaking up the sun on a lounger.

'Is that lesson still on, Giacomo? Do you have time?' she asked, after they'd exchanged greetings. He'd sounded pleased to hear from her again.

'*Certo!* Of course, and we'll combine it with lunch. I'll pick you up in one hour and take you somewhere special,' he said over a crackly line. 'Wear something casual and bring your costume.'

In her room, she dressed again. Over a dry bikini she pulled on a pair of denim shorts and a loose white cotton T-shirt. When she checked herself in the gilded cheval mirror she looked out of place in the opulent surroundings. The room deserved a flowing silk or satin dress with retro accessories, maybe even a tiara set on her dark hair. *But the mirror is fake. French-style repro*, she consoled herself. *We can't all be perfect.* Anyway, Giacomo had said to come casual. Somehow, she didn't think that opulent would be his style. He had that open-air, sun-kissed look with his tousled hair. She wondered if he might know something about the history of the hotel. These two weeks were going to rush by and she needed to find out as much as she could from whatever source.

Picking up her sun hat and pushing a thick towel and a tube of Factor 30 into her beach bag, she left her room. In the living room, she moved the glass candle holder to one side and picked up the curled-up papers. But they were sheet music. The crotchets and quavers were not going to tell her anything about the past. She moved over to the photographs on the piano. They all showed Mario and his wife in groups of different people, and peering closer she recognised a shot of the Royal Festival Hall and another of the Sydney Opera House.

There was nobody at the front desk and she jumped when she heard a crash of falling china upstairs, followed by a woman shrieking. Emma emerged from the kitchen, wiping her hands on her apron, muttering something under her breath. Susannah watched her hurry up the stairs to the upper floor, marked *PRIVATO*.

CHAPTER 18

Three blasts of a tinny horn diverted her attention and she stepped outside to see Giacomo astride a turquoise Vespa. He waved and held out a helmet.

'*Buongiorno,* Signorina Susannah. Climb aboard and hold on tight. Are you ready for your total immersion Italian lesson?'

She had to grip his body firmly as he negotiated the bumpy track. He smelled of woodsmoke and spices and there was not an ounce of spare fat on his broad torso. After a while, he took a left turn down an even bumpier, narrower track that descended to the sea. As the Vespa brushed against waxy green vegetations, the scent of mixed herbs and flowers filled her nostrils, the whine of the Vespa's engine loud in her ears so that conversation was impossible.

Eventually, he stopped as the road ended at gates with a sign forbidding entrance: *VIETATO ENTRARE.*

'It was my father's property. These are his olive groves.' He gestured behind from where they'd driven. 'He had a dream to build a house on here one day, but permissions take forever and now my parents have passed away, nothing more has been done and I'd have to apply again. Bureaucracy is a big headache in Italy and I doubt planning approval will happen,' he said.

Susannah climbed from the pillion and pulled off her helmet. 'So, we've both lost our fathers... it's hard, isn't it?' The sea lapped the edges of a sandy beach and there was nobody else in sight. 'Wow, what an amazing spot.'

Jutting out of the sea ten metres offshore, rocks formed a series of arches, like backbones of a sea monster. It matched one of the postcard images.

Giacomo unlocked the padlocked gate and pushed his Vespa inside, locking it behind him. 'As you can see, it's remote and before I fenced it off, people camped and left rubbish. There's been a rave held here and a break-in, but I leave nothing valuable in this place.'

He climbed the wooden stairs of a veranda leading to a small cabin and unlocked its double doors, opening them wide. 'This is our beach hut. What do you think?'

'It's a little piece of heaven,' she said, taking in the bunk beds, table and chairs. Against one side of the wall was a counter holding a two-ring camping stove fed from a small gas bottle underneath. 'In England, we have beach huts, but we're not permitted to sleep in them.'

'I know,' he said. 'I had a girlfriend from Scarborough, but *brrr!* the North Sea does not compare.'

He fetched a couple of bags stowed under the Vespa seat and transferred them to a cool box beneath the cabin table. 'We have no electricity, but ice packs do the trick for a while to keep beer cool. But, now, you are going to have to work for your lunch. Come!' He pulled off his T-shirt and shorts to reveal a tight-fitting costume which hid no secrets. His body was toned and strong and she averted her eyes as he looked her up and down.

'Did you bring something to wear in the sea?' he asked.

She stepped out of her shorts, conscious of the difference

between his tanned body and her winter-white legs and after removing her T-shirt, she followed him to the water's edge where a sailing boat was anchored in the shallows.

He looked at her. 'I hope you have sun protection. It's very easy to burn. The breeze disguises the sun's heat.'

'Of course I have,' she said and started to rub lotion on her legs and arms.

'Let me do your back.'

The thought that she was on her own with a relative stranger, miles from anywhere, and was thinking of allowing him to touch her body brought her up with a start. 'I can manage,' she said, although it was almost impossible to spread the cream evenly on her back by herself. As she struggled, she was conscious of him grinning at her efforts. 'Oh, here!' she said, handing him the bottle and turning her back to him.

He laughed as he said, 'Don't worry. I have three younger sisters and I'm an expert at this.'

He rubbed her back almost roughly. There was nothing seductive about his touch and she felt like his fourth sister.

'There you are. All done. *Ecco! Tutto fatto*. Repeat after me. We'll start these Italian lessons right now.'

When she tried, he told her to say it again. 'Make your vowels sound less English, Susannah. Get your mouth round them. Exaggerate, like we do.' He waved his hands about and then it was her turn to laugh.

He applauded her second attempt. 'I'll use as many Italian words as possible today, but if I see you're floundering with my method, I'll use English.'

'*Grazie*, Giacomo.' He was being so kind and generous with his time. She wondered if he was as kind to his sisters. Whatever his intentions, she was happy to enjoy his company. It had been a long time since she'd felt so at ease with a man. It was the happiest she'd felt in the bleak months since losing Daddy.

He sailed the boat further out, instructing her how to jibe

and move smoothly from one side of the boat to the other, telling her to dip her head and shoulders under the boom as they zigzagged their way out of the bay. On the distant shore of the next bay, she noticed a platform at the edge of the sea and she asked if it was used for fishing.

'*Sì. Un trabucco.* Sometimes called *trabocco.* The fishermen lower nets in the shallows. They're very effective.'

She took a couple of photos of the spider-like structure and he told her that a few were now converted into fish restaurants. 'They're very popular. I can take you some time, if you like.'

'I'd love that. *Grazie!*'

The wind was keen further out to sea and the boat built up speed. When they reached a sand bank some way from shore, he cast anchor.

'*Prendi.* Take,' he said, handing her a mask and snorkel from a bag under the seat. 'First we will snorkel and after we will fish for our lunch. *Facciamo la pesca.*'

He helped her put on the mask, showing her how to brush back tendrils of her hair so that water would not leak in and patiently instructing her at the surface how to blow through the snorkel.

They didn't have to swim down far. The sea was as clear as glass, weeds waved in the current and tiny fish darted in shoals here and there like in an Attenborough wildlife film. Giacomo carried a small harpoon and he gestured to her to follow through channels in the rocks. She watched as he speared first an octopus and then two different types of fish, placing them in a string bag secured to his belt. He pointed to an amphora resting on the sandy bed and took her a little way further from shore, where a statue stood erect just below the water. The rays of the sun streamed through the sea's surface, bouncing from the head of the stone woman like a halo.

When they returned to the boat and he hauled her up beside him, she was effusive.

'That was the best. It's a whole new world under there,' she said, a little breathless from the exercise. She was unused to swimming wild. Lengths in the public swimming pool didn't compare. 'What's the story behind the statue? Is she very old?'

'*La Madonna del Mare?* No, not old compared to some of the artefacts I've discovered on my dives. She was put down there in the early 1950s as a memorial to a plane lost beyond this bay. They never found any survivors, or indeed bodies. Every year in July there's a small ceremony to remember all those lost at sea during the last war and the priest blesses the spot and flowers are cast on the water. The *Madonna del Mare* is not particular to here. Such feast days are celebrated for one reason or another in many places along the Italian coast.'

'There's a Catholic church in Hastings where I live. St Mary, Star of the Sea. But I've never heard of similar celebrations.'

'Yes, I noticed that in England. You go crazy over Christmas – not in a very religious way. And you have your fireworks on the fifth of November. But that seems to be it. I remember seeing men and women dressed up and dancing in the street once.'

'Morris dancers?' She smiled. 'With sticks and bells and handkerchiefs. I think they dance to banish winter around harvest festival time. But you're right, Giacomo, now I come to think about it. We don't have many traditional feast days in our calendar.'

'It might be because our summers are hotter and longer, the weather more dependable. Or simply because we like an excuse to celebrate – and more specifically to eat good food together. We're a Catholic country but not in a particularly fervent way. It's kind of accepted as part of our make-up. But not so many people attend church anymore. I don't.' He gestured to the sea. 'I feel closer to a higher being, or whatever, when I'm in a place like this. I don't need to worship in a church.'

'I know what you mean.'

It was another world here but mention of the church in Hastings had brought her thoughts back to why she had come to Puglia. Once they had returned to shore, she would show him the photo of her father's painting and ask if he knew anything about the hotel's past.

'You're very quiet, Susannah. Are you hungry?'

She tore her gaze from the turquoise ocean. 'Starving. That swim used up a lot of energy.'

He touched her shoulder. 'You need more lotion on here and then we'll gather firewood.'

This time when he applied the sun cream, he was gentler. Nevertheless, her skin smarted. Whether from sunburn or his touch, she wasn't sure.

Over their simple meal of grilled fish with tomatoes, and a salad of Tropea onions and olives, he told her how much he'd missed Puglia when he was in Manchester.

'You don't realise what you've got until you don't have it on your doorstep.' He passed her rings of charred squid as he talked.

'Does the wine bar belong to you, Giacomo? You managed to be here today. I do appreciate that.'

'It's my pleasure. Yes, the bar is mine now. My father left it to me and I'm trying to bring it up to date and diversify. I want to attract more foreign tourists. Apart from offering traditional cooking and local products, my dream is to add a package of walks and tours around our countryside. I thought of Puglia Wild for a brand name. What do you think?'

'It certainly fits this rugged countryside and the wild sea.'

'And "wild" is a word young Italians recognise too. There is a demand for something different nowadays than straightforward beach and city holidays.'

'Well, I wish you well, Giacomo. And if you want to experiment and take me to more wild places, then take advantage of me while I'm here.'

It occurred to her as soon as she'd said the words that they could be misconstrued and she blushed. *Take advantage of me. Go wild with me.* But Giacomo didn't bat an eyelid. He simply said, '*Grazie*, Susannah,' and opened another beer.

'Do you miss England at all?' Susannah asked.

'I miss the girls.'

'The girls here are very beautiful.'

'Yes, but they can be… needy,' he said, searching for the right word. 'Quite high maintenance. I find English girls easier company.'

'Easy company or easier?'

He grinned. 'That would be telling.'

He took a swig of his beer and stared out to the sea. 'Here in the south – as soon as you go out with a woman more than a few times, her family starts to plan the wedding. It's harder to have friendships with someone if they're thinking of putting a ring on your finger. It makes me feel like a bull tethered by a nose-ring.'

'Goodness, Giacomo, that surprises me for this day and age. How old are you anyway? And don't ask me to guess. That's what old people do and when you get it wrong, they're always offended.'

'I'm thirty-six.'

Susannah had him down as younger. She was two years older but she felt far more. Maybe living in Italy was kinder to the body and mind.

'To me it sounds as if you haven't met the right person,' Susannah said, picking at the red grapes that Giacomo had produced at the end of the fish course.

He turned on his side and stretched out to face her. 'What about you? Do you have a right person?'

She shook her head. 'No.' She left it at that. Reluctant to expand on her disastrous relationship with a married man who had constantly promised to leave his wife for her... She fiddled with a couple of blue stones in the sand. No point in telling him more. That was in the past.

He held up his bottle and the sun glinted off the green glass. 'To you and me,' he said. 'That we find what we are looking for, even though we might not be looking.'

She laughed. 'Very philosoph... philosophical... Two beers and I can't speak properly.'

'I've enjoyed today, Miss Susannah. *Mi sono divertito.* Repeat after me, but you say: *mi sono divertita*, because you are a woman.'

'Yay – I'm a woman. *Mi sono divertita.*'

'Let's have a quick swim before I take you back to the *masseria*,' he suggested, pulling her to her feet.

'Oh, talking of the *masseria*,' she said, rummaging for her phone in her beach bag and bringing up Maureen's text. 'Look at this. It's hanging on my wall back in England. What are the chances of this happening?'

He peered at the screen. His hair was full of sand, his skin burnt to a mahogany colour. For the first time she noticed a tattoo of a tiny scorpion on the back of his left shoulder.

'Is that a painting of La Torre?'

'I showed it to the owner, Mario, and he thinks it probably is,' Susannah said.

'Who did the painting?'

'My father. *Mio padre*,' she said and he smiled.

'So, he has been here too.'

'Actually, never. My father painted it from a postcard he was given as a young boy. I've brought it with me. He always wanted to visit Italy. I found the hotel on the internet and obviously I had to come. For my father.'

'*Mi dispiace.* I am sorry he couldn't be with you. And your mother?'

'She died giving birth to me. My grandmother brought me and my sister up. *La mia nonna.*'

He smiled and nodded his head.

'Unfortunately, my grandmother has never told anybody who sent the postcard and she has dementia now, so maybe she will never be able to tell me. There's more though, Giacomo...' She paused, feeling suddenly shy about opening up so much. He was a relative stranger. But, for all that, she felt safe with him. 'I found another postcard, with writing... and a note. Addressed to my grandmother, but hidden... and I want to find out who wrote them and what the link is between my grandmother and the postcards showing the *masseria*.'

'So, you have a mystery to solve. But maybe your *nonna* would not want you to solve the mystery. If she hid these things... then maybe they are love letters?'

'So, do you think I'm awful in wanting to find out. Poking my nose in?'

He sighed. 'I can see why you are intrigued... I would be too, I suppose.'

'I can't help it.' She paused. 'It feels to me as if I *have* to find out. As if I'm meant to...'

'Well, if you need a Doctor Watson, I am happy to help you with your magical mystery. What about the present owner? Can't you ask him if he knows about the history of the *masseria*?'

'He's not local, Giacomo. And he hasn't owned the place for long.'

'Well, if you come across anything that needs translating, I'm here for you. Now, how about that swim?'

The swim developed into a lesson from Giacomo on how to do handstands in the sea without swallowing water. Although missing her father was always in the back of her mind, she couldn't remember the last time she'd felt so carefree.

CHAPTER 19

Lying flat on her stomach on the bed that evening because her shoulders were sunburnt, Susannah called Maureen for a catch-up.

'It's been a brilliant day. And the fish tasted so good grilled over the fire. Giacomo caught sea bass and a little red fish they call *tordo*. It means "thrush" but I haven't the foggiest what the fish name is in English. Oh yes, and I'm learning Italian. Total immersion... a bit full-on, but it's amazing how much easier it is to pick up when you're actually in the place.'

'And what's your private instructor like? A young Italian god?'

Susannah laughed. 'Nothing like that. He's very sweet – got three sisters. I feel like a fourth. He's easy company and he's offered to help me find out more about this place. I need to know that the postcards are not just a coincidence.'

She winced as she turned over and her shoulders grazed the sheets. 'Can you imagine having lunch caught and cooked for you on a deserted beach on an ordinary holiday? I don't really want to come home at the moment, if I'm honest. And definitely not until I've sleuthed more information about the sender of the cards. If I can. Maybe I'll extend my stay.'

'I'm pleased you're enjoying yourself, Susi. Not that I don't want to see you again, but you were overdue some me-time. Make the most of it. The rain hasn't stopped drizzling here and the weather is dismal for August. Hardly anybody's put their nose in the shop, so I've been sorting stuff. You've space for new furniture. We can look out auction venues when you return.'

'You're an absolute angel. What can I bring you back?'

'Nothing. Yourself! Safe, sound and refreshed. Night night and have fun, Susi.'

'*Buona notte.*'

'Get you. You sound like a native.'

The last thing Susannah heard before she switched off her phone was Maureen's deep chuckle.

Mario was seated at a breakfast table in the olive grove, engrossed in a copy of *la Repubblica*, propped against a Moka coffee pot. He looked up when Susannah made her way over the gravel path to a table deeper in the shade.

'*Buongiorno*, Susi. I hope you slept well.'

'The bed is very comfortable but...' She pointed to her red shoulders. 'I tossed and turned last night.'

'Maybe give the sun a miss today?' He picked up his newspaper and walked over to her table. 'I am going up to Monte Sant'Angelo in half an hour if you'd like a lift. I need to place an advert at the employment agency for a part-time manager. It's an interesting hilltop town and you should visit our UNESCO heritage cathedral.'

'*Grazie*, I'd love that. I thought I'd be fine now I've returned my hire car but I didn't reckon on the hit and miss bus service.'

'You need something to cover your arms and shoulders. The nuns in the cathedral prowl around looking for transgressors;

they're very hot on modesty. I'll wait for you at the front of the house. *A dopo!*'

She added that to her stock of ever-growing phrases. '*A dopo*,' she said, practising the words. It meant 'until later'. Very useful. Hopefully she would get the chance to quiz Mario on what he knew about the history of the *masseria* while they were out.

Her transport this morning was very different from Giacomo's yesterday. Mario was waiting in a two-seater classic red Ferrari sports car. The top was down and his fingers tapped on the steering wheel in rhythm to an operatic aria. It wasn't her type of music but he seemed transported.

'My wife,' he said when she opened the car door. 'One of her best recordings from *Tosca*. Better than Callas, in my opinion. But I am of course biased.'

He snapped off the CD player and pulled a silk shawl from the glove compartment. 'Take this, Susi. For your hair while we drive, and for the cathedral *dopo*.'

She sank into the red leather seat and he turned the key as she tied the soft scarf around her hair. The car started with a throaty roar before purring down the drive. He drove fast and she couldn't help pressing down her feet as he took the bends, the tyres squealing on hot tarmac. The engine was loud and people turned to stare and nudge each other as the Ferrari drew into the main square and she felt self-conscious but simultaneously thrilled.

Susannah sensed from the beginning that, by the end of the day, she would fall for Mario's charm. It started with the atmosphere in the grotto deep down in the hillside where worshippers gazed in rapture at the image of St Michael the Archangel. The basilica was packed and she found herself pressed against strangers: the woman next to her fanned her face, spreading a whiff of stale perspiration on polyester, and she almost gagged. Up until fairly recently, during the pandemic, everybody had been advised to be no closer than two metres from each other, but there was no chance of social distancing in this claustrophobic space. Mario must have sensed her rising panic. His hand stole into hers as he leant close to whisper in her ear that there'd been cult worship ever since the fifth century in this church. The cave walls seemed to bear down, the scent of dozens of lilies arranged stiffly in vases on the altar was cloying and she shivered.

'Let's get into the sunshine,' he muttered, guiding her from the crowd, his hand firmly round hers as they climbed the long flight of stairs hewn from rocks.

When they were outside, she tilted her face to the sun and breathed in gulps of fresh air.

'It seems to affect people in one of two ways,' he said. 'My wife loved this church, but I have to say it gives me the shivers too.'

'Amazing as it is, I was uncomfortable down there. I felt... trapped.'

'Then we will have to make you feel better. Come!'

Mario guided her from the busy main street thronged with tourists, through labyrinths of narrow alleyways where washing hung from windows like colourful flags. Plumbago plants and geraniums trailed against white walls in splashes of blue and pink. A couple of women stood at their doors chatting and Mario exchanged greetings. They smiled back at the handsome man and the beautiful young woman who walked past.

'*Eccoci!*' he said finally, after they'd climbed further through the old town. 'Here we are.'

Susannah stored this new phrase in her head as he drew her through the entrance to a small bar and onto a generous balcony at the back. She feasted her eyes on the tumble of roofs stretching out like a springboard to the sea in the bay below and when he put his arm around her, she relaxed against his side. It felt good to be held by an attractive man after too long.

'What a place. I'd never have discovered this on my own.'

'Sometimes it's good to let somebody else help you, Susi.'

Their eyes locked and she felt a frisson of anticipation.

As Susannah sipped on the Aperol Spritz from the tall glass that the waiter set down on their table, she let herself sink into the intoxicating day. They didn't talk much but there were plenty of looks swapped and one hour later, her head light, her thoughts ignoring warnings that this could only end one way, she allowed Mario to take her somewhere else she would never have discovered without his help.

A couple of doors further up from the bar, he stopped at a whitewashed house and pulled a key from under a pot holding a topiary bay tree. From the outside the house was nothing special but when he pulled her through the door, she gasped at the interior. It was furnished oriental-style with jewel-coloured tapestries hanging from the walls. Huge iron lanterns stood on the floor holding thick ivory candles while a bed piled high with velvet cushions took centre stage. Mario threw open painted shutters to reveal a portrait of the sea. Then he pulled her into his arms.

'May I?' he whispered, his kisses starting on her forehead, down her cheeks, then he was nuzzling her neck and before she could say, 'you may', his lips were on hers and there was no going back.

That was the moment when she should have pushed him away. But she didn't want to. There was an inevitability to all of it. She'd go back to Hastings and he'd likely forget all about her, but the man was beautiful, seductive and she gave in to his love-making and surprised herself with her wanton response.

Afterwards, their legs a jumble on the rumpled covers, she leant up on one elbow and gazed down at him. His eyes were closed and she drank in the sight: an older man with more expertise in bed than the couple of lovers she'd been with before. He was in excellent shape – the only telltale signs of age were slightly puckered skin at his armpits and fine lines around his eyes and mouth. She longed to run her hand through his mop of silver-white hair, but she didn't want to wake him. It was cut well and she wondered if the highlights were natural. She imagined he visited an expensive barber.

His eyes flickered open.

'What are you looking at?' he asked.

'You.' She traced her finger round his left eye, down his cheek and when she circled his lips, he caught her hand in his.

'You will have to wait a while if you want me to make love to you again. I'm an old man, after all.' He chuckled and she wondered if she were supposed to contradict him.

'Is that what we have just done?' she asked. 'Made love?'

He huffed then. 'Are you going to analyse everything and go serious on me, Susi?'

'No, not serious. But... I need you to know that I don't usually fall into bed so easily.' She tugged the sheet over her breasts.

He sat up then, pulled a velvet cushion behind him to sit against the headboard.

'I didn't force you.'

'I know. I'm not complaining. Simply telling you I'm not usually this sort of woman.' She pulled him down and kissed the tip of his nose. 'But I like it. You cast a spell on me.'

'So, what sort of woman are you? A nun? My wife is no longer with us, you know. We are both adults. Free to do what we want.'

He got out of bed and started to gather her underwear from where it was strewn about the floor, like little sins.

'Come. It's time to take you back.'

'I'd prefer to make my own way back,' she said, as if wanting to prove her independence to this man who had crashed in on her like an unexpected storm.

He shrugged his shoulders. 'Whatever you like. Maybe we can talk later?'

'Maybe. I'll have a wander and catch a bus back.'

She needed to be alone for a while – to gather her thoughts, rein in her giddy emotions.

Mario locked up and they went their different ways. She watched as he stepped into the glaring heat of the day. The streets were quiet. In August, Italians sensibly rested in the afternoon. Later on, as darkness fell, the town would be busy again with people taking the air, dressed in best clothes for the *passeggiata*, parading up and down the main street. *La bella figura* still counted here in southern Italy, where what you looked like and who saw you was important. Giacomo had explained this to her yesterday and told her he hadn't missed this practice during his time in Manchester. She wondered what he was up to now. If he was clearing up after his lunch customers or resting, enjoying his siesta in the arms of a pretty girl? She shook her head as if to rid herself of these confused thoughts, like a dog shakes itself dry after a downpour. Why should she be thinking of Giacomo when she had just been to bed with Mario? Maureen would most likely remind her that she'd said she'd prefer to cuddle up to a hot-water bottle than a man... what was Puglia doing to her?

In a piazza at the top of the old mediaeval quarter of Rione Junno, Susannah found a tiny grocer's shop that stayed open all day. A *signora* was crocheting something in gaudy colours on a stool behind the counter and she got up to prepare her a *panino* with mortadella sausage, wrapping it in brown paper for Susannah to take away. She also bought two dark purple figs and a bottle of mineral water and went to find shade to eat her lunch.

Beneath a linden tree, its scent still lingering despite the end of the flowering season, she ate her simple and delicious picnic. A couple of ring-necked doves pecked between cobblestones, daintier than the more common pigeons and she scattered crumbs for them from her *focaccia panino*. She needed a shower; she could smell Mario on her. Before too long she would be back in Hastings, over a thousand miles away from here, but she didn't regret going to bed with him. For an hour, she had wantonly lost herself with an expert Italian lover and she hugged the memory to herself. She'd intended to ask him more about the *masseria*, but the whole delicious interlude had been an escape which she'd abandoned herself to, her mind empty of everything except their lovemaking amidst the velvet cushions.

In a sense, she considered it compensation for years of not caring for herself. Her tiring commute to and from London, working in the chaotic world of investment banking where she'd burnt herself out. Then, looking after Grandma Elsie, bedridden, constantly thumping on the ceiling with Grandpa Cedric's walking stick that she kept by her bed, summoning her to bring cups of tea, change wet sheets, retrieve the remote control she'd lost within the bedclothes. Susannah wouldn't have minded if Elsie had thanked her once in a while, but she was always complaining. 'What are you doing down there, Susannah? Watching television, no doubt. Stuffing your face with chocolates while I'm suffering up here alone.'

With Dad it had been different altogether. She'd cared for him out of love, not because of a sense of duty. But she'd become so rundown trying to keep Cobwebs going, hurrying back and forth to tend to him during her lunch hours. Her sister, Sybil, always seemed too busy to help out with the hands-on care and she really did not want him to go into a home, like they'd been forced to send Elsie in the end. When the police had come into her shop one afternoon and told her they'd found Elsie wandering barefoot along the seafront in her nightie, she'd been advised to find professional dementia care. Dad had been fine in the head. It was the cancer in his body that hadn't been fine. She'd cared for him herself in their home up until he'd died two days after being admitted to St Michael's Hospice.

Mario was the first man she had slept with in a long time and she'd enjoyed every minute of it. And when he'd reminded her that he was a widower, she'd felt a whole lot better. Even if it never happened again, it had been wonderful. She stretched her arms to the sunshine like a cat and began to make her way back to the hotel.

Back at the *masseria*, she rinsed the silk scarf Mario had lent her and went to hang it to dry on the line near the olive grove. Once again, she was the only guest staying in the boutique hotel that night and once again she and Mario dined at a table for two. Any slight awkwardness she might have felt was immediately dispelled by his friendly manner. He was gentlemanly, solicitous, pouring out her wine, showing her how to eat their starter of tiger prawns and expertly filleting her seabass, while asking her about life in England. He talked of his plans to renovate an old outbuilding in the grounds, presently used as storerooms. It felt like a husband and wife catching up over their evening meal.

'How did you get on at the agency, Mario? Any luck with finding someone to manage the place?'

He shook his head. 'Nobody suitable. I need a fluent English speaker for the party of American guests arriving soon, whilst I'm away in Rome. But there's nobody on their books at the moment. Youngsters all want city jobs.'

She leant forwards, elbows on the table, hands cupping her face, a rush of inspiration hitting her. 'What about me? Would I do?'

He gave her a long look. 'But you're on vacation.'

'My holiday could be extended into work,' she said. 'I worked in a hotel in London when I was younger. I'm sure I could manage.' It was as if she was hovering above herself, listening to somebody else proposing this crazy idea that had popped into her head. Staying longer would give her the perfect opportunity to probe the origins of the postcard sender. And, with Mario off the scene, she would have freedom to explore the *masseria*. It was perfect.

'What about your work in England?' he said, his finger tracing the rim of his empty wine glass. 'Your antiques?'

'The shop is my own,' she said. 'And I have an excellent assistant whom I trust completely.'

She mentally crossed her fingers, hoping that Maureen wouldn't mind.

When Mario spoke, it was as if he was ticking off his reasons for accepting. 'You wouldn't have to do anything domestic. Emma sees to that side of things. Your task would simply be to care for the guests, do some administration – but you could call me if there was anything complicated to deal with. I'm not expecting more enquiries because we're no longer on the booking website.'

He leant forwards, clasping her hands in his. 'If you want it, the job is yours. For one month.'

Mario fetched a bottle of Prosecco from a glass-fronted cupboard. 'Let's seal the deal with a glass of this excellent Valdobbiadene.' The cork popped in a celebratory sound and he proceeded to outline her job description, only half of which she absorbed.

She declined more Prosecco, left him sitting at the table and made her way back to her room, reeling a little at the sudden change to her plans, hoping she'd made the right decision. Cobwebs would be in good hands and Maureen seemed to revel in taking the reins but there were limits to friendship and she didn't want to take advantage. Susannah left the door unlocked. If he came to her later, she knew she was ready to allow him into her bed.

A full moon hung low in the sky as if caught between the limbs of the olive trees and she fetched her phone to take a picture. She stood for a while at the window gazing at the silvered grounds. Footsteps scrunched down the gravel path leading to the pool and she leant out further to see who it was. She made out the shape of a woman running. Susannah lost sight of her as she disappeared into the shadows. *Probably Emma in a hurry to get home to her family. She works so hard.*

She pulled the shutters to and picked up her guidebook to Puglia. The cover showed a street of *trulli* in Alberobello, a town she wanted to visit one day to discover more about these strange conical dwellings. With her new job, she would have more time.

Before she undressed, she exchanged a series of texts with Maureen.

What do you say to looking after the shop for me during September?

Tell me more, dear girl. What are you up to?

Long story.

No problem, but??? imagination in overdrive???

Been asked to caretake here.

With a Latin lover?

Ha ha! Later.

She shut down her mobile to stop Maureen asking more questions and went to sit at the dressing table to remove her mascara. The reflection in the oval mirror showed a young woman with glowing skin and soft, dreamy eyes. *The sunshine of southern Italy is doing me good,* she thought as she applied cleansing lotion to a cotton pad. *Or is it Mario and this place?* With its attention to detail, the room dressed like a stage, candlesticks on either side of the dressing table, an antique vanity set, a vintage black-and-white poster of a floury-faced clown advertising a performance of Enrico Caruso in *Pagliacci*, sitting in this bedroom was like waiting for the curtains to swish open and the next act to begin.

In the mirror, Susannah watched the door to her room slowly open. Mario entered and turned the key behind him in the lock. She stayed quite still as he walked towards her, carrying a dress over his arm.

'A present for you. You will look stylish in this for my American guests,' he said. 'I know it will suit you.' He held up a black dress, the folds in the skirt and across the bust soft and beautifully stitched. After hanging it from the antique hat-and-coat stand in the corner, he stepped towards her and bent to lift her loose hair to kiss the nape of her neck.

Scooping her from the dressing-table stool, he carried her to bed without a single protest passing her lips.

In the morning when she woke, he was gone. In one sense she was relieved. This fling with Mario was in danger of becoming too intense and she needed to slow down. She tried on the little black dress, gasping when she read the well-known but hitherto inaccessible designer label. In the mirror, a sexy young woman stared back, cleavage peeping from the crossover folds, the material soft, caressing her naked body. Did accepting the dress mean she was a kept woman? She shrugged the garment off and donned her ordinary clothes, telling herself not to get carried away. It was only a dress. In her shorts and cotton T-shirt, she went to fetch the borrowed silk scarf from the washing line.

It was in tatters, fronds rippling in a slight breeze like taunting fingers. As she removed the pegs and untangled the shreds, she wondered what night creature might have done such damage. There were huge tears in the fine material, as if a bird of prey had ripped it with claws.

CHAPTER 20

PUGLIA, 1946

THURSDAY, AUGUST 15, 1946.

Even the signora grows tipsy as the afternoon progresses in the dining room of the Masseria della Torre, but I remain stone-cold sober, concerned about these British RAF boys who seem to know me. I am definitely on the back foot. Whenever I approach their table to serve, they fall silent. One of them glares at me, muttering comments about lack of moral fibre and going AWOL when I lean over to clear dishes or fill glasses. I cannot wait for the day to end, but Eva and Maria are in their element flirting with these handsome foreigners. One of the servicemen has found the baby grand the signora uses as a sideboard for arranging glasses and bottles of liqueurs and he's singing the words to 'It's Been a Long, Long Time'. Eva and Maria twirl and sing '*La, la, la*' to the music, their skirts rising above their plump knees to the accompaniment of wolf whistles and cheers. When the pianist croons the lines about kissing his girl twice, there are more raucous shouts and banging of spoons on the table.

I retreat to the kitchen followed by the girls but Signora

Pinto shouts at them to stay in the restaurant and to pour more wine for the party. 'Today we make money. Keep those men happy.' She shoos them back but they really do not need much encouragement.

'Roberto, you can go home early. Take the evening off. We'll be fine without you,' she tells me, swaying as she speaks, a little cross-eyed. 'My girls will look after them.' She wraps half a roasted chicken and a couple of stuffed peppers in brown paper and shoves them in my hands. '*Buona festa*. Take this with you and have tomorrow off.'

I don't need telling twice and I wheel the bike across the courtyard, through the wide doors past three parked Jeeps. I stop for a few seconds to take in the dusty windscreens, the RAF roundels on the side, once again trying to pin from where I am getting this knowledge, remembering the airman's words.

He'd asked if I was Billy. Am I Billy? Should I have questioned him further? What is stopping me? What happened to me to make me want to forget? I am beginning to believe that my mind does not want to remember, that something dreadful happened to me, like Anto once said. The bike wheels fizz along the dusty track, and as I pedal, the rush of cooler air after the hot kitchen is welcome. If I hurry, Anto and I can catch an evening swim.

At the end of the track, a kitten darts across my path and I skid to avoid trapping the little thing under my wheels. When I stop it approaches, its mewing far louder than its size merits, its little tail pointed straight up like a cartoon cat. On further inspection I cannot see its mother or other kittens, so I find myself lifting it up. *I am going soft*, I tell myself. But I know Antonella will love a cat about the place. She's been complaining about rats invading the hen coop. I drop the kitten down my tucked-in shirt. It doesn't complain, settles warm on my stomach and in twenty minutes I am back at the *trullo* and handing over the little animal.

'She's so pretty. *Che bellina*,' Antonella coos, holding her up and talking to her. '*Grazie*, Roberto. How clever of you. This one will be my huntress, won't you?' She talks to her as if she is a tiny human and I smile.

'No need to cook this evening,' I tell her, holding up the signora's gift. 'She was in a good mood, but her head will be complaining tomorrow morning. Let's have a swim and a picnic on the beach,' I suggest. 'I'm in sore need of a dip.' For some reason I can't tell her what happened just yet.

The kitten follows us down to the beach and even puts a paw in the sea, mewing plaintively as we leave her behind when we both dive in and strike out towards the grotto. This time I win when Anto challenges me to a race. I am growing stronger in this horseshoe-shaped bay. It's brought me luck: the sea air and fresh diet of fish and vegetables are doing me good. As well as the company of this lovely girl. We sit for a while on a flat rock, watching the setting sun. Before darkness falls, we swim slowly back to the beach, the kitten mewing a welcome, darting between our wet legs as we set about building a fire from driftwood.

To wash down the chicken and peppers, we drink an unfinished bottle of Primitivo I took from one of the dining tables. The sound of the sea washing the shore's edge is soothing and the kitten curls up in Anto's lap as she leans against me, staring into the flames. I'm so delighted that she feels safe enough to do this and I dare not move in case I dislodge her. I could sit here for hours with her sitting close. My heart is full. But then I spoil it by opening my big mouth.

'Anto,' I say, tentatively enough I think. 'The other day... in the market... when you introduced me to that woman as your husband...'

Before I can say anything else, she springs away from me and inside my head, I curse at my clumsiness.

The mood is broken and she starts to clear the remains of

our picnic into the basket. 'It's late and I'm tired,' she murmurs. She picks up the kitten, seeming to totally ignore the words that spilled from my mouth.

'I'm going to call this little signorina Birba. I can tell she's going to be a mischievous one. Did you see how she tried to nick my piece of chicken? Birba, Birba, Birba,' she says, tickling the kitten under her chin, ignoring my earlier questions.

Later that night, after she has said goodnight and shut the door to her *trullo*, I sit smoking for a while in the cooler night air. I haven't mentioned to her how the airman asked me if I was Billy. Is it because I'm anxious what I will discover about myself? My life here with Antonella is good. Why would I want to change it? But equally, do I want to carry on living like this forever? Am I a coward for not wanting to face up to my past, when months ago I was desperate to find out who I really am?

FRIDAY, AUGUST 16, 1946.

Midway through the morning, I am hoeing weeds between tomato plants when I hear a motorbike approach. From the corner of my eye, I see Anto pick up a bowl of salad leaves she is cleaning outside the *trullo* and dash inside, the kitten scampering after her.

When the rider sees me, he cuts the engine, swings his leg over the bike and pulls it onto its stand. It is the young RAF serviceman who spoke to me yesterday in the restaurant. He walks over, holds out a hand and I take it, conscious of my grubby paw gripped in his, clean and smooth.

'I never introduced myself properly,' he says. The way he stares at me is as piercing as yesterday and my stomach churns.

'I'm Phil. If you want the whole caboodle, it's Pilot Officer Philip Sanders.' He looks at me quizzically, adding, 'RAF?' The question in his voice lingers.

'My name is Roberto,' I reply in English. With less assurance than this young Englishman standing before me.

He sighs. 'Look here. Can we sit and talk? So bally hot.' He wipes sweat from his brow and I indicate the bench over by Anto's *trullo*, shaded by the laden fig tree.

'We'll have to mind the wasps,' I say, leading him over. 'But it's the coolest place at this time of day.'

'Could I have some water, do you think, old bean? Last night was a bit heavy on the old vino.'

'Of course. Sorry, I should have offered.'

When I stick my head around the *trullo* door, Anto is hunched on a stool in the corner, terror written on her face.

'Can you bring us fresh water, Anto?'

She shakes her head and I tell her not to worry, I will deal with it. I busy myself with finding the jug and, conscious that my hands are shaking, I fetch two tumblers draining on the side of the sink.

Outside, the pilot pulls a brown envelope from his jacket, which he then hangs from a fig branch.

'The ants will take up home in that,' I say, transferring the jacket to a hook in the wall beside the *trullo* door where Anto dries hot chili peppers. The material is thick in my hands, good quality, and the blue matches the grey-blue of the pilot's eyes.

He tips out photographs from the envelope. 'Take a dekko at these, old bean,' he says, handing them over.

In the first, three young men stand at ease, grouped beneath an aeroplane. The name Liberator immediately springs into my mind. They are wearing battledress blues and smiling at the camera, their fresh young faces eager and confident. The one in the middle is shorter than his two fair-haired companions. He has dark hair and his hands are thrust deep in his pockets. It could be me. I look at Philip and he nods his head encouragingly.

'Don't you see? It's you. Billy,' he says. 'That was taken

shortly before our first practice exercise, back in Morpeth. The sprog crew. Remember? You were as sick as a dog and had to fork out one pound to ERKs for cleaning out your turret.'

I shake my head. 'I would like to say I remember, but... I don't.'

'Let me see if I can jog your memory and then I'll tell you what *I* think happened. We called you "old bean" all the time, because that's what your pa called you in his Italian. *Fadgelino,* or something like that. You told us it meant "bean". And that you loved eating them. So, you were officially christened "old bean" in the Mess. We wasted good beer over your head at the ceremony. Remember?'

I look blankly at him and he continues.

'And you told me you'd always wanted to join the RAF. Ever since you were a small boy and you saw what you thought was a pterodactyl flying across the sky. You joined the cadets. You were hellishly relieved, old bean, when they let you in, because you thought you might not be eligible – your dad being a macaroni. But your mother is English. Remember any of this?'

Again, I cannot remember anything but I continue to listen, wondering if something will chime.

'You told us how lucky you'd been but how unfair the system was. Because your dad was locked up at the start of the war for being Italian, when Churchill said to collar the lot. Remember, Billy? You were incensed that all Italians were rounded up together with other foreigners who were considered as aliens – even those who'd lived all their life in Blighty.' The young man called Phil stops, peers at me, waiting for my reaction.

I shake my head, numb. There is nothing in his words that I recognise. He continues to tell me more about myself. But if it is me he is talking about, I am a stranger.

'You never made it to pilot because you were an ideal candidate for a gunner: short, stocky but not so stocky you wouldn't fit in the turret. So, what happened to you, Billy? You and I were on a different craft that night. Your Liberator pranged and ditched in the sea. We were told you'd all bought it, but you must have got out somehow.'

He looks at me again, a crease between his brows. 'Christ, Billy, it's so good to see you again, but... won't you let me take you back to the base at Amendola? Get you seen by a doc? You've got amnesia, old thing. I'm sure of it.'

He stands up. 'Look, I've got to dash but... what do you say I leave these snaps with you and you can take your time checking them over in peace and quiet, after the shock of me turning up like this has worn off? You can keep them. I have the negatives if I want to make copies. They might ring some bells. I'll come back to see you again very soon. Tomorrow, even. We've got to solve this, Billy old bean.'

I try to interrupt but he holds up his hands. 'I won't take no for an answer and I'm not giving up on you either, Billy. I've made up my mind. To me it's as obvious as bloody daylight. And besides, I owe you. Big time! You're probably going to tell me you don't remember, but I'll always be grateful to you for chivvying me that time when I was absolutely frozen on the beer lever and wanted to jack in the whole show.' He clamps a hand on my shoulder. 'You were an absolute brick and, well, now it's my turn to repay you. As wonderful as this is,' he says, gesturing at our surroundings, 'I can't see you wanting to live in this desolate place forever after.'

I take the photos and watch as he climbs back on his motorbike. At the first kickstart, the engine roars into life and he disappears down the track in a trail of dust. I stand gazing into the distance long after he is out of sight.

Only then does Anto come out of her *trullo*. 'What was all that about?' she asks.

I hand her the photographs and she sits where the man

called Phil sat moments ago. She sifts through the photos, spending longer on some.

'These are photographs of *you*, Roberto,' she says, looking up at me with such sadness that I want to take her in my arms and comfort her.

'What are you going to do?' she asks.

'I'm not sure.' I take the pictures and shuffle them like cards. 'That man. He's a pilot. He was dining at the *masseria* yesterday and said he recognised me. He tells me we were in the same squadron together. But, Anto, I can't remember a thing about it. It's like listening to another man's story. I admit there have been times recently when my mind has taken me to a locked door and it's opened a fraction... but then... almost immediately, it slams shut.' I run my fingers through my hair. The flesh on the back of my head is still tender. I'm in a limbo world. 'The man, the pilot called Phil, he suggests I go with him to the camp to see a doctor.'

'I knew this would happen. That you would leave me too. Why didn't you talk to me about it last night?'

I shrug. Not sure myself why I didn't. Maybe I thought that by ignoring it, the problem would go away by itself. I watch her return to the *trullo* and then I pick up the hoe to continue weeding. My hoe stabs at the dry soil and after a minute or two I realise I'm doing more damage than good, slicing the bases of tomato plants which will now wither and die. I've done half a row before I tell myself to stop.

What is the point? What am I doing here, propped up by a nineteen-year-old girl who deserves someone better? A girl for whom I have growing feelings that are not reciprocated? I'm playing at life. Hiding from the world like a coward, frightened of what I might discover if my memory returns. I've been kidding myself I am protecting Anto, but it is really the other way round. I fling the hoe to the ground and march into the *trullo to* find her.

She is in the corner, crying. But she wipes the tears from her eyes with the backs of her hands as soon as I enter and gets up from the stool.

'There is something I have to tell you, Roberto,' she says, standing up tall, her chin jutted forwards. 'Nonno's box... I hid the contents. I didn't want you to see those things, in case you found out who you were and left. But it was wrong of me. I know that now. I'll take you to where I put them.'

'Anto,' I say, reaching out to her, wondering if after all she has feelings for me, but she slaps my hand away and marches out of the *trullo* in the direction of the beach and I follow at a trot. 'Slow down, Antonella,' I call, but she ignores me, her feet flying over scorching shale, the noisy cicadas jeering at me as I trail behind under the blazing sun.

Instead of descending to the beach, she leads me towards the far edge of the cliffs, weaving her way through a meadow of coarse grass where crickets creak their relentless song, and abandoned olive trees are distorted from the force of sea winds.

'Watch yourself along this next bit,' she says, turning as we stop in front of a dense thicket of prickly pear plants. 'The thorns will tear at you if you don't step exactly where I do.'

We pass through what seems to my eyes an impenetrable barrier. We hold our arms up high to avoid inch-long grey thorns, and brush past orange and pink fruits sprouting on fleshy cacti leaves, before we reach a circle of boulders.

'Follow me carefully,' she orders as she begins to descend a path that pitches down from within this circle to a hollow. I can hear the sea crashing below. We have entered what resembles the lip of a huge cauldron, the sea below us a frothing, churning soup thirty metres or so beneath.

Antonella shouts above the roar of the waves. 'Don't look down; hold on to the rope and follow slowly.'

A thick length of rope is secured to rusting rings in the sides of the rocks. After descending three metres we enter a cavern set back from the top of the grotto where we swam to the other day: Antonella's special place. At the very back of this cavern, under the shelter of a canopy of rocks, is a ledge, wide enough for one man to lie down. Hanging from wooden hooks are a few dented aluminium implements: a frying pan, a kettle, a ladle and a tin that holds candles as well as a couple of spoons and forks.

'My brother and I used to play in here for hours. It was our secret place. I told you one day I'd show you.'

She shoves her arm deep within a crevice and pulls out a sack.

'These are yours, Roberto. What you were wearing when Nonno found you in the sea.'

I pull out bulky, dirty white overalls, one of the legs torn and singed. And I know, even before I hold them up, that they will be heavy from heating element strips and buoyancy pads strategically placed on knees, behind the head and on breast pockets. How often have I been assisted into this piece of flying kit in the dressing room? Plugged in and tested for short-circuiting before a mission? I turn stone cold. My hands begin to shake as Antonella holds up a chain: an identity tag. I grab it from her. Engraved on it is a name and a number: Sergeant William Pica, RAF. 1584477.

'My name is Billy,' I tell her. 'Not Roberto.'

She hangs her head.

Silence between us while the sea in the grotto below slaps and slops against the rocks.

'You will leave and I'll never see you again,' she says.

'Will you mind so very much?'

She looks up at me with such pain. The next second, she is hugging me close, tears pouring down her face.

'Don't leave me, Roberto. Please don't leave me.'

Her body is shaking, her words tangled with her tears and I

try to calm her, rubbing her back, smoothing her hair from her face but she continues to sob.

'He'll find me. I know he will,' she weeps. 'Salvatore beat me so badly that my bruises took weeks to heal. You have seen for yourself the scars on my back that he caused with his belt. But... he did more. You know he did more.'

I wait for her crying to abate, I continue to hold her, whispering '*Shh, shh,*' as if she is a tiny child, telling her that not all men are evil like Salvatore, that I am so, so sorry, and I promise to protect her. At that, she tugs at my shirt, stares up at me. 'How can you promise such a thing? You will go away, back to England. How can you look after me?'

'I'll go to see this camp doctor. I will sort something. *Shhh*, don't worry, Anto. I can't bear to see you like this. I won't abandon you.'

'You cannot promise me anything,' she says, pushing me away again.

And then she moves towards the edge of the cavern, turns to look at me, her brave face on again as she poises above the drop to the grotto.

'Come,' she says, her eyes glistening with tears. 'I'll take us back a quicker way. Leave your stuff here. It will be safe until you pick it up later.'

I drop the tag with my name on top of the sack and move to stand beside her at the edge, the sea beneath us a swirling green and blue.

'Jump after me,' she says. 'Wait until I've swum out of the way and then jump.'

And then she is gone, the back of her head as black as the glistening rocks at the edge of the sea where she sinks in the water below. I watch as she resurfaces and starts to swim towards the mouth of the grotto. 'Jump, Roberto. Jump now,' she calls.

I am less graceful as I fall. At the last minute, my feet skid on moss at the edge of the stones, so that I land face first in the ocean instead of feet first – the pain in my head is an explosion of lights. I swallow water on impact, disorientated as I rise through bubbles to the surface, fighting for breath as I thrash around in panic and sink again.

Images flash before my eyes: a twinkling of lights that form themselves into streams of tracer, a pyrotechnic of cannon fire and red blotches of explosion, an icicle hanging from my mask, acute pain in my leg, cramp and finally my mother's face, her mouth forming words of encouragement as I sink, sink, sink, trying desperately to hang on to my life. *Is this all there is, then? What about the rest? I'm only twenty-five for fuck's sake. Do I never get to tell this girl that I love her?*

I'm aware of drifting towards a place of peace and comfort, when arms interrupt my reverie and grab me with fingers that pull at my hair. I feel the kick of somebody's legs against my torso as I am dragged to the surface and when I thrash about as we break through, Anto is shouting at me to lie still else we both drown and I obey her when she tells me to stay on my back, to kick my legs as she guides me through the waves, hauls me through the shallows, my body scraping and scratching on the stones where we collapse. I gulp in huge mouthfuls of air, coughing and spluttering saltwater from my lungs. Dazed, shattered, I watch her as if in a trance as she heaves wood scattered by the tide and builds a fire with matches fetched from Nonno's cave. When it is ablaze, she pulls off my wet clothes. Once again, I am as helpless as an infant, nurtured and cared for by her hands.

How can I leave this girl? This is the second time she has given me back my life.

Sometime later, when we are huddled together under a sail by the fire and I feel stronger, I whisper my thanks and she touches my cheek with her mouth before resting her head on my chest.

'Please don't leave me,' she murmurs. I fold her in my arms, holding her tight as she falls asleep.

Fragments of my past dribble back to me, like snapshots from a photo album, as I lie there on the sand, listening to the rhythm of the sea sucking and pulling on the shore as I finally remember where I have come from, what I was doing and knowing what I have to do next.

CHAPTER 21

SATURDAY, AUGUST 17, 1946.

Phil is outside the *trullo*. He's come to collect me and I ask him to switch off his engine while I go inside to say goodbye.

'Anto, I have to return to England to sort out a few things. I'll be back as soon as possible...'

She carries on chopping a carrot, dicing it small. From a pot on the sill she grabs a handful of basil, her fingers guiding the knife as it moves up and down at lightning speed. Then it's the turn of the onion as she slices.

'Anto. Did you hear me?'

She looks over her shoulder, her eyes watery, tears running down her cheeks. 'It's the onion,' she says, 'always does this to me.' And then she turns back to the sink, slicing so fast that onion rings fly to the floor.

I move towards her, wanting a reaction, but her back is stiff, unresponsive.

'Go if you're going.'

'I'll be back, Anto. I promise.'

Silence.

Phil sounds the hooter. I cram my few possessions into my pockets. The notebook where I've kept a record of my time here, a piece of broken seashell that Anto gave me, shaped like a flying bird, its eye a tiny piece of blue-black sea glass. She told me when she pushed it into my hand that my memory would fly back to me one day like a bird. I throw a last glance at her back, at the hair at the base of her neck where her curls now touch the collar of her blouse and then I leave.

The doctor at Amendola Airbase gives me a thorough examination, spending time on my head wound, testing my eyesight, jotting notes, asking me question after question, many of which I am unable to answer. He warns me I will most likely suffer from headaches in the future.

'Your brain will have an overload of information as your memories return. It will be like a full-on assault. Don't expect life to be smooth for a while, Sergeant.' He folds his notes and puts them into a yellow envelope, writing *To Whom it May Concern* on the front. 'Give this to the doctor when you get back to the camp in Blighty,' he says and then I am dismissed.

Phil spends all his free time with me and talks to me about the past, the scrapes we got into, the ops I flew with him before we changed crews. I get that he's willing me to remember the rest of my past but I talk to him about the present and tell him I want to return to Italy as soon as I'm able. He's due to remain in Puglia a while longer. There is still mopping-up work to do here in Foggia with the displaced, but I am being sent back on the next possible flight, probably in a couple of days. The squadron is slowly depleting as men are demobbed. Most of the time I stay in the sick bay, looking at more photographs that Phil fetches me.

And slowly, more recollections return like a jerky old film. An intermittent slide show of memories. Glimpses of the old me. At night I dream. Of a restaurant my Sicilian father owns in a seaside town in England. Of a girl called Elsie whom I walk out with. Of night missions when none of the young men I fly with dare to hope to return alive. When I wake, I sit up, staring through the windows of the sick bay at the almost empty airfield in Amendola. My hands shake as I realise that what I dream is the truth.

Other memories flood in as I perch on my hard bed, the scenes of my life flickering in my head. The bedsheets are drenched in sweat, my head is hammering like the doc warned. And, as my memories travel back in time, I realise my life is more complicated than I could ever have imagined.

CHAPTER 22

PRESENT DAY

For the first weeks while Mario was in Rome, the American guests kept her busy and Susannah had little time to research the postcards. She was used to English invoices from her Cobwebs business but Italian bills were different – containing more information – and she had to concentrate on not missing anything. She'd told Mario that she'd worked in a hotel. But hadn't told him that it was as a cleaner in her student days. There were times when she'd felt out of her depth in the last fortnight, regretting her crazy suggestion. She'd had no time for anything else and was beginning to worry that she would not be able to discover anything about Elsie's postcard writer. Most of the group was pleasant, but one demanding woman complained about the air conditioning; there was no gluten-free muesli at breakfast; the mosquito net above her bed did not keep away the insects and the quiet nights kept her awake. Eventually Susannah booked her a room in a modern hotel and from then on the group vibe picked up. Two young couples in their early twenties asked about walking in the area and she thought immediately of Giacomo and phoned him. There'd been no time for another Italian lesson, unfortunately. Apart from needing one, she had missed his company.

'The bar is shut for plumbing modifications tomorrow, so I could take them on a trek in the afternoon – a walk past a traditional coastal watch tower. The path runs through a nature reserve. Do you think they'd like that?' he asked.

She could hear plates being set down in the wine-bar's kitchen and the sudden hiss of oil hitting a hot pan.

'Sounds *perfetto*. They're really keen to do it before they leave in the next days. While I'm on, can I book the group in for a meal on their final evening?'

'*Certo!* A last supper.' He chuckled. 'And will you come on the walk tomorrow?'

'You don't need me to be there for interpreting, do you?' She laughed. 'Not that you would struggle, Giacomo.'

'No. But it would be great to spend some time together.'

'I'd love to catch up with you when I can, but I've loads to do here. More than I bargained on.'

She was flattered to hear he wanted to get together again, but she had something else in mind. Emma had asked to take off the following day to look after her grandchildren if she left a couple of *lasagne* to pop in the oven, and Susannah had already given her permission. So, tomorrow, with most of the guests off the premises, she would be able to poke about the *masseria* undisturbed. Mario had mentioned he'd inherited bits and pieces upon purchasing the farmhouse. Perhaps she would find something to link to the sender of the postcards. What, she had absolutely no idea. But any lead would be good. And if she found nothing, that was another box to tick off her search.

'That's a shame, Susannah. Are you sure you don't want to tag along?' Giacomo persisted. 'The coast tower is really interesting. It dates back to the fifteenth century and—'

'I'm quite sure. Perhaps another time? I need to finish a bundle of paperwork for Mario,' she lied.

'I'll fetch them at nine-thirty. If you change your mind...'

'I won't. Maybe another time?' She ended the call, hoping she hadn't put him off, but as much as she would have liked to spend a day sightseeing, she needed tomorrow to concentrate on her hunt.

She waved goodbye after reminding them to take plenty of water for their walk, fussing around them like a mother hen, despite not being much older than most of the party. Then, checking that those who had stayed behind were happily ensconced by the pool, she went to the kitchen. Hanging from a hook was a bunch of keys that Emma usually carried in her pinafore pocket. Mario had talked about converting the store-rooms into extra accommodation and after scouting round the rest of the house, she planned to investigate that area.

In the living room a huge bookcase took up most of one wall. She'd earmarked a shelf of leather-bound albums. Once again, she wished her daddy was with her. He had a logical, methodical brain, despite being untidy round the house. In no time he would have helped her formulate a plan. Most days he'd managed to complete the *Times* cryptic crossword, even in the latter stages of his illness. Susannah knew he must have been feeling really rough when he'd stopped asking her to buy news-papers. She pictured him sitting in the old brown armchair in the shop during their coffee breaks, chewing on his pencil, sometimes closing his eyes to concentrate on a tricky clue and then shouting, 'Eureka! Why didn't I think of that before? It was staring me in the face.'

But how could you be logical and methodical when you didn't know what you were looking for? Postcards of this farm-house had been sent to Grandma Elsie. Fact. The letter and card both expressed a longing to meet up again. '*My heart will never be complete without you*' were the words she knew by heart – words written with love. Fact. It was why and by whom those words were written that she wanted to uncover. She knew she was thrashing about. But she had to make a start.

One of the albums in the bookcase was a visitors' book and she turned the stiff pages, some stuck together and spotted with mildew. She ran her finger down the few comments for 1947, the date on the handwritten postcard, but nothing spoke to her. Not many guests had stayed that year and she wondered if it was too soon after the war. The card had been written in perfect English. Was the sender an English guest or someone fluent? He might be a German, in which case he had once been the enemy. Had he been made welcome? Maybe he was French or Italian? How on earth had Elsie met him? In effect, he could be of any nationality in the world. What was the link with the *masseria?*

Was the sender perhaps an Italian POW who'd been marooned in England but then returned to his homeland after the armistice of 1943? From a distant history lesson at school, she remembered there were thousands of Italians in British camps until the 'Eyeties', as they were commonly called, changed sides. 'Macaroni!' she said aloud. Grandma Elsie had muttered that word when she'd visited her in the care home. Italians were called macaroni by some British soldiers during the war.

Sighing, her mind racing with too many possibilities, she replaced the visitors' book and pulled out two photograph albums. But these were no help either. One was empty and the other contained saucy black-and-white postcards: plump women at the Viareggio seaside in the 1930s wearing long knickerbockers and half-buttoned camisoles, revealing ample bosoms. There was one of a priest cavorting with a nun in bed and another with a couple canoodling under a ping-pong table.

Susannah replaced the albums and ran her fingers over the titles of the books on the next shelf. She came across a couple of

English poetry books and she opened the front page of the first slim volume. A hand-written inscription: *To my darling, 'How like a winter hath my absence been?'* A dried rose fluttered to the floor.

Replacing the faded flower in the book, she hurried to her room to compare the handwriting on the postcard.

January 1, 1947
In my dreams I imagine the day when we shall be reunited. Until then, I hope my letters will fill the gaps. All my best love xx

The sentiment of being parted was the same, but the writing on the card and letter was different, the letters rounder, untidier, the 'e' totally unlike the swirly, old-fashioned, careful script in the poetry book. The date on its frontispiece was 1857. Over one hundred years earlier, not that it necessarily meant the message had been written then.

Sensing that she was allowing herself to drop down rabbit holes, she snapped the book shut and returned it to the shelf in the living room.

It took her frustrating moments to match the correct keys from the ring, but in none of the six other bedrooms did she find anything of use. Sepia photos on the walls showed groups of workers standing erect in front of a threshing machine; in another, a terrified-looking young bride cowered beside an older man with long whiskers. There were hand-tinted photos of the basilica of Monte Sant'Angelo and more recent images of the *masseria* undergoing reconstruction: Mario in the foreground, stripped to the waist, halfway up a ladder, waving at the photographer. But nothing to give her a lead as to the identity of the postcard sender.

Think this through, Susi, she told herself. *You have absolutely no idea what he looked like.* Or if he was a he. It could just as well be a she. Had Elsie fallen for a woman? Anything was possible but nothing was clear as questions jumped into her head.

A tap on the living-room door interrupted her search and she jumped.

'Sorry to startle you, my dear, but is there any chance of a coffee? But not espresso. My wife and I could do with a long one, like we drink back in the States,' the elderly classics professor of the party asked.

'Of course, sir. Give me five minutes.'

In the kitchen, she set a pan of water to boil and found a filter jug. While she waited for the coffee to brew, she doodled on a shopping list pad on the counter: a huge question mark, surrounded by who, why, where and when. Easy when you reduced a quest to these four short words. Hard when you weren't sure how to proceed. As she scribbled, she noticed a box with several pots of tablets and vitamins sitting on a tray with a pill organiser like she had used for Dad and Gran and she wondered who they were for. Mario and Emma both seemed as fit as fiddles, but you never knew.

She carried the tray with coffee and chocolate almond biscotti to the husband and wife sitting in the shade by the pool and promised to arrange a visit to the basilica for them on the next day.

'We have to pace ourselves, dear, at our age,' said the professor's wife. 'One day on and one day off. But we're having a swell time. And John adores all the antiquities.'

Susannah stayed chatting for a while, impatient to continue her sleuthing, but conscious that the guests were her responsibility. Eventually she made her escape.

In the sunny courtyard, she stooped to stroke the hotel cat, fat and sleek from leftovers, stretched along the threshold of one of the storerooms. Three doors faced her. The first was ajar but when she tried to push it open it jammed and, poking her head around the half-rotten wood, she saw sun rays streaming through cracked tiles, and a precarious fallen beam. It took time to fumble for the key to the second. With a click, it turned in the stiff door, which she shoved open with her shoulder. Inside it was completely dark, the shutters barred and she yelped as something furry scuttled over her sandal. To search this room, she would need a torch and she reached for her phone in her pocket.

'Signorina. *C'e qualche problema?*'

Emma stood behind her, hands on hips.

'A cat...' Susannah stammered, making a mewing sound. '*Gatto.* I think one of the cats got in... I h-heard it yowling... *miaow, miaow.*'

The look on Emma's face told her that she didn't understand or most likely believe her explanation and Susannah continued to stutter out the first words that came into her head.

'Did you have a good time with your grandchildren? *Nipotini? Tutto bene?*'

In response, Emma held out her hand and Susannah gave her the keys.

'*Grazie,* signorina.'

She hadn't expected Emma back so soon and her lack of Italian and Emma's lack of English made the situation even more awkward. Susannah shrugged her shoulders and made her way to reception, feeling like a naughty child caught mid-act, frustrated that she was no further forward with her mystery.

No other opportunities presented themselves in the next couple of days and Susannah began to worry that, with Mario returning, she had reached a dead end. After lunch on the guests' final day, she helped clear away dishes and carry them to the large kitchen.

'*No, no,*' Emma said, still frosty, insisting she didn't need help. Susannah ignored her and set to, loading the dishwasher.

'*Il Signor Andreani torna quando?*' Susannah asked in halting Italian, wondering if Emma might have a firmer idea of Mario's return.

A deep slow shrug of the shoulders, followed by a '*Boh!*', told Susannah that Emma did not have the faintest idea. She liked this simple expression, guessing it translated as 'dunno'. Her list of colloquialisms was growing with each day that passed.

It was obvious that Emma was not going to be more communicative, so, making sure her guests were all happy to have a lazy afternoon before the evening at Giacomo's that she had planned, she walked to the beach through the olive groves, drinking in the view of the calm sea and the strange fishing platform that Giacomo had told her was a *trabucco*, jutting from the shore's edge. She was looking forward to seeing him again, she realised, as she brushed her fingers along strands of wild rosemary growing along the path. The scent was more potent than the bush growing in a pot in her patio garden back in Hastings. It would be another world when she returned to her English routine after her Puglian adventures. The month was rapidly drawing to an end and she needed to get her brain into focusing on the reason she had stayed on. The second and third storeroom still beckoned but she needed Emma out of the way first. She settled herself on the beach, a book on her lap. But she couldn't concentrate, her eyes drawn to the *trabucco* where a couple of fishermen were hauling up a huge net in smooth movements. Drowsy from the wine she'd enjoyed at lunch, she stretched out in the sun and was soon asleep, her dreams muddled, interspersed with images of fishing platforms and her grandmother dancing by the sea with a handsome young Italian sailor.

She woke later with a dry mouth and her legs stinging from

sunburn. While she'd been asleep, the sun had moved so that she was no longer in the shade. Plunging in the water for a quick swim, the saltwater stinging her limbs, she returned to the hotel for a shower, slathering her shins with aloe vera cream. Desperate for a cup of tea, she went to the kitchen and helped herself with a teabag she'd brought in her luggage – Maureen having delightfully warned her that tea in Italy was as weak as gnat's piss. The kitchen was spotless, Emma nowhere to be seen, and she boiled up water in a tiny saucepan, as kettles didn't seem to feature in Italian kitchens.

Waiting for the water to boil, she saw the housekeeping keys were back on their hook. *Now or never, Susi. Time is running out.* Without thinking twice, she left the pan on the gas and, snatching the keys, hurried to the remaining storerooms. The torch on her phone showed the second was completely bare, save for curtains of cobwebs and trails of droppings. In the third, her eyes took a while to adjust to the gloom but she made out a few sticks of furniture, including an old single bed with metal ends that stood against the far wall. As well as a bundle of rusting tools in the corner, her gaze took in a wooden chest and a chair riddled with woodworm. A bee buzzed against grimy panes and, standing on the chest, she worked the window open to let it fly free. Stepping down, she saw a piece of silky white material protruding from beneath the lid, and the finger of a pair of thickly padded gloves. Raising the lid gingerly, she saw a pair of goggles, the rubber around the rims perished and a chain with a name written on a tab, tangled in a ball of string. She worked it loose and brought it closer to her eyes, the letters too hard to distinguish in the gloom. She needed the phone on her torch, but, annoyingly, that was sitting on her desk in the office. Underneath was a bulky garment and she pulled at it. There was a label on the collar and she managed to make out: *A.M. size medium.* There were numbers and a crown symbol next to the words *Stores Reference.*

Emma yelling, 'Signorina Susannah?' shattered the after-noon air. Susannah jumped and pushed the box under the bed.

She smelled burning. *Shit! The pan of water on the stove.* She'd forgotten about it and it must have burnt dry. Pulling the door and shoving the keys into the back pocket of her jeans, she shouted, '*Arrivo.* I'm coming.'

CHAPTER 23

She'd blown it with Emma, probably never to return to her good books, but Susannah didn't care. The writing on the garment in the box was English. Was there a connection to the old post-cards written in English? Was the answer yes, or was she simply wanting it to be yes? She needed more evidence... It took some time to pacify the woman as she ranted and railed, pointing at the scorched pan and waving her arms about in a tirade of Italian that Susannah couldn't translate. But while Emma made a great play of taking the pan to the bins outside the kitchen door, Susannah sneaked the keys back on their hook.

In her room, she applied eyeliner and mascara with shaking hands and decided to wear the little black dress Mario had gifted her for this evening's party at Giacomo's. She couldn't wait to discuss her find. If the white material was a parachute, then the other stuff she'd glimpsed could have something to do with the war. The date on the card was January 1947 – not too long after war's end. Had it been in that box ever since? What was the name on the tag? It would have to wait until after the party. The guests had asked to be taken out for a typical *pugliese* meal and Giacomo had booked a local group of folklore artists to perform in his wine bar for the event.

Dressed and ready, she checked her reflection in the cheval mirror, pleased with how the designer dress clung to her body. It fell from the hips to the floor in soft folds, slimming her curves and covering her sun-scorched legs. She dreaded to think how much it had cost, but Mario seemed well off and probably used to purchasing such luxuries. Emma had arranged a perfumed red rose in a vase on the dressing table and at the last minute, Susannah pinned it to one side of her head, feeling exotic and different. She'd used a washout shampoo colour and the blue blended well with her black hair, like the sheen on a starling's feathers. Checking her watch, she hurried to the pool where drinks had been arranged before the arrival of the taxi to take the little group up to Giacomo's wine bar for their farewell dinner.

The setting was perfect, Susannah thought, as she made her way down the gravel path: spotlights artfully arranged so that the pool water was gently lit up from beneath the surface, fairy lights garlanded through white oleanders planted in huge terra-cotta urns along the path and a calming Bocelli aria playing in the background. She would miss the place, so different from her mundane life in Hastings.

Emma arrived with a tray of glasses of Prosecco and Susannah moved to help her.

'Dio mio,' Emma exclaimed as she let go of her tray, the crash of splintering glass on the tiles round the pool stopping conversation as everybody turned to stare. Emma spoke in rapid Italian, pointing at Susannah, shaking her head, waving her hands about and when Susannah approached to pick up the shattered pieces, Emma turned on her heel and ran towards the house, still ranting.

Susannah found her in the kitchen.

'Disgraziata! Puttana!' the Italian said, shaking her fist.

Susannah didn't understand the words, but Emma's anger was evident.

'*Che c'è?* What is it?' Susannah asked.

Emma picked up a fold of the black dress, disgust on her face. '*Non è il suo.*'

'*Non capisco,*' was all Susannah could manage. 'I don't understand.'

Muttering to herself, Emma gestured to Susannah to follow, spitting words as she stepped quickly to the lounge.

Emma picked up the photo of the group with Mario and Pavarotti, pointing to the woman on the other side of the famous star. The dress that the woman wore was identical to the dress Susannah was wearing. Susannah hadn't noticed this before.

'*Questo vestito è della signora. La signora è molto malata,*' Emma continued slowly, tapping her head.

Susannah was confused. '*La signora?*'

'*Sì, sì. La signora Andreani.*'

If she'd understood correctly from her basic Italian, Emma was telling her the black dress belonged to Mrs Andreani and that she was very ill. But Mario had told her she was dead. What the hell was going on?

Susannah tried again. '*Signor Mario Andreani è...*' She racked her brains to explain what she meant and then remembered she'd heard the English word used by Italians. '*Signor Mario è single, vero?*'

Emma waggled her finger. '*No, no. Non single. Il signore è sposato.*'

'*Sposato?*' Susannah repeated, feeling like a parrot. This was another new word.

Emma held up her left hand and pointed at her ring finger. '*Sposata.*' She pointed at the woman on the other side of Pavarotti, her fingernail tapping on the glass accusingly.

'*Signora Anita Andreani. Bellissima.*' She held the photo to her bosom and shook her head sadly.

'*Viva?*' Susannah asked, plucking the word from somewhere: the Italian for 'long live', or 'alive'...

Emma nodded and followed it with a grim expression and a gesture to the head. '*Povera signora. Malata.*'

So, contrary to what Mario had told her, his wife was not dead. She was sick. The pills she'd noticed in the kitchen were most likely for her. And Emma seemed to be intimating that she was sick in the head.

Utterly confused but unable to communicate anything more complex, her immediate thought was to ask Giacomo for help but he would be busy preparing for the group's arrival. One thing was certain, she needed to immediately change out of the little black dress that Mario had given her. She left Emma and hurried to her room, stripping off the second-hand dress as if shedding a snakeskin. She threw it onto the bed – the bed that Mario had carried her to and literally laid her on top of the covers. His wife had probably been somewhere else in the building at the same time. And then Susannah remembered how she had heard shouting from the top floor before Mario left. The shouts of his wife most likely. His wife had been on the floor above while in this room Mario had slowly undressed her, made love to her, whispering how beautiful she was, how her skin was like a velvet peach, how her breasts were firm, how he wanted to kiss every centimetre of her body...

And the scarf ripped to shreds on the washing line. Had Mario's wife done that? Susannah hurled a couple of cushions across the room as she recalled everything. Mario hadn't made love to her... he had used her for an easy fuck. How stupid and gullible she had been to fall for his Latin-lover charms. But she remembered his words plainly. 'My wife is no longer with us.' And she'd believed him and felt sorry for his loss. What a bloody liar. What a bastard. If he'd been around at this moment, she would have confronted him, wife or no wife present, and left the *masseria* there and then to catch the first plane home.

But he wasn't back yet. God knew when he would deign to return.

And it wasn't the fault of the American guests this had happened. She didn't want to ruin the last evening of their holiday and leave Emma to manage by herself. But she wouldn't stay one minute longer than necessary. If Mario phoned, she would not hold back on what she thought. He would receive an earful. For now, she willed herself to calm down. She pulled the rose from her hair, dragged on a pair of jeans and a plain white T-shirt, sprayed her favourite Jo Malone scent behind her ears, and, taking a deep breath, she re-joined the group.

'Not sure what's wrong with Emma,' she said, in answer to their queries. 'But she's gone to lie down. Some family problem or other. Change of plan: we'll have our *aperitivi* at Mo Vini instead. Giacomo has a really well-stocked bar. And he mixes a fantastic Aperol Spritz.'

Susannah was relieved that Giacomo had managed to find musicians for the evening. Their playing was loud and stopped her from engaging in polite conversation. He was kept busy in the kitchen and they hardly talked to each other while she ferried plates to the table, her guests increasingly merry as the generous carafes of bubbling white Lizzano and courses of home-made seafood pasta kept coming.

But while she worked, her head was full of the fact that Mario's wife was still alive: that he had been simply using her for sex. She hadn't complained at the time but if she'd known he had a wife, she wouldn't have gone there. It had tainted everything. She felt stupid. The physical attraction had been strong, and she'd not had sex in so long and now she put what had happened between them down to pure lust. The man was an expert lover. And he'd known how to trigger her responses.

The youngsters wanted to go on somewhere else at the end of the evening.

'Where can we go to dance, Giacomo?' an attractive girl called Shona asked, leaning into him. 'Is there anywhere with a good vibe in town?' He'd steadied her as she swayed and phoned for a taxi. After unsuccessfully trying to persuade Susannah to join the party, they'd left in a swirl of embraces and laughter, squashing themselves and a group of Italians they'd befriended in the restaurant, into the seats of the Fiat Multipla, bound for a nightclub on the cliffside out of town.

'I'll help you clear up and then I'll be on my way, Giacomo,' Susannah said, surveying the debris on the tables. She would tell him about her storeroom discoveries the next time they met. For the moment, the sour taste of Mario's deception had tainted everything.

'*Grazie*. I'd appreciate help. But let's have a drink ourselves before we get going again. It's thirsty work watching other people drink and I think we deserve it. I'm pleased with how the evening went, are you?'

'It was a success. *Grazie*, Giacomo.'

They sat on the terrace at the back of the bar and he pulled out a packet of Marlboro, offering her one.

'I gave up years ago. But... yes, please.'

He cupped his hand round the cigarette in her mouth as he flipped his lighter open and she drew in a lungful of nicotine.

'What's up?' he asked. 'You're subdued this evening.'

'I've decided to cut short my stay, Giacomo,' she said as she stubbed out the cigarette. 'Gross. Why did I ever smoke in the first place?'

'Why are you leaving early? I still have so much to show you. And... I thought you wanted to find out more about your painting and the cards...'

'Yes. I do. I...' She hesitated, not knowing how much she

wanted to confide about Mario with this kind guy. 'Let's just say I don't want to stay at the *masseria* any longer than I have to.'

Giacomo raised his eyebrows and with his cigarette still in his mouth, popped open the cork to a new bottle of white. 'Try this. A very good year. I think you'll like it. In fact, I think you need it.'

After two more glasses, it was easy to open up. Susannah had always been a lightweight drinker. A cheap date, she'd been told by her university boyfriends. After the fourth glass she hinted about having slept with Mario and discovering afterwards he was married. 'Age-old story,' she said, her words slurring, the room spinning like a merry-go-round. 'But I'm not that kind of girl. Really I'm not.' She spared the finer details.

Giacomo listened without passing judgement.

After she'd drunk the most part of the bottle, she forgot what she had and hadn't told him and he suggested she stayed in his spare room and to leave the tidying up until morning.

'Your guests are capable enough of sorting themselves out and getting to the airport without you. I presume you already booked their transport. Stay here tonight.'

'Did I ever tell you how kind you are, my big brother? Remind me to tell you of another dis... coverage I've made...' she started to say, throwing her arms around him, hiccupping loudly and covering her mouth as she swayed. 'The words won't come out ploperly, Jack... Jack's much easier to say than G-Giacomo. I shall call you Jack from now on, but let me tell you about my English box...'

He laughed. 'Whatever your box is, you can tell me tomorrow.'

The tap on the door next morning added to the army of hundreds of hobnailed creatures doing an Irish jig on the insides of her temples. She lifted her head warily from the pillow, groaning as the room spun.

'Good God,' she muttered as Giacomo stepped in, bearing a glass of very dark liquid. She clutched the sheet around her naked breasts. 'We didn't... did we?'

He grinned. '*Sfortunatamente no, cara* Susannah. It's not my style to seduce a girl who is legless... I learned that expression quite quickly in England.'

She peeped under the sheet and saw she was completely naked. 'But who...?'

'Not me. It was all down to you. I had a job gathering all your various bits and pieces from the terrace... I'm afraid your knickers landed on the balcony below. They are at this very moment draped on the signora's washing line next to three pairs of large *nonna* knickers.'

She buried her face in her hands and groaned. 'I'm never drinking again... I am so, so sorry, Giacomo.'

'Don't be. It was funny – especially the pole dancing display in the kitchen with the mop, the bucket on your head.' He set the tray on the bedside table. 'Get this down you. It will help calm your stomach.'

'Nothing will calm my stomach. Ever again. Let me just lie here and die.' She picked up the glass and sniffed at it, pulling a face. 'What the hell are you poisoning me with?'

'Fernet-Branca. A *digestivo* that contains at least twenty-seven herbs.'

'Yuck,' she said. 'It smells like floor cleaner mixed with cough mixture. Do I *have* to?'

'It is of course totally up to you, but I suggest you do. And after you've showered and dressed, I'll prepare you another tried and practised Italian cure for hangovers.'

She groaned again. 'And what might that be?'

'*Spaghetti aglio, olio e peperoncino*... with garlic, our best

Puglian olive oil and spicy pepper. Carbs to counteract nausea and chili to kick-start your metabolism.'

Her stomach heaved. 'I don't want to kick-start anything. I want to disappear...'

'*Coraggio*, Susannah. Come on. I promise this will help, chased up with an extra-strong double espresso.'

Still feeling delicate – and knickerless beneath her jeans as she hadn't the courage to knock on the downstairs flat to retrieve them – Susannah sat on the restaurant terrace with Giacomo and ate most of the surprisingly delicious spaghetti.

'In England, it's usually curry after a heavy night,' she said, putting down her fork in surrender.

'And which do you prefer?'

'You have to understand this is all most unlike my usual behaviour, Giacomo. In fact, I lead a simple life back in Hastings.'

He smiled. 'It's good to be brought out of yourself once in a while.'

'Yes, but not like this. I'm so embarrassed.'

'What's to be embarrassed about amongst friends?' He got up and removed her plate. 'Coffee?'

'What I'd really love is a strong cup of builder's tea.'

'I can do that for you. I brought back tea leaves from England. Got into the habit of drinking it myself.'

'You are a wonder-man, do you know that?'

'Keep dishing out the compliments. I like them.'

She followed him into the kitchen and watched as he set a pan of water on the stove for tea. 'You know, Susannah: what you told me about Mario. It won't be the first time a *straniera* is seduced and it definitely won't be the last. I'm afraid it's a kind of sport for young Italian men, chasing foreign girls.'

'I know that. Apart from the fact that he's not a *young* Italian, I didn't want it to be me: the foreign-girl-on-holiday cliché. I misjudged Mario totally and thought he genuinely liked me. And he reminded me of that Venetian guy who presents the TV programmes about Venice: same steel-grey hair, cheeky grin – a kind of anything-is-possible-if-you're-with-me guy...' She blushed as she thought about the possibilities that Mario had shown her in bed.

Giacomo frowned. 'Not sure which TV guy you're talking about, but I'm sure Mario does genuinely like you. What's not to like?' He handed her a cup. 'Here's your tea.'

'Let's change the subject, Giacomo. And... thank you for looking after me.'

'My pleasure. By the way, you christened me with a new name last night. Jack is the new Giacomo.'

'Did I really? Jack is less of a mouthful than Giacomo, but... I don't remember much about last night.'

'It's what my English friends used to call me too. So, Jack I am. They used to say I was Jack the lad – whatever that meant.'

Her head sore, it was too difficult to explain. 'Don't think you're a Jack the lad. Hope not. Couldn't cope.'

'Whatever! Listen – I can drop you back to the *masseria* this morning. I need to go that way to see one of my suppliers.'

'Thank you so much. I kind of regret returning the car hire now. I didn't think I needed it anymore. Jack, there's something I want to show you when we get there.'

'Oh yes. You did say something about a box. But I wondered if it was some kind of euphemism.' He winked at her and she swiped him with a tea towel.

'Don't be ridiculous! I had a snoop in one of the outbuildings and I came across a box with what I think might be British gear from the war. I need a second opinion. I found a tag with a name too, and I need to take another look, because I was interrupted by the housekeeper.'

He gave a low whistle. 'Interesting. I'm no expert, but I'll certainly take a look when I drop you back. Do you think any of this is linked to your letter writer? Is that what's on your mind?'

'Got it in one. But it's only a hunch. I haven't anything definite to go on.'

'I hope you're not disappointed. What's the expression? Looking for straws?'

'Clutching at straws... but I have so little time left.'

'Extend your stay!'

'But I've been here more than a month already. I have a life back in England, you know.'

Giacomo left her to prep a fish stew in his kitchen and she sat for a while longer on the terrace, sipping at water to rehydrate. The view of other roof terraces and the walls of the castle in the old town were very different from the Hastings roofline. Glancing at her watch, the time one hour later than in England, she reckoned Maureen would be opening Cobwebs right now. Maybe it was time to go back. Accept defeat. Accept that she was never going to get to the bottom of Elsie's secret. Mario was a lost cause and she was still fuming at his deceit but, still, she wasn't ready to go home. Not yet.

Giacomo called that they could leave in ten minutes. She downed the rest of the water and went to join him.

CHAPTER 24

Emma was sweeping dead blossoms from the main entrance as Giacomo and Susannah drew up on his Vespa. She glared at Susannah.

'I'll call you later, Jack,' she said, realising that with Emma on the patrol, there would be no chance after all of showing him the contents of the box. '*A dopo!* Later!'

She watched as the blue Vespa left a trail of dust in its wake. Her head was still smarting and she needed more water. Ignoring Emma's mutterings, she entered the cool of the *masseria*.

The Americans had left. A note had been slipped under Susannah's door, wishing her well. *Best holiday ever,* the pretty girl called Shona had scribbled. *Give my love to cute Giacomo. Tell him I'd love to come back and have him show me more wonderful photo opportunities on his tours.* She'd scribbled three large exclamation marks afterwards and a heart with an arrow through it.

Is Jack cute? Susannah asked herself. *Laid-back, kind... but cute?* She hadn't thought of him in that way.

The sound of hoovering from the upper storey told her

Emma was busy in Mario's apartment. Susannah wondered if he was about to return and if she would get the chance to meet his elusive wife, Anita. She was tempted to pack her bag and slip away without saying goodbye, but as annoyed as she was with him, he hadn't paid her yet and she couldn't afford not to take the money. Plus... there was the matter of the box in the storeroom to clear up... she couldn't leave now.

The little black dress was gone from her room, and Emma had tidied up: a fresh rose placed in the vase on her dressing-table, bed made up with clean sheets, the cushions she had hurled across the room arranged neatly against the pillows.

She wasn't hungry and, still feeling hungover, she didn't fancy roasting by the pool to read. Instead, she scrolled through Maureen's messages until she found the photo of her father's painting. *I'm here, Daddy. At the very place you painted, I'm sure of it. And I found a box with English stuff from the war, but not sure where that's going to lead me – if anywhere. Wish you were here to help me distinguish guesswork from truth.* Her eyes began to close and she flopped back against the cushions to snooze away her hangover.

The roar of a car engine and a man's frantic shouts interrupted her rest. Her heart sank. Mario was back. At first, she wanted to stay hidden in her room but then her sensible head kicked in. *You can do this, Susannah,* she told herself, a frown on her face as she planned how she would stand up to the man, what she would calmly and coolly say. There would be no angry voice, no undignified fishwife swearing. She would behave with style, show her disdain for him in an adult way and leave with her head held high.

Shouting, shrieking and the barking of a dog made her hurry to the entrance. Susannah watched a woman streak from the car. Mario shouted at her to come back, while his Dalmatian lolloped after the woman. The woman was barefoot and her long hair streamed behind her as she ran, swearing in English at the top of her voice. Susannah stepped outside to see if she could help and was almost knocked over by the dog, followed by the woman, who rushed round the corner towards the terrace, Mario in hot pursuit.

'Help me catch her. Please, Susi,' Mario shouted.

Susannah overtook her, holding out her arms to block the path and yelped as her outstretched arm was scratched by the woman's long fingernails. She pushed Susannah over as she barged past. 'Out of my way, bitch,' she screamed.

Susannah scrambled to her feet. Mario had been joined by Emma, who was wringing her hands and crying, trying to add to the chase. The whole scene resembled a burlesque comedy.

'*La povera signora,*' Emma cried. 'Poor madame.'

Mario managed to catch hold of the woman. He held her tight while she wriggled to escape.

'Help me get her into the house,' he called over his shoulder. And then he said something to Emma in Italian and Susannah caught the word '*ambulanza*'.

The woman kicked at Mario as she struggled to get free and as Susannah approached, she saw her dig her teeth into Mario's arm.

'*Ahi, Anita. Ma smettila.* Stop it. That hurt.'

Her hair a tangled mane, her face an angry grimace, the poor woman, who Susannah now realised was Mario's wife – his *living* wife – was totally different from the sophisticated, elegant apparition in the photo with Pavarotti.

Between the three of them, they managed to manhandle Anita into the *masseria*, thankfully empty of guests. Mario held her tight and Susannah watched as Emma injected her mistress in the arm. Slowly she calmed, Mario still holding her, his voice soothing as he murmured, stroking her untidy hair from her face. The siren from an approaching ambulance sounded in the distance and when the paramedics took over, Susannah, feeling helpless, made a quiet exit and went to pack her bag.

A knock on the door half an hour later, followed by Mario asking if he could come in, had Susannah jumping from her bed. 'No, Mario, you can't.'

'Please, Susi. We need to talk.'

'I don't think we do. There is absolutely no point.'

There was a thump on the door, like a kick. She listened as he walked away and then she sat to gather her thoughts. *No need for a talk. It changes nothing. Shower and check out.*

Half an hour later, her suitcase packed, her hair still damp, she called Giacomo to ask if she could possibly cadge one more lift, but it went straight to voice message.

In reception, Mario was busy on his laptop.

'I'm leaving,' she said. 'I need you to call me a taxi. I'll leave you my bank details so you can pay what you owe.' She scribbled them on a piece of paper and put it on the desk.

'Why are you leaving so soon? I'm sorry about the scene with my wife.'

'Are you sorry about the scene? Or because I discovered you lied to me?' Her earlier resolve to stay calm had deserted her and she was intensely annoyed at his arrogance.

'I never lied, Susi.'

'Don't call me Susi. Only the people I respect call me by that name.'

He rolled his eyes and that maddened her even more.

'You *did* lie, Mario. You told me your wife had died.'

'That was no lie. It was a figure of speech. You've seen what she's like. The wife I once knew is dead.'

'You're playing with words like you played with me. You're a waste of space and I'm stupid for letting you seduce me.'

'As I recall, you seemed to enjoy it.'

There was nothing she could say to that, so she pursed her lips and pushed the bank details towards him. She couldn't bear to be in his presence any longer and told him she would wait for the taxi outside.

'I regret it had to happen this way,' Mario said as Susannah shoved her phone into the back pocket of her jeans. 'I was going to explain to you in good time.'

'There would never have been a good time, Mario, and there is no need to explain anything to me. I don't want to know a thing more about you and your wife.'

He ignored her and ploughed on. 'I've been trying to keep Anita with me for as long as possible. Putting off the day when she would have to be sectioned, but' – he sighed deeply, holding out his hands in a gesture of hopelessness – 'she is deteriorating fast. I thought the clinic in Rome would have new treatments we could pursue. Emma and I cannot cope with her any longer.'

'You don't have to tell me any of this, Mario. It makes not the slightest difference. If you had explained the truth to me at the beginning, then maybe I might have been sympathetic, but I don't like being used.'

'You are a beautiful young woman. I like you. I think you liked me too. Where was the harm?'

'You *liked* having sex with me. But I don't make a habit of screwing married men and especially married liars.'

She swept out of the *masseria*, glad he didn't attempt to follow. The September sun beat down, her suitcase was heavy and perspiration trickled between her breasts. Where Anita had scratched her with her long fingernails the skin smarted. Blood had dripped onto her white shorts and she felt a wreck, inside and out. The sensible thing would be to ask Mario if she could wait in the cool of her room, wash her wound and dab the blood from her clothes, but she wanted no more favours from him and nothing about the man made her feel sensible anyway. There was no point in sitting at the edge of the road under the midday sun either – and she didn't feel like hitching a lift, so she slipped back into the courtyard of the *masseria* to wait in the shade of the palm trees.

The storeroom was still unlocked from the last time she'd been in there. Slipping inside, she lifted the lid of the box again and pulled out the tag and the rest of the contents.

On the base, underneath the tangle of string, and sticking out from a sheet of old newspaper, was a frayed brown envelope. She opened it. Inside were half a dozen black-and-white photographs and she moved nearer to the door to shuffle through the images. They all showed young men in their twenties. One photo showed a group of seven dressed in flying kit, next to an aeroplane. One of the young men sat astride the cockpit, a cheeky grin on his face. The plane had a circular symbol on the side of its nose and she peered more closely at hand-drawn images of bombs crudely drawn beside the roundel. She was certain that the photos were of a young aircrew, maybe RAF, and, from the style of trousers, together with the fact that they wore what she supposed were life belts or parachute harnesses, the photos most likely dated back to World War Two.

Her heart began to thump as she sensed she was closer to a missing link. In the nursing home, Elsie had talked about a Billy, and an 'airyplane', as she'd put it. Susannah wished again that she had tried harder to wheedle more information out of her grandmother before coming to Puglia. But, like an animal senses its prey, Susannah felt she was getting nearer. Elsie's secret lover could well be one of these airmen, who for some reason had left his equipment at the *masseria*. The next question was why. Elsie's letter and card were dated 1947. Not that long after the war. Could all these bits of information possibly fit together?

· · ·

The taxi would arrive soon and before closing the chest, she wondered for a moment about taking the contents. But her hands were already full with her luggage, and besides, no matter how she felt about Mario, she couldn't very well steal from him. Instead, she took photos of everything to show Giacomo, making sure to be extra careful as she copied the photos, in the hope that she could research the RAF presence in the area. There was little point in phoning Sybil to ask her to question Elsie, so she would have to find out as much as possible in Puglia before she returned to England.

CHAPTER 25

Giacomo set a cool glass of Aperol Spritz before Susannah. 'I reckoned tea wouldn't hack it today,' he said, drawing up a chair opposite her and sipping from his Moretti beer. 'Spill! You look shattered. What's up?'

'You're becoming my regular sounding board, Jack. *Grazie e cin cin!*' she said, taking a slug of the delicious cool drink.

She brushed over her confrontation with Mario and concentrated on the latest discovery in the box. 'Look at these.'

He stood behind as she scrolled through her photos. She was conscious of his breath on the back of her neck.

'Those are *definitely* RAF crew,' he said. 'There were many bases for the British and American air forces in Puglia. Especially round Foggia. I believe Canadians and South Africans were here too. We could take a trip one day next week.'

'I need to seriously research about the war in this area, Jack, but I've made up my mind to leave. I can't stay at the *masseria* a day longer. That man, he's impossible...'

'There are no flights until Monday. Strikes – it's all over the news.'

She ran her fingers through her hair, hot, bothered, thwarted.

'Is it such a problem to wait a few more days until the strikes blow over?' Giacomo asked. 'Stay in my spare room – preferably not after pole dancing in my kitchen – and see if you can get to the bottom of the identity of your postcard writer and determine once and for all the link with your *nonna*. To me it's a no-brainer.'

She laughed out of embarrassment at his comment about pole dancing. 'Are you sure? I'll help all I can in the wine bar and try not to get in your way.'

'I wouldn't suggest it if I didn't want you to, Susannah. And, if I'm honest, I'm hooked now and as eager as you to solve your mystery. I can be your Doctor Watson.' He scrolled through her other photos of the box contents and looked up.

'This is an identity tag, Susannah. Have you read the name?' Giacomo moved his fingers to enlarge the image.

She leant over him, her breath mingling with his. 'It's a bit rusty and dirty, but I think it says Sergeant William... the rest is impossible to read.'

'Any signatures on your cards?'

'Afraid not. Just a line of kisses. Not a William in sight.'

'Well, that doesn't prove anything. But it doesn't mean that this William *didn't* write your cards, either.'

'You're talking like a riddle, Giacomo.'

'Riddle?' he asked, puzzled.

'A line, or lines that are said in a way you have to keep guessing,' she said. 'Like a cryptic clue in a crossword.' She sighed. 'Daddy would have solved it in no time.'

'*Coraggio*, Susannah! Don't give up. One step at a time.'

'And two steps back.' She took back the phone. 'Thank you, Jack. I don't mean to sound negative. I'll call Maureen now to see if she minds looking after the shop a while longer. She's owed big-time when I get back. I think I need to look at that box again.'

'It's all absolutely fine by me, darling girl. I am thoroughly enjoying Cobwebs and your bookshop Jonathan is not such a bad old stick, you know. I dropped in a couple of first editions and ended up staying an hour in his lovely fusty shop chatting.'

'He's not *my* Jonathan.'

'That's a relief because he's invited me to dinner on Friday. Said he makes a mean fish pie. No, seriously, Susi. Please don't worry about hurrying back. The shop's fine, I'm fine and all is well with the world in Hastings. I've even watered your spider plants and cut back the rampant climbers on the patio.'

Susannah brought Maureen up to speed about Mario as well as her subsequent discoveries in the outbuilding. 'If possible, I want to see if I can pin down who sent the postcards and wrote that lover's note while I have these last few days here. I don't suppose you could accidentally-on-purpose drop by Sybil's and ask if she can find out more for me from Gran? Chances are she won't be keen. But it's worth a go. She might catch her on a good day.'

'Leave it with me. I'll see what I can do. Take care, Susi, and don't do anything I wouldn't...' Maureen's deep laughter travelled down the line. 'So, that means you have my permission to let rip. Be very Italian and do *everything*! *Ciao*, darling.'

Giacomo had a full house that evening for a special meal deal and Susannah was kept busy until closing time. It was an excellent way to practise her expanding Italian vocabulary and she only went astray with a couple of orders. The customers were friendly and understanding, one of the men teaching her a new phrase:

'*Sbagliando si impara,*' which Giacomo promptly translated as 'we learn by our mistakes'. *So very true,* Susannah thought, thinking back to her interlude with Mario. *And it isn't the end of the world.*

Giacomo locked the restaurant door at one o'clock in the morning and he and Susannah unwound over a glass of red Extroso *pugliese,* made from Montepulciano grapes.

'Thanks so much for your help tonight. It meant I could concentrate on the food prep. You did well, Susi.'

'I enjoyed it. And I only boobed once.'

His eyes twinkled. 'Yes, you won't be making that error again in a hurry. It caused much hilarity at table six. Remember for the future – I prepare *torta di fichi,* not *fiche.*'

'I shall NEVER forget. I thought that elderly gentleman was going to choke on his fig tart.'

Giacomo roared with laughter. 'Yes, you offered a slice of fanny tart to our illustrious mayor.'

Susannah buried her face in her hands with embarrassment. 'Don't you dare tell me you never made mistakes when learning English.'

'You mean when I told the customers in the Manchester restaurant that the crap starter was excellent?'

She laughed. 'One letter makes a big difference.'

'And how I told a girl in a pub she could massage me.'

At Susannah's puzzled look, he explained. '"Message" was what I was trying to say.'

He cut her a slice of fig tart. 'Time for you to savour my fanny tart,' he said.

'*Fico, fico, fico.* I shall be saying it in my sleep. Masculine not feminine. We don't have that problem in the English language.'

'Don't get hung up about it. The important thing is to have a go and communicate.'

The fig tart was delicious, the addition of lemon zest and a dollop of fresh mascarpone bringing out the flavours of fruit and almonds to perfection.

'What do you have lined up for tomorrow?' Giacomo asked. 'I'm free if you need my help. Take advantage of me.'

She spluttered on her tart. 'Now, that has double meanings too, Jack.'

'You think I don't know?' His grin was cheeky but she wasn't going there. No more dalliances. Not after Mario.

'I need to make a list. I can hear my father asking why I didn't do it earlier. And I need to buy a thank you gift for Maureen. She's been so good about the shop. If you're still free in the afternoon, then, yes please, I'd love your help. As wobbly as I feel about going back to the *masseria*, I have to see if Mario can shed light on the contents of that box. I remember he said he inherited stuff, but he also trawls antique markets, so if he brought it in, that box might not have anything to do with the *masseria* and I am barking up the wrong tree.' She held up crossed fingers. 'But I'm hoping otherwise. And then, as I said, I also need to research about the RAF in this area.'

'Sounds like a plan. You can use my laptop for that and...' He paused before suggesting that he could act as her chaperone if she wanted him to go with her to the *masseria*.

'You're very kind, Jack.'

He stood up and stretched. 'I'm all in. That's me done for today.' He glanced at his watch. 'Time for bed. *Buona notte* – or, really, *buongiorno*.'

'Night. And *mille grazie*.'

'*Prego*.'

As soon as her head hit the pillow, Susannah was out like a light.

After a lazy breakfast on the terrace, of *caffelatte* served in hand-painted cups that were more like small soup bowls, and fresh almond biscuits fetched that morning from the *pasticceria*, Susannah started on her list. Giacomo was busy in the kitchen and every now and again he broke into song. He had a good voice, uninhibited by Susannah sitting nearby. Italians had bucket-loads of self-confidence, she thought. It was the way they were brought up. She'd noticed how young children were allowed to stay up far later than British children. Parents were strict about good behaviour but encouraged their offspring to join in with conversations. Last night there had been young children sharing dinner with family at a couple of tables, their tastes sophisticated as they grappled with shells and wound spaghetti expertly round their forks, large white serviettes tucked round their little necks to catch splashes.

Her list of Things To Do grew:

1. Check with Grandma Elsie. Who was Billy that she mentioned at my visit to the home?
2. RAF – WW2 presence in Apulia?
3. Who stored RAF items and photos at Masseria della Torre? And why? Who was William on the ID tag?

'Strike while the iron is hot. I want to get the meeting with Mario over and done with, Jack,' she called. 'Is your offer still on?'

As it happened, when they turned up at Masseria della Torre in Giacomo's work van, what could have turned out to be awkward was lost in Mario's distracted state. Three large suitcases waited in reception where he was throwing files into a packing box. For the first time, Susannah thought, he looked old, his hair lank and greasy, jeans grubby, sweat staining his crumpled cream shirt. When she started to ask about the contents of the box in the storeroom, he waved his hands about. 'I have no idea, *cara* Susi, and no time to concern myself with such trivialities at the moment. I told you I inherited a load of junk with this place. I've never got round to sorting it all – and now, with Anita being so ill, I doubt I shall find time. Take it, take it, my friends. It will be one less thing to throw away.' He turned to climb the stairs to his private wing. 'I'm closing the place down again and returning to Rome for a while, so take it with you today. I don't know when I'll be back.'

Feeling sorry for the man, despite his treatment of her, Susannah led Giacomo to the storeroom to hunt for anything else that might give her more clues. But a couple of empty wine barrels, a rusting hoe and balls of string told her nothing.

'Why was the box stored in here? Under an old bed?' Giacomo said. 'Maybe the airman was hidden? Crash landed and rescued by the owner of the *masseria*? The sheltering of allies and refugees, it happened all the time during the war.'

'Quite possible. But we still have no link to Elsie's postcard. Nothing to say that this airman wrote love letters to her.'

'Well, why did she have a postcard image of the *masseria* sent to her?'

'I was thinking that too but I just feel I'm going round in circles, Jack. I wonder if I'll ever discover the truth,' Susannah said. 'No matter who wrote these cards, Elsie would never have admitted to having a lover. She cared very much what people thought and loved keeping up appearances. There's no snob like a nouveau riche snob.'

A couple of scorpions scuttled into the corner as they dragged the box away from the wall, and Susannah wrinkled her nose. 'I hope there aren't more inside.'

'They're not like scorpions in horror movies, Susi. In fact, traditionally, they are meant to ward off harm.'

'Is that why you have a scorpion tattooed on your shoulder?'

He smiled. 'You know me and my love of nature, Susi. Scorpions are part of the wild and the overall pattern. And their venom is used in medicine too. There's room for all creatures in this world. We humans think we are the owners of everything and it annoys me. Maybe I had my tattoo done in defiance.'

'I hear what you say. Nevertheless, if you love scorpions so much, I'll let *you* unpack the box.'

'No problem. Let's hope you find more clues inside.'

With a low whistle, Giacomo carefully pulled out the goggles, gloves and a pair of thick coveralls, which he shook out and laid on the metal bed. There was a hole in the arm, stuffed with straw where a mouse had once made a nest and he brushed it away, together with little black droppings. He lifted the envelope from the bottom and added it to the pile.

Susannah shuddered as she picked up one of the thick leather gloves and a spider scuttled out of the thumb.

'This is a definitely an old flying suit,' Giacomo said. He prodded the knee pads. 'In quite good condition. These are buoyancy pads for keeping a man afloat in the water.' He examined the label. 'Can you read what this says? Is there a name on it, maybe?'

'AM,' she said, peering at the label. 'Some of the letters are worn away from mould. Let me see if I can find details on Google.' As she brought the garment closer to her eyes, there was the sound of metal falling to the stone floor and Giacomo bent to retrieve it.

'Air Ministry,' she said, eventually. 'You're right, Jack.'

Her phone pinged as she started to scroll for more information. She read the message from her sister.

Stop bothering Gran. Your friend pestering with questions. Gran poorly. Leave her be.

'My sister's asked me to leave my grandmother alone. In her typically blunt way. So, if I'm going to find anything else out, it's now all down to me.'

Giacomo held up a chain holding a metal tag. 'This is the identity tag, Susannah. And it has a name on it.'

'Yes. It says William. I found that the first time.' She took it and read out, 'Sergeant William Pica, RAF. 1584477.'

'Does that name appear on your postcard?'

'No. I looked already.'

'Just because they aren't signed doesn't mean they weren't written by someone called William.'

'Yep, you said that before, but it's too easy, Jack. I need more than guesswork.'

'Guesswork can lead to answers, you know.'

'It can also lead us up the garden path.'

'How I love your quaint English expressions.'

'What would you say then?'

He thought for a moment. 'Catching butterflies?'

She smiled at the image.

'The museum in town would love this stuff. They have a section devoted to memorabilia from wartime,' Giacomo said.

'That's another place to add to my list then. I need to find out more about the man who wore this gear before handing it over.'

'We're getting closer. I can feel it,' Giacomo said, folding the suit back into the box before running his hands round the brown paper lining of the box. But there was nothing concealed save a couple of cobwebs and the dry carapace of a beetle.

Susannah liked his use of the word 'we'. It made the task lighter to have somebody to bounce ideas off. Daddy might not be here, but Giacomo was a good second best. He hoisted the box onto his shoulder and as she followed him to the van she tried to picture what the wearer of the flying suit would have looked like. Was he in one of the photos she'd found in the box? Was his name written on the back of one? She still had a lot of delving to do and she wasn't going to give up.

And then it came to her and she hit her head with her hand in exasperation: 'Billy!' she shouted.

'What's up, Susannah?'

'In English, Billy is a shorter name for William.' She took hold of Giacomo's hands and danced him round as she jumped up and down. 'Don't you see? That's the link. My grandmother mentioned a Billy when I asked her about the postcards. William Pica is Billy... Oh, Elsie, you naughty girl...'

CHAPTER 26

PUGLIA, 1946

And so, like water that seeps unseen through a crack in a reservoir wall, Roberto's former life flooded back as the dam finally broke. While he sat on his hard bed in the hospital hut at Amendola airbase, his head was back in England. It was April 1945, and he was listening to Elsie: his girl from another life. His other life.

ENGLAND, 1945

'Everybody's talking about the end of the war coming soon. Gawd, I hope so, Billy, 'cos at the moment it's all pie, pie, pies – with potato peelings instead of meat, and cakes made from parsnips. And I have no stockings left. We paint our legs with tea, Billy, I ask you – or draw lines to pretend we're wearing nylons. Madge next door always manages to get hold of a pair. But she has lots of Canadian soldier friends. All right for her with her cleaning job at their digs. All she does is wiggle her bottom a bit when she's down scrubbing the floors, and Bob's your uncle...'

Elsie had that pinched look on her face again, Billy thought as he listened to her whinging, her mouth turned down, her voice like a squeaky violin. He couldn't wait to get into the fresh air and cycle up to the castle for some peace. At the rate he was going, with his shot nerves, he could picture himself living alone on a smallholding in the middle of the Sussex countryside if he survived this ruddy war. A little house, land to tend, no more bone-jolting rides as a rear gunner, waiting for death in the dark sky.

'You're not listening, are you, Billy? You're somewhere else. Are you thinking about your poor mum? God bless her. Or is your head in the clouds in your airyplane?'

Her childish use of the word rankled. The Liberator he and his mates crewed was no toy. He was proud of what he did. In his position at the back of the plane, it was like sitting in a coffin, his breath turning to icicles as he strained his eyes through the gap in the canopy the ground crew had cut for better all-round vision. In temperatures of minus 30, when the Perspex turret was smeared with ice and oil, it had been nigh impossible to track enemy bandits. Hunched at the rear, isolated from the crew, their conversation muffled, he felt he was the protector of all the lives aboard and it weighed heavy.

No amount of lucky charms could help keep them alive, in his opinion. Take Monty for instance, their navigator. He always carried his girlfriend's knickers in his pocket. But Billy held no truck with all that stuff. Survival was down to him, not to talismans: he had to stay alert, thickly gloved hands poised on the Browning machine guns.

This second short break back to Blighty after completing thirty-five combat missions – how the dickens they had managed this was a bloody miracle, he kept marvelling – had coincided with his mother's funeral. It should have been a time to switch off. But it was impossible to relax. Even when he slept he was on alert, his dreams loud with the bang, shake and rattle of the craft as it took off for another night mission.

Elsie's voice dragged him back to the present.

'They're showing *Love Story* at the ABC, Billy. Starring Stewart Granger. He's so handsome. Madge told me it's about an RAF pilot going blind—'

'Joyful!' Billy muttered.

'I thought you'd like it, being about the war and everything. We could have a cuddle in the back row too,' she said, fluttering her eyelashes. 'Couldn't you have been a pilot, Billy, instead of a gunner?'

He sighed. It really was time to call it a day with Elsie. They'd been together since school, but his life was different now. The war had opened up new paths and he'd left her behind a while ago. They'd turned into a habit.

'Elsie, it's a beautiful day. I don't want to be cooped up in a cinema. I spend too much of my time rammed in a tiny space.'

Elsie pulled a face, her plump, lipstick-red lips turned down. 'Please yourself.'

Hands in his pockets, he waited for her to fetch her coat and join him for a walk round the park. He'd rehearsed in his mind what he was going to tell her. That there was no guarantee from mission to mission that he would survive. She was better off finding someone else. Then, he would tell her that he didn't feel the same anymore.

The last time he was on leave, he'd let himself get carried away. They'd done more than heavy petting when he'd kissed her goodnight. One thing had led to another against the back wall and he felt bad about that. He'd enjoyed the 'naughty', as he and his RAF mates put it. And Elsie hadn't objected; in fact she'd encouraged him, whispering in his ear about how a girl had to give a brave airman some comfort before he left. But that was in the past and he was going to have to break it gently to Elsie. It was over.

He stamped his feet in the cold as he waited. In Amendola, he'd left behind blue skies and balmy spring days. Nights in the sky were freezing once they climbed above five thousand feet, but winter in Puglia was drawing to a close, blossom appearing on the cherry trees in the plains, stripes of white a landmark on the early mornings when they returned to the airfield after night sorties.

Elsie slipped her arm through his and they walked down the pavement, past the line of houses with their blackout blinds. Progress was slow because of her high-heeled shoes.

They sat on the veranda of the County cricket pavilion where Billy had fielded for the second team on many a sun-filled Sunday afternoon. His Italian father sometimes came to support, but had no idea what was going on. His English mother provided refreshments from the restaurant and the opposition had been heard to say they enjoyed the fixtures at Hastings purely on account of her generous corned beef sandwiches and walnut and coffee sponge cakes. The pitch had been dug up to use as a potato patch now and a team of middle-aged Home Guard were hoeing between the rows.

He pulled out a packet of Woodbines and offered one to Elsie but she shook her head.

'No, ta. Gone off 'em,' she said. She leaned nearer and lowered her voice, even though the nearest person was an old man at the far end of what used to be the green, walking a manky-looking mongrel.

'I've got something to tell you, Billy.' She looked behind her. 'I think I'm... you know.'

'No, I don't know. What do you mean?' He exhaled smoke into the crisp air.

She bit her lip. 'I'm in the family way,' she whispered.

His heart skipped a beat. 'Bloody hell, Elsie...'

'That night – before you left for wherever it is you are at the moment.'

'Italy,' Billy reminded her – for the umpteenth time.

He did a mental calculation, counting back. A fleeting visit

six weeks previously, or thereabouts. Early February. Before the
crew's posting to Amendola Airfield, near Foggia, in southern
Italy. His mother had been gravely ill and, as it happened, it was
the last time he'd seen her. Bloody hell. It was the one and only
time they'd gone the whole way. He cursed himself for not
using protection but she'd been more amorous than usual. He'd
lost control. When you were young and facing death each day,
you did stupid things. Like on the many beer-soaked nights in
the Mess, where things got a bit barmy: chairs overturned,
fellows leaping over them like racehorses. The pilots were
generally the craziest. Each day was like the last day of their
young lives.

'Shit, Elsie. Are you *sure* you're pregnant?' Billy asked, his
arms resting on his knees as he slumped on the bench next to
Elsie.

'You were all over me, Billy. Couldn't keep your hands off of
me. Yes, of course I'm sure. You weren't wearing nothing, was
you? We'll have to get married, Billy. My parents will kill me. I
can't bring up a kid on me own.'

He was trapped. He didn't love her. But he would see Elsie
right. That was the way he'd been brought up. It was his duty.

'We can get married quickly before you go back,' she said.
'I've sorted a marriage licence and I've got Gran's ring. And
we're allowed two pounds of cooked ham on rations.'

'You seem to have it all worked out, Elsie,' he said.

'A stitch in time,' she said, patting her flat stomach. 'Nobody
will realise if the baby's a bit early.'

Billy went through with it, awkward in his suit that no longer
fitted him now that he had beefed up with extra muscle from
service training. Elsie wore a pale blue two-piece and a
borrowed pillbox hat with a veil. There was no money for a ring
for him, but he slid his own mother's ring onto her finger. It

should have been a special day, but to Billy it seemed like the start of a sentence and at twenty-four he felt like an old man already. But duty was duty and he would be a father to this unborn child.

His heart ached to think about his mother. Her funeral was the following day. It seemed a cruel twist of fate. She would have been mortified about the registry office wedding. A regular churchgoer at St Clement's, she would have wrung her hands and cried. She'd have worried about what the neighbours thought of the mean, curled-up Spam sandwiches and dry seed cake served with stewed tea afterwards. The only guests were Elsie's parents and Billy's father, his face expressionless. He squeezed his son's hand afterwards and muttered something about his Peggy, how he still missed her; that she should have been at his side today.

There was no time for a honeymoon and the wedding night was spent in Elsie's single bed, Billy grateful that she felt too sick to go through the actions. The one saving grace was that he was going to be a father. He would have to do his best not to croak on future missions. There were too many babies born to missing fathers.

Forty-eight hours later, after enduring a funeral and a wedding, both as tragic as each other, Billy boarded a train at Hastings Station to start his journey back to Amendola. Heavy hearted, he waved goodbye to Elsie until she disappeared from view, enveloped in a cloud of steam from the train.

CHAPTER 27

AMENDOLA AIRBASE, PUGLIA, MARCH 1945

So, on his return to Amendola, Billy Pica was a married man. No ring on his finger but legally married, spliced, hitched. And he was going to be a father.

'Ops on tonight,' their navigator Monty said as they queued for tea in the Mess. 'Large do from what I've heard. Briefing at seventeen hundred hours.'

Billy had known something was up. The phone booth had been secured with a padlocked wire, preventing outward calls: indication of an imminent briefing. He was relieved to have something to distract him, his mind switching instantly from domestic problems to the job in hand.

Half an hour later, the whole squadron was summoned to the lecture room. The doors were closed, blinds pulled down as Wing Commander Bishop began to explain that night's mission. These briefings always seemed dramatic but secrecy was of top importance, 'careless talk costs lives' being the mantra constantly rammed home.

Lights were switched off and a blue haze from dozens of cigarettes mingled with the beam of the projector illuminating a map on the opposite wall, showing the target for tonight's op.

The wingco limped over to the image, pointing to a small field by a church at the edge of a forest near Ljubljana, Yugoslavia. 'Tonight's operation involves a substantial force. Fifty-six Wellingtons. Thirty-five Liberators. A single Pathfinder Halifax. The containers you will drop hold guns and explosives for partisans helping Tito in his ground war against Fritz in the areas code-named Cuckold and Toffee.'

At the next slide, Monty copied down a series of map coordinates carefully, his notebook resting on his thigh. Bishop twisted a strand of wool about a number of pins along the route, each pin marking a turning point. He waited while notes were taken, before finishing with, 'You have four hours' petrol and a flight of three hours, so conserve your fuel carefully.'

He stood to one side to let the senior meteorologist begin his forecast. 'Take off at twenty-one hundred hours. No moon, but clear visibility. A bomber's sky tonight.'

Billy breathed a silent sigh of relief. Nobody liked going up in a full moon – it was tantamount to a death sentence. You might as well fly by day.

'Any questions, men?' Wingco Bishop asked, before wrapping up the briefing. 'Otherwise, I wish you all good luck and Godspeed. See you when you report back.'

After he'd left, murmurs grew to a crescendo and there was a general move to the exit. A sergeant stood behind a table outside the lecture room, reminding crews to check their pockets, to empty them of small change, cinema stubs, bus tickets, cigarette packets – anything that could be a useful clue to the enemy as to where they had flown from if they were shot down and interrogated. Then, they filed past another table, where their intelligence officer issued them with escape equipment to zip in their flying suits: a compass, European currency, including *dinari*, maps and condensed Horlicks tablets – in case they had to bale out on the other side.

And then there was a rush towards the Mess. The men

had almost two hours before take-off and it was always a good idea to line the belly. After a supper of stew and boiled spuds, they hung around, coffee flasks, helmets, oxygen masks cluttering the tables, the clunk of billiard balls and music from the radio in the corner mingling with the chatter of a few. Some were quiet, writing letters in case they didn't return. In one corner a pilot grabbed forty winks, his arms pillowed on his parachute on the table, heavy fleece-lined boots waiting beside his chair.

The waiting was hard and Billy's thoughts kept turning to Elsie, a heavy lump in his stomach like an undigested dinner. But he knew that once they were in the air, he had to banish home concerns and concentrate on the job. The lives of all his crew depended on him and he had to bolt all other thoughts to the back of his mind.

At 20.30 hours he and his crew loaded themselves into a truck to take them to the planes at the dispersal area. It was driven by a tall WAAF, her sun-bleached blonde hair reminding Billy of Elsie. Elsie, his wife, his pregnant wife. He must stay alive to look after his young family.

Get a grip, Billy. Stop frittering away energy. Get a bloody grip.

The time for leaving was almost upon them. He was already sweating in his layers: long-sleeved vest, long johns, battle dress of jacket and trousers, then heated waistcoat plus padded flying suit – all topped off with a Mae West lifejacket and parachute harness. Heated gloves, thick socks and eventually padded boots and leather gauntlets would complete his cumbersome armour once he was aboard.

Bats swooped between the crew as they gathered round the plane, the balmy Mediterranean air in sharp contrast to what it would be like thousands of feet in the clouds. Billy joined a couple of the men to have the traditional piss against the rear wheel of *Mamma* and then the drumming of engines started up around the airfield as, one by one, each plane shuddered into action.

Inside the plane Billy carried out his own checks, the voices of Monty and the bombers on the other side muffled, the hiss of oxygen in his mask distorting all sound. As the chocks were pulled away and the plane started to amble out of dispersal to queue along the runway, Billy noticed WAAFs and ERKs waving in the distance and he popped a piece of gum in his mouth by way of distraction.

And then they were airborne, everything shuddering and banging as they moved. The undercarriage thudded up and the craft shook and rattled, ammunition jostling and rattling in the fuselage, his turret swaying and vibrating as they ascended. The momentary fears that always threatened to paralyse him dissolved as soon as they were underway and his brain adjusted to pure oxygen as he fastened on his mask. Cold air began to penetrate the layers and his electrically heated suit tingled into action in his cold coffin at the rear, draughts whistling past the opening the ground crew had cut out of the Perspex.

'Permission to fire the Brownings, sir,' he asked Skipper over the intercom and with that granted, he fired a short test burst from the guns, his fingers encased in three layers of gloves. He was relieved when all four guns instantly responded. From that moment onwards, his mind worked in automatic as he trained his eyes through his turret, searching the darkness for enemy fighters: above, below, rotating the turret all around, ever-searching, never relaxing, comforted by the dark shadows of other Liberators flying alongside their craft in the black void.

One hour in and Billy shouted, 'Flak and searchlights starboard – bags of them.' Then a terrific crack rattled about the craft as flak burst alongside the Liberator, stunning him for a moment. Flares blinded his eyes momentarily and he widened them to adjust his focus. Skipper's voice crackled over the intercom as he warned he was taking evasive action and Billy was thrust back against the capsule as the Liberator plunged, tumbling thousands of feet, spiralling round and round, so that his stomach churned and he regretted the extra helping of stew he'd shovelled in at supper.

Skipper righted the craft and now Billy's eyes were on stalks as he readjusted his sight, swivelling the turret all the time, searching for bandits in the sky. He listened in as Monty communicated with Skipper, setting the course again to find the rest of the squadron. On their own they were easy meat for hunting fighters, the posters in the flight section at base warning them all: 'Don't be proud – stay with the crowd'. Five hairy minutes passed before they were back with the other Liberators and Billy breathed a small sigh of relief.

Another thirty-five minutes and they were above their target, pinpointed by a square of bonfires lit by partisans in the field below. The bomb aimer's voice was distorted and crackly over the intercom as he instructed Skipper to position for the drop. 'Left, left, left a bit. Steady... steady. Hold that... Okay, Skipper, bomb doors open.'

Billy felt the updraught of air through the doors and heard a piece of fabric flapping. When the call came through: 'Container gone,' he smiled and cheered mentally as Skipper's voice announced, 'Mission accomplished, chaps. Another sixty minutes or so, with the wind behind us, and we'll be back in Amendola, downing a beer or three. Keep your eyes open, Billy. We're not home yet.'

A mission was never truly accomplished until the moment the plane was safely landed back at dispersal. This was the time to be on maximum alert.

Billy turned and turned in his capsule, his nerves taut and jangled, scrutinising every angle of the sky for enemy. An icicle had formed on the end of his mask and he knocked it away with his gloves. One more bloody hour until they were back.

At times it felt to Billy that the plane was not moving at

all – that they would never land. He began to fight sleep, feeling woozy in this cold black final hour, the plane cushioned in clouds that looked as soft as bedclothes. Twenty-five long minutes dragged by. He popped a Benzedrine tablet in his mouth to keep awake and glanced down at the never-ending expanse of sea below. Once again, the memory of Elsie and her shattering announcement entered his mind, his concentration diverted. He shook his head to rid the thoughts. He couldn't wait for the moment when he could at last remove his oxygen mask and light a forbidden cigarette, enjoying the ecstasy of knowing he and his fellow crew had survived again.

The Liberator flew into a bank of fog and Billy sharpened his reactions, searching for shapes, stretching wide his eyes to peer into the white mist. Suddenly there was a violent shake of the craft and the plane banked abruptly as Skipper took evasive action. A huge shape slid by. Billy's heart hammered in his suit as he caught a glimpse of the square tips of the wings of a German Me-110. Too late he shouted through the intercom, 'Hostiles approaching at zero. Go, Skip.'

He heard Skipper's command, 'Prepare to corkscrew.' Billy pressed the firing buttons in a prolonged burst but he could no longer see the bandit.

And then the instruction to abandon ship came, Skipper's voice no longer calm as the plane shuddered and went into an uncontrolled spiral.

An explosion of lights, streams of fire, bullets piercing the capsule while the helter-skelter descent continued, the plane tossed about like a leaf. Billy's last thoughts before he struggled to reach the release-handle in the door behind him was that they were going down for good. He thanked the bloody stars he'd been recently equipped with a pilot-type parachute. Exit would be easier. His vision was blinded temporarily by a ball of fire as he struggled to rotate the turret and push the doors open to bale out. The door flapped closed and slammed against his head and the stars he saw were not from the sky.

He jettisoned himself into the void, blood streaming from his head. He craned his neck to see through sticky eyes if the others had made it, but everything was black and fuzzy. Down, down, down he fell before yanking on his ripcord. And then darkness was lit up like fireworks as the Liberator exploded. Before Billy splashed into the ocean, he uttered part of a prayer from his childhood: '*If I die before I wake, I pray to God my soul to take…*'

Cold water took away his breath. He resurfaced. He was vaguely aware of the fluorescent pad ripping open to release the yellow dye that would indicate where he was floating, and then further out to sea behind him there was another immense explosion. He watched in horror as, silhouetted against the flames, the Liberator tipped and sank below the sea's surface. There was an awful silence. He shouted but nobody answered.

CHAPTER 28

ENGLAND, LATE AUGUST 1946

Billy Pica's memories had returned with a vengeance. What a mess his life had turned out. In many ways, he thought, it would have been far easier to have remained forever as Roberto Bruni, spending the rest of his days with Antonella. But his conscience would not allow him to do that. He knew now he had a wife and child back in Hastings and he would never rest easy if he didn't carry out his duty to them.

The medical team had put him through the mill at the airbase at Foggia where he'd reported with Pilot Officer Phil, his companion from early RAF days. Eventually they'd concluded he was not a deserter and that he truly had suffered retrograde amnesia caused by a blow to the head when ejecting from the fated Liberator in March 1945. Now he found himself back in Blighty, preparing to go through the tedious process of demobilisation.

As the train rattled north from Croydon Airport where he had landed with a handful of personnel from Foggia, he cleaned a patch of steamed-up window and peered at the grey world of southern England. There were more houses flattened than standing. Those that remained were mostly damaged, some of the gardens set out in large vegetable patches, others reduced to piles of rubble, an occasional apple tree rising above the bricks, the fruit a splash of colour in the drab surroundings. A group of children waved from where they were scrambling over a pile of masonry. One of the boys stuck out his tongue before turning and dropping his short trousers to reveal a white bottom to the train passengers. Billy grinned and settled back against the seat, wondering if he had produced such a child. A little person capable of confronting the world with spirit and audacity. He and Elsie hadn't communicated since their wedding day. Had she been missing him for the last year and a half? And was he father to a son or daughter?

His immediate destination after finalising demobbing was Hastings. During this zigzag journey – to RAF Warton in the north, one of the few demob centres still running, then back south again – he would attempt to persuade himself that Italy had been an interlude. He'd left a whole chunk of his heart there, but destiny had other plans for him. He had to accept this and if he didn't, he would go crazy, torn constantly between two worlds. *So be it, Billy my old pal.* His heart listened reluctantly to his sensible advice and the roundabout journey mirrored thoughts that would not lie still. He hadn't understood anything about broken hearts until he met Antonella.

The service uniform hurriedly put together for him in Amendola was too tight and he undid the top button of the shirt, scratchy against his flesh, more used as he was to one of Nonno's loose, patched linen garments.

He looked more Italian than a member of the British Services. He felt more Italian. The expression 'fish out of water' came to mind as he dwelled on the months spent living on the beach with Anto. Despite trying to banish thoughts of her, he couldn't help wondering how she was and what she was doing at this moment. Her face kept appearing in the window. But it was Elsie he was returning to.

He dragged his gaze from the sight of post-war England and tried to concentrate on his copy of the *Daily Express*. The front page had a full review about an Air France plane bound for London that had crashed moments after take-off. Twenty people dead. He thought back to his fellow crew members, wondering why he should have been the lucky one to survive. Gloom enveloped him like the steam belching outside from the train. At least if he'd died with them, he wouldn't have to face the tangle his life had become. What a ruddy awful mess.

At Preston Station, he climbed into a taxi. The driver took one look and started to speak slowly and deliberately, until Billy cut him off and told him he was English.

'Thank gawd for that, mate. We've had a few foreign airmen come here who don't speak the lingo that well.'

'My father is Italian. My mother English. I was born in England, pal,' Billy said.

'Thought you might be one of them greasy dago macaronis. Do you ever get grief about that, mate? The Eyeties aren't looked on too well here, you know. What with changing their minds halfway through the war and that. Been away long, have you?'

'Seems like a lifetime,' he replied, leaving it at that. How to explain to this stranger that to him it *was* a lifetime. When he'd lost his memory, his former life had been shed like an animal moulting its winter coat. Billy wasn't him anymore.

He half-listened as the driver rattled on, delivering a patter doubtless used on countless other passengers.

'In a funny way,' he said, half turning to Billy from the driver seat, 'we miss the war. Don't know what to do with ourselves now, do we? Lost a pattern. The army gave me a structure. But I wouldn't go back, neither. I was at Cassino...'

Billy let him talk. Cassino had been hell. Over 50,000 men killed. Obviously when the crew were up in the air, they were up there to cause death. But when they dropped their bombs through the clouds, they tried not to let themselves think about civilians and the devastation below. It was the only way to get on with the job.

At RAF Warton he was told to leave his baggage and report to the orderly sergeant in the NAAFI waiting room.

'Slow trickle now,' the middle-aged sergeant said, issuing Billy with a leaflet and a map of the camp. 'Demobbed thousands here. We'll be winding up soon, no doubt.'

The Brits are good at sorting and filing. They love it. For a moment Billy wondered at the way his mind was observing: as if from the eyes of a foreigner. Maybe the blood in his veins had turned Italian after months of living in Puglia with Antonella. Billy took in the details of the series of huts he had to pass through, the signs above the doors describing their various functions: accounts, post, medical, clothing and then, finally, advice. Would they have guidance for a man who was married to somebody he didn't want to be married to, in a country he no longer wanted to live in? Would there be a leaflet to tell him to go straight back to Puglia and bigamously marry the girl whose absence he was keenly feeling and whom he knew he should be forgetting?

Naturally, none of these thoughts were to pass his lips. But if pills existed to make him magically fall in love with his English wife, then he'd ask for a triple dose in the medical hut.

The process took longer than he'd imagined and the first night in Warton was spent in a hut at the far end of the base, five minutes' walk from the canteen. A plate of beans, chips and a rubbery fried egg, washed down with strong dark tea in a chipped white cup and he felt as if he'd never been away.

'Fill yourself up, lad,' the weary-faced man sitting opposite him said. 'The missus has already warned me food is scarce out in the real world. She has to queue every day for basics. All she got the other week from the butcher was a slab of whale meat. Said it stank the house out for days.'

Billy watched the man shovel in his food, before pushing away his plate and lighting up. 'These are about the only things not rationed,' the man said, offering Billy a fag.

He was a strange dining companion. More like a tramp than an ex-serviceman, greasy hair with dandruff on his collar, his clothes hanging from him like a scarecrow. Neither of them asked each other about their time in the war and they made their way back to the dormitory hut to their narrow beds, exchanging cursory good nights before switching off the light. Billy lay awake for long hours, listening to the rattling of his neighbour's snores, wondering what Elsie would make of his return. He reckoned the child would be about nine months old now.

He'd given scant details at the base about his wife and asked for no notifications to be sent to next of kin about his return. 'I want to surprise them,' he'd explained. 'Easier than a letter turning up after all this time.' As he lay awake, he examined his decision not to announce his arrival. In his heart of hearts, he knew he'd been leaving himself an escape route. With Elsie not knowing he was on his way, he still had the option to disappear completely. Get on a train for anywhere except Hastings. Start a new life somewhere with a new identity. Pack up his troubles in his old kit bag, like the old song went, and see where his feet took him... But it felt cowardly. Billy had a child to consider as well as an ageing, widowed father trying to run a business alone, now his mother had gone. He wondered what his father would say when he turned up? It would be good to hug the old boy.

Next morning, dressed in flannel trousers too long in the leg, a single-breasted cotton tweed jacket, the arms too short, and topped off with a pork pie hat on his head, he was on his way again, officially released from duties with the RAF. Over his arm he carried a raincoat. In his cardboard suitcase he had a tie, two shirts with matching collar studs, a ration book, a release resettlement comprising pension details and a warning from the commanding officer never to wear a mixture of uniform and civilian clothing. This abuse, he was told, would diminish the hard-won admiration and respect earned by the Royal Air Force. He was also given sweets and cigarettes just before catching the bus back to the station, like a child given a treat to take home at the end of a birthday party, he thought ruefully. His days as a serving officer with the RAF were over.

He imagined his future rested in taking over from Pappy in the restaurant that his parents had started off as a humble café with three tables in their front room. By the time Billy was a teenager, people had travelled from far beyond Hastings to eat his delicious Italian food. Billy would spend his days in Angelos and return to Elsie in the evenings. Years stretched before him like a bleak, never-ending horizon of muddy clouds.

It was close to midnight when the train pulled in at Hastings. A full moon hung in the sky and a keen wind whistled round the station precinct, a couple of sheets of newspaper twirling and scuttling about the platform in the draught. It was too late to turn up on anyone's doorstep. Billy found himself following the path up to the castle – a favourite haunt as a boy. Stalling the moment when he had to announce his homecoming, he decided to sleep rough and sort himself out in the morning.

The raincoat came in useful and he wrapped himself up and dossed down under a large rock near the gateway to the castle. He'd carved his initials here when he was a teenager, to merge in with dozens of others. The hollow under the rock kept away the worst of the biting sea wind. Below him, town lights twinkled – unlike the last time he'd been up here, when blackout had smothered houses. The women's toilets at the edge of the castle grounds had housed anti-aircraft guns, much to the hilarity of the soldiers manning them. Tonight, the moon cast a silver-grey glimmer over the sea – the same moon that would be casting its light over the horseshoe bay below the *trulli*. He closed his hand over the shell bird in his pocket and pictured Antonella curled up alone, Birba the kitten snuggled on the bed next to her. He'd promised Anto he would return, but that was impossible now. Somehow, he had to contact her to let her know he wasn't coming back. But although he'd taught her all the letters of the alphabet, she was a long way off from properly reading and no postman ever came out that way anyway.

The notion to walk to the edge of the cliff and throw himself into the sea tempted him for a few seconds. His heart felt wafer thin, his future like a prison sentence.

Get a grip, Billy. Stop talking fucking nonsense. Stiff upper lip and all that. Life goes on. You have a child to care for.

By the time birds woke him, dew soaked his raincoat and his body was stiff. Ravens wheeled around the ruined castle walls like huge bats, their cries echoing from the castle stones glistening in the morning light. He lit a full-strength Capstan, the smoke curling up to join a swirl of thin sea mist and walked along the barbed wire fencing round the castle until he reached the point where he could look down over Old Hastings. Out at sea, a horn blew a long, echoing blast. He watched fishermen setting out from the Stade on the shingle beach below, where dozens of tall fishing huts stood like black giants. Pappy would be opening up his café soon, starting his day with a double-strength espresso from the machine he'd imported before the war. A novelty that only a few customers enjoyed, strong brews of treacle-brown tea the preferred drink served to most of his customers. Billy planned how he would nonchalantly turn up, push open the door to Angelos, the bell tinkling as he entered. He would lean against the counter and call out, 'Double espresso for me too,' and then wait for the look on Pappy's face. Would the sign swinging above the café have been altered yet? The apostrophe missing before the 's' that Billy had nagged him about over the years? 'Angelos makes you sound like a Greek taverna,' he'd continually told him. 'Let me get out the ladder and write in the apostrophe.' But his father wouldn't have it. Stubborn old git, his pappy.

Billy dragged his fingers through his hair and felt the stubbly growth on his chin. He'd borrow Pappy's old straight razor and tidy up once the greetings were over. But as Billy trod down the path, the view of the old town in the hollow below shocked him. Another gaping hole, like a missing molar, showed where more houses had been eliminated since his last visit in 1945. Near the start of George Street, he stopped in horror.

Where his parents' business and home should have stood, there was nothing except a pile of mud and stones. Rubble and wooden props supporting the buildings on either side were all that was left of the Italian restaurant and the flat where Billy had lived with his parents.

A woman walked by and he grabbed her arm as she passed. She shrugged his hand off. 'Do you mind?' she said but, noticing the look on his face, she changed her tone. 'You all right, mister?'

'What happened here?' he asked.

'Unexploded bomb. At the end of the war. Almighty explosion. And before that we were besieged with doodlebugs. Don't know how many times they dropped them on the town. As if they were experimenting on us.'

'What about the people?' He pointed to the gap.

'Killed. Nothing they could do for them, poor devils. Happened in the night.'

Now it was her turn to clutch his arm. 'Did you know them, dearie? Can I do anything?'

He shook his head. 'No. There's nothing you can do.'

She continued on her way, turning once or twice to stare back at the young man gazing at the crater, standing like a statue in the middle of the pavement as people going to work pushed past him.

. . .

Billy walked as if in a dream up the alleyway to St Clement's where his mother had always worshipped. She was Anglican. Pappy had tried to introduce Billy to his own religion and taken him occasionally to the Catholic church at the foot of the hill. But when he was eleven years old, he refused point blank to attend Mass or any kind of church service any longer.

'You can't make me believe in all that Virgin Mary stuff,' he'd told his parents. 'And dead people rising up again.' And Pappy had thrown his hands in the air Italian-style, telling Ma that they couldn't exactly drag him to church screaming. But each Sunday morning, Billy had to mop out the restaurant instead, while his mother worshipped at St Clement's and Pappy went on a Sunday constitutional, as he called it: his once-weekly circular walk towards Fairlight Cove and back. Billy hadn't minded. He'd enjoyed being on his own and helping himself to cigarettes from the box behind the counter while they were out, turning music up loud on the wireless set, dancing around, using the broom as a microphone to sing favourite songs and attempt a tap dance like Fred Astaire, changing the sign on the door to CLOSED.

There were several new graves in the tiny cemetery opposite the church that sheltered beneath the steep rise to the houses above. Next to his mother's stone was a new mound, weeds beginning to push up in the soil and he knelt down to touch the earth, pulling out stray strands of couch grass, remembering Pappy's cheerful manner; the way he welcomed his customers with a broad smile; the way he was always on the lookout for new recipes. There was the time he'd found mushrooms in the fields on his Sunday walk and tried them on the family in a risotto. They'd spent the night trotting back and forth to the privy in the yard. Thank God he had tried it on them first before his customers.

His father had worked too hard, starting off selling ice cream in the streets between Hastings and St Leonards, pedalling a tricycle holding a large ice box painted with a sign: *Angelos Cornettos*, the apostrophe missing there too.

'We no have this *sistema* in Sicilia,' he would tell Billy, who, at ten years of age had already attended school for longer than his father had and was keen on improving his pappy's English. 'We say the *cornetti* of Angelo. *I cornetti di Angelo*. How you expect me to learn all these stuff?'

It was embarrassing when Pappy made mistakes, but his English mother told him it didn't matter. 'The way he speaks, it makes it sound more Italian for our customers,' she'd tell her son. 'Leave Pappy be. It's in his heart what matters, not how he speaks English, son.'

Billy stayed for five minutes beside his parents. They hadn't deserved to die before being able to enjoy their retirement years. 'I'll sort you a proper stone, Pappy,' he whispered. 'Just as soon as I can.' He patted the earth. Pappy was what he'd called him since he was very little. A mixture of the Italian Papà and English Pa.

Billy took the steps back down to the High Street, past Brook's tobacconists where he'd spent his halfpenny pocket money on a Friday after school, past George Reeves' furniture warehouse, the sign, *Pianofortes Sold or Exchanged*, in need of a touch-up. The houses up here were narrow, packed in like a row of wonky boxes. He was making for number 78 where he and Elsie had spent their one and only unconsummated night as a married couple in her parents' house.

He glanced at his watch. Almost eight thirty – Elsie would probably be making breakfast. He wasn't hungry. His stomach churned with nerves. Shortening his steps, he delayed the moment when he would reach out to knock on the door of the tiny fisherman's cottage, and witness Elsie's startled expression.

Only a few paces remained, when the door was pulled open and a pram started to emerge.

'See you later, Mum.' Elsie's voice reached him before she stepped out to the pavement, the sides of the pram scraping the narrow door frame. She tutted and bent to examine the shining new Silver Cross perambulator.

Elsie wore a mink coat, a couple of blonde curls escaping from a matching headband; her shoes were red leather, three straps crossed over the instep. He took in all these details before his eyes slid up to her face, her mouth smeared thick with her customary red lipstick.

'Elsie,' he said, approaching her.

She brought both hands to her mouth and the pram rolled towards the edge of the pavement. He moved fast to stop it from dropping to the road.

'Gawd. Is it really you?' she said, her voice a half whisper. 'But... you're dead.' She looked round. The street was deserted. 'Nobody must see you, Billy. Leave us alone.'

'How about that for a greeting?' he replied, disappointed at her reaction, but not surprised. It was a shock for her after all.

He trailed after her as she hurried away, increasing her speed, the pram bumping over the rough pavement. When they turned down an alley, she stopped.

'I've got another life now, Billy. You can't just turn up out of the blue like this. You're supposed to be dead. I got a letter from the War Office and all.'

'Can't you spare at least five minutes to talk, Elsie? Let me see our baby.'

'Follow me at a distance,' she hissed. 'If there's nobody in the park, you can tell me what the hell happened to you and where you sodded off to all this bleeding time.'

He left a gap and had to hurry to keep her in sight as she pushed the big pram a mile away from Old Hastings through the streets towards Alexandra Park. At the bandstand, she put on the pram brake and climbed the steps. She didn't want to know him anymore, that was obvious. But all this cloak and dagger was killing him. And he wanted to see his child.

'Five minutes,' she said, checking a gold watch on her wrist.

He bent over the pram before climbing up to join her. The child was asleep. All babies looked the same to him. 'Did we have a boy or a girl?'

'A little boy. I nearly lost him. He was born early. I named him Frank,' she said, her arms crossed over her bosom as she tapped her foot impatiently. 'He's blond – takes after me. Right little active nipper he is too. He's toddling now, in and out of everything... and his morning sleep in the pram is one way of giving me some peace. He wakes me early every bleeding morning, so I push him up to Mum's to tire him out and to try and get me figure back. What do you want, Billy? Turning up like this out of thin air. I've married again. And I'm doing all right.'

That floored Billy.

'*Married?* But what about our son?'

'You've not bothered to keep in touch, have you? As far as I knew, you were dead. I got a letter in one of them yellow envelopes telling me just that. What was I expected to do? There aren't enough men to go round as it is. I had to take my chance when it was offered.'

'I had amnesia,' he told her, changing the words when she looked puzzled. 'I lost my memory. The plane I was in went down in the sea. The others died.'

'Yes, I know about the plane crash. But they *told* me you were dead. How was I supposed to know you'd drop from the sky like a bad penny?'

She pointed to a row of smart Edwardian villas lining the road opposite the park. 'I'm not Elsie Pica now, Billy, I'm Doctor Ferguson's wife and I live over there in The Laurels. His first wife died in a doodlebug raid. Hastings was tormented by the buggers—' She broke off, a frown puckering her powdered forehead. 'Your dad. The café... Do you know about that?'

He nodded his head. 'I found out this morning.'

The child started to whimper and Elsie came down the steps to rock the pram. 'Gawd! This is the only time of day I get a bit of peace and quiet to myself,' she said, rocking the pram more vigorously. 'He normally sleeps longer.'

'What are we going to do about this mess, Elsie?'

'I want you to go away and pretend you never came back.'

'But what about Frank? Our son?'

'He's got another father now. He doesn't need two.' A tone of desperation entered her voice now. 'Please don't ruin everything for us, Billy. We've got a good life. I don't have to worry about working no more. Frank will go to a private school. You could never give me what Cedric does.'

'Do you love him?'

She shrugged. 'I'm fond of him, yes. He's all right – a kind man. Older than you, of course. He's generous. He's good to Ma as well. We don't want for nothing no more.' She corrected herself, putting on a posh voice. 'We don't want for anything. Cedric is paying for me to have elocution lessons, don't you know.'

Billy looked towards the pram. In a way, Elsie was giving him everything he'd dreamed of in his worst moments: a get-out clause, an escape from a life he never wanted. But it felt all wrong somehow. Now he knew he had a son, he wanted to be a part of his life, see him grow up and give him the same happy childhood he had enjoyed.

'At least let me write to him. Keep in touch. He's my son too, after all. And you could send me a photograph or two. Show me how he's getting on.'

'What's the point of that? It will confuse him if he thinks he has two fathers.'

'*I'm* his father.'

'Not any longer you're not.'

Billy went to lean his hand into the pram and gently touch his son's blond hair. The little boy stirred, opened his eyes and looked at Billy. Then, his mouth wide open, he started to bawl.

'Now look what you've done, Billy. Just go away and leave us alone.'

He watched her push the pram away, over the damp grass and back to the path. He followed at a distance through the arboretum, listening to the child's wails and Elsie shushing him and telling him to bloody well go back to sleep. He felt like running after her to tell her not to shout at his son. A son he was having to leave, through no fault of his own. It was an almighty mess and he had to tell himself to get a grip. How many times up in the sky had he told himself to control himself, to steady his nerves. But this: abandoning his child to Elsie and her new husband – it was different. Gut wrenching, if he was honest.

He leant against a tree to watch her push his son out of his life. Once out of the park gates, she crossed the road to a grand house with large gleaming windows and a feature-tower attached to one side of the building. A well-tended lawn stretched before it and rhododendron bushes separated it from the leafy road. Billy made a mental note of the address: The Laurels, 85 Lower Park Road. From behind an alder, he watched Elsie turn a key in the lock and manoeuvre the pram through the smart blue door and shut it firmly behind her. Billy stood there for a few moments. He thought he glimpsed her face at one of the top windows of the tower but it could have been the shadow from copper beech branches swaying in the breeze. He needed a stiff drink.

CHAPTER 29

PUGLIA, 1946

Almost three months had passed since Billy had left. For Anto, he would always be known as Roberto. However hard she tried to pack the memory of him into a closed box, turn the key and throw it away, he kept popping into her head. She eventually steeled herself to a strange routine: sleeping during the day, waking late in the afternoons when the day was well past its peak. At night she had found it impossible to sleep, hence the reversal of her days. For the first time in her life she was totally alone; night noises stung her senses, filling her with fear and imagined danger, so that when the morning came, she was always exhausted.

At first, she had tried to lull herself to sleep at night by listening to waves brushing the shore below the *trulli*. She had drunk infusions of fennel to settle her insomnia after she had finished Nonno's store of wine. Drinking two or three glasses calmed her at first, but finished by making her maudlin, bringing on tears and self-pity, and she had no wish to venture into Mattinata to buy more. Anto lived on what she found about her: the last of the salads and tomatoes from the *orto*, prickly pears from the wild, snails when it rained and eggs from her hens. Fish was her staple food and on the couple of occasions she'd worked on the fishing platform, straining unsuccessfully to haul up the heavy net, she'd missed Roberto by her side.

She came to realise her feelings for him were way deeper than she'd wanted to admit. It was not the silence in the *trullo* or inability to work the *trabucco* that aggrieved: it was the solid, loving absence of him beside her. In the evenings, she resorted to pushing Nonno's boat into the shallows to sit alone, waiting for fish to nibble, watching sunset colour the horizon. She shouted in anger at gulls who tried to steal her catch, her throat sore, the words strange to her ears after days of silence. Perspiration poured from her as she hoed and dug the vegetable patch, trying to tire herself out so she could sleep. But her efforts served only to fill her body with aches and pains. The pickaxe became her main weapon as she angrily broke up stones, pulverising them to gravel to sprinkle on the paths. But the night still brought no rest: only space for memories of days spent with Roberto.

His patience, his quiet voice, the way his muscles rippled on his stocky body as he worked, his brown eyes that crinkled when he laughed, the way he threw back his head, his mouth wide open, his joy filling her. The smell of him: masculine, musky. On the first nights after he'd left, she'd worn his work shirt to sleep in, breathing in his male scent. But she'd washed it on the fourth morning, pounding it in wood ash and water paste until his smell was gone. Gone, like him. He would never come back. He had promised, but she had never dared to believe in his promises. She'd always feared his past would steal him away from her. And it had. Nothing wonderful lasted forever in this life. She had learned that over the past years.

Sleep continued to elude her. Every time an owl hooted in the black night or a pair of mating foxes shrieked, she jumped, her nerves taut as the wires on Nonno's *trabucco*. Birba was no use to her either once the sun went down. She disappeared to hunt in the olive groves, setting down gifts of half-chewed shrews or grass snakes at her door in the half-light of dawn. And so it was easier for Anto to rest by day when the sun was up, and to endure the nights by sitting in the kitchen, moths dancing round the single candle stub that she lit to keep herself company. Soon she would have no more to burn. She continued to embroider on a large piece of the parachute that she'd measured out to make a cover for her bed. Dividing it into squares, she continued to sew the story of her life, turning it into a picture book of events, omitting the episode with Salvatore. But in a scene where Nonno and Roberto fished together from the *trabucco*, she embroidered an ugly black cormorant perched on the edge of a pole, telling herself the bird was Salvatore waiting to steal from their catch. The material was slippery, but she took pains to wash her hands before she worked and to keep her stitches neat, the effort of concentrating on the needle that pierced the cloth back and forth calming her a little, the silk a warm layer over her knees.

In the first square where Roberto appeared, she remembered Nonno Domenico's description of him arriving like an angel from the sky over the sea and she sewed an image of the Angel Gabriel she had seen in the church of the Addolorata in Foggia where she'd been baptised.

Just before nightfall, she took to walking to the edge of the cliffs where Nonno was buried and sat nearby, talking or singing to him in the salty breeze, the only reply returning to her from shrieking gulls and the sea crashing on the glistening rocks below.

By the start of the new year, her supply of flour and rice had completely gone. She lifted the pot from the chimney breast where Nonno had kept their savings, and tipped it upside down. A few coins rolled onto the table. Twenty lire in total.

One kilo of flour cost at least thirty lire, rice fifty. She would have little to eat over the winter months. Antonella needed a job, otherwise she would starve.

She let herself into the small *trullo* where Roberto had slept. The patched trousers she had darned for him hung from a nail on the wall and she ran her fingers over the material before turning to the bike. The tyres were flat and she took a while to pump them up and, instead of using that day to sleep, at eight o'clock she pedalled along the clifftop to seek employment at the *masseria* where Roberto had worked.

The huge double doors to the courtyard stood open and she wheeled the bike through and propped it against a palm tree. A woman was shouting somewhere inside the building and she stepped towards the angry cries, the clatter of pots and pans almost drowning the words.

'Can't you do anything properly, Eva?' the woman yelled. 'Or do I have to do everything for you? *Mannaggia*, your mind is always on that scoundrel, damn him. You're a good-for-nothing apology for a daughter. What good are you to me in this state?'

Roberto had often recounted the day's events after his shift at the *masseria*. Anto knew a lot about Signora Pinto and her two daughters, Eva and Maria. His descriptions of the three women had made her double over with laughter in the evenings as they ate together.

There was more wailing and shouting as Eva retaliated. 'It's not my fault, Mamma. I feel so sick.'

'Well, whose fault is it, then? Not the Holy Ghost's, I'm sure. If you hadn't opened your legs for that man, then you wouldn't be in the mess you're in now. *Gesù Maria*, you're lucky your father isn't alive to give you a thorough beating.'

Anto lingered at the entrance to the kitchen, taking in the huge copper pans of water boiling away on the vast stove, the baskets of aubergines and peppers on the table. Signora Pinto pulled Eva away from the sink where the girl was bent over a pile of fish and pushed her daughter away.

'Go and lay the tables. At least that won't make you puke.' She shouted at the top of her voice, pushing a strand of hair from her flushed face, 'And tell that lazybones Maria to get in here this minute.'

Eva brushed past Anto, her hands clutched to her mouth and Signora Pinto shouted at Anto, 'Are you the girl from the village? You're late. Get in here and clean these fish.'

There would be time to explain later, Anto thought, as she rolled up her sleeves and set to, descaling a pile of mullet and bream and sorting through a slippery heap of sardines. It was work she could do standing on her head and when the signora inspected her progress a little later, Anto earned a grudging, '*Brava!* When you're finished there, you can slice those aubergines for the *parmigiana*.'

Thirty minutes later, a thin girl of about thirteen turned up at the door. '*Scusate*, signora,' she said, twisting her skirt, her pinched face screwed up with worry. 'Our donkey is lame, and I had to run all the way here.'

'Who are *you*?' asked the signora, looking back and forth between Anto and the young girl.

'Rosa,' she replied, 'my mother sent me. Agnese, from the village.'

'Oh, *Santa Maria* and all the *angeli*. This place is like a mad house today.' She threw up her hands in exasperation and then thrust a broom into Rosa's hands. 'Go and sweep the dining room. And see if my daughter needs help with setting the tables.'

Lifting a large basket of tomatoes and courgettes onto the laden kitchen table, she turned to Anto. 'I don't know who you are or who sent you but you're a fast worker, I can see that, and you can stay now you're here. We have a wedding party arriving in less than three hours and I need all the help I can get. If you're not Rosa, who *are* you?'

'My name is Antonella, signora. Roberto told me you might have a vacancy.'

Fibs came easily to her mouth when needs must.

'Ah, Roberto. He was a good man. It's a pity he had to leave,' the signora said, slicing courgettes with a mandolin cutter as she talked. 'We miss him.'

For the next two hours, Anto worked hard, banishing her fatigue. She listened to Signora Pinto's moans, which ranged from complaints about Eva, who'd got herself in the family way, but without a family. 'The scoundrel promised her a new life in the city but he disappeared as soon as she told him about the baby.' She held up her kitchen knife. 'He told her he was a *conte*, you know. She would have been set up for life. But if he turns up here again, the little aristocratic shit, once I've dealt with him, he won't have the wherewithal to continue his family line. And Eva should have known better than to give in to his promises and part her legs, but I'm kept so busy here now that my *marito* has passed' – she made the sign of the cross against her pillowy bosom with her knife – 'that it's been difficult to keep an eye on everything.'

Anto made all the right noises as the signora told her about the bunions on her feet that were as large as *patate*. 'They'll be the death of me,' she complained. As well as her bunions, she had haemorrhoids to contend with, which would also be the death of her. And as for her daughters, they'd been sent by *Gesù Cristo* to test her, although she didn't deserve any more testing because she'd been tested enough in her life. Her parents had christened her with the name of Fortunata, but luck had been thinly spread in her life so far and she was looking forward to a change in her fortunes... Her voice became part of the background after a while for Anto, blending with the chopping and slicing, frying and bubbling and the barked instructions to Eva and Maria.

Anto was exhausted by the end of the day but more than pleased with the fifty lire she'd pocketed, together with a bag of leftovers and the request for her to come again and help out on the following weekend, when there was an even bigger wedding party to cater for.

'I don't know what I would have done without you, *ragazza*. Tell Roberto if you ever see him, if he needs a job again, there's always one waiting for him here.' She added half a loaf and a lump of *cacciocavallo* cheese to Anto's bag of food. There was little point in telling the woman that Roberto wasn't coming back and Anto decided to keep up the pretence of being in contact with him. It was best if word didn't get out that she was living on her own.

It had been a good day and for the first night since Roberto had left, with her stomach full and, appreciative of the silence at the *trullo* after the busyness of the *masseria*, Anto slept the whole night through. At first light she walked to the cavern and sat for a while, listening to the ocean pounding at the rocks below. The weather was cooler now and there would be no opportunity to swim with winter approaching. It was well past the time to harvest olives and she wondered how she could cope with the backbreaking work on her own. She walked back through the olive groves, willing herself to stay strong.

You will be fine, Antonella, she told herself. *Time will help and soon you will forget about Roberto.* She tried to persuade herself the ache she felt in her heart would pass. Like a fever, it would rage and eventually die down.

On the following Saturday, Antonella helped again at Masseria della Torre with wedding preparations. There were two hundred guests expected. 'They're coming from the city,'

Signora Pinto told Anto as they plucked feathers from a couple of dozen hens. 'If we put on the finest meal, then word will spread and I can start to put money aside to repair this place. It was my husband's dream.' She wiped a tear away and Anto felt sorry for her. She was not such a bad sort, for all her shouting. There were many mothers who would have turfed out a pregnant daughter and sent her to the nuns, but Signora Fortunata Pinto had a warmer heart than she first presented. She had found a dress and a skirt for Anto that no longer fitted Eva or Maria and insisted Anto ate more. 'You're all skin and bones, *ragazza*. How do you expect to find a husband if there's nothing to get hold of in bed? *Mangia, mangia, ragazza.* Eat more, girl.'

In a strange way, Anto began to enjoy the hours spent in the company of these three women. Fortunata made her laugh and the girls, who hated being stuck in the middle of nowhere and longed to live in the city, were friendly enough to Anto, especially when she did their jobs for them.

'I don't know why Mamma doesn't sell this place and be rid of it,' Maria said to Anto as they folded linen napkins into swan shapes to set on the table. 'There's no way she can carry out Babbo's plans.'

'What plans were they?' Anto asked.

'Our father worked in America for five years as gardener for a bigwig in films before he married Mamma, but he felt homesick for his Puglia. He hit on the idea of attracting rich *americani* to come here and spend their holidays. He told us there were plenty of *italo-americani* who would love to spend nostalgic holidays by the sea. But this place is a dump,' Maria said, pointing at the rough stone walls of the dining room and the wonky, dilapidated furniture. 'Why would rich people want to come and spend their time and money here when there are luxury hotels in the cities?'

'Life in a big city is busy,' Anto told her. 'It's peaceful here.'

'Have you ever been to Foggia?' Maria asked. 'I *long* to live there. They tell me there are *ristoranti* where orchestras play every evening. And a special room in the Café Roma just for ladies, with plush red velvet seating and Persian rugs on the floors.'

Anto ignored Maria's question as to whether she'd been to Foggia. 'I doubt any of those cafés still exist. I've heard bomb raids completely flattened the city.'

'Oh, but I'm sure they'd be rebuilt by now, won't they? I long for a bit of *life*. To sit and sip coffee from dainty cups and watch ladies and gentlemen walk by in their fashionable clothes. There's nothing to do here. Don't tell Mamma, but I shall run away at the first opportunity. Eva was foolish to rush at the *conte* but I will pick my opportunity more wisely.'

'Don't believe that life is always better elsewhere,' Anto told her, picking up a pile of polished cutlery from the sideboard. 'We'd better hurry with these tables. If you go and pick roses for the vases, I'll finish off here.'

It was true what Maria had said about the *masseria*. Anto looked round the dining room at the damaged mirrors, mottled streaks showing where the silvering was fading. The place was ramshackle, stuffed with furniture from the last century and gloomy dark paintings of unhappy-looking women and men wearing powdered wigs. There was no comparison with the cafés and restaurants in Foggia that Anto had glimpsed. She'd gazed through their windows at the marble counter tops and polished chandeliers that glittered in the evenings, where the rich and famous of Foggia congregated.

Signor Pinto's pipe dreams to lure guests to Masseria della Torre were empty. The signora was an excellent cook; the food was delicious, that much was true. But it was not enough to build a healthy business. There were plenty of excellent eating places all over the region but Puglia was a long way from Rome for *stranieri* to travel overland from train stations. She reckoned there would be no rich *americani* coming to stay in this *masseria* any time soon. But as long as Anto had work and money coming in, that was all that mattered and she kept all negative thoughts to herself.

Anto had told Fortunata from the outset she was happy to work behind the scenes but would not serve at table, despite her attempts at persuading her otherwise.

'But you're a pretty girl, Antonella. It's a pity about your hair. But that will grow if you only let it, instead of hacking at it all the time.' She tilted Anto's face to the light. 'Look at those beautiful big eyes and lashes that could sweep my kitchen floor. *Ma sei bellissima*. You're really beautiful. With a face like that before them, my customers would be so distracted, they'd order the most expensive dishes and wine. And think of the tips they would leave you, *ragazza*.'

'Please, signora,' Anto said, ignoring what she considered to be ridiculous compliments. There was no way she could explain her reason for lying low, but the fewer people who knew where she was, the better. Word spread like mould in these parts and fear of Salvatore knowing her whereabouts was always in her mind. 'Don't let me loose in the dining room. I'll only drop food in people's laps and knock over wine glasses. Maria and Eva are far better than I will ever be at waitressing. *Per favore*. I'm more use to you in the kitchen.'

She was quick at her job, flipping meat on the griddle, seasoning dishes perfectly, adding finishing touches to salads, plating up orders without smears on the edges of the dishes, washing up without having to be told twice.

'*Va bene*, Antonella. Fine for now. But the time will soon come when Eva has her baby and then you will have to step in to help.'

Anto put off that thought for the time being and whilst the wedding guests enjoyed their starters, she busied herself with arranging baked chickens on huge oval platters, sprinkling the golden pieces of meat with roasted sage leaves, arranging stuffed peppers and aubergines so that they resembled the petals of a huge flower. She still had to finish off a tower of profiteroles and arrange tiny rosebuds around its base. As she worked, she hummed one of Nonno's songs, oblivious to the rowdy guests in the dining room as Eva and Maria bustled back and forth from the kitchen, carrying in the dishes and commenting about the handsome men they were serving.

Anto was fast asleep under her blanket when the sound of a motorbike approaching down the track to the *trullo* woke her early next morning. She sat up and stretched her arms above her head. Maybe Roberto's pilot friend was bringing her a message from Roberto in Inghilterra. She jumped out of bed and pulled on her skirt and blouse, splashed her face with cold water and grabbed a scarf to tie round her head.

Through the narrow window above the kitchen sink, she saw a man walk towards the *trullo*. It was not Roberto's blond pilot friend. Her heart began to pound and from the table she grabbed the paring knife she used for gutting fish, slipping it into her pocket as she waited for Salvatore Zuccaroli to knock at the door, her worst nightmare come true.

'*C'è nessuno?*' he called. 'Anybody there?'

Anto held her breath, as if by holding it he wouldn't see her. He pounded on the door again and when she didn't answer, she watched in horror as he forced it open. Her stomach churned as his bulk blotted light from the doorway.

'Ah, *finalmente*! You're a hard one to track down, aren't you?' His smile was cruel as he looked her up and down and moved further into the room, his heavy bike boots and jacket making him appear bulkier than he was.

Anto's hand crept towards her skirt pocket as Salvatore pulled a chair from the table and sat down, making himself at home. 'I'm very thirsty after my long search for you. The roads are terrible round here.'

She willed herself to remain calm. 'There is water outside in the well.'

'Hah! Hospitable as ever.'

'I will have to fetch more for you. My husband finished the jug just now.' She prayed that Salvatore would believe her lies. 'He's busy preparing to harvest olives in our grove.'

Salvatore sat up straighter, drumming his fingers on the table. 'So, you are a signora now. And who is the unfortunate man?'

'Let me fetch you water from the well. I'll call my husband to join us from the olive grove.'

Once out of the door, Anto ran for her life. She was fit from her swims across the bay and Salvatore was wearing heavy bike boots that hampered him, which gave her a head start. He didn't know the lie of the land and she was banking on outwitting him and hiding where he would never find her. There was no time to think of what would happen later. Her immediate thought was to flee from the presence of this evil bastard, with his unfinished business.

The olive trees were thick with unpicked fruit, the branches hanging heavy in the grove and she hoped she would be camouflaged as she sped towards the cliffs. Her skirt snagged on wild *rosa canina* branches and she tugged to free herself, slowing her progress. Behind her she heard Salvatore's heavy steps as the distance between them shrank, his voice angry as he bellowed.

'Don't think you can run away from me again, bitch. This time you won't get away.'

Her ruse of a husband being nearby had not worked. Anto's panic heightened and she urged herself on, leaping over stones, pushing through juniper bushes, the scent of wild fennel and mustard strong as she stamped over plants. She tripped once, her ankle snared by a bramble and as she picked herself up, Salvatore's shouts grew louder as he shortened the gap between them. At last she reached the thicket of prickly pear plants marking the opening to the cavern above the grotto. She turned to see where Salvatore was. She seemed to have lost him and she pushed past the cacti plants that hid the entrance, their long thorns snagging at her skirt which ripped as she pulled at it, desperation mounting as she struggled to tear free. She slid on her bottom down the slope to the cavern and squeezed herself behind a rock, her breathing loud in the space, her heart battering her ribcage, biting her lip as she listened to waves swirling in the grotto below her. The sea was choppy today. No fisherman would ever set out in such a storm and she prayed she would not have to escape by jumping from the cavern and swimming ashore. When the waves were like this in the grotto, you could be easily carried out to sea unless you were an extremely strong swimmer.

Stones slithered into the cavern and Anto held her breath as the sound of Salvatore's heavy steps approached.

His cruel laugh echoed in the cavernous space. 'Very clever, Antonella. You almost evaded me, but not quite. If it hadn't been for the telltale ribbon of material snagged on the plant, I wouldn't have found you. More's the pity for you.'

Anto heard the metallic flick of a lighter before light bounced from the glistering rock surfaces. He would spot her at any minute, corner her where she crouched, the cliff face behind her a trap unless she moved immediately. She darted from her hiding place towards the edge of the gap that opened to the sea.

'How did you find where I was living, Salvatore?' Anto shouted above the waves, her fingers finding the handle of the kitchen knife. If she engaged him in conversation, it might be possible to distract him a few moments longer.

'Your aunt in Foggia told me – eventually – about your

trullo near the sea. It took a little persuasion. Unfortunately, she passed out before I could get your exact whereabouts.'

'You're a *bastardo*. Did you hurt her?'

'Not as much as I would have liked to. It was bad timing your cousin turned up when he did.'

'What do you want?' Her hand was tight around the knife now. If he came near, she would plunge it in his heart.

'To settle scores. This war might have passed but I don't forget a grudge. You caused me lots of trouble, you know. I lost my job with the *carabinieri*. My apartment was taken away. My wife left too. All because you reported me.' He spat, but his spittle didn't reach her and he took a step nearer. 'One bad turn deserves another, pretty Antonella. *Bbèlla*.'

'I paid for what happened already. Or have you forgotten? I was a virgin until you laid your filthy hands on me. You're nothing but a bully and a coward. You think you're so big and clever. But my aunt will report you and then *you'll* be the hunted one. You were stupid when you were a boy at school and you always will be.' Anto's words were loud, anger outweighing common sense and soft talk, persuasion abandoned from her original plan of talking herself out of danger.

'If you want me, come and get me, *big man*.' She taunted him, her eyes fiery, hatred contorting her face as she held out the knife.

With a roar, he picked up a stick where it leant against the cavern wall and lunged. At the last minute, he tripped on a half-buried rock and she stepped sideways to avoid him falling against her, watching with a mixture of relief and horror as he staggered, scratching at air as he tried to regain his balance and then plunging over the edge to the frothing sea below.

'*Aiuto, aiuto*. Help me,' he screamed, his voice echoing in the hollow of the grotto. 'I can't swim.'

For anybody else, Anto would have jumped. She knelt over the opening, watching as Salvatore resurfaced through the foaming waters, his arms stretched towards her before he sank again into the boiling sea. Twice more she glimpsed the top of his head as he came to the top, the last time no longer shouting for help. She stayed watching, waiting for the moment when the waves would suck him out of the grotto, pull him out to sea in the whirlpools of current. She wondered how long he would stay out there in the ocean. When his body was found, what would his face look like once fish had nibbled at his eyes and water bloated his body? She hoped his corpse would be washed up unrecognisable, far away from her bay, in another country on the other side of the Adriatic. In those first moments she felt no guilt, no responsibility for his death. He had deserved to die and she had fulfilled her vow to kill him without even having to lay a finger on him.

Antonella sank to the ground, sobbing. She saw bloodstains on her skirt and on her fingers. In her horror and panic she had gripped the blade of the kitchen knife. Her blood, not his, but she knew she would have plunged the blade deep within his heart if necessary. Her blood dripped onto the sand where she knelt, and she rubbed at it with her hands, trying to smudge the grains into the floor of her favourite place.

Flinging open the lid to Nonno's box she'd stored in the cavern, she pulled out the flying suit, hugging it to her, rocking backwards and forwards on the dirt floor, whispering Roberto's name, feeling abandoned and lonelier than she had ever felt.

CHAPTER 30

Anto trailed home along the cliff, carrying the contents of the box, clinging to them as if they were part of Roberto. She kidded herself she was doing so because they would rot in the damp cave, but in truth she needed to hold on to something of his, to feel him near. Sapped of energy, she stumbled more than once. It began to rain and when she arrived back at the *trullo*, her clothes were soaked and she couldn't stop shivering.

She bolted the door. The catch was stiff, as Nonno had rarely locked the door to the *trullo* and she struggled with her injured fingers. Lighting the fire proved difficult and she broke several precious *cerini* wax matches until she managed to start a feeble flame. Cupping her hands round a hot fennel tisane, she pulled Birba close, the little kitten squirming as she held her tight, but she couldn't get warm. Even when she draped a blanket over her shoulders and pulled her stool closer to the hearth, she continued to shiver. Darkness fell and rain turned to hail, pelting the little windows. She fastened the shutters, imagining Salvatore's face leering at her through the panes. Raindrops hissed onto the fire from the wide chimney. After a while the thin flames petered out and she was too terrified to go outside to replenish the supply of sticks.

Anto curled up with Roberto's flying suit in her arms after heaping all the covers she could find on top of her and willing sleep to come and take her away from the sound of Salvatore's anguished cries. She lay awake all night and at first light, she was still chilled to the bone.

Letting herself outside to fetch more wood, she opened the door warily, craning to check that Salvatore had not somehow turned up from the sea. The rain had stopped and mist rose from the earth as it heated up in the early morning sun. The olive trees loomed as if draped in shrouds and she gazed all around, checking Salvatore's ghost had not returned to haunt her. With a sharp intake of breath, she took in his motorbike propped against a tree near the entrance to the property. Last night she had completely failed to notice. What if somebody came to look for him and spotted the bike? She had to get rid of it.

Antonella hurried to the small *trullo* where the tools were kept and grabbed a pickaxe and a long-handled spade. It was no good trying to push the motorbike into the scrubland. A shepherd would find it and anyway the machine was far too heavy and she did not know how to start it.

It took most of the day to dig a hole deep enough near the olive tree next to the bike, her sore hand hampering her, the ground packed with stones. Rain had softened the top layer but underneath, it was rock hard. She used the pickaxe to break up the earth, every sinew in her arms and shoulders screaming with effort as she lifted the heavy tool above her head and brought it crashing down on the packed earth, over and over again, imagining she was striking Salvatore's body with each blow. When she thought she had made the hole deep enough, she mustered all her strength to push the bike into it, but she hadn't bargained on the handlebars. One side protruded about twenty centimetres above the level of the ground. She wept with frustration. All her energy was gone and now the bike was lying on its side in the hole, it was impossible to gouge out more stones and earth from beneath. Anto screamed to the sky, startling Birba. The terrified creature scuttled up the nearest olive tree, mewing plaintively, her back arched like a witch's cat.

'*Dio buono*. Good God! Why are you doing this to me?' Anto railed. 'What have I ever done to deserve all this? No more, no more... I can't take it.'

And then a calm descended on her and she lay on her back in the dirt, taking deep breaths as she watched shapes of storm clouds passing above: swirls of dark blue on grey, patches of white breaking through like beacons. An image of herself as a little girl came to mind, when Nonno would calm her during thunderstorms which had always terrified her, inventing stories about the clouds: that one was a giant, the other looming behind it was a bull, the white streaks were angels' rays coming to the rescue. After ten minutes or so, she rose to her feet and she summoned her last forces to shovel dirt back in to the hole. The handlebar still protruded from the earth like a skeletal limb and she fetched stones, one by one, that Roberto had piled at the other end of the grove, and relocated them to cover the handlebar, making the journey dozens of times until there was no visible trace of the bike.

Back in her *trullo*, she was too exhausted to eat or wash. From time to time she pulled the photos from the envelope the *inglese* pilot had given to Roberto, running her fingers over the blurred image of his young face, wondering if she would ever see him again. She lay wide awake for a second night, the door bolted fast but she let Birba wander free outside this time. There was no point in punishing the little cat.

. . .

Next morning, Anto packed a few belongings into a basket and shoved Roberto's air force items into a sack. His identity tag fell to the floor and she picked it up, running her fingers over the letters of his strange English name. It would not do to leave them in the *trullo* in the event the place was searched and they were found. What would the authorities make of her and Nonno having harboured a foreigner? The war was over but people still waged battles against each other, bitter with simmering hatred and resentment at what neighbours had done or not done. And like a baby needs a comfort blanket, or a widowed woman clings to a husband's clothes until she is ready to let them go, Anto, in her anxiety, needed something of Roberto near her. Finally, she tugged the shutters on the *trullo* window closed and, after padlocking the doors to both buildings and throwing extra corn to her hens, she stepped out over the fields, leading the goat laden with the sack containing Roberto's belongings. Little Birba trailed behind her, darting into the undergrowth from time to time, but always returning to mew and check her mistress was still there.

Eva was hanging out tablecloths when she stepped onto the estate of Masseria della Torre. As the girl stretched up to peg linen on the line, the bulge of her stomach was obvious. Anto put down her basket, tethered the goat to a tree and went over to help.

'You look terrible,' Eva said. 'Are you sure you're fit to work today?'

'Time of the month,' Anto said. 'I'm fine.'

'Wish it were mine. But at least I've stopped puking up. It carried on for so long. But Mamma said it was a good sign. It means the baby is strong. He ruddy well kicks like a strong 'un.'

'How much longer do you have?'

'Not long. Less than a month, maybe. Mamma is being surprisingly nice to me. She's even started knitting little vests and socks.'

'She's a good woman,' Anto said. 'I was scared of her at first.'

'She likes to shout, that's true.'

The two girls wandered over to the kitchen and Anto was immediately enfolded in Fortunata's embrace. Her hands were covered in flour from the ear-shaped *orecchiette* pasta shapes she was making. Anto moved over to the sink, which was filled with a mound of turnip tops.

'Shall I wash these for the sauce, signora?' she asked.

'Our little cherub has returned,' Fortunata announced. 'But you look ill. Whatever is the matter?'

'It's only my monthlies, signora.'

'You need a good dose of iron inside you. Mackerel and spinach for you today, *ragazza*. And dried apricots for afters. I can't have my workers fainting on me.'

'And I didn't sleep well,' Anto continued. 'There's a hole in the roof at home and until I can get it repaired, I was wondering if I could stay, and use Roberto's room for a while. I can do extra jobs for you, signora. There's no need to pay me. And I brought the goat with me, for milk and cheese.'

'*Grazie, cara.* It will be good to have you with us, dear. And once Eva gives birth, perhaps you can take over her responsibilities.' Fortunata kissed the gold crucifix on the chain round her neck. 'The Good Lord has provided again.' She lifted her head to the ceiling and made the sign of the cross. '*Grazie a Dio.* Now, go and settle yourself in Roberto's old room.'

In the narrow storeroom that gave onto the courtyard, Anto felt protected. Even though she believed Salvatore was gone now, she never wanted to feel as vulnerable as she had last night. The windows were high in the walls and barred; there was a lock on the thick door. She pushed the sack containing Roberto's possessions and photos into an old box containing twine far under the bed and for the first time in many hours, she began to breathe evenly, her heart no longer fluttering like a bird trying to escape.

. . .

As winter advanced, custom at the Masseria della Torre dwindled to a dribble. Rainfall had churned up roads that were still in need of repair since war's end and fewer vehicles passed now. Eva grew plumper and lazier as her time approached. Without being asked, Anto made a start on tidying the unused rooms in the old farmhouse. She came across leather-bound books in an old trunk covered in mildew and cobwebs and she turned the pages, delighting in the illustrations and tracing the words slowly with her finger, mouthing the letters until she was able to decipher their meaning. Roberto had helped her learn her alphabet in the evenings when they sat together. She was a willing and able student, proud that she could now say she was no longer *analfabeta*, but there had been no books for her to practise on at the *trullo*. She took pleasure at the *masseria* in dusting the books and filing them onto shelves. A whole new world opened for her as she uncovered stories. Her favourite was Alessandro Manzoni's *I Promessi Sposi – The Betrothed –* and at night, by the light of a candle in the little storeroom, she filled her head with the tale of a poor young couple who had wanted to marry. Don Rodrigo, the rich villain who had his eyes on the bride and prevented the marriage, morphed into Salvatore for Anto. When the young lovers ran away to Milan, Antonella devoured the descriptions of the city, reconciling herself to the fact that she could only ever travel to these places through pages of books. Occasionally she found herself thinking, *I must tell Roberto about this.* Or, *I wonder if Roberto has read this book,* before reminding herself not to be stupid. *You will never see him again. Put him out of your mind.*

CHAPTER 31

PRESENT DAY

On the drive back from the *masseria*, Susannah kept glancing back at the old box, as if to make sure it was still there.

'It's not going to jump out and run away, you know,' Giacomo said, turning to her with a grin.

She smiled. 'You never know... but there's something magical and mysterious about all this. I can't wait to look through everything again.'

'Let's hope it doesn't turn out to be a Pandora's box.'

'Who knows? There are so many unknowns. I mean... I've been thinking about the link between Elsie's mention of a Billy and the William of the ID tag. If this was a film, it would fit nicely with some viewers, but others would scoff at the huge coincidence...'

'So, what sort of viewer are you, Susannah?'

'A bit of both, I suppose.' She was quiet for a moment, staring out at the sea beyond a straggle of holiday houses lining the beach. 'There's nothing to say he *wasn't* her lover. And there were many doomed love affairs during the war, weren't there? Young people from different cultures and classes, in circumstances very different from normal. The war must have given an urgency to life. Not knowing if tomorrow would come. Grabbing at comfort...' She rubbed her head. 'But... there's nothing to say, either, that he *was* her lover. Uff! My brain hurts, Giacomo, too many questions swilling around. Can we stop for a coffee?'

He pulled in at a bar on the edge of Monte Sant'Angelo and Susannah took photos of the views over the town, the sea in the distance. She removed her jacket, enjoying the sun's warmth. 'I'm going to find it hard to leave all this,' she said.

'It's not going anywhere, Susannah. You can always come back.'

'Please call me Susi.'

He raised his espresso to her. '*Va bene*, Susi. My door is always open.'

They arrived back at Giacomo's wine bar at about six o'clock. Checking he needed no help, she popped along the street to the local museum to check out anything she could discover about the area during World War Two. She didn't hold out much hope, but she was sure Daddy would have pursued every avenue. *Be scientific, Susi,* she could hear him say. *Use your imagination. What you are searching for might be under your nose, but always use a grain of scepticism.*

The past was ever-present in her mind as she wandered round. In the back room, lists hung on the walls with names of the dead from both world wars and she peered at the photographs, wondering if William Pica could possibly be standing amongst the huddles of uniformed men. She peered at a censored postcard dated 1941, sent from Egypt via the Red Cross to inform a mother that her son was imprisoned. Susannah thought how the war had wrenched simple people from their simple lives.

She gazed at an old poster for a film – *Donne Senza Nome* – and read the translation beneath.

The film, Nameless Women, *was made to show the plight of women after the war. Italy was destroyed – especially our forgotten south. Mothers had to put bread in their children's bellies. Sleeping with the enemy was one option. Many displaced women were arrested for prostitution and incarcerated in primitive conditions.*

Nobody should be nameless, Susannah thought, her mind on her postcard writer. Maybe she would never put two and two together: he would remain one of the nameless and she would have to let go of her unsolved mystery. But she was going to do the best she could in the little time left her. It would niggle her if she didn't and she'd feel as if she'd failed her daddy.

Susannah studied another display of photos, noting the impoverished people waiting in line for food next to the rubble of bombed houses piled high. She tried to put herself in the picture and to imagine how difficult it must have been for ordinary people to get by.

And then she came across an incongruous black-and-white photo: a motley group of men and boys dressed in white, one of them holding a cricket bat. She wasn't a particular fan, but she was sure this sport wasn't played in Italy. Her mind flew to the reference to whittling a cricket bat in the letter she'd found at Elsie's. And the little sketches... Could there be a link? What was going on here?

She peered at the names of the players. The captain was a Roberto Bruni. A newspaper article was framed and positioned beside the photo. The same Roberto Bruni, a few years older, held up a contract of some kind, a beam on his face. The Italian was beyond her understanding. The girl on the desk spoke no English and she called up Giacomo.

'Are you free, Jack? Only I've found something strange here in the museum and I wondered if you could spare five minutes to translate something for me.'

'*Certo*. I'm all good here. I'll pop down. Maybe we could even grab an *aperitivo* in the bar next door before the mad rush starts.'

While she waited for him to come, she wandered into a back room where a large black-and-white banner announced a *mostra* of the work of Antonella Saponaro. She managed to understand the gist of the Italian – it was an exhibition of a lifetime's artwork.

The walls were covered with an assortment of unusual driftwood art: fish crafted from varying widths of wood strung up to wriggle as if caught in a current, a row of framed pebble pictures, a lamp stand constructed from seashells, a large heart formed from odd pieces of beach debris. The pieces were whimsical, unusual and there was something about their style that captured her interest.

A particular part of the display in a cabinet stopped her heart: an angel, its wings studded with blue, green and white fragments of sea glass. She scrabbled in her bag and pulled out her own talisman, her travel charm shaped like a gull, and matched it with the angel. The crafting was very similar.

She hurried to talk to the girl at reception, holding up her gull, speaking in very slow English, pointing behind her at the exhibition room, but the girl shook her head, smiling apologetically. 'Little Eenglish,' she said.

Giacomo arrived when she was attempting again. 'Brilliant timing,' she said, dragging him with her to the back room. 'Look what I've found.' Once again, she held up her lucky charm against the dozen similar pieces. 'These are more sophisticated, but I think it's by the same artist. Can you ask the girl if she can tell me more about her?'

She listened to the pair, frustrated that her knowledge of

Italian was so poor, and then Giacomo translated for her. 'It's all work by a very popular and respected local artist.'

He spoke again to the girl, the conversation flowing back and forth without Susannah understanding.

'Lidia here says there's a shop in town devoted to her work. She says it's best if you pop in there to find out more. Where did you get yours from?' Giacomo asked.

'I've had it since I was a little girl. My father told me an old man gave it to me in the park. Please, let's go to the shop.'

'I'll ask Lidia to phone the shop to tell them we're coming.'

Another rapid Italian exchange, the girl smiling at Giacomo and scribbling something down on her notepad. Giacomo had such an easy manner about him, Susannah thought. Everybody seemed to warm to him but he didn't seem to realise the effect he had. She wondered who was flirting with whom. The girl tossed back her hair and reddened a little before Susannah tugged at his sleeve.

'There's something else I want to show you in here.'

She took him over to the corner devoted to the war and its aftermath, pointing to the photos and articles that had particularly interested her. After scanning one of the newspaper cuttings, Giacomo explained, 'This is about a local salesman who represented one of the new olive co-operatives. He was responsible for forging links with England.'

'This is the same man in the photo of the cricket team, is it not?' she asked, pointing at the team photo.

Giacomo nodded. 'Looks that way. It says he set it up from scratch but it didn't last long. Not enough interest in the sport.'

'So – who was this Roberto Bruni?' Susannah asked. 'And how did he know about cricket? It's played by countries that were once British colonies. He's got to have lived in England, or something. Do you think he's the one who wrote about cricket and wanting to be together with Elsie again?' She quoted again from the letter: '... my heart will never be complete without you at my side...'

'Do you know all the words by heart, Susi?'

'Almost. They're so romantic, heartfelt. Imagine having something like that written about you...' She peered at the photo of Roberto Bruni again, a dark-haired young man, a friendly grin on his face. A good looker. 'If only there'd been a signature or something on the cards and letter and it read: Roberto Bruni. That would solve everything.' She huffed in frustration.

'I agree about the cricket team in a place like ours. It's weird. Nobody plays it in Italy. But you're leaping to conclusions if you think this man knew your grandmother, Susi. You need to be logical. I thought this William, or Billy, was the man you had lined up? Listen, why don't you see if you can track down this man's relatives to find out more? And possibly eliminate him from your quest? But Bruni is a really common surname. Like Smith or Brown in your country. It won't be easy.' Giacomo read through more articles and then suggested they forget about the *aperitivo*.

'If we hurry, we can go straight to the driftwood shop before it closes. It's not far.'

He took her arm as they walked briskly, stepping into the road once or twice to avoid dawdling tourists on the narrow pavement. 'I read in that article that the British still had a strong presence here in the immediate war aftermath. Helping with the displaced and relief work,' he said.

'Could Roberto Bruni have been a helper for the Brits, perhaps? Because he knew English? Somehow he learned about cricket? Got interested and tried to set up a team?'

'Random, I think. More likely he experienced cricket on his trips to England as a rep.'

At the gift shop, Susannah pressed her nose to the front window, taking in a row of houses made from blocks of sea-washed wood, candlelight flickering through their tiny windows. They were arranged on a contorted plank shelf studded with barnacles.

'Oh, my word,' she whispered. 'Magical. I need to go in.'

The shop owner spoke good English and after explaining that she had owned her piece for over thirty years and wanted to know if it could possibly be by the same artist, he produced a magnifying glass and turned the shell gull over. 'Yes, signorina. It's by the same woman.' He pointed to a tiny scratch on the back: a curly letter A. 'Signora Antonella Saponaro.'

'I've never noticed that before.'

'With the naked eye it's almost impossible to see. A pin scratch, that's all, but the flourish is the artist's own. Was this bought here in town? It's an early work, I believe.'

'It was a present when I was little. In England.'

'The artist is still alive, signorina. But she no longer makes these pieces. They're popular. We'll soon run out and then they'll become collectors' items.'

Susannah turned to Giacomo, her face alight. 'Incredible, don't you think?'

'Did your parents give it you?'

'No.' She bit her lip as she recalled her father's explanation. 'It was from an old man, apparently. I fell in the park and he gave it to me to stop my tears. I was very young and I don't remember much about it. But... I've kept it ever since... as a lucky charm.'

'Seems it's still bringing you luck. Guiding you,' Giacomo said.

'Or confusing me... Do we really believe in that stuff, Jack?'

'To say we do might be considered crazy. But to say we don't might be crazier.' With an Italian shrug of the shoulders and hands outstretched, he said, '*Chissà*? Who knows?'

She supposed she should be feeling excited about today's discoveries. But her brain was in overload with all the possibilities. How to distinguish them from red herrings? She wandered round the shop, gazing at the displays, wishing an explanation would jump out at her. *Why aren't you here, Daddy? You'd know what to do. Am I being ridiculous? Tell me if all these discoveries are links... or mere coincidences that I'm reading too much into.*

Eventually, she pointed to a pair of colourful starfish earrings that would do perfectly for a gift for Maureen.

'*Li prendo,*' she said in her best Italian. 'I'll take these.'

As the owner wrapped up her gift, spending time over creating an elaborate bow, he mentioned casually, 'Signorina, I am sure this lady will be fascinated to know that one of her pieces of art landed up in England. She loves to communicate with her fans. Why don't you get in touch with her?'

Susannah and Giacomo looked at each other as the owner sorted through a pile of cards on the counter, before handing Susannah one.

'There is an email address on the back. Let me know how you get on if you decide to contact her, signorina.'

'It is going to the top of my list of things to do,' she said, as they left the shop. '*Buonasera e grazie,* signore.'

CHAPTER 32

PUGLIA, LATE FEBRUARY 1947

Billy jumped down from the overnight bus in the main piazza of Monte Sant'Angelo. The other passengers were mostly pilgrims, destined to visit the underground sanctuary of St Michael the Archangel. He was over ten miles from Antonella's *trullo*, and after purchasing a few provisions from the grocer in the square, he was happy to walk the rest of the way. It would buy time to prepare for his arrival and what to say to her. He thought of it as a homecoming but he was unsure of the reception he would receive.

Back in 1943, when they'd all been issued on their arrival at Foggia base with *A Soldier's Guide to Italy*, he'd read the pamphlet that warned them about venereal disease and the 'warm-looking attractive women in Italy'. There were no pages dedicated to advice about how to apologise to a warm-looking attractive Italian woman to whom you'd made empty promises.

As he descended the mountain it was the colours – the blue-jade of the sea merging with the brilliant azure of the sky – that captured his attention, and the shimmering silver-grey leaves of olive trees stretching for kilometres down the slopes, like a silk cloth spread over the land. It was all so different from the granite-grey sea off Hastings. It had taken him months to save money for this journey back, doing any jobs he could snatch in Eastbourne and other coastal towns far enough away from Hastings: washing dishes in cafés, gardening, labouring on building sites. He'd bought a foot-passenger ferry ticket to Calais and managed to hitch most of the way over Europe, sometimes having to wait days for a truck driver to agree to let him travel in the cab.

Even though it was late February the sun was warm enough to stuff his raincoat into his knapsack and roll up his shirtsleeves to relish warmth once more on his skin. An early bee buzzed sleepily on a tall clump of yellow helenium at the side of the road. He stopped for a moment to drink in the view, lighting a cigarette from what he hoped might be his last tin of Capstan Navy Cut. That is, if he was allowed to stay. An old man approached from the other side of the road, leading a donkey laden with a basket of geese. They stretched their long necks towards Billy and honked angrily. The old man nodded as they crossed by and Billy exchanged a smile. Already it felt good to be back. There was no denying his Italian roots. In England, his dark looks and complexion had invariably been treated with suspicion, but it was easier to merge in here. As he walked on, it was as if each step left Billy behind and the old Roberto returned to occupy his head. He was Roberto here. Roberto Bruni.

He kept up a steady pace, stopping to sit and lean his back against a shrine at midday to eat his slice of cheese and crusty *pugliese* bread. He drank fresh water from a spring and lit up again after his simple meal, drawing nicotine deep into his lungs. Only three more kilometres and he would be with Antonella again. He began to feel nervous.

The shutters at the kitchen window of the *trullo* were closed, the door secured with a padlock. It was eerily quiet. He wandered round the back and immediately there was a squawking from two scrawny chickens. The gate to their run was open, the water bowl empty and shells of broken eggs lay here and there. A couple of dead birds lay on their sides, their feathers ruffling slightly in the breeze. Spinach and fennel gone to seed in the vegetable garden was all that was left to show from the work he and Antonella had put in. The hens needed corn but that was stored in the smaller *trullo*, also padlocked.

'Anto!' he called, although it was obvious to him she was not here. No way would she have left her hens to fend for themselves unless she was desperate. The only response was the sigh of olive branches in the breeze, fallen, wizened fruit littered round the bases, lying where they had dropped.

Something bad had happened. With mounting fear, he strode down the track to the beach. Maybe Anto was sheltering in the *trabucco*, within the little hut on the fishing platform. She loved the sea, had told him how she didn't realise quite how much she had missed it until she and Nonno had left Foggia for the final time. There was no way she would have returned to the city. Or was there? Had something happened to her aunt? Had she travelled back to the city to help look after her young cousins? It would be typical of her – the way she thought of others before she thought of herself. He imagined how terrified she would be of bumping into that bastard policeman again.

The *trabucco* was deserted too. The door to the hut was banging in the sea breeze, the catch sheared off. He would repair that, but not now. Now he had to concentrate, remain calm and work out where Antonella could be.

Maybe she had left him a note. He'd taught her how to write simple words, and he had promised to come back after all. He hurried back to the *trullo*. The chickens flocked towards him in a panic of feathers, squawking round his feet, pecking at his boots. He found a stout stick and wrenched open the flimsy padlock to the smaller *trullo*. He filled a small bucket with corn and went to scatter dried yellow grains for the hens, and they clucked in glee, scratching at the ground, pecking hungrily to search for more.

The padlock on the main *trullo* was sturdier and he fetched Nonno's screwdriver from the small *trullo* to unscrew the door handle to release the chain. A dirty cup and plate sitting in the stone sink told him that Antonella, normally neat and tidy, must have left in a hurry. Where the devil was she? What had happened to cause her to leave?

And then it came to him: she might be in her special place – the cavern above the grotto. For some reason she was camping there. He remembered noting the ledge she and her brother had used as a bed, and the cooking utensils. Yes, she had to be there.

His feet flew over the scrubby grass on the clifftop. A single boar scuttled from behind a juniper bush and he stood stock-still for a few moments, staring out the animal. Eventually it turned tail, grunting as it fled. As he drew nearer the edge of the cliff, he lost his bearings for a few seconds. Everywhere looked the same, the edges lined with prickly pear cacti in a natural barrier.

'Anto. *Dove sei?* Where are you?' he yelled, scrutinising the landscape, searching for a telltale spiral of woodsmoke emitting from the cliff surface.

Nothing.

'Anto! It's me. *Sono* Roberto,' he yelled again. Still nothing, save for the startled two-note crow of a cock pheasant as it flew for cover, and the crashing of waves against the rocks below.

Pushing through the nearest clump of cacti plants, he nearly fell down the concealed path to the cavern entrance, grabbing hold of the crude railing at the last minute. There was no sign of life down here. He bent to touch the ashes within the circle of stones. Cold. There was no blanket extended on the sleeping shelf. Nobody had camped in here recently. He moved to the edge from where he and Anto had jumped all that time ago and as his gaze fell towards the sea, he noticed dried bloodstains in the dirt by his feet and his heart stopped still.

Roberto hurried along the couple of kilometres to La Masseria, hoping Fortunata might be able to fill him in with any goings-on. It was his last option. He doubted very much Antonella had returned to Foggia and he hoped not to have to travel there himself. Finding her in a big city would be a task and a half.

There were no vehicles parked outside the old farmhouse. A cockerel and a handful of chickens, far healthier than the hens back at the *trullo*, scratched in the grass outside the main entrance. From inside he could hear the lusty cries of a baby and despite hammering on the door, nobody came to answer.

He made his way across the paved courtyard to the kitchen, from where the crying came. Fortunata was bent over Eva, coaxing a baby to suckle from her daughter's breast and he knocked on the door to announce his presence.

Fortunata looked up. 'Roberto? Is it really you?' she cried and immediately hurried over to envelop him in her plump embrace. 'Where have you been all this time? *Vieni, vieni*,' she said, encouraging him to enter. She pulled a chair from the table and hollered to Antonella to hurry and come to see who had turned up.

'So, she's here,' he said.

'Yes, she's here. And right miserable she has been since you disappeared. She doesn't say as much, but you can read it from her body. She has lost her spark, *povera fanciulla*.'

He was shocked by Antonella's appearance when she sidled into the kitchen. It had been coming on for eight months months since he'd seen her. The bloom on her face had gone. There were dark shadows under her eyes and she had lost weight. She reminded him of a startled animal frozen in headlights, not knowing in which direction to bolt.

'Anto,' he said, approaching her, his hands outstretched in welcome. He watched in dismay as she visibly shrank into her body, her shoulders slumping, her eyes downcast. A tear trickled down her face and she swatted it away as if it were an annoying insect.

'Go and take a walk, you two,' Fortunata said. 'And when you come back, we shall sit in the kitchen and eat together. There are no guests today. We shall celebrate Roberto's return.'

He gave silent thanks for Fortunata's sympathetic reading of the situation as Anto hurried slightly ahead of him through the olive groves. Each time he drew nearer, she increased her pace.

'Anto, slow down. I know you're angry with me, but please let's talk.'

She stopped and turned. 'Why did you come back, Roberto?'

'Why do you think?'

'I don't know what to think.'

They continued to the empty beach and she perched on a rock at the very edge of the water, her back to him. The only way he could see her face was to roll up his trousers and paddle round in the shallows to stand opposite her.

'You're sulking, Anto. But can't you see I had to go back to England? To sort things out.'

'And why are you back here now? Was there an English-woman there who didn't want you anymore?'

'Actually, that is exactly what happened. She wanted me gone. There is little love lost between us. And she doesn't want anybody to know I am still alive.'

'So, I'm second best, am I? If you can't have her, then I will do.'

He sighed. 'That's not how it is at all, Anto. How do you know what is going on in my mind?'

'Any woman in her right mind would come to that conclusion.'

A huge wave washed ashore, causing him to lose his balance and fall back in the rolling shallows.

Antonella smothered a giggle from behind her hands and he was pleased to see something of her old spirit. He splashed her and she squealed. One splash developed into another and before long they were both drenched.

How she ended up in his arms, he couldn't remember, but she responded to his kiss before pushing him away, her breathing as heavy as the desire he felt.

They sat together on the sand for a few moments, a small distance between them. She was the first to speak.

'I truly believed you wouldn't return.'

'I can understand why you are so upset. In all honesty I didn't think I would be able to return.' When she turned to him, hurt in her eyes, he quickly added, 'Not because I didn't want to, Anto. It was so hard to leave you last August.' He fiddled with a couple of stones from the beach, tumbling them round and round in his hand. 'There is so much to talk about. I don't know where to begin.'

They were both soaked through. Antonella began to shiver and he pulled her to her feet.

'Let's go back and get you out of those wet clothes,' he said.

She let go of his hands and once again moved ahead of him up the path, distancing herself, saying to him over her shoulder, 'Let us see what you have to talk to me about, before anything else happens between us, Roberto.'

He knew then that he would have to work hard to win her over, make her believe she could trust in him. He would be the same if the shoe was on the other foot. It would have to be a slow and honest courtship to win Antonella. And, God knew, he wanted her. How he was going to tell her about his son was going to turn this courtship into a minefield. And he wasn't sure how he was going to walk it.

When they entered the kitchen, there was much wringing

of hands at the sight of their wet clothes. Fortunata dragged them both over to the stove where pans of boiling water waited to receive pasta for the midday meal.

'Warm yourselves while I find dry clothes for Roberto. My husband was roughly the same height – but not the same width.' She laughed. 'He loved my cooking too much.'

She called for Maria to take Antonella to find a dry dress and to fetch trousers and a shirt from the chest at the end of her bed, interspersing her instructions with comments about the state of the pair of them. 'How did you both get so wet? Did you fall in? Who rescued who? What were you thinking of? You might have caught your deaths, you silly pair. You wouldn't see me go into the sea unless it was the middle of August, and then only up to my ankles. You're like *bambini*, you two. *Alla Madonna e tutti i santi...*' This last invocation was followed by a steady stream of other saints' names and she finished up by making the sign of the cross against her huge bosom with a ladle that she then proceeded to use to stir up sauce in a copper pan. 'Today we have *sugo* made from the hare we eventually caught in the vegetable garden. He was eating all my greens, the rascal. Well, at least I know he's been fed with good produce, *Madonna buona...*'

It was fortunate for the pair of them that they couldn't get a word in edgeways and there was no opportunity to explain why or how they had ended up in the sea and in each other's arms. Roberto concentrated on securing Fortunata's husband's wide corduroy trousers with string and rolling up the flapping shirt-sleeves and he was pleased to see a smile on Anto's face at his appearance. He told himself if it made her happy, he would dress like this for the rest of his life.

There was no space for self-consciousness as they sat round the kitchen table and Roberto felt he was part of a family. Fortunata had placed him and Anto at opposite ends of the table and he watched as colour seeped back to her cheeks. At one stage she took Eva's baby in her arms to let her eat her pasta in peace and when the child began to whimper, she stood up, rocking the baby to sleep like a natural as she paced the kitchen floor. Watching her, he felt a pang of regret about his own son back in Hastings but Elsie had made it abundantly clear he was never to be part of that family picture. Maybe one day when Frank was older, he would be able to explain how he had not wanted to abandon him. In the meantime, regular letters would hopefully link him to his son.

At the end of the meal, when Anto rose to help clear the dishes, Fortunata stopped her. 'Take the rest of the day off, *ragazza*. I'm sure you two have a lot to catch up on. Leave the clearing up to us. *Andate*. Shoo! And we'll see you later.'

Maria piped up with a laugh. 'Maybe I should be a chaperone? We already have one unexpected baby in this house.'

Anto glared at her. 'No need for a chaperone. We are just friends. Aren't we, Roberto?'

Fortunata gave him an old-fashioned look when he replied with, 'Si! The *best* of friends.'

They wandered into the olive grove. The sun played through the leaves and they sat opposite each other, leaning against the thick trunks of two twisted trees.

'Where do you want me to stay now I'm back, Anto?'

'Not here. The signora has given me your old storeroom to sleep in.'

'Would it help if I stayed in the small *trullo* where I used to sleep? I could tend to the hens, dig over the vegetable patch for you and carry out repairs. Why did you leave your *trullo* anyway?'

There was a moment's hesitation before she answered. 'It was too lonely on my own. Too many memories. Whenever I passed by where we buried Nonno, I was upset. It made sense to stay here at the *masseria* where there's work and company.'

'What if we went back to like it was before? I could sleep in the small *trullo*, and you could sleep where you always did. I could provide company.'

She pulled at tufts of grass at her side before she looked up at him. 'I'm not ready to return.'

'Does that mean you might return one day?'

A shrug of her shoulders and she was back on her feet. 'Who knows, Roberto? Shall we walk to the sea?'

'As long as you don't push me in again.'

'I never...' she started to say and then stopped when he laughed.

A couple of fishermen were mending nets on the beach below the *masseria* and at the far end of the bay, a new small *trabucco* sat near the rocks. Shading his eyes with his hand, Roberto made out busy figures of men pulling on the square net, gulls wheeling above, waiting to steal from their catch.

'Nonno's *trabucco* will need tending to,' he said. 'I can work on that and see if the net needs repairing. Maybe we could take a picnic there on your next day off.'

'Maybe,' she said.

She walked away from him along the sea's edge, stooping every now and then to pick up a shell or a piece of sea glass and he let her be. *Softly, softly, catchee monkey,* he told himself. It was not that he wanted to catch her. That was not his way. If she came to him, it must be because she wanted to. At the moment, from the signals she was giving out, he was not sure it would happen. Instinct told him he should not crowd her. She was more fragile than she made out. He needed, above all, to be very patient. Anto had endured hardship and violence at the hands of an evil man. He thought back to the day she had told him about Salvatore raping her – just before his memory started to come back and he had to return to England. Such bad timing. Why did life put obstacles along the way at the wrong moments? He sighed and lay back on the sand. He'd drunk a couple of glasses of wine with Fortunata's excellent pasta, followed by a large portion of succulent roast hare and, with the sounds of gulls and the washing of the tide lulling him, he closed his eyes against the glare of the overhead sun and within seconds, he was fast asleep.

When he opened his eyes, the sun had slipped to the horizon and a breeze ruffled the sea with lacy breakers. He was alone on the beach. He stood up, brushing sand from his clothes and hair and, picking up his jacket, he trudged up the path back to the *masseria*, cursing himself as he walked. A fine start he'd made of wooing the girl, falling asleep like that. Not the best strategy for romance.

Fortunata was in the kitchen, her hands busy with knitting. She looked up when he came in. 'There's coffee in the pot if you want, Roberto?' she said. 'Did you have a lovers' tiff? Antonella came in a couple of hours ago and went straight to her room. I've put her where you used to sleep, you know.'

'*Grazie*, Fortunata. She told me. No, we haven't quarrelled. I fell asleep on the beach.' He added wryly, 'And we are not lovers.'

'*Madonna Santa.* Falling asleep in a girl's company after months of separation is absolutely not the way to her heart.' She roared with laughter. 'Pour me a coffee too while you're at it.' She pointed to a shelf of bottles. 'And fetch down the Kümmel. It soothes my stomach after a meal.'

The liqueur was strong, and flavoured with cumin seeds. Roberto knocked it back in one. It went well as a chaser to the strong, black coffee.

'Anto told me you went back to Inghilterra. Did you find out what you needed? I always thought you weren't properly Italian,' Fortunata said, her needles clacking as she talked.

'There is nothing left for me there. My mother passed away from illness two years ago and my father was killed by an unexploded bomb.'

'*Mi dispiace, figlio mio,*' she said, the needles stopping between stitches. 'Poor boy. And is there no *fidanzata*?'

'No,' he replied. 'No girl to stay for.' He wasn't ready to explain details of his hurried marriage to a girl he hadn't loved – that he was also the father of a son his wife didn't want him to have contact with. That to all intents and purposes he was dead. He hadn't even talked to Anto about all this yet. He needed to pick the right moment.

'So, you are planning to make your life here in Puglia?'

'Yes, Fortunata. That is my plan. Whether it works out is another thing.'

She placed her cup firmly on the saucer. 'I didn't take you for a defeatist, young man. The best way to make your future is to create it. If life is too easy, if everything drops into your lap, then it's usually not worth holding on to. *Su. Coraggio!*' She waggled a plump finger at him. 'There are two mistakes in life: not beginning something you want to do and not striving until the end.'

Fortunata was right. He knew that.

She continued knitting as she told him, 'I think Antonella is waiting for you, to be part of your plan. She just doesn't realise at the moment.'

CHAPTER 33

It took Roberto long hours to carry out the tasks he'd set himself at the *trulli*. He put his back into weeding the vegetable garden and preparing the soil for spring planting. Someday very soon he would go to the market in Mattinata or Monte Sant'Angelo and buy tomato plants, radishes and maybe a few salad seedlings. The weather here was milder than in England and there was no need for bringing seedlings on in a glasshouse. He needed more hens too and oil for the pulleys on the fishing plat-form. Every night he fell asleep wishing Anto was in her *trullo* across the way and every morning over coffee and a hunk of bread he missed her presence. Before his memory had returned to him like a bad apple, they had been getting on so well: sharing breakfasts at the table in the yard, helping each other with domestic tasks. He'd enjoyed listening to her as she went about her chores – scattering corn for the hens or sweeping the kitchen, singing while she worked. They'd hauled in fish together and swum to the grotto towards the setting sun. He wanted to be at her side again. But would she want *him* after he revealed he was married and father of a baby boy?

Ten days later, she turned up at the *trulli*, leading the goat on the end of a thick rope. He heard her coaxing the animal before he saw her, cajoling it to walk on. '*Cammina, dai, cammina!*' Her kitten Birba running at her side was bigger than the last time Billy had seen her.

He walked towards her and she smiled shyly. 'Fortunata doesn't want the goat about the place anymore. She eats her roses and baby Livio doesn't need the milk. I thought I'd better bring her home.'

She tied the goat to the ring on the side of the *trullo* and looked about the place. 'You've been busy.'

'I've enjoyed it and it has given me time to settle. But I need to make a trip to town soon for tools and corn. Perhaps you would come with me?'

'If you walk over to the *masseria* tomorrow, you can hitch a lift on Fortunata's cart. She goes every Wednesday to Mattinata for provisions.'

She looked in the vegetable garden before leaving, and inspected what he had done, nodding her satisfaction at the tidy patch and he thought afterwards that maybe returning the goat was an excuse and she had turned up to see if he was still around. After all, he had disappeared before.

That night as he lay waiting for sleep, his head was full of Anto: how beautiful she had looked when she'd turned up out of the blue, her hair grown long enough to tie back from her face, no longer the skinny young lad he had thought her to be when he'd landed in this place. He had a plan up his sleeve. This morning she had been slightly easier in his company, obviously more relaxed on her own territory. She was still wary of him but there had been one or two moments when it almost felt like before. They'd shared a mid-morning snack and she had taken over in her kitchen, slicing fresh bread and soft buffalo mozzarella she'd brought with her from Fortunata, fetching sprigs of basil from the old sink by the door and chopping the leaves to sprinkle on top. This, with a handful of bottled olives she'd pulled from a shelf in the *trullo*, completed their simple meal, washed down with spring water. It was chillier that day and they'd eaten inside and he'd lit a fire in the hearth. She'd tutted at the dust everywhere and he'd told her to ignore it.

'Dust will always be there, but time will not. Relax, Anto! I bet they keep you busy at the *masseria*. Breathe a little.'

She'd smiled a thanks and leant back in her chair. 'The signora is very good to me but, yes, you're right. I am never completely at my ease at the *masseria*.' She looked at him. 'There is no place like your own home.'

He'd been encouraged and so he had it in his mind to prepare her a special treat. 'Next time you come to visit, it will be my turn to prepare a simple meal for you, Anto.'

She nodded. '*Grazie*. My free day is always Tuesday.'

He was not to be alone with her until then. From the moment he arrived on the following morning at the *masseria*, he was swept up into Fortunata's kingdom as she ordered him about, telling him to sit next to her at the front of the cart. 'People will think I have a young lover,' she said with an impish grin as she urged the horse on with a click of the reins. 'Let's get chins wagging in Mattinata.'

And in town, she had him scurrying here and there to fetch items and lift shopping onto the back of the cart. Antonella was dispatched to the chemist to buy medicine and cotton nappies for baby Livio and when they stopped for a coffee at the bar in the piazza, Fortunata made Roberto sit next to her while Antonella sat opposite. When all her shopping was finished and stored safely on the back of the cart, he was given twenty minutes to buy items he needed at the hardware shop while the signora and Antonella went to look round the stalls for dress material. It was as if Signora Fortunata was deliberately keeping them apart. On the way home, he was ordered to drive the cart back and he needed all his powers of concentration to listen to her instructions and to steer the cart, never having done it in his previous life.

'Unless you are rich enough to own a motor car, then you will need to learn how to control a horse and cart,' she'd told him, adding, 'especially as you've told me you intend to stay here in Puglia, *figlio mio*. How else will you manage your errands?'

The weather could not have been kinder for the special day he had planned for Antonella, the sky the blue of a child's painting, the sea calm, massaging the shore. He had bought a bottle of sparkling white Malvasia wine to go with the shellfish pasta dish he had asked Fortunata to secretly prepare. She'd slipped a light almond cake wrapped in a cloth into his hands and told him it was Antonella's favourite. The day before, he had decorated the cavern at the top of the grotto, her favourite place she'd told him. He'd cut candles to fit in empty jam jars to dot around natural shelves in the niches and picked armfuls of spring flowers to decorate the space. Early that morning, he had carried the food over to the cavern and laid a fire, collecting sticks and small branches from the clifftops. He would light it when they arrived. The stage was set and he couldn't wait to see her face when he revealed how he had arranged her favourite place.

The day would begin with freshly ground coffee and Fortunata's almond cake. He hunted for a clean cloth to throw over the table outside the *trullo*, adding another bunch of wild flowers he had picked, shoving them in a pitcher, knowing that Anto would have arranged them better. But it was the thought that counted, he told himself.

She was wearing a dress he'd not seen before. The pale pink suited her, making her hair seem darker, her skin softer. She smiled shyly at him when he pulled out the chair for her to sit down.

'*Grazie*, Roberto.' She fingered the tablecloth. 'Nonna made this cloth. It's good to see it again.' She nodded with approval as he carried out the cake and a tray holding two cups and a Moka pot of steaming coffee.

'It's like going to a bar,' she said.

'This is only the beginning, Anto.' He poured coffee and handed her a cup. He hoped his words didn't sound corny. For his part, he truly hoped they could begin again. All of a sudden, he felt tongue-tied. But he forced himself to continue, stuttering a little as he started.

'I never told you what happened when I returned to England,' he said as he sat down.

'I probably didn't give you the chance. Tell me now.' She picked up the knife to cut two slices of cake.

He drew a huge breath and dived in. 'When my memory came back, I realised I was a married man.'

She reacted just as he feared. The knife clattered from her hands onto the plate and she slumped back in her chair.

'In one sense I am not surprised, Roberto,' she said, her voice low. 'It was always in the back of my mind and I prepared myself for this, but as you said nothing about a wife when you returned, I began to hope...'

She rose from her seat. 'I must go...'

'Please don't go, Anto. Please listen to what I have to say.'

'What is the point?'

'For me there is every point. First of all, the woman I married has told me it is better if I do not exist. She has a new life. She believed I was dead and she prefers it to remain that way. She was shocked when I turned up. And... I never loved her anyway, Anto...'

'Then why did you marry her?'

'Because of the oldest reason in the world. She was pregnant. Carrying my child.' He paused before adding, 'I am a father too.'

There. He had told her everything. It was out in the open. This was when she would storm off and he would lose her for good.

But she sat down again, her eyes flashing as she leant forwards to speak.

'You men,' she said. 'You say you never loved your wife. Then why is she pregnant?'

'I'm not proud of it.'

She sighed. 'It means nothing to you men, does it?'

'The war—' he began and she interrupted.

'Do not blame it on the war, Roberto. The war is not the reason why men take women to bed, but it is always the women who pay for the consequences. It is *always* the women and the babies they bear who suffer.'

'It isn't easy for me to know I have a son whom I shall not see grow up, Anto. Believe me.'

'And so why does she not want you anymore? What did you do to make her feel that way?'

'She found a man who is richer than I can ever be. A rich man – a surgeon who can provide her with a lifestyle that I never could. And she didn't want me to take that away from her.'

She paused. 'When two people love each other, money shouldn't count. So, she didn't love you either.'

'I was going to finish with her anyway and then she told me she was pregnant. So, I stood by her. We married in haste and I went back to war the next day. My plane crashed. Nonno found me and you know the rest.'

'*Madonna*! What a mess. *Che pasticcio*.'

'It needn't be a mess, Anto. I didn't love Elsie.' He got up, moved away from the table raking his hands through his hair.

'This is not happening how I wanted it to: it's not the way I wanted to explain how I feel about you.'

'And how do you feel?'

He turned to face her. 'I love you. You must know that already. I want to be with you for the rest of our lives. I want to look after you. I came back to see if we could make a life together, but I feared it might not happen.'

'I have always believed that for two people to truly love each other, there has to be trust. Why didn't you tell me all this as soon as you returned? It makes me ask myself what else you are hiding.'

'There wasn't the opportunity to talk to you alone. You know what it's like with Fortunata. It's impossible to get a word in edgeways.'

'We went to the sea together. You could have told me then.'

'You are right. I could have. But... I was so happy to be with you again... and I was scared of losing you.'

There was a long silence. He watched her, the breeze ruffling strands of hair around her face in a soft frame.

'I am not yours to lose,' she said eventually.

She stayed in her chair, giving him a strand of hope to continue.

'Anto. Can we start again perhaps?'

Another silence. A silence filled with the sound of a hen laying an egg over in the coop, birds singing, a breeze stirring the branches on the olive trees, ordinary sounds that replaced the words he found so hard to muster.

'So, what name do you go by in Inghilterra?' Anto asked. 'Is it Billy?'

'I was christened in England as William Pica. Do you remember the tag Nonno removed from round my neck? But I have always been known as Billy. Born to an English mother and a Sicilian father who emigrated to England to find a better life. That is why I speak Italian.'

'So should I call you Billy now?'

'Billy is someone from the past, Anto, whom even I do not recognise now. I would like to be known as Roberto.'

Another silence.

'Is there any hot coffee left?' she asked, lifting her cup and popping another morsel of cake into her mouth.

He felt his shoulders relax and the breath he hadn't realised he'd been holding slowly release as he picked up the Moka pot. 'I'll brew some fresh. This has gone cold.'

When he came outside, she was no longer at the table. She'd wandered over to feed the hens, talking to them as she scattered corn. As she walked back to him, she wiped her hands down her dress before taking a cup of fresh coffee from the tray. The breeze stirred, scattering blossom from the almond trees and some of it settled on her hair, like wedding confetti.

'If you'd like to,' he said, 'I thought we could take a walk later. I have a surprise meal prepared for you.'

'Yes. I'd like that.'

Instead of rushing ahead of him, this time they walked abreast. She was full of questions concerning his life back in England and he filled her in about his parents' popular restaurant built up from nothing, about his time in the RAF and how he and Elsie had walked out together since they were teenagers.

'But once I joined up and left Hastings, I quickly realised we weren't meant for each other. We were very different from the children we'd been.'

'I'm sorry about your parents,' she said. 'We have both lost our families. Sometimes I dream that my mother is brushing my hair by the fireside and it breaks my heart when I wake up and she's not there. But to know you have a son who is alive and you cannot share... that will be painful for you.'

'I intend to write to him.'

'Won't it be confusing for him? To have two fathers?'

'That's what his mother said. So, what would you do if you were in my shoes?'

'I'm not sure. He won't be able to read your letters for a long time. I think you have to hope his mother – Elsa, is it? – that she will explain to him one day when he is older.'

'She's called Elsie. Who knows what she will decide to do? I rather think she will keep him in the dark. Why would she want to upset her comfortable life and tarnish her reputation?'

'Are you intending to write these letters for your son – or for yourself? To ease your conscience.'

He stopped in his tracks. 'It was not my intention to abandon him. My conscience is very clear, Anto. I did not lose my memory on purpose. I went back to England to take up my role as a husband and father – even though I didn't love Elsie. Do you think so little of me?'

She touched his arm. 'Forgive me. There is so much to understand about each other. And... I *do* want to understand, Roberto.'

They walked on in silence. In the olive grove, she stopped to examine the branches, the first shoots of new growth appearing.

'These were not pruned last autumn. We will have to make sure it's done this year,' she said.

Roberto was confused. One moment, she talked of the future, seeming to include him by using the word 'we', and yet she was still distant with him. It was complicated. But he wasn't going to give up.

CHAPTER 34

'So now is when I blindfold you and we embark on our mystery,' Roberto told her, pulling out a neckerchief from his pocket.

Antonella laughed. 'What are you up to?'

'If I told you, it wouldn't be a mystery. Trust in me. I'll guide you.'

When he was sure she could not peek from the blindfold, he hooked his arm through hers and led her along the clifftop. She stumbled once and he drew her closer and he noted that she didn't complain or pull away, just giggled. 'If I break a leg, then you will have to do my chores for Signora Fortunata,' she told him.

'Don't worry, Anto. I'll make sure that does not happen.' He breathed in her scent of lavender, rosemary, the salty sea, her body warm against his side.

'I can hear the waves,' she said. 'You're not going to push me over the cliff, are you? Maybe you're a murderer. How would I know any different?'

He chuckled. 'Me after your vast sums of money?' He made a mock growl and she laughed.

'You do not scare me one little bit, signore. Seriously, where are you taking me?'

'Two more minutes and we shall be there. I want you to sit quietly and wait for a couple of minutes while I do some finishing touches. Promise me you won't peek and spoil my surprise?'

'I promise. But you're quite crazy.'

Inside the cavern, he lit the candles in their jars and uncovered the food on the stone ledge, before setting a match to the laid fire. The place looked cosy, he thought. Romantic even, and he hoped she would like what he had done.

'For the last stretch I shall have to hold on to you tightly,' he said, panting slightly after the climb back up from the cavern.

She was sitting on the grass, plucking at the blades. 'I was beginning to think you'd abandoned me. One more minute and I'd have tossed the blindfold away,' she scolded.

At the entrance to the cavern above the grotto, he turned and took both her hands in his and guided her carefully down the slope. At the last minute, she gave a little shriek and uttered a *no* before slithering into his arms. It was all he could do to not kiss her.

He'd noted the change in her as soon as the cool air of the cavern hit them.

'Roberto,' she said, 'where have you brought me? I...' She tugged off the blindfold and put both hands to her mouth and, with dismay, Roberto saw her horror straight away.

'*Dio buono,*' she muttered, turning to scrabble her way on all fours, up and out of the cavern.

'Anto. Where are you going? Whatever is the matter?'

When he emerged on the clifftop she was already far ahead, running as fast as he had ever seen her. He gave chase, calling to her to stop. 'What is wrong, Anto? What have I done?'

But she didn't answer. She continued to pelt across the scrubby grass, through the olive groves and across the *trullo* yard. He caught up with her as she fumbled with the bolts but she slammed the door in his face and refused to let him in.

For almost one hour, he sat outside the *trullo*, his back against the door, wondering what he had done to cause such panic. He'd believed the cave was her favourite place in the whole world. When she emerged, her face was pale, her eyes still wide with alarm.

'What did I do to upset you so badly?' he asked. 'Please let me help you, Anto. You told me we should trust each other. Can you not find it in your heart to tell me?'

'I did something dreadful,' she said, standing opposite the table where he now sat – where they had shared coffee and cake earlier that day.

'Talk to me, Anto. You listened to me and by listening you helped me. Tell me what was so dreadful, Anto,' he urged.

She fiddled with the material on her skirt and when she started to talk, she avoided his eyes.

'While you were away, I committed a terrible crime and every day I wonder if somebody will find out...'

She clammed up and he waited patiently.

'I was completely alone. When a motorbike came down the track, I thought it was your English friend come to bring news of you.'

She looked up when she told him this. 'I missed you when you were gone, Roberto.'

Hearing her say those words gave him hope. It was the first time she had expressed feelings for him, but the tenderness in his heart was replaced with anger when she revealed what had occurred.

'It was Salvatore. The *carabiniere* from Foggia. I told you about him.'

He stood up. 'What happened, Anto? What did he do to you?' His hands balled into fists as he moved closer.

'He didn't do anything this time. I ran away. But...'

'What? What happened? For Christ's sake, Anto. What happened?'

Her head bowed, she told him about the horrific episode in the cave. How she had tried to hide from Salvatore, but he had found her. How he plunged into the sea when he attempted to grab her and she had done nothing to save him when he fell.

'And each day I think his body will float ashore and the *carabinieri* will work out it is him because he's been missing for so long and then they'll find out I was his killer.'

He took her hands in his. She was shaking. 'You did *not* kill him, Anto. He fell. He was going to attack you. You didn't lay a finger on him. He drowned.'

'But I didn't jump in afterwards to save him. He shouted that he couldn't swim. I stayed where I was and watched him sink...'

'Nobody would be expected to save a man who was intent on doing them harm. You did *nothing* wrong, Anto. I *promise* you.'

A hand to his head, he apologised. 'And me with my big feet, I took you back to the place you least wanted to be. I am so, so sorry, Anto. For not being here for you.'

'How were you to know he would come and find me?'

She was still shivering violently and he suggested he made up the fire inside the *trullo*.

'And while you stoke it, I'll fetch the candles and supper. Get warm and we'll eat our meal here.'

Neither of them had much appetite for Fortunata's rich fish pasta, but he opened a bottle of wine and they sipped it by the fire. Antonella was quiet, staring into the flames and he let her be, hoping that his presence, rather than words, would comfort her. The silence was filled with the crackle and snap of twigs burning and slowly, colour returned to her cheeks.

'I don't think I can ever go back to my grotto,' she said.

'We can find another place to swim, Anto. You don't need to return to that place.'

'I haven't been in the sea since that day. Only in my dreams do I swim. But before I wake, I'm always hampered by weeds and when I tear them from my face, his face looms before me and his eyes are open and staring. And when he floats nearer, there are holes in his head and his mouth is open and he has no teeth and a sea snake slithers out from between his swollen blue lips...'

He took hold of her hands. 'Let me stay in the *trullo* tonight with you, Anto. I'll take Nonno's bed.' He topped up her wine. 'And tomorrow we will start afresh.'

'*Grazie*, Roberto.' She sank back as if the fear that had kept her going until this point was slowly seeping from her.

In the middle of the night, he stirred as Anto slipped into his bed and he moved to make room for her. She curled up, her back to his chest and he pulled her close, his arms around her waist, spooning her with his body. Before too long she was asleep, her breathing even and deep.

He was alone when he woke next morning. Only the dent where her head had been on the pillow and a strand of dark hair showed that she had shared his bed. The door was ajar and he could hear her talking to the hens outside as they clucked and he lay there for a couple more minutes, listening as he came to.

'Lazybones,' she said, pushing the door wide. 'If you get up now, I'll prepare a *frittata* for breakfast. The hens are pleased I've returned. There were four warm eggs to greet me this morning. And one with a double yolk, I'm sure.'

He stretched and yawned. 'And if you were a really good person, you'd brew me a strong coffee to go with the eggs.'

'Now that would be going a step too far. I don't want to be spoiling you, do I?'

A blue sky heralded warmer weather for later, but for now

it was crisp cold. After breakfast inside, they chatted. 'Signora Fortunata will be sacking me if I don't return today,' she said.

'I think she will forgive you this one morning off,' he said. 'She told me you haven't been happy for a while. She's a mother of two daughters and I think you're almost like her third. I'll walk you back later.'

'What are your plans, Roberto? Are you returning to England?'

'There's nothing for me there now. And...' He stopped. Roberto wanted to tell her again that he loved her. Why would he want to go back to England? But she was distant again this morning. He was terrified of losing her before he had even begun. He was at a loss as to how to proceed. He'd been a gunner in the back of a Liberator, for Christ's sake, where he'd known exactly what to do, but this? Knowing what to say to the woman you loved. He did not know how to navigate this one. He'd read somewhere that love was like the falling of dominos. How many dominos had to fall before everything fell into place? Was love ever smooth?

'So how do you intend to get by?' she asked, distracting him from his scattered thoughts.

'Good question. Up until now there has always been some-thing: my parents' restaurant first, then the Air Force.'

'You speak English and you know about running a restau-rant. That's a start.'

'Maybe in the big cities where it's possible to capture the tourist trade, but not in this far-flung corner of Puglia.'

'Do you want your job back at the *masseria*? There's so much to be done to stop it falling down.'

'If Fortunata will have me, then as long as I can bring in enough money to manage from day to day, then that will be fine. I have no great ambitions, Anto. The war knocked that out of me. Survival, happiness, health and a degree of freedom suit me fine.'

'Then, we shall ask her this afternoon.'

He helped her clear up and then suggested a walk to the *trabucco* to see what repairs were needed.

He carried a small bag of tools as together they made their way down the path to the sea. Halfway, she stopped to gather sprigs of rosemary.

'We can catch our lunch and grill it on the beach. If we're lucky, February brings squid and red tuna,' she said.

On the *trabucco*, Roberto busied himself with securing a couple of wires that had worked loose on the net frame and after oiling the main column, they lowered the net and sat and waited on the platform, their legs dangling above the water.

'Anything extra we catch, we can take to Fortunata,' he said. 'To earn us a few lire.'

She was quiet and he saw that she was looking towards the grotto. He took hold of her hand. 'Anto, it's been months now. His body will not turn up.'

She turned to him but let her hand rest in his. 'I hope not. It's a relief to share the burden. But promise me you'll tell nobody, Roberto.'

He squeezed her hand. 'It will be our secret alone. But you need to banish it from your mind.'

'It's not easy.'

The water round the net began to bubble and swirl, the gulls swooped to poach and they were kept busy for the next half an hour retrieving the catch.

While Anto sorted the fish, shooing the birds away as she did so, Roberto made a fire from driftwood scattered about the shore. He added a simple barbecue to his list of things to build in the coming weeks. There might come a time, he thought, when living from day to day proved insufficiently stimulating, but for now he was perfectly happy to immerse himself in the rhythm of the seasons. He didn't dare to imagine Anto by his side. But that is what he hoped for.

Later, as darkness began to fall and the stars came out to silver the shallows, they ate their simple meal. The spring air grew chillier and Roberto fetched an old sail to throw over a wigwam of large, bleached driftwood branches he had assembled earlier near the fire. They moved inside to shelter from the nippy breeze.

Their view was the sea and the moon glistening on its surface. Roberto lit up, offering a cigarette to Anto and she shook her head.

'Look at that spectacle. People pay good money to go on holidays for such a view,' he said.

She wriggled nearer, shivering a little and he drew her to sit close so she was cradled between his legs. She leant back against his chest.

'I feel happier than I ever have, Roberto.'

Roberto wanted this moment to go on forever. She was warm against his body and he was waiting for the moment when she would pull away, retreat from him like she had so often, like a vixen he had once observed, circling a dead rabbit, sniffing at it, jumping back, approaching, looking round to see if this was a trap. But Antonella stayed still and it was he who moved first this time.

He dropped a kiss on the top of her head, courage pouring into his heart. 'Anto, we have to stop this tiptoeing around each other. Let's get married.'

She turned to face him. 'But you're already married. How can we?'

She wasn't saying no. He wanted to pull her into his arms and do a merry jig around the fire. She wasn't saying no... Instead, he took both her hands in his, controlling his excitement and quietly, logically, spoke to the girl he loved so much. 'The only people here who know I returned to England are Fortunata and her daughters. They don't know I'm married. All they know is my parents are gone. Think about it, Anto. How many people's lives have been torn apart by the war? Papers lost, churches and municipal records bombed or burnt? To thoroughly check everybody's documents is going to be nigh impossible. Nobody here will know I am already married. I love you. I want to marry you. And I want it to be a proper marriage, a partnership between two people who love each other. Not like the sham Elsie and I started.'

She lifted herself to her knees and wound her arms around his neck. 'If you're asking me to marry you, then I accept.'

Their kisses grew more passionate. He wanted more than anything to make love to her on the sand beneath the starry sky, but as his fingers stroked the softness between her thighs, he felt her tense up and he stopped, respecting her reaction, wanting more than anything else to protect this girl who was so much more fragile than anybody knew.

'Anto,' he murmured. 'I can wait. We shall wait until we are properly married.'

Only too aware of the damage Salvatore had done to this beautiful girl, he wanted the first time they consummated their love to be perfect.

With another kiss, Anto fastened the buttons on her blouse and smoothed her skirt down over her legs.

He pulled her to her feet and Anto picked up one of the candle jars to light their way back to the *trullo*.

She gave a little cry of joy as the beam picked out the shape of an intricate shell close to where they had sat moments ago. '*Perfetto*,' she said, picking it up and showing it to Roberto. 'And see – it has a tiny hole here that I can use to pull thread through and make a necklace. It will be a souvenir of the happiest evening I have ever spent.' She tiptoed to kiss him on the lips, her eyes glistening.

'There will be a lifetime of happy evenings, *amore mio*,' he said, his heart brimming as they made their way together up the coastal path.

CHAPTER 35

PUGLIA, APRIL 1947

Fortunata was having none of it. 'If there's to be a wedding, then we're going to celebrate it properly.'

'Please, signora, no fuss. Roberto and I want a quiet wedding.'

'Am I saying it will be a fuss? No, Antonella, I am not. But a special meal, a little music, good wine. Even if it is only us, we must mark it, *ragazza*. Are you ashamed of getting married? God in heaven and all his *angeli* know that I cannot wait forever for my two girls to find good men. Let me at least celebrate for you. I won't take no for an answer. Roberto loves my *pasta al forno* with my famous rigatoni and sausage-meat sauce. And there must be a wedding cake. What cake do you like, Antonella?'

Her girls, unknown to Antonella, had cornered Roberto when he came to scythe the back field and clean the pool of algae and they'd explained his duties for the nuptials. He was expected to arrange for Antonella's bouquet. But he was not to worry because they would make it for him. Antonella had said she liked the pale pink roses that grew over the ruins of the pigsty and they would weave her a garland of daisies and sweet-smelling fennel flowers to place on her head. And had he thought about a garter for her to remove from her thigh to throw to the guests? Because as sure as the sun rose and set every day, she wouldn't want to throw her right shoe away, as was another custom that *pugliese* brides used to follow. Not when shoes were so hard to come by after the war.

'Anto only has one pair of working boots,' Eva cut in. 'She can't wear those on her wedding day. So I'll look out a pair of my shoes. Her feet are smaller than mine and I have some that pinch my toes.'

'Don't you worry, Roberto, we'll help you with all the details,' Maria added.

Roberto had not been worrying. Not one little bit. Until they had started up their fussing and organising. But he let them carry on. If it was all going towards making the day special for Antonella, then so be it.

And Antonella let the sisters help her too. If it was making it easier for Roberto, who probably did not know about half the wedding customs and traditions on account of his having been brought up in Inghilterra, where everything was likely to be different, then anything to ease the day for him would be a great help.

The priest who married them in the chapel of Holy Maria of the Light, in the middle of a small olive grove, was newly ordained. An enlightened young man, he had fought with partisans and, post-war, was anxious to instil independent thinking in his small nucleus of parishioners. He understood not everybody, especially younger members, liked the strong hold that the church had on society and he had confided this to Roberto and Antonella when they had gone to ask permission to marry.

'We fought hard for freedom,' Fra' Francesco told them. 'And we should hold on to it with all our might.'

He was tolerant of the fact that documents were missing, understanding only too well how war had complicated people's lives, but he was keen to understand their reasons for marrying.

'Is this something decided in haste?' he asked Antonella. 'Are you pregnant?'

'No, *padre*,' she answered immediately. 'We want to marry because we love each other. Is that not so, Roberto?' She turned to him and took his hand.

'That is exactly it,' Roberto said. 'Love is the reason.'

Fra' Francesco nodded and completed the necessary paperwork. 'Then you have my blessings. Remember, "Love is patient, love is kind. It does not envy, it does not boast, it is not proud. It does not dishonour others, it is not self-seeking, it is not easily angered, it keeps no record of wrongs."' He quoted from the Holy Bible without faltering, finishing off with a question to them both. 'Do you agree with all this, my friends?'

Antonella and Roberto looked at each other and nodded.

'Then I am very happy to marry you.'

There were six of them at the wedding breakfast at the *masseria*, seven if you counted baby Livio. Fra' Francesco turned out to be an excellent dancer and after they had finished Fortunata's feast, he helped Roberto push the table to one side. The merry little group held hands and rotated clockwise before reversing direction as 'La Tarantella' blasted from a crackly record on a wind-up gramophone discovered in one of the top rooms.

Gone midnight, Antonella lifted the skirt of the dress she had sewn from the rest of the angel parachute, which had brought Roberto to her, and threw her garter in the air. Eva caught it. 'But who will possibly have me?' she wailed. 'A girl with a baby?'

'I will,' her sister Maria replied and, laughing, the two girls performed a polka round the room while everybody applauded, Fra' Francesco singing along in his fine baritone voice.

Fortunata clapped her hands for silence and made a speech, her words slurring from the third glass of home-made fennel liqueur served with the almond and orange cake decorated with mascarpone and pink sugared rose petals.

'These two good people are family to me. Some would say my family is a strange mix. Let people think what they will. This war has blown us to all corners like dandelion seeds in the wind, to plant ourselves wherever we landed. So, let's raise a glass to all the *figli* – all the lovely babies that, God willing, will be added to our beautiful family.'

'*Alla salute! Tanti figli maschi!*' rang round the kitchen and when Fortunata deliberately dropped her glass onto the tiled floor, she announced, 'As is the custom, this glass has broken into many pieces. Which means that Roberto and Antonella will have as many happy years together as the fragments in my kitchen.'

It was time to take their leave and return to the *trulli*. Fra' Francesco offered the newly-weds a lift in his dented Fiat Topolino, but they wanted to walk.

'It's not cold this evening, Padre,' Antonella said.

Fortunata wrapped a soft cream shawl around her shoulders. 'And Roberto will keep you warm, won't you, *caro*?' She winked, with difficulty, both eyes squinting, her body swaying a little as she hugged them close and kissed them soundly on their cheeks, her breath sweet from fennel liqueur.

It was a clear night, the moon a pearly crescent above the sea as they walked in silence towards the *trulli*. When an owl swooped in front of them, Anto jumped and Roberto pulled her close.

'I'm not afraid,' she said, babbling a little, 'only a little nervous on this special night. I'm used to owls – they fly above the vegetable garden to catch moths. We call them flying cats because they catch mice too. Do you find the hooting of the owl melancholy, Roberto? I want to know everything about you...'

He squeezed her hand. 'No,' he replied. 'Owls don't worry me. It's a normal night sound. Far worse is the howling of the dying. When I was being checked over in hospital in England, I slept near the burns unit.'

'You haven't told me about your time in hospital.'

'It was tedious more than anything. I've been lucky, Anto. I met men who couldn't remember a thing and who probably never will. My memory came back eventually and I didn't have to retrain it.' He stopped, bending to find her lips. 'I don't want to take anything for granted now. Having seen what war did to so many, I know I am a lucky man. The luckiest man in the world to have found you.'

'When your memory returned, I thought you wouldn't want me anymore.'

'Oh, Anto... you really don't realise how much I love you, do you?'

He kissed her gently at first and then parted her lips with his tongue, his heart racing as he felt her respond.

They were at the *trulli* now and, releasing her, he opened the door and scooped her into his arms. 'This is when I carry you over the threshold, signora.'

Inside, he closed the door behind him with one foot and carried her to the bed, lying down beside her.

'Signora,' she whispered. 'I can't get used to you saying it.'

'Will you be all right, Anto? You said you were nervous. I mean... if you don't want to—'

She stopped his words by pulling him to her. 'No more words, Signor Bruni.'

If she was being brave, if she was overcoming a dread of what was to follow on her wedding night, it didn't show. They made love as husband and wife in the dark, thin moonlight shining through the narrow window on their naked bodies.

He pulled the covers over them afterwards and held her hand until he was sure she was fast asleep, and after that he slept until the birds woke them early next morning and they slid into each other's arms to make love once again.

CHAPTER 36

PRESENT DAY

A new email popped up in Susannah's inbox, one she had been hoping for. A reply from the driftwood artist. Since moving into Giacomo's spare room, she had hung her gull talisman up next to the bed and she glanced at it before running downstairs.

Giacomo was in the kitchen, singing along to the latest Tiziano Ferro hit and he didn't hear her approach. She tapped on his shoulder and he swung round, the knife he was using to chop red peppers dangerously near her stomach.

'Woah, Susi. Don't do that to me. I'm armed...'

'Sorry, but I had to tell you straight away. There's a reply from that artist.' Her eyes were like saucers as she gabbled. 'At least, it's not actually from her, but from a Bella Bruni. *Bruni*, Jack! The same surname as the cricketer and the olive rep, the one you said was such a common name round here. Do you think there might be a connection? And she wants to meet me. In Vasto. Where is that?'

She jumped up and down like a child and he grinned, switching off the radio but continuing to remove seeds from the peppers.

'Woah! I'd love to see you on Christmas morning, opening

your presents... Vasto is further north up the coast. In light traffic it takes about an hour and a half to drive there.'

'Could I catch a bus? I only have three days left before my flight. It'll have to be tomorrow.'

'If you can wait until tomorrow afternoon, then I'll close the bar that evening.'

Her eyes shone. 'Really? Would you do that for me?'

He smiled. 'Of course, Susi.'

She flung her arms around him and for a moment as he pulled her into a hug, she thought he was going to kiss her, but then he murmured, 'I have a knife in my hand, Susi. Get in touch with that woman now and arrange everything.'

They used Giacomo's delivery van on the following afternoon. There was a light drizzle and Giacomo told her he never relied on his vintage Vespa for long trips. 'I need to make sure we get there,' he'd said.

They had trouble locating the address – a four-digit number along a busy road leading to Vasto centre. But when they eventually found the partly concealed dirt track leading towards the edge of the cliffs, the busy traffic behind them was forgotten in an oasis of palm trees and the rich purples and ruby-reds of bougainvillea. Number 1006 was a whitewashed building surrounded by walls supporting a tangle of jasmine and roses. They pressed the intercom and a woman's voice answered. 'Chi è? Who is it?'

Susannah had unaccountable butterflies in her stomach while she waited. And then, when a young woman opened the door to the seaside house, for a moment, Susannah stood stock-still. She could have been her twin. It was like looking in a mirror. They remained staring for a moment at each other, before falling into an embrace.

'I'm Bella. Bella Bruni,' the woman said eventually, disentangling herself from Susannah and stepping back.

Still shocked, she babbled her reply. 'Susannah Ferguson and... my friend, Giacomo.'

'*Piacere*. A real pleasure. Please come in. My grandmother is asleep at the moment. She dozes a lot these days, bless her.' Bella drew them into a spacious open-plan room decorated with rustic wooden furniture and large ceramic plates on the walls, painted in colours of the sea.

Susannah and Giacomo followed Bella to a garden room at the back of the house. An old lady was asleep in an armchair in the corner, large windows framing a view of a wide terrace and an infinity view of the Adriatic. Plants and ornaments made from driftwood and seashells sat on shelves or hung from hooks on the walls.

The old lady stirred and sat up, peering at her guests. Her steel-grey hair was cut in an urchin style, her fringe chunky and chopped, her eyes a deep brown, alert and smiling.

'*Vieni, vieni*. Come,' she said, her arms outstretched in welcome. 'I am so pleased to meet you.'

Giacomo and Bella stood back as Susannah crouched before her.

'*Sono* Susannah,' she said in halting Italian.

She reached up to stroke Susannah's face and then clasped one of her hands. 'It is wonderful that somebody from Inghilterra has come all this way to see me. I feel very flattered.'

Susannah didn't want to pierce the old lady's bubble and she smiled at her. It wasn't hard: Antonella radiated sweetness, her deep brown eyes alight, warm.

'My granddaughter tells me that you wrote about having one of my early pieces. May I see it?'

Susannah had wrapped it carefully in tissue to bring along today and as she removed it, Antonella moved forward in her chair, her hand to her mouth.

'Where did you get this?' she asked. 'Pass me my glasses, Bella. Please!'

Susannah watched as, with trembling hands, the old lady brought the shell closer to her eyes. 'It is,' she said. 'It is...'

'What is it, Nonna?' Bella said, bending to put her arm around her grandmother.

'It is the one I gave to your grandfather. To my darling Roberto.'

She turned to Susannah, beckoning her to draw closer, once again reaching to stroke her face. 'It's like a miracle that you found us.'

'I don't understand. What do you mean?' Susannah said, looking over to Giacomo. Bella translated for her and Susannah wondered if maybe the old lady was suffering from the same affliction as Elsie, her mind gone astray with the years.

'Your *nonno* gave you this, my darling,' the old lady said.

Bella translated for her and Susannah gasped. 'My grandfather? What do you mean?'

'Your *nonno* Roberto,' Antonella said. 'Roberto Bruni. He told me that he had given you his lucky bird. That's what he called it. I made it for him. And he left it with you in Inghilterra.'

'My *nonno*?' This was crazy. Or the old lady was crazy. Susannah looked from Giacomo, to Bella and finally back to Antonella, feeling like she was part of the Mad Hatter's tea party.

The old lady picked up a battered notebook from the occasional table beside her, and flicked to a page at the back.

'This is a notebook your *nonno* kept from the first days when he arrived injured on our beach many years ago. My own grandfather carried him to our *trullo* and we looked after him. Read the name written here. My eyes are not as good as they used to be and anyway, it's difficult for me to pronounce. He always laughed at my attempts.'

'William Pica,' Susannah said, stalling over the name, written in rounded capital letters, the ink faded.

She turned to Giacomo, her eyes round in amazement. 'The same name as on the tag in our box, isn't it?'

Giacomo nodded and she turned to the old lady. 'I still don't understand. I'm confused, Signora Antonella. You said his name was Roberto and this tag says William. But my grandfather was called Cedric. How can this man be my grandfather?'

The old lady was clearly confused. Susannah decided to calm down and sit back and play along, but the next thing she came out with threw her again.

'He told me he was known as Billy in Inghilterra, but to me he was always Roberto.' The old lady selected a photo from the side table and handed it to Susannah. 'This is your *nonno*.'

William. Billy... Could the old lady be telling her the truth?

Incredulous, Susannah peered at an older version of the young man she'd seen in other photos – grouped amongst fellow RAF servicemen in the photos found in the envelope. The same man from another photo where he'd stood amongst cricket players and in the article about the olive co-operative. But in this photo, he was standing at the door of a *trullo*, his shirt-sleeves rolled up to show strong, sun-kissed arms, a pitchfork in one hand, a pipe in his mouth, a straw hat pushed back on curly dark hair. Could Roberto be Elsie's Billy? It was all so complicated. Too complicated to be true?

The old lady's laugh was like the tinkle of a bell, her slender fingers tracing the features of the man after Susannah handed back the photo. 'He had no idea of working on the land when he arrived with us. Clueless! But he soon learned. He had to.' She caressed the photo. 'How I miss him. *Povero* Roberto.'

Susannah looked again at the man the old lady had told her moments ago was her grandfather. William Pica, also known as Billy, had been in the RAF – that was what the identity tag showed – but here in Puglia, for whatever reason, the same man was known as Roberto Bruni. A man with a double life. The old lady's affection for this man was obvious. But Susannah was baffled. How could this beautiful woman accept that her husband had had an affair with an English girl, her grandmother Elsie, and not be bitter about it? An affair that had apparently produced a baby: her own father, Frank, for this is what the old lady called Antonella was telling her.

Thoughts swirled and swooped in her brain like bats in a cave. She wanted to ask the old lady these puzzling questions but she was reluctant to upset her. If the man in the photo was truly her grandfather, had Grandpa Cedric known about him? And had he known Frank was not his son? The carefree man in the photo, whom this old lady claimed was her real grandfather, wore a pair of faded shorts, his hair tousled, his head tossed back in laughter. Grandpa Cedric had always been smartly dressed: a stiff, formal gentleman. As far as she could remember, she'd never seen him in a pair of shorts. His shirts were expensive, his trousers folded neatly every night in a press. And he always wore a tie or a cravat, no matter the weather. In the few minutes she'd been with this delightful lady, the past she had always known had been scattered like a row of skittles.

'Your *nonno* Roberto made me laugh every single day,' the old lady continued. 'He was my *amore* with his glass always half-full, despite our many ups and downs over the years. I was very unhappy until he came into my life, Susannah *cara*. But with him I was complete.'

She looked up at Susannah with watery eyes. 'How he would have loved to be with us today to meet you and your father. He is called Frank, is he not?'

Susannah shook her head. '*Mi dispiace*. I am so sorry. My daddy passed away at the beginning of the year.'

The old lady was quiet for a moment. 'Such is life. Nothing lasts forever. I shall be the next to go and I will have so much to tell them when I join them in *paradiso*.' She laughed when she added, 'If I'm allowed in.' Her eyes crinkled, her smile and laughter lighting up the room.

Susannah broke the silence that followed these words. 'Signora, this is such a shock for me. I'm finding it hard to take in. And I don't understand how you could know that I am your husband's granddaughter.'

'You are so formal with me. No need to call me signora.'

'What shall I call you? I'm so bewildered.'

'What else but Nonna?' The old lady threw up her hands as if astonished such a question should be posed. 'Though we are not blood-related, we are connected through the heart. Through Roberto, the father of your father. And just look at you. You have your *nonno*'s eyes and his dark, curly hair. You don't look like an *inglesina* at all. You could even be Bella's sister. *Mamma mia.*' The old lady clasped her hands together in delight. 'It's so wonderful that you're here. A missing jigsaw piece of Roberto's English family.'

Giacomo, who had been quiet in the background, spoke up. 'I've been thinking that too, signora. About the resemblance between Susannah and Bella. It's quite remarkable.'

Still unconvinced, Susannah persisted with her questions. 'But how could you know for sure?'

'The shell gull you have showed me just now. Roberto told me how he gave it to you when he was back in Inghilterra and you were a little girl – how difficult it was for him not to pick you up and smother you with kisses. How he had to keep quiet when his own son appeared before his very eyes and he couldn't tell him who he was. He always hoped that one day his English family would know about him. It never happened. But... here you are now.'

She turned her attention to Giacomo, gesturing to him to come nearer. She clasped his hand in hers.

'And tell me, Susannah. Who is this handsome *giovanotto*? Is this young man your *fidanzato*?'

Susannah shook her head, embarrassed that Giacomo had been mistaken for her fiancé. 'No, no. We're simply good friends.'

Giacomo leant down low and dropped two gentle kisses on Antonella's papery cheeks. '*Piacere*, signora. Delighted to meet you.'

'Well, if I were you, young Susannah,' the old lady said with a chuckle, holding tight to Giacomo's hand, 'I would never let this simple friend slip from my grasp.'

'Nonna!' Bella, who had been translating all the exchanges for Susannah, brought her hands to her face and laughed. 'You can't say things like that.'

She turned to them and apologised. 'I'm sorry. Nonna is apt to say the first thing that comes into her head.'

'If everybody was as honest as I have learned to be, then life would be more straightforward, don't you think? If I can't say what I want to, an old lady approaching one hundred years, then there's no hope left for the world. And as I said before, young Susannah, you can call me Nonna. My husband was definitely your grandfather and we were definitely married – so I am certain I can be a *nonna* to you. And if you find it so very difficult to call me Nonna, then I'm also known as Anto. Short for Antonella. You decide for yourself, *cara*.' As she talked, Antonella's dark eyes were full of emotion.

'*Grazie*, Nonna,' Susannah said, leaning in to kiss both her cheeks. '*Grazie*.'

Susannah's eyes glistened too. In the few minutes she'd been in Nonna's sparkling company, she felt closer to her than she ever had been with Grandma Elsie. Something had clicked between them. She'd found a missing tie she didn't know she'd been searching for. She hadn't expected to find family in her hunt to identify the writer of the cards and letter and there were still many questions she needed to ask before she could truly accept these amazing revelations.

While her *nonna* was lost in a private moment as she gazed at her husband's photo, Susannah looked at the cluster of photos in their frames. She bent to examine one that showed her grand-father in much later life: greyer, stockier, beaming as he stood in the middle of people, a traditional *trullo* behind them.

'That was taken outside our little house. With our family,' Nonna said and then almost immediately she corrected herself. 'Your family too.'

Susannah waited a little before asking her next question, wary of offending the woman who wanted to be known as Nonna.

'So, this man. Your husband. I'm still finding it hard to understand how he could possibly be my grandfather? Can you explain more about what happened?'

Anto handed over the notebook, its cover a faded charcoal-black, the curling edges torn.

'I'm tired now. It's a long story and too complicated to explain in a few minutes. This notebook is for you, *cara mia*. Roberto wrote in this most days from the time he arrived on our beach. After we were married, there was little time left at day's end. We were busy and then our children came along. Read it. It's his story. And it's a story for you. It's no use to me now. He wrote in *inglese* anyway which I can't read or speak.'

She pressed the notebook into Susannah's hands and she flicked through the front pages, noting little sketches here and there and neat handwriting, the pencil strokes faded. A couple of the pages were stuck together. She would have to prise them open carefully later. Her eyes wide, she looked up at her newly found *nonna* and shook her head. 'I don't know what to say.'

'Don't say anything. Read it, drink it in and then we shall talk some more.'

'I'd love that,' Susannah said, 'but the day after tomorrow I have to return to England.'

'Then you must come back to us one day very soon,' Nonna said.

Nonna's eyes began to droop. She leant back against the cushions and her body relaxed into sleep almost immediately. They left her alone and retired to Bella's sitting room to chat.

'Nonna was struggling at her *trullo* on her own,' Bella explained. 'She was very reluctant to leave and come to Vasto to live with us, but it was the only way. Whenever we can, we try to take her to visit, but she feels ill in the car, poor thing. She has deteriorated a lot in the last months.'

From a drawer in a desk she extracted a bunch of keys, removing two. 'I have a favour to ask of you, Giacomo. The *trulli* where Nonna and Nonno lived are nearer you than us. If you could check on them occasionally, I would be so grateful. I find it hard to get over there these days with work commitments and caring for Nonna. If you think anything needs doing, perhaps you could call me. The buildings are isolated – it would be a shame if vandals broke in.'

'*Certo*, Bella,' Giacomo said, taking the keys. 'It will be a pleasure. I often walk those clifftops. It's part of the wildlife reserve. I'm honoured you trust me.'

'I can tell you're a good man,' Bella said. 'Our family is scattered now because of work. With the state of the Italian economy – especially post-pandemic, we have to go wherever there is employment. It's not like in the past when people stayed close to their roots.'

They chatted a while longer and, after exchanging details, promised to keep in regular contact. Nonna woke moments before they left. She asked Bella to translate carefully what she wanted to say to Susannah.

'Nonna said it is important that you know your father was loved deeply by Roberto, even though he left England to start another life. He wrote many letters but never received a single one in return. Not being able to see his son was a thorn in his heart, but you turning up today is wonderful. He was a good man. She says thank you and asks you to please come again soon.'

'Now that I've found you, I won't let you go. Bella, I'm so grateful you replied to my email,' Susannah said after more hugs were exchanged.

'It was Nonna who asked me to respond. She doesn't always bother, especially to the begging letters, but she was excited that somebody from England wanted to visit her. She won't stop talking about your visit for days now. I haven't seen her so animated in weeks. But...' Bella bit her lip and lowered her voice. 'Make sure you come back soon. She's frail.'

In the van, Giacomo and Susannah sat for a couple of moments before moving off.

'My heart is so full and my brain is fit to burst with everything I've discovered today. Can everything I've learned be true? I've been thinking that Elsie had an affair with this Roberto – or William or Billy as his real name was. But I still don't understand how or when. It's all such a muddle at the moment but I didn't want to ask Nonna for more details. It's a puzzle. What have the postcards of the *masseria* – and the painting, for that matter – got to do with anything? I started off to find out about that, and I seem to have ended up with a new family. But isn't she lovely? My *nonna*... if that's who she really is. It's so strange to say out loud.'

'She's given you the notebook. That will likely hold keys to your puzzle.'

'I can't wait to read it,' she said, feeling in her bag to make sure the notebook was still there.

'It's like a film,' Giacomo said. 'Maybe I should be on hand with wine and tissues while you read it.'

She smiled. 'Thank you so, so much for today, Jack. You've been amazing.'

He squeezed her hand and started the engine. 'It's been a blast. And a privilege. It's not every day I'm involved in a family story like this.'

For the first half of the journey back to Monte Sant'Angelo, Giacomo left her to dwell on her thoughts and she was grateful for his sensitivity. She kept glancing at the notebook sticking out of her bag, but the road was full of bends and she knew if she started to read, she'd be carsick.

They stopped for a drink on the outskirts of Foggia, Giacomo having decided they would take a longer scenic route another time during daylight. At a bar in the city centre, they sipped wine spritzers. In front of them a building with a façade in the shape of an M dominated the busy piazza. 'The *fascisti* built it in honour of Il Duce. It's the town hall now,' Giacomo explained.

'The place gives me the creeps, if I'm honest. The buildings loom over everything with their ornate columns and embellishments. Everything's a faded dirty white, like... a symbol of a murky past.'

'The city underwent massive reconstruction after the war,' Giacomo said. 'There were over twenty thousand victims of the bombings and most of the original buildings were flattened. There's a lot in the history books about Rome and the northern Italian cities during World War Two, but our south tends to be forgotten. The airfields dotted around the Foggia plains attracted bombers from both sides.'

'As usual, ordinary people are those who suffer,' Susannah said. 'What must it have been like living through those times? People have said living through Covid-19 was like being in a war, but they didn't face bombs and starvation. Terrifying,' she murmured, as the roar of half a dozen passing motorbikes blasted the air.

'Pardon?' Giacomo said.

'Just rambling,' she replied. 'And I've been thinking about my father. How he never got to know about his real father. And how hard it must have been for his father too, not seeing his son grow up. Antonella said he wrote letters but never received a reply. It's all very, very sad.' A tear ran down her cheek and she wiped it away. 'Let's hurry back, Jack. I miss your corner of Puglia. I can see why Bella says my *nonna* was happier living there. I'd love to visit Nonna's *trulli*, but time is running out.'

'But there *will* be a chance another time, won't there, Susi?' he said, the question in his tone like a hint he wanted her to return, a hint that this newly found family would not be the only pull in Puglia.

CHAPTER 37

MARCH 1945.

*My eyes are open. I bring my hands to my face. They're bound
in rags and when I try to pull at them, the pain is so bad that I
yelp. My head drums and thumps and I'm nauseous.*

Susannah read late into the night, Billy's notebook slowly
revealing the story of her real grandfather. She was totally
absorbed from the first lines, transported to a period in history
she knew little about. It was by no means a complete account of
his life but now she understood what had happened and why
Grandma Elsie wanted to hide her past. What had sounded to
Susannah like demented ramblings from her grandmother that
day in the home had indeed been true: how she'd wanted the
best for her only son, expressing a tinge of regret for giving him
the postcard. She had even mentioned a Billy too. Somebody
who kept disappearing in his airyplane. At the time, Susannah
had discounted all this as nonsense. She almost felt sorry for
Elsie, who had most likely destroyed all the letters Billy had

painstakingly and lovingly written to his son, because she was fearful of the revelation of her double marriage. From everything she had read in Grandfather Billy's notebook, she knew now that he too had married bigamously. Her daddy had known nothing about all this. To all intents and purposes, his father and Nonna and Elsie and Cedric had carried on their lives against the law. Grandma Elsie in England had wanted the reappearance of Billy kept quiet, and not purely for legal reasons. Elsie had preferred her bread to be buttered by Grandpa Cedric's bank accounts. On the other hand, Billy's and Antonella's had been a true love story. And surely the war must have given rise to many similar bigamous relationships.

Five long years of battle caused ripples of change as a result of enforced separations. She thought back to a television documentary she'd seen about the effect of families torn apart. There were moving shots of couples reunited at railway stations but while there were plenty of couples happy to be reunited, there'd been interviews with women who admitted they didn't know their husbands anymore when they returned. Their men, coming home from the awful conditions in camps and on battlefields, were changed forever. Another woman talked about the war opening up her life, making her realise she had never known what love was until she'd met her handsome GI. Bigamy was an imprisonable offence; divorce was only granted upon proof of adultery back in the day, with much stigma and shame. Susannah sighed, thinking it was best not to dwell on that side of things. It was love that mattered – not whether parents were married legally according to bits of paper. In her grandfather Billy's case, she liked to think love was above the law and had conquered all. Her own father had grown up believing he was someone else's son... but he'd still had a good life.

It was three o'clock in the morning and she didn't want to stop reading the last few pages but her eyes were telling her otherwise. The writing started to swim and her head nodded to her chest. Tiptoeing down the stairs to Giacomo's kitchen, she brewed herself a pot of strong espresso and added a handful of his hand-baked *pugliesi* dunking biscuits to her snack tray to keep up energy levels. Back in his spare room, she plumped up the pillows and resumed her read.

There were only two more entries after the description of the happy wedding day and she imagined his life must have been contented and fulfilled as well as busy. Nonna Antonella had told her as much. With Antonella, he had found his destiny. Flicking through the final pages, she noticed the final pages were dated far apart.

SUNDAY, NOVEMBER 5, 1950.

Today is my English son's birthday – for that is how I find it easy to differentiate between Frank and little Italian Leo, who was born to us two years ago. I hope one day they might meet each other but I have not once received a reply to any of the many letters sent to Elsie.

A lot has happened since I last wrote in here. And as time passes, I find myself thinking in Italian. English words come slowly to me.

For a few months after Leo's birth, Antonella was poorly and so most of my time was spent caring for the baby. I have a strong bond with Leo. Sometimes I think I doubled my efforts with him because I could never care for Frank in this way. How many times have I rocked Leo to sleep, gazing on his features, wondering how Frank looked: whether he had the same button nose or how he might gurgle when I pulled faces or played peek-a-boo. Elsie has sent no photos or descriptions of his progress, so I have to imagine my English son. Maybe it's for the best – but it still hurts and I console myself with the thought that no news is good news. Nessuna nuova, buona nuova.

Antonella is better now and every market day she sells her artwork in the main piazza of Mattinata. One day I hope to have earned enough money to buy a small shop so she doesn't have to carry her pieces back and forth. We have also managed to purchase a donkey and cart. Only the rich drive about in Fiats and Lancias but we rarely see them on our dusty roads. The cockerels calling us at dawn and the braying of our donkey for his breakfast are our early morning alarm clock. Antonella makes jewellery from seashells and pictures from driftwood that she combs from the shore. Tourists have started to come on holiday to Puglia and Americans especially – those who have relatives living in this part of Italy. They love her work and buy plenty to take back in their suitcases as souvenirs of the places where they were born and from where they emigrated.

My work at Masseria della Torre has come to an end because Fortunata and her daughters moved back to the city when business dwindled to nothing. We miss our extended family. They visited us in our trullo last August, but there is little space. Thank goodness I manage to pick up work here and there. I teach English part-time at the local school and whenever anybody needs a waiter for a special event, I make myself available.

A new venture is my participation with other olive grow- ers. I have helped set up a co-operative and we now sell our precious first-pressed oil for ourselves, bypassing those big companies who used to give us next to nothing for our harvests. When I lived in Hastings and helped Father with the restaurant, olive oil was hard to come by. I remember him telling me when he first came to England, the main use for English people was to rub olive oil from the chemist on babies' heads when they had cradle cap. Now, I could wash my hands in it.

Susannah looked up from the notebook, thinking about these new relatives that Nonna Antonella had talked about. Was Leo perhaps Bella's father? It would be great to meet the rest of her Italian family. The thought of returning to Hastings and her very English life was strange. At the age of thirty-eight she had discovered Italian blood was in her veins and she smiled at the happy realisation: part of her belonged to this amazing country.

The final entry was dated many years later, the writing different from earlier passages: in parts barely legible, the letters crooked and incomplete as if written with a shaking hand. Susannah did a mental calculation. Her newly discovered grandfather would have written the lines when he was about seventy years old. Not an old man, but ill maybe.

SUNDAY, JUNE 12, 1988.

After many years' silence, I am compelled to write again. I stopped updating my notebook when it was apparent I would never receive replies to any of my letters. At first, I thought something dreadful had happened, that Frank had succumbed to a childhood illness. But now I know he is still alive and it is more than likely Elsie has never given my son any of my letters. I like to think that is why Frank never acknowledged them over the years and not because he hates me for aban-doning him.

But at last I have seen him again with my own eyes. He has a family of his own. Last week in Hastings I saw for myself. With little time left to me, I couldn't keep away.

For several years I have continued to work for the olive-

growers' co-operative, which I helped set up in our town during the late 1950s. Under Mussolini's regime, from the 1920s, the fascisti exacted heavy levies from the co-operatives. They hit the members, ruining the concept of fairness built up behind the movements, denying rights that had taken so long to establish. I was proud to do my bit.

People remembered from the end of the war that I spoke English. In small towns like ours, maybe the sparrows spread news as well as the women gossiping at the washing fountains. Certainly, in the osterie, men's tongues loosen with each tumbler of wine and there are few secrets. The townspeople remembered how I'd spoken with English soldiers and airmen at the end of the war. They didn't know everything about me for even I have begun to forget much of my past. The mind is a clever organ; it denies or accepts what it wants to know.

My visits back to England began because I was asked to work as the representative for the English market. The co-operative wanted to expand and I was their man.

I was strict with myself. I didn't go anywhere near Hastings on my early visits, although I was tempted. I didn't want to upset the apple cart, as my English mother used to say. But when my health declined at the end of last year, I knew my travelling days were coming to an end and so, with the excuse that perhaps I might find more outlets for olive oil further south of London, I boarded the London to Hastings train.

The town had not changed much. The defences on the beaches were no longer there – dragons' teeth, we used to call them, designed to prevent invasion of the Sussex beaches. There were new amusement arcades on the sea but the centre was down-at-heel. I believe the English prefer to spend holidays abroad now in places like Italy, Spain and Greece. I bought a coffee in an Italian café but the coffee was different: weaker than how we drink it back home. There – you see – I call Italy my home now, and more specifically Puglia. At one stage, in the early years, I felt neither one thing nor the other – né pesce, né carne. Neither fish nor fowl. I was caught between two worlds, but my Italian blood flows strong in me now. I even speak English with an Italian accent. When I struck up conversation with an Italian café owner, he didn't understand me at first. And when we tried Italian, I didn't understand his anglicised version. Our world has become an interesting hotchpotch of cultures.

I remembered where Elsie lived from over forty years ago and I hoped she might still live in the same grand house opposite the park. Most likely Frank would live somewhere else, in another city perhaps – with a family of his own. But I had to at least try.

God was on my side that day. I am not a religious man, but lately I have found myself turning to my Creator in moments of crisis. Maybe it is hypocritical to do so when I know I have little time left: like a drowning man who clutches at the nearest wreckage. I have read accounts where men who find themselves in the direst of straits call out to God for help, and I have become one of them.

I'm rambling. I do that more and more these days. Antonella tells me so in the kindest possible way. But it's good to put down my thoughts and explain myself. It would have been better to have done so face to face with my son, but in the end, I lost my nerve. Too much time had passed; it would cause too much upset.

I sat on a park bench for a while gathering courage, staring at the house, at the path where I had last seen baby Frank pushed in his pram by Elsie as she hurried to escape from me. And then the door opened, and a little girl ran out through the porch: maybe five or six years old – her hair a tumble of dark curls. I watched as a fair-haired, middle-aged man followed, stopping to kiss the cheek of an older woman, her blonde dyed hair at contrast with her lined face. It was

Elsie and I was shocked. The woman I had married towards the end of the war looked more worn than my Antonella. The little girl was already down the garden path and across the road into the park when the man, who I now realised was Frank, turned round. He shouted for her to wait, to be careful of the cars, and she ran up to where I was sitting on the bench.

'I'm playing hide-and-seek,' she told me. 'Don't tell my daddy I'm here.'

And then she hurried to crouch in the middle of a flowerbed that in Italy would have been planted with vegetables, rather than flowers arranged in soldierly lines of blue, white and red. 'Is he coming?' she hissed at me.

'Yes. Keep very still,' I replied.

And then Frank was there, in front of me. My son. A smile on his handsome face. 'Have you seen my little scamp?' he asked.

I shrugged my shoulders and then there was a squeal and the little girl stood up, crying and holding her leg. 'Ouch, Daddy. It stung me. A nasty bee stung me. It hurts.'

Frank scooped her up and came to sit next to me on the bench as he soothed her. Without thinking twice, knowing from my own granddaughter how it is sometimes easier to calm a child through distraction, I pulled out the seashell bird that Antonella had given me years ago when we first met and which I always carried in my pocket when I travelled. I held it up to show my granddaughter.

'If you hold this tight in your hand,' I said, 'it will help the pain go away.'

Her little face unpuckered and with a sniff she took the charm and wrapped her fingers around it. 'Is it magic?' she asked.

'Yes. Very.'

'Can I keep it?'

Frank told her off then and I shook my head and told him not to worry.

'Let her keep it,' I said. 'Maybe one day your daughter will visit Italy and see where it came from.'

'You're very kind, sir,' he said, a smile on his face. A good-tempered face, his eyes blue-green like the sea that laps the shores near us. His fair hair, speckled grey, the same wiry hair as mine, receding from a high forehead. But my hair is dark – like the little girl's: my English granddaughter.

Should I have opened up then and told Frank who I really was? Suddenly it seemed wrong to do so. Selfish. What would it achieve? He seemed happy. My bombshell might have disrupted many lives. In the end, I decided to leave it be. I had seen Frank and I'd seen my pretty granddaughter and that would have to be enough.

The little girl leant up and put her arms around my neck and kissed me on the cheek.

'Your cheeks are whiskery like Daddy's,' she said as she moved away, the shell held fast in her fist. 'But you have more wrinkles. Thank you for my magic present.'

We said our goodbyes and I watched my English son walk away down the path and disappear between the lines of trees towards the lake, his little girl skipping at his side.

Susannah placed the notebook on the bedcovers and leant back against the pillows. So this was what Nonna Antonella had mentioned. She remembered now the kindly face of the elderly gentleman in the park, with his dark hair streaked with silver. She had said to her daddy that the man looked like Badger in her *Wind in the Willows* storybook, with his striped hair and fat little body.

'Why does he talk in that funny way, Daddy?' she'd asked and Frank had told her it was not funny – that he was from another country, from a place called Italy and that one day perhaps they would holiday there and swim in the warm sea and eat Italian ice cream and spaghetti.

'Spaghetti hoops?' she'd asked and Frank had replied that the spaghetti in Italy would be far nicer than from a tin.

Susannah reached for her talisman, which she now knew had been made by her Italian *nonna*. She gazed on the shell bird and its sea-glass eye. She'd kept it all these years, little realising the elderly man who had given it to her was her grandfather. Her flesh-and-blood grandfather.

Her eyes watered. She was angry that Elsie had denied her daddy knowledge of his father and never passed over his letters through the years, even though from what she had read in the notebook, there was little love between her and Roberto – or should she call him Billy? William was the name her grandfather had been christened with. That was what his identity tag showed. In his notebook, he referred to himself as Billy, but mostly Roberto. She was sad for her father that he never knew he was half Italian and resolved to do her best to make up for this huge misunderstanding. All her life she had felt something was missing, that she didn't really belong, always wondering what she had done to upset Grandma Elsie. Maybe with her dark hair, she had reminded her grandmother too much of the man she had wanted to erase from her life. But it wasn't her place to judge, and the stirrings of an understanding for why her grandmother had behaved the way she had stole its way into Susannah's thoughts. She'd never experienced a war, never had to fend for herself, like so many desperate women all over the world, victims of terrible circumstances. Elsie had done the best she could; she'd provided her only son with a comfortable upbringing. If all her love had been poured into Frank and there'd been little left for her granddaughter, then so be it. It was what it was. Life moved on.

. . .

Next morning, Giacomo brought a cup of tea to her room, strong how she liked it, English-style. He lifted the notebook from her face where it had dropped as she fell asleep.

'Hey, sleepyhead,' he said, placing the cup on the bedside table. 'You're still wearing your clothes. Did you not go to bed last night?'

She yawned and stretched her arms above her head. 'No. I went into the past instead. Oh, Jack, I have so much to tell you. I don't know where to begin. I've read the whole of my grandfather's notebook.'

'So, you've made up your mind that Roberto Bruni was definitely your grandfather?'

'Yes. Unbelievable as it all seemed to me at the time, I know now. The notebook has unlocked the mystery. The names and dates and places all match up. My father, my grandmother Elsie, their house in Hastings... so I know I'm partly Italian, Jack. What do you make of that?'

'I want to know more. Why don't you have a shower and you can tell me over breakfast. Will scrambled eggs and fresh coffee do you?'

'You do know that you're the best Italian friend I've ever had,' she said. 'I could get used to this, you know.'

He gave her a look that she found unfathomable and left her to get dressed.

Downstairs, a pretty girl with a figure to die for and long dark hair cascading down her back was manning the bar and she smiled sweetly at Susannah. As she turned to reach for a bottle on the shelf, her short skirt rode higher up her legs and Susannah felt a twinge of jealousy. She was probably Giacomo's latest. She immediately banished the annoying twinge. She had absolutely no right to feel that way.

'*Buongiorno,* signorina,' the girl said. '*Sono* Loredana.'

'*Piacere,*' Susannah replied.

After Giacomo had set down her breakfast, he hugged

Loredana and the pair chattered away in dialect, Loredana laughing and punching him playfully at some comment Susannah didn't understand. It felt like a preparation for resumption of her ordinary life. She left them alone and went upstairs to finish her packing, part of her wishing she could stay.

CHAPTER 38

HASTINGS, ENGLAND, PRESENT DAY

A vase containing white delphiniums and deep-rust sedum sat on the scrubbed pine table in Susannah's kitchen in Hastings, together with Maureen's cheerful welcome home note.

Good to have you back. Can't wait to catch up with ALL your news. See you tomorrow in the shop. M xx

Rain had not stopped falling since she'd touched down at Gatwick Airport. Today, as she stepped down the damp alleyways towards Cobwebs, water splashed up her legs, soaking her jeans. The last roses of summer hung over walls, their sodden petals like pink blotting paper scattered in puddles and by the time she reached Cobwebs, she matched the look of the land-bound gulls huddled within their forlorn feathers. The town was empty of holidaymakers, schools having begun the new academic year. The grey sky and sea were oppressive and the air smelled of damp dog.

'Good morning, good morning,' Maureen said as Susannah pushed open the shop door. She stepped towards Susannah for a hug, and rapidly retreated. 'Drowned rat look is it today? Poor you. It's been gloriously sunny up until two days ago. I'll put the kettle on. I'm dying for a good chinwag.'

Susannah hung her jacket round a mannequin she'd not seen before. Next to it was a leather suitcase overflowing with colourful clothes. 'You've been busy,' she called to Maureen in the galley kitchen.

Setting down a teapot and two mismatching cups and saucers on a tray, Maureen filled her in with what she'd been up to. 'I think you'll be pleased when you examine the books. It was really busy over Bank Holiday and I've had to take in new stock. I thought these bits and bobs of chinaware would be wonderful for when we serve teas.'

'So you think it's viable, do you? Your café idea?'

'Absolutely. But I thought we'd go more tea room than café. More olde worlde. Maybe with an old-fashioned tea party theme, encouraging customers to dress up a bit? Hats and gloves, a boa or two? Of course we need to discuss it, but my initial customer survey suggests it will work well.'

Susannah sipped on her Earl Grey, her mind drifting to Puglia. At this time of morning there would be a congregation of shop owners in Giacomo's bar. They'd have locked their shops, turned their signs to *CHIUSO* for a fifteen-minute break, enjoying what was essentially a quick Italian breakfast-on-the-hoof of coffee and fresh pastries. Italians weren't generally big on breakfasts first thing, she had discovered.

She shook her head back to the present when she realised Maureen had said something which she hadn't taken in. 'Sorry, Maureen. Wasn't concentrating. I'd say I had jet lag, but a two-and-a-half-hour flight isn't excuse enough, is it?'

'I'll give you time to adjust back, although you know I am aching to hear what you've been up to in Italy. Tell me all about these dishy men you've snared.'

Susannah frowned. 'God! You make me sound like a nymphomaniac. I let one snare *me*, as you know, but I quickly disentangled myself once I realised what he was really like. Giacomo is a friend. A good friend, more like a brother. My big news is far more important than dishy men, Maureen.'

'Do reveal.'

'Get ready for a real-life saga. It all starts with the fact that Elsie was married to two men at the same time.'

Seeing the look of confusion on her friend's face, she paused. 'Let me start from the beginning...'

It was fortunate that no customers came into the shop during the next hour, as Susannah proceeded to relate everything she had found out from the notebook and her newly discovered Italian family. Maureen kept stopping her with questions and entreaties to slow down as the details became more complicated.

'Wow,' Maureen said, when Susannah had finished. 'I *think* I've understood. Complex, or what? Far, far stranger than fiction... So that message on the postcard you found. The one that we thought must be from her lover. And the note or letter, whatever – they were never meant for Elsie. They were meant for your *father*.'

'Absolutely. I know most of the words by heart: "In my dreams I imagine the day when we shall be reunited. Until then, I hope my letters will fill the gaps",' Susannah quoted. 'And "my heart will never be complete without you at my side". But Elsie never passed on a single one of his letters to my daddy.'

'That wording – easy to interpret as the words of a lover.'

'Words of love written by a father for his son,' Susannah said wistfully.

'Does your sister know any of this?' Maureen asked.

'No, not yet. The only communication Sybil and I have had recently is her texting me to leave Grandma Elsie alone. I'll have to tell her sooner or later, I suppose, but knowing her, she will probably think I'm inventing it to stir things up.'

'So your grandma married bigamously.'

'Yes. As did my real grandfather – William – or Billy, as he was known here in England. His parents owned a café in Hastings along George Street. It's so sad – the place was destroyed by an unexploded bomb and his father was killed. His mother had died shortly before that from cancer. You know that gap where people hang out along George Street? With the benches and the new trees? It was there.'

'Goodness. Sybil will be shocked. She won't like you revealing a family scandal.'

'Oh, Maureen, these scandals, as you put it, must have happened far more than people realise during the war. Goodness knows how many women gave birth to babies whose fathers were not their husbands.'

'I imagine quite a few. Divorce was not really a consideration back then either, was it? Think of all the GIs over here when the husbands of many of our women were over there on the Continent. I mean, my own mother fell for a Canadian, after all. What was the saying? "Overpaid, oversexed and over here"? So many young people in the wrong places at the same time. And love was about the only thing that wasn't rationed.'

'Agreed, Maureen. Although it probably wasn't always love. More like lust and loneliness. I suppose if your man is away, missing presumed dead, and somebody offered you marriage, kindness and an easier life, you'd most likely take it.' Susannah sat back in the rocking chair that Maureen had pulled out for her when she arrived. It was a new item. Quite comfortable. The kind of chair that a traditional, storybook grandmother would sit in. Elsie had never been one of those, in Susannah's opinion. Nevertheless, discovering all this had made her think slightly differently about her behaviour. She couldn't condone it, but maybe she could find it in her heart to forgive.

'It's hard for us to imagine what it was like having to manage the trauma from day to day in those times, isn't it, Maureen? Nowadays there's counselling for far less, but people kept quiet about their sufferings back then, didn't they? What makes me really sad is that Daddy never knew anything about his real father.'

Susannah paused and finished the rest of her tea. 'Do you know, I've always felt different; that part of me was missing? Discovering this new Italian family Daddy should have known about is one of the most precious gifts I've ever received and... it's like a part of me has been unlocked. And I fully intend to make up for what Daddy missed and return to Italy as soon as I can.'

'Frank would approve of that, I'm sure. He often talked about how he wanted to travel in Italy. I even suggested we went together.'

'Really? We talked about going too. I hadn't realised...'

'... that your dad and I were very fond of each other? We'd planned to do the Piero della Francesca trail in Tuscany. But then he fell ill.'

Susannah set down her teacup and looked at Maureen. Never had she imagined a romance between the two of them. But when she thought about it, why not? They'd have made a perfect couple and her daddy would have been very happy.

'So many things going on behind the scenes I've never guessed at, Maureen. Well, I shall make one of his wishes come true. Albeit belatedly.'

'What do you mean?'

'As he was a quarter Italian, I've decided to scatter some of his ashes in Puglia, and the rest here, probably up on the cliffs near Fairlight where he used to love walking.'

'Susi, that's a *wonderful* gesture. So fitting. Will you have to get permissions?'

Susannah winked. 'Who knows? I am following what my heart tells me and maybe I'll bypass rules and regulations.

Goodness, I'm beginning to *think* like an Italian. Giacomo told me most Italians believe rules are invented to be broken.'

The door pinged and a very wet customer entered the shop and popped his umbrella in the stand. Maureen rose to greet him.

'Good morning, ladies. I'm looking for a present for my girl-friend, who loves anything to do with the 1920s,' he said.

'Does she like antique jewellery?' Maureen asked. 'Let me show you what we have in this box over here.'

Susannah left her to it and cleared away the teacups. Maureen seemed to belong to Cobwebs. Where did *she* belong?

'Hello, Gran.'

No response. Susannah could barely make out the shape of Elsie beneath the sheets of the hospital bed. There was nothing to her. The respirator sucked and cranked with its regular mechanical beat, blotting out other sounds as she watched the unnatural rise and fall of her grandmother's chest.

'Hello, Gran,' she said, louder this time.

'I'll leave you alone for a while, dear,' the nurse said. 'Talk to her. Hearing is one of the last faculties to go. I'll be back to check on her in a few minutes. If you need me, there's the buzzer.'

The nurse's shoes squeaked over the floor and Susannah was alone with Elsie and the machine. Rivulets of rain streamed down the window that looked out over an expanse of grey building and more rows of windows.

'Gran, I found out about Billy. Or William. William Pica, as he was christened.'

There was no change from Elsie as the machine continued its work of keeping her alive.

'I met his other wife. In a roundabout kind of way, when all I was doing was snooping, really. I wanted to know about those postcards... and the letter, addressed to you. That you hid in your dressing table. Not meant for you at all. Meant for my daddy. Anyway, Billy's wife is lovely. He was happy, you know, in Italy. Really happy. He had two more children. I'm going to meet them one day soon.'

Susannah didn't really know why she was telling her grandmother these things. Maybe it was a way of explaining it to herself.

'Antonella – that's his wife's name – she said I look like him. I have his dark hair and eyes, apparently. He's dead, Gran. I managed to visit his grave before I left Puglia last week. In Italy they put enamelled photos of the deceased on the stone. He was very handsome, but you know that yourself, Gran.' She paused. If Elsie could hear her, as the nurse said, she wasn't showing any signs.

'Is that why you don't like me very much, Gran? Because I remind you of him? Sybil is blonde. You always favoured her, didn't you? I look Italian. Maybe you were scared I might have given away that you were once married to an Italian. When I was in Puglia, lots of people mistook me for a native. I was even asked the way once. I had to say, "*Mi scusi, sono straniera*. I'm a foreigner."'

Susannah knew she was rambling, but there was a lot to say.

'Italian is a beautiful language. I think Frank would have picked it up quickly if he'd visited his father. If he'd been given the chance.'

No response.

'It's a pity my daddy didn't know his real father.'

The machine worked on. Elsie remained stiff and motionless under the starched sheets. Outside, rain fell relentlessly, streaming down the windows.

'It doesn't matter though, Elsie. It really doesn't anymore. You were worried about your life with Grandpa Cedric falling apart, weren't you? You destroyed all those letters Billy sent to

Frank, didn't you? You were frightened. I think I get that. Although I can't understand everything. How could I? I've not lived through a war, have I? I don't know what I'd have done in your place. It was a mess.' Susannah fiddled with her hair, winding a curl round and round her index finger.

'But you could have shown me a little more love, Gran. You were quite nasty to me at times.'

In, out, in, out. The machine did its job of breathing. Keeping what was left of Elsie alive.

'But don't worry, Gran. I'm fine. I'm happy, although I do miss Daddy.'

Susannah rose and bent over Elsie's comatose body. 'I'm going now. I forgive you, Gran,' she said slowly, deliberately.

The slightest twitch of Elsie's eyebrows might have meant something. Susannah would never know if Elsie had registered her message.

'Goodbye, Gran.'

As she opened the door, the kindly ICU nurse, busy with a machine plugged into another patient, turned towards her, acknowledging her with a nod.

'Are you all right, my dear? Your grandmother hasn't long now. I'm sure she knew you were there.'

'Thank you for looking after her, Nurse. I'm absolutely fine. Goodbye.'

The rain had almost stopped, drops on the silver birches at the entrance like glittering jewels. She walked away, her heart lighter.

CHAPTER 39

Every now and again, Giacomo texted Susannah from Puglia, sending mouth-watering photos of new dishes and cocktails he'd concocted for his bar, or scenes he'd captured during his walks. He texted her. *You must come to this cove and swim* or *Take in this view. Over the border into Basilicata. Matera. A great place to visit.* This, of a huddle of houses described as cave dwellings. Susannah couldn't wait to return to explore her roots further. She planned to visit Antonella too and had made up an album to show her photos of Frank taken over the years.

Ten days later, on a freezing evening when Susannah was reading by the log burner, wrapped in one of her father's lumpy Aran sweaters that she hadn't wanted to send to the charity shop, there was a knock at the door.

'Special delivery,' a man said, his face hidden by an enormous bouquet of white roses. He thrust it into Susannah's arms.

'Giacomo, what on earth?' she stuttered, wanting to hug him, the flowers in the way. 'What on earth are you doing here?'

'If you let me in out of the sleet, I'll tell you.'

His hair was plastered to his face, his jacket wet through

and she pulled him into the living room to sit by the fire. 'Take your clothes off,' she said and he roared with laughter.

'Now that's the kind of welcome every man dreams of.'

'Idiot! You know what I mean. Here, put this on. I'm as warm as toast now. It was Daddy's.' She knew she was rambling, thrown by his presence. As she pulled the thick sweater over her head, she wished she wasn't wearing her sloppy old jogger pants and her father's thick darned walking socks. 'Let me make you a hot chocolate and you can tell me why you're here. Do you actually like hot chocolate?'

'Anything hot would be welcome.' He moved nearer the stove, warming his hands in the glow. Frank's sweater fitted Giacomo's broad back perfectly and for a moment her eyes watered as she remembered how she'd loved to snuggle up to her daddy when she was small and listen to him reading, pointing out illustrations in her storybooks.

She arranged the roses in an enamel pitcher while she waited for the milk to boil, peering at her reflection in the window. Her hair was lank and greasy but she hadn't been expecting visitors, least of all a handsome visitor from Puglia.

Giacomo was sitting in Daddy's old chair, his legs stretched out. She noticed a small hole in the toe of his left sock and found that endearing and rather homely.

'It's lovely to see you again. But to what do I owe this visit? Is it work related?'

He gave her a long look. 'I'm glad you're pleased to see me, Susi.' He pulled an envelope from his jacket pocket. 'Bella wanted you to have this letter from Antonella as soon as possible. Our postal system can't be relied on. An email wouldn't do for your *nonna* and so Bella phoned me for advice. And here I am – your special messenger.'

He handed it over and she slit open the slightly damp envelope.

Vasto, il 21 settembre

Dear Susannah,

I hope you are well.

I write this to you rather than emailing or texting, as Nonna insisted she wanted me to send a 'proper, old-fashioned letter', rather than doing it the 'lazy way', as she calls emails and text messages. She also insisted on signing the letter herself, after I had assured her more than once that the English words say the same things as she dictated. She sends her love and is looking forward to seeing you as soon as you are able to return to Puglia.

Finding you has been very important to all of us.

'I can die happy now in the knowledge that Roberto's family knows what happened to him.' Those are Nonna's exact words. She drops frequent comments recently about leaving this earth, so don't delay your return. (Obviously, I did not say I was writing that comment.)

Nonna wants you to have the trulli where she and Nonno Roberto lived for many happy years. She is drawing up documents with our lawyers to cover this bequest. You may of course think twice about the responsibility of owning a house so far away and want to sell the property, but, in any case, it would be best if you travelled to Puglia sooner rather than later to see what she is offering. There is much to discuss and Nonna is already planning a big family party. So, be prepared!

I look forward to hearing what you think. There is no need to write a letter in reply to this, but I know that Nonna would love to receive a postcard of England in the post and see the place where Roberto came from. You know my number. WhatsApp me to talk about anything.

Very best wishes,

Bella

P.S. *The rest of the family are very excited to meet you.*

With shaking hands, Susannah looked at Giacomo.

'This is incredible. Do you know about the contents?'

He nodded.

'Well, do you want this hot chocolate or shall we drink something stronger to celebrate this amazing news? I have some warming whiskey. Will that do?'

They sat next to each other on the settee, sipping the fiery spirit and Susannah had to read the unbelievable news twice more. There had only been one meeting with Nonna Antonella, and her generosity was incredible.

She looked up from the letter and followed Giacomo's gaze. He was staring at her father's painting.

'So that's it,' he said.

'Yep. All started because of a postcard that Grandma Elsie so easily could have thrown away, but for some reason gave to my father when he was little. And because of that, look what's happened: I've discovered a part of my roots that might never have come to light. Grandma Elsie never passed on any of the letters sent from Puglia. Goodness only knows why she passed on the one she did. Guilt, maybe? I went to talk to her but she's on life support.'

'Well, I for one am very glad she didn't throw away the card. I would never have met you otherwise.'

'That's very sweet, Jack. The feeling's mutual.'

She didn't often drink whiskey. It was strong and it felt the most natural thing in the world to lean into him after he'd said that, resting her head on his shoulder encased in Daddy's thick Aran.

'It's that destiny thing again,' she murmured.

'What? You and me?'

She sat up, the room spinning a little. 'I meant finding out about the family secret. Maybe I was always meant to discover it.'

He stood up, removing the sweater. 'I should get going, Susannah.'

She noted the longer version of her name. She'd upset him.

'Don't talk rubbish, Jack. You're not the only one with a spare room. No need to go to a hotel. It's too late now, anyway. I'll make up Daddy's bed. Think of all the nights you put up with *me*. And I'm going to be cadging a room off you again soon.'

Giacomo was quiet over breakfast while Susannah chatted over arrangements for coming to Puglia.

'I'll give you a whistle-stop tour of Hastings if you like,' she suggested when she'd cleared away the dishes.

'I have to get back. I promised Loredana I wouldn't be away long. She's still getting to know the ropes in the bar.'

'That's a shame. Mind you, it's raining again. Not the best weather for sightseeing, anyway.'

At the door, she went to hug him but at that same moment he bent to pick up his rucksack and, awkwardly, they bumped heads.

'Let me know when you plan to arrive,' he said.

'Of course.'

After he'd gone, the house felt empty and she sat for a while in the living room, the fire in the stove burned down and cheerless.

'Well, what do you think of all that, Daddy?' She spoke aloud to her father's ashes in their ugly plastic pot on the chimney piece. 'What a turn-up, eh?'

. . .

One week later, still undecided as to whether she would ever tell her sister about Elsie's past, Susannah left Cobwebs again in the capable care of Maureen. She packed hand luggage for a long weekend in Puglia. Most days since receiving her letter, she'd spoken to Bella. Nonna Antonella was not very well; Susannah should come soon. One by one, the elderly folk in her life were passing on and Susannah felt sad, even for Elsie still lingering in hospital.

At the last minute, she transferred half of Frank's ashes into an empty plastic talcum powder container. She knew her father would have smiled and approved of this practical idea. Online she'd discovered that a certificate from the funeral directors was necessary if taking ashes abroad, but there'd been no time left to sort these regulations. She felt quite Italian as she concealed the container between her T-shirts and underwear in the middle of her case.

CHAPTER 40

Bella was unable to join Susannah on her first visit to the *trulli*, but as Giacomo already had the keys, he took her on his Vespa. Susannah clung tight as he navigated the bumpy dirt track that led to Nonna's place.

The strange little buildings were exactly how she had imagined from the sketches in Billy's notebook. The cluster of stone *trulli* resembled pixie hats or mushrooms sprouting from the stony ground, with their conical roofs. She imagined how, if she were to pull on one of the stones, the building might collapse, like a Jenga game. And yet from everything Giacomo had told her about their construction, she knew they were sturdy buildings.

A gust of wind swept through the branches of the laden olive trees, swaying in a welcoming wave as she climbed from the Vespa. She pulled off the helmet and scraped her fingers through her thick hair, taking in the view of what would become her properties once all legalities had been finalised. A cluster of three conjoined *trulli*, surrounded by fig and almond trees, and beyond, almost hidden by the thick, twisted trunks in an olive grove, a smaller *trullo*. In the distance the sigh of the sea and cries of seabirds called to her.

'Great setting, isn't it?' Giacomo said.

'It's very remote. I'd need my own transport.'

It took a while to open the door of the main *trullo*, but Bella had passed on instructions from Nonna about how to wiggle the key to the right and then to lift it fractionally while listening for a click.

It was like stepping into the pages of her grandfather's note-book and Giacomo smiled at her low whistle as he joined her.

'*Che meraviglia,*' he said. 'It is wonderful, isn't it? Stuck in time. I've been here to check a couple of times but it still moves me. So many of these old places have been done up with no thought to tradition.' He moved to the low sink and ran his fingers over the rough stone.

'Wow! Just wow!' Susannah said, turning to take it all in.

Hanging from hooks above the old-fashioned cooking stove were shining copper-bottomed pans, a blackened griddle, ladles of varying sizes and hand-carved wooden spoons. There was a dusting of soot on top of the stove and a battered, coffee-stained Moka pot, but apart from that, the little house gleamed. She recognised more of Nonna Antonella's distinctive driftwood and shell ornaments arranged on a shelf. A basket of old toys, a couple of wooden chests and a baby's cradle took up space in a small alcove, curtained off with gingham material. A ladder leant against a higher area where baskets and a tin bath were piled.

Behind another curtain, embroidered with seahorses and gulls, stood a double bed with a decorative metal headboard painted with flourishes of wild flowers. The counterpane was made of a pale, pale silk and divided into squares.

'It's their story,' she cried. 'I remember this from my grand-father's notebook. He wrote that Antonella spent evenings sewing scenes onto the material of his parachute.' She ran her fingers over the fine stitching. 'How wonderful! But I wonder why she didn't want to bring this to Vasto?'

'Maybe she felt it belonged to this place,' Giacomo commented. 'Her home of happy memories.'

'I can ask her myself when I visit her. Let's take a look at the small *trullo*,' she said, moving out into the sunshine. 'It's where my *nonno* slept when he first arrived.' Today was one of those balmy, misty autumn gifts, the air warm, filled with birdsong and the lazy hum of the last bees.

The second key opened a large padlock on a chain. As she pushed the door open, a mouse scuttled across the floor and disappeared behind a pile of sacks. She wrinkled up her nose. 'I'd make this into a guest room. But the rodents would have to be evicted first.'

He laughed. 'You're already planning a guest room, eh? And I thought you said the place was too remote?'

'Yes, well. It's absolutely charming, isn't it? What's not to like? I don't know about recharging batteries... I could recharge *everything* here. Perfect for a get-away-from-it-all holiday.'

'The beach is a stone's throw. Shall we explore?' he asked.

Thyme grew along the path, lined with umbrella pines and rosemary plants with their scattering of the last pale blue flowers of the season, the colour of sea mist. Susannah ran her hands along the aromatic bushes, the view of the sea below framed by the tall trees, their fallen cones strewn along the way.

'Late autumn at home, it's never as warm as this,' she said. 'Is there anything not to like about your beautiful country, Jack?' She stopped for a moment, drinking in the view of a couple of fishing boats in the distance, framed through the trees. 'It will be a steep climb back,' she said, suddenly breaking into a run. 'Race you.' She laughed as she set off, but Giacomo overtook her easily.

He was waiting for her at the bottom, the sand on the beach clean and deserted. She did three cartwheels. 'This is so, so perfect. I feel so freeeeeee...' she shouted, pulling off her top and jeans and running into the sea in her underwear.

He caught her enthusiasm and joined her, getting his foot stuck in one jean leg and toppling over in his haste. She laughed and when he had sorted himself out, he performed a shallow dive and swam out to where she was doing backstroke. He plunged beneath her and resurfaced alongside.

'To tell the truth, it's a little chilly for me. I prefer to swim in the heat of August. You are mad, Susi. What's got into you?'

'Who knows? Maybe because it all seems so crazy and improbable – to have been inside a *trullo* where my father's real father lived. To find out I am partly Italian, so part of me belongs here. Maybe I'm happier than I've felt in a long time... who knows why?' She shouted above the sound of the surf and then struck out further towards the horizon. When she turned back, she could see Giacomo on the beach, dressed again, sitting on a rock, watching her. He waved and she swam towards him slowly, savouring what would likely be the last hours in the sea until next summer, pushing Hastings and reality to the back of her mind.

He'd hung his boxers on a driftwood stick to dry and she laughed. Then, as he gazed at her, she suddenly felt embarrassed about her skimpy knickers and turned away from him. 'No peeking while I put on my jeans.'

With his back turned, he called out to her. 'Are you up for dinner in my favourite restaurant? And it's my shout this time.'

'I'd love that. But I've only these old jeans and...'

'No knickers. Yes, I know. Not the first time, either.'

'Don't remind me.' Then she giggled. 'I wonder if the old lady downstairs ever wondered if her knickers had shrunk when she found mine draped on her line. How do you say "knickers" in Italian?'

'*Mutande,*' he said, his face one wide grin. 'But I meant tomorrow for dinner. Plenty of time to find dry ones.'

'*Mutande,*' she repeated. 'I'll add it to my list.' She laughed. 'And I gladly accept your invitation for tomorrow. *Con piacere. Grazie.*'

With Giacomo it was easy to be herself because he was so laid-back. It was great to be in his company once again. When she'd accepted his invitation, his smile was more of a beam. She'd forgotten how gorgeous he was. She felt tingly inside as she continued to pull on her clothes over her wet limbs and it had nothing to do with the cool air.

CHAPTER 41

Susannah woke at five thirty next morning, unable to sleep in, her mind filled with thoughts of her own father, of Elsie, of Roberto and Antonella, and reeling with ideas for the *trulli*. Giacomo and Loredana were up already, lingering over coffee and she joined them. Giacomo's hair was tousled, stubble on his face. He looked as if he'd passed a sleepless night and she tried not to imagine why.

'Tonight we're dining al fresco,' Giacomo announced. 'Wear jeans and your fleece.'

'Ooh exciting. My last night. Is Loredana joining us too? Where have you booked, Jack?'

'Don't worry about the details, Susannah. See you later. Got a busy day.' His chair scraped along the floor as he got up.

She noted the use of Susannah, rather than his usual affectionate Susi. He was strangely distant and prickly, in a rush to get to one of his new suppliers, she supposed. He gave Loredana a quick hug on his way out.

'If you prefer, *Giacomo*,' she said, playing the same card as he put on his leather jacket, 'we can call off tonight.'

'*A dopo,*' he said, as he picked up his car keys. He was out of the door before she could say anything else.

Loredana didn't want any help and Susannah slipped away to take pictures of the sun rising over the sea. She walked to the topmost quarter of Monte Sant'Angelo along the quiet alleyways. Through the shutters of some houses, she caught the sounds of people stirring: a tap running, the hushed murmurs of early risers. The morning chill made her breath steam in the empty street and she was glad of her fleece. A couple of cats eyed her hopefully from their shelter beneath the castle walls but they didn't pad over. Strays mostly inhabited rundown corners of town and generally weren't treated well, wary of people. Giacomo always left trays of leftovers outside his kitchen door, explaining the cats were useful for keeping down vermin, but she had caught him more than once stroking them.

Pleased with her images of the sun's gold wake on the sea and fishing boats setting sail for the day's catch, she was ready for breakfast. The sweet aroma of fresh bread and sweet rolls enticed her through the door of a small bar. As she dipped a delicious *pastarella* in her cappuccino, she considered where and when to scatter her father's ashes. She bought a picnic for lunch and as she walked down towards the sea, she decided she wanted to visit Antonella. She would ask Loredana to book her a taxi. Blow the expense; some things were more important than money. She dialled Bella's number to ask if it was convenient to come over.

Bella enveloped her in a warm hug at the door. 'It's so good to see you again, Susannah. I haven't told Nonna, so it will be a special surprise.'

A bed had been moved into the garden room overlooking the sea, pillows propped up behind Antonella's back so that she could gaze at the waves tumbling to the rocky shore below the house.

Susannah sat beside her new *nonna*, hoping she would wake up soon but not wanting to disturb her. Her eyes were closed, her face serene in rest, her olive skin smooth for a woman of her age. Susannah looked around the sunny room, at the brightly coloured crochet blankets draped over the chair where Bella sat, the spider plant hanging from a hook by the window, bursting with its babies, the unusual driftwood creations on the walls. It was a room filled with life.

'What are you thinking about, *cara mia*?' Antonella's voice was barely audible as her eyes flickered open.

Susannah bent to gently kiss her cheek.

'I was hoping you would come,' the old lady said, catching Susannah's hand in her own. 'How wonderful!'

'I *had* to see you. How could I not? Not only to thank you for your wonderful gift, but to see you again. *Grazie*, Nonna.'

'You are so welcome. I had many happy years in my *trullo*. There were difficult times too. But, overall, I was happy. You will find happiness there too, Susannah, *cara*.'

Bella was quietly interpreting for the two women and Antonella smiled, wagging her finger as she told Susannah she must learn to speak Italian soon. 'I know one or two words only in English, but of course Roberto spoke perfect Italian, so there was no need. But you've read his notebook, haven't you? By now, you know our story.'

'And I treasure it, Nonna.'

'The notebook cannot tell you everything, though,' Antonella continued. 'You can't know how I anguished about what to do for the best at that time. We were taught as little children to accept what came along. But our world was turned upside down. How could I accept everything that followed in those terrible years?'

She stopped talking, her breathing laboured and Bella came over to pour her grandmother a glass of water.

'Don't speak, Nonna,' Susannah said. 'It's enough just to sit with you, to be with you.'

Antonella shook her head. 'I need to tell you, my darling.' She sipped more water and settled back against her pillows, once again taking Susannah's hand.

'For a long time, I had to fend for myself. I trusted nobody. So that when your grandfather Roberto came along, I couldn't bring myself to trust him either. I didn't listen to what my instincts were telling me, because my trust in life had been shattered. But he was a good man. I nearly lost him. I needed calm to listen to the small voice inside my head that was trying to speak to me... You two girls, my girls, you should take time to listen too, and go with your hearts, otherwise you could miss what is waiting for you.'

Her eyes closed and Susannah sat for a while longer, until she was sure that Antonella slept. Then, she gently released her fingers and tiptoed from the room with Bella.

The two young women embraced, staying in a long hug. When they pulled apart, both of them had tears in their eyes.

'I wish I could stay longer, Bella, but I shall be back as soon as I can.'

'I'll keep you posted about Nonna. Thank you so much for coming to see us. Take care and we must keep in touch.'

Outside Mo Vini, a carriage was parked, its bridled horse eating from a nosebag. The beautiful animal turned his head when she approached and the harness clinked.

Giacomo came out, carrying a basket, which he stored in the back. 'Hurry and change into something warmer,' he said. 'Loredana told me you'd gone to visit your grandmother, but I thought you'd run away back to England when it began to grow dark.'

'Sorry, Jack! I simply had to go and see her. But on the way back, there was so much traffic coming out of Vasto and the taxi driver didn't want to hurry as he'd already got a speeding ticket last week.'

'Well, you're here now. I thought you'd like to try one of our popular methods of tourist transport before you leave.'

'Wow! How brilliant. Where did you rustle this from?'

'A friend of a friend. When you stay in one place long enough, you build up useful contacts.'

Fetching her fleece from the spare room, she hurried downstairs. In the bar, Loredana was rinsing glasses and the girl waved a hand.

'*Buon divertimento*, Susannah. Have fun!'

'Won't Loredana mind?' she asked Giacomo as he helped her into the carriage. For a crazy moment she wanted to keep hold of his hand.

'Why should she mind?' He indicated where she should sit. 'If you're cold, there's a blanket.'

'I feel like a *nonna* being taken out for an evening outing,' she said.

'If you want to act like a *nonna*, then feel free.'

He was still tetchy and she didn't comment on his strange reply but sank back into the padded seating and watched while he climbed onto the front of the carriage. He sat up straight and picked up the reins, a whip set in his right hand. Making a clicking noise with his tongue and commanding the horse to '*Cammina!*', they moved off down the road.

After a while, he took a dirt track and talked to her over his shoulder. 'This horse is a Conversano, originally from a famous breed called Lipizzano, brought here in the sixteenth century from Austria.'

'How do you know all these facts?'

'I worked as a tourist guide when I was a student. And I love my area. Are you comfortable back there?'

'So comfortable I could nod off.'

'Like a *nonna*?' he asked, throwing a cheeky grin over his shoulder.

She wanted to tell him she felt anything but a *nonna* and that she'd prefer to have him sitting close beside her in the back while he pointed out the various tourist hotspots. But she didn't. It was crazy the effect Italy had on her, making her feel romantic and gooey. And anyway, he had a girlfriend. A girl-friend with long legs, long hair. And very short, tight skirts.

Giacomo stopped a couple of times along the track to point out plants: sea daisies growing from cracks in the cliffside like a natural garden and, further along, white lilies dancing in the breeze.

'We call this section of the coast *la terra delle fate*, land of the fairies. Don't you think the plants look like tiny dancing figures? Their Latin name is *Pancratium maritimum*.'

She was impressed with his knowledge and told him so.

'I include these facts on my Wild Tours.'

He moved on and pulled up at a semi-ruined tower at the edge of the sea.

'This is where I brought your American tourists. There are many of these towers along the coast,' he explained. 'Fifteenth century bastions against looting Saracen pirates searching for riches and galley slaves along the coast. When we were naughty children, my *nonna* used to threaten that if we weren't good, the *saraceni* would take us away in the night.'

'Where's the restaurant?' she asked, looking round, picturing him as a curly-haired urchin.

'There isn't one.' He helped her down, his breath warm on her cheeks as she leant towards his outstretched arms.

Her eyes were drawn inexplicably to his mouth and she realised he was growing a moustache. That explained the unshaven look of this morning. What would it feel like against her skin? She shook away the idea as he set her down.

'I've brought supper to eat al fresco. Follow me.'

He fetched the basket from under the seat and led her to the top of the squat tower, having tied up the beautiful Conversano horse to a ring in the stonework.

'A fire would be lit up here on this flat area as an early warning system if pirates were about. Then the next tower would follow suit and so on. There were eighty or so along this coast.'

He laid a rug down and opening the lid of the basket, he produced a bottle and silver-foil containers.

'Mm! There's something delicious in there. I can smell it. I've said it before, Jack. You are such an *amazing* friend.'

He stopped in his tracks and she noticed how his shoulders tensed.

'What have I said, Jack?' she asked.

There was a brief silence before he replied. 'Let's eat and drink.'

He knelt opposite her on the rug and busied himself with opening the bottle of red wine, sniffing the cork and nodding in approval. 'Primitivo. I hope you like it. New on this autumn's bar list.'

From the wicker basket, he produced wine glasses and poured two generous measures.

'*Cin cin,*' she said, clinking hers against his and he responded with, '*Alla salute.* Good health... wishing you a happy life, Susi.'

'That sounds like a goodbye but I'm coming back, you know. I'll be a very happy *trulli* owner soon. We can celebrate again when I've signed the contract.'

She watched as he expertly served up starters of rolled aubergines stuffed with ricotta and fresh herbs, using a fork and spoon in one hand to place them on white dinner plates.

The sun was low in the sky, the coastline bathed in a misty light. They perched side by side, leaning their backs against the base of the tower as they ate.

'I love that we're not using paper plates or plastic beakers for our picnic,' she said.

'What else did you expect?'

Waves crashing onto the rocks below filled the silence after his remark and she felt awkward in his presence, not for the first time today.

'How did you make this starter?' she asked, to fill the space.

'My cousin Lori made it. She's an ace at inventing *antipasti*. Whenever she comes, she freezes down batches for the restaurant.'

'Lori? You mean Loredana? Your *cousin*. I thought... I thought she was your girlfriend.'

He roared with laughter. 'Never. I can't believe you thought that. Quite apart from the fact we're related, she's very different from any girl I'd want to go out with.'

'I thought so too. But it's not the kind of thing you say, unless you know somebody really well.'

Giacomo didn't comment and busied himself with serving up slices of meat bathed in a creamy white sauce. '*Vitello tonnato*,' he said. 'Have you ever tried it?'

'No. What is it?'

'Okay. The ingredients are a strange combination, so just taste and see.' He cut her half a slice and fed it to her with a fork. Some of the sauce dropped on her chin and he wiped it away with his thumb.

'Mm. Lush! What is this?' Susannah blurted out, taken aback by the intimacy of his fingers touching her face.

'Veal with a sauce of tuna, fresh mayonnaise, anchovies and capers. Coming back into fashion. Just like *nonna* used to make,' he said, not moving away.

'It's to die for. I need the recipe, Giacomo. Fish and meat together. Who'd have thought?'

'We Italians. That's who. We are good at many things.' He paused. 'But not everything, unfortunately.' He topped up her wine, a testiness in his voice.

She felt slightly woozy, but she was enjoying feeling uninhibited.

'I shall miss you, Jack, when I go back to Hastings, but I hope you'll come and visit me when I stay in Nonna's *trullo*.' She laughed because the full moon was shining silver onto his head so that it looked like a halo. 'Is there a Saint Giacomo? Because if there isn't, you are the perfect candidate, my friend.'

He put down his glass and hunched his knees to his chest. 'You really don't get it, do you, Susannah?'

She was beginning to understand that when she upset him, the name Susi didn't exist.

'Get what?'

He flung out his arms, the calm, laid-back Giacomo that she had got to know over the past weeks turning animated, his eyes flashing as he spoke. 'Yes, I'm your *friend*, Susannah. I am happy to be your *friend*, but it's not enough. I thought you knew by now what I feel. But it's pointless. It's good you're leaving tomorrow before I fall any deeper.'

Her mouth open, like a fish gasping for water, she didn't know what to say as he continued.

'From the day you walked into my wine bar, I fell for you. I didn't want to act like the stereotypical Italian who falls for the pretty *straniera*. But I did. You were different. You... you light me up. How many times have I shut my bar to share time with you? My customers are beginning to complain I'm no longer reliable; they don't know when I'll be open. But none of that mattered because I wanted to be with you. You make me laugh. You're beautiful, interesting... but I'm beginning to feel like a fool. And if I'm honest... used, as well: like a chauffeur, ready to drop everything when you ask a favour. Loredana keeps warning me but I don't want to listen, because my heart tells me not to.'

He stood and walked to the edge of the tower, hands deep in his pockets and she rose to stand next to him.

'I'm so sorry, Jack. I didn't know. It's a surprise for me to hear this. A *wonderful, glorious* surprise. I mean, I never imagined we could get together...'

'Why not?'

'I thought you had little respect for me because of Mario, for one thing. And then there are the practicalities: I live in England. You live in Italy. There's my work. Your work. So much to think about.'

'Practicalities! Work!' He spat out the words. 'Then that spells to me your feelings aren't the same. Otherwise, all those considerations wouldn't matter. You don't see me like I see you... To me, love knows no frontiers...' He broke off and paced about the roof, his voice raised against the sound of the surf. 'We talk about *un colpo di fulmine* in our language when we fall for someone. It's like lightning and you're powerless to do anything about it. And that's how I felt.'

'You mean love at first sight?'

'Yes.'

'I don't know what to say. I've been cautious because of what happened with Mario, but...' She moved near him and her hand crept into his. 'Kiss me, Jack.'

A frown on his face, he turned. 'Don't play with me, Susi.'

'If you won't kiss *me*, I'll kiss *you*.' She placed her hands on his cheeks, drawing him down until their lips met, Nonna Antonella's words ringing in her ears: *listen to your heart... otherwise you could miss what is waiting for you...*

His mouth didn't move at first, almost stubbornly she imagined, but very quickly his arms were round her and he was pulling her close. As their kiss grew deeper, she tasted desire and then she giggled.

'Are my kisses so ludicrous?' he asked, drawing back.

'They're like lightning,' she said, pulling him close and after that no more words were spoken. *Love conquers all, doesn't it?* she thought, as she concentrated on the matter in hand, trusting her instincts, like Nonna had eventually done.

CHAPTER 42

MONTE SANT'ANGELO, MONTHS LATER

In Casa Vintage, Susannah opened the clasps on a gentleman's nineteenth-century Asprey leather travelling case and pulled out six cut-glass bottles with silver tops. The bag would sell easily. Who might have used it? she wondered, as she reached for polish to buff up the tarnished tops. Had the owner taken it on a grand European tour a hundred years ago? Would Puglia have been part of the itinerary? She paused in the unwrapping of these treasures from England before carefully arranging a set of Victorian rose-patterned teacups on her marble shop counter. On her visit to Puglia, Maureen had stayed in the small guest *trullo* where Billy had slept during the early days after his arrival with his angel wings. She'd driven over various items of bric-a-brac from Hastings and small pieces of furniture in her van. The fact that there were new import and export regulations in force since Brexit was no great problem as this was a new venture and they had nothing to compare with.

It is what it is, Susannah thought as she unwrapped a teapot lid from tissue paper. There was a similar saying she'd learned in Italian: *è quello che è*. She had found a lady in town to sew various cross-stitch samplers for her with similar mindfulness quotes to hang up in Casa Vintage and many of her customers preferred the English-language versions. In fact, her style of shop was a novelty here in southern Italy and she'd been kept busy since opening. She followed the same pattern as in Cobwebs and set out goods in scenes that told part of a story. Her Italian was better with each week that went by as she used it every day and Jack didn't always correct her handwritten price tags.

'*Non importa*,' he told her. 'It doesn't matter. They know you're *inglese*. The errors are cute and a talking point for clients.'

Many customers were surprised when she opened her mouth to speak, because although her Italian was improving all the time, she hadn't managed to shake off the unmistakable accent. She probably never would. 'But you look Italian,' they would comment, 'with your dark hair and olive skin.' And then she would reply that her *nonno* had been half-Italian. 'It's a long story,' she'd tell them. 'Someday I will write a book about it. Our children will need to know their roots.'

Her fears of losing her independence and identity by moving to Puglia and acclimatising to a new life had been converted to a sense of adventure that still thrilled her with each new day. She glanced at her favourite cross-stitch Italian sampler behind the counter, and smiled. She knew it off by heart:

Non so dove vada la mia strada, ma cammino meglio quando la mia mano stringe la tua. I don't know where my road is taking me, but I walk better when my hand is tightly clasped in yours.

Giacomo's hand was always there when she needed it. He wasn't flowery in the way he showed his love. There were no extravagant words of passion but when he said something, she knew instinctively that he meant it.

'I love you. We're good together aren't we, Susi,' he'd whispered to her this morning as they lay in bed. He'd stroked her tummy, just beginning to show her three months' pregnancy. 'And this little one will feel the same for his *mamma*,' he murmured as he gently kissed her. She felt cocooned by his love. It was the small, unexpected gestures she appreciated. Arranging impromptu suppers on his day off at their favourite spot by the old watchtower, taking her on magical mystery tours to quiet corners of Puglia: like Massafra, a town riddled with caves and canyons, or a walk deep into the Gargano forest, or a visit to the giant olive trees of Ostuni. A lifetime of discoveries awaited her to share with her new husband.

Casa Vintage was located six shops along from Mo Vini but Giacomo had moved in with Susannah to the *trullo* before their wedding, preferring to separate home life from work.

'We will buy an old *masseria* and fill it with beautiful *bambini*,' Giacomo had whispered to her after she'd told him she was pregnant.

On a fine evening, the sky painted scarlet and amber, Giacomo helped her scatter Frank's ashes on the same ridge where Nonno Roberto and Nonna Antonella had laid her great-grandfather to rest. Nonna Antonella had passed away in her sleep not long after her last visit. On this beautiful, still night, Susannah thought of the plucky girl who had nursed a complete stranger back to health. A stranger who, unknown to her and him, had another life back in England. And a son, her own father. How strange and tangled were the paths that life presented. And how wonderful too.

'God bless you, Daddy,' Susannah whispered as she let his dust sift through her fingers to join the earth of the cliffs. 'Forever in my heart.' A slight breeze danced him away as she spoke aloud: 'You're in Puglia now.' She brushed away a tear. 'He was a good man, Giacomo. I'd love to name our son after him. Franco. Do you mind?'

Giacomo came over to stand behind her, embracing her, enfolding her from behind with his love – protective hands placed over her tummy. 'It's a perfect name, *tesoro*,' he said, kissing the top of her head.

She stood for a while longer, marvelling at how much love she felt for this man and her new homeland. *And there's room in my heart for more*, she said to herself. Standing here was like standing on the edge of the world. *No*, she corrected herself, *it's like standing on the edge of the beginning*.

A LETTER FROM ANGELA

Dear reader,

I want to say a huge thank you for choosing to read *The Postcard from Italy*. If you did enjoy it, and want to keep up to date with all my latest releases, just sign up at the following link. Your email address will never be shared and you can unsubscribe at any time.

www.bookouture.com/angela-petch

I hope you loved *The Postcard from Italy* as much as I enjoyed writing it, and if you did I would be very grateful if you could write a review. I'd love to hear what you think, and it makes such a difference helping new readers to discover one of my books for the first time.

The inspiration behind *The Postcard from Italy* came from an old black-and-white family photo of my uncle, dressed in his RAF uniform. His beautiful eyes are haunting, his face fresh. Sergeant William Francis Beary, 1584477, was my mother's only brother in a family of four girls. Twenty years of age, a rear gunner, he was shot down on the night of November 5th 1944 over what was then Yugoslavia. He and his crew members (five RAF and three RCAF) were on a mission with 178 Squadron to drop containers near Ljubljana, now in Slovenia, for partisans behind enemy lines. They flew in their Lockheed Liberator from Amendola, one of a complex of many military airfields in the wide flat area of land around Foggia and Bari, in southern Italy. Their plane crashed to the ground in flames in Gornji Grad, Zagreb (now Croatia), shot down by a German Messerschmitt night fighter.

When we researched further, the Ministry of Defence replied: 'Tragically the aircraft failed to return and all the crew were designated as Missing... At war's end, the squadron undertook enquiries to establish the fate of KH100 and it was established that the aircraft had come down in Gornigrad, Yugoslavia, and that the crew had been buried there in a communal grave.'

I never met Uncle Billy, as he was known by family and friends. How I would have loved to. So, I invented a story where I could. I have him surviving, but suffering from amnesia.

I myself had a frightening attack of transient global amnesia three years ago. Four hours of my life were completely lost to me. Only my family can fill in what happened during that time. Billy's bout lasts for longer and led to complications, but I've wondered since what I might have done in my missing hours if I hadn't been hospitalised.

I visited Puglia with my husband in 2019 and I was captured by the wild beauty of this region. Having written four books set in Tuscany, it was time for a different setting and a story slowly wove its way into my imagination. I hope you are tempted by my descriptions of this captivating area and will visit. Masseria della Torre is based on a real boutique hotel, but the owner is far from being Mario...

War wreaked havoc on relationships. In writing *The Postcard from Italy*, I did extensive research about rear gunners in the RAF, from accounts written by veterans of World War Two, but one particularly amazingly intimate book about the women left behind at home went to my heart. Julie Summers' *Stranger in the House: Women's Stories of Men Returning from the Second World War* helped form the character of Elsie.

Elsie is understandably shocked when Billy turns up out of the blue after the war. Britain had changed in his absence and so had Elsie. There were many 'war-confused' unions like hers and Cedric's. By the end of the war, love was about the only thing left unrationed it had to be grabbed whenever and wherever possible. And Elsie grabbed it. Hasty wartime marriages resulted in 34,000 divorces in the UK in 1945–6. I do not judge Elsie for trying to find happiness with a new man. Adaptability was the key for many women whose lives were profoundly altered as a result of World War Two.

Hastings, in Sussex, is another location I have drawn upon. My father loved antiques, a passion started during the war, when he and my mother married and hated the utility furniture issued to them. It was definitely not a fashion at that time to buy second-hand, but they loved old furniture and Daddy, like Frank, loved repairing what others considered rubbish, even rescuing discarded furniture from the side of the road. As children we spent many Saturdays trailing round the junk shops of Old Hastings with them. There is a little bit of myself in Susannah's character and Daddy did actually make me a rather large dolls' house one Christmas. I have played artistic licence with some of the Hastings settings, so I hope I am forgiven for having shoehorned certain venues and events into my story. But I do have a soft spot for this old fishing town.

I love hearing from my readers and I always do my best to reply. I would love to hear what you think about Billy, Antonella, Elsie, Nonno, Frank, Susannah, Giacomo, Mario and the others – you can get in touch on my Facebook page, through Twitter, Goodreads or my website.

Angela Petch

KEEP IN TOUCH WITH ANGELA

www.angelapetchsblogsite.wordpress.com

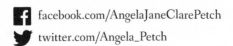 facebook.com/AngelaJaneClarePetch
twitter.com/Angela_Petch

QUESTIONS FOR READING GROUPS

1. Susannah travels to Italy and is quickly seduced by Puglia. At the end of the story, she is living in Italy with Giacomo, who says, 'Love knows no frontiers.' Do you agree? How easy would it be to uproot and move to a different country, a different culture? Can you think of any difficulties you might encounter?
2. During the war, Antonella becomes involved with Salvatore and the black market. Do you approve?
3. Antonella buries her grandfather without notifying the authorities and, similarly, Susannah scatters her father's ashes without gaining official permission. Did these two events upset you?
4. How important are the settings in this story? Would you like to visit Puglia? Have you ever visited Italy?
5. Elsie and Frank marry bigamously. How would you have reacted in their situations if you were either of these characters? Would you have made the same decisions?
6. Billy was taken in by strangers and nursed back to health. Poor country people in Italy harboured

many prisoners-of-war and refugees during World War Two, even though if caught, they could face the death penalty. Do you think you could do this, faced with the same situation?

7. The author uses a lot of Italian expressions in *The Postcard from Italy*. Is this annoying or do you think it enhances the story?

8. Do you have any favourite characters in *The Postcard from Italy*? If so, why? Similarly, are there any characters you do not like?

ACKNOWLEDGEMENTS

Thinking about whom to thank makes me anxious. Will I forget somebody? My books might be the result of my own research and imagination, but there is far more involved in giving birth to 100,000 words than my efforts alone.

My faithful, trusty editor, Ellen Gleeson, is always there with her wonderful insight and so she and the whole Bookouture team (aka the Family, without wishing to make them sound like the Mafia), are top of my list. Thank you. Without you, I would have far fewer bruises from where I've been pinching myself over the last couple of years, but I would not be reaching so many readers either. Italian kisses on both cheeks to you all and thank you for helping me realise a long-standing dream of publication.

My brother, Patrick Sutor, keeps himself busy researching family and I am grateful for all the information he provided about our uncle Billy. It was supplemented by books written by rear gunners who wrote about their experiences during World War Two. These very human records of courage are important memories, so thank you to aircrew members Don Charlwood and Ron Smith. I'm also grateful for a thesis I read by Dr Amy Louise Outterside: 'Occupying Puglia: The Italians and the Allies, 1943-1946'. Her work helped me visualise those years and understand more about the difficulties ordinary people dealt with during that period.

My Italian *amici*: Antonella (yes – I pinched her name!), Silvia and Marcello advised on correct Italian usage and customs, responding quickly to my desperate WhatsApp messages. Any mistakes are my own. *Mille grazie* to Isabella and Maurizio for creating their beautiful guest house, B & B Alla Canale. I fell in love with the Vasto coastline and the azure sea echoed in their blue terracotta planters. I knew I had to use this location sometime and it became one of the springboards for *The Postcard from Italy*. I've used artistic licence to pick up the fishing platform (*trabucco*) you can see silhouetted against the sunsets from their amazing terrace and place it further along the coastline. Similarly, the *trulli*, which are not really seen on the Gargano Peninsula, where Antonella and Roberto lived, have been spirited geographically to help paint my settings. My husband and I stayed in a quirky *masseria* guest house (Barone Gambadoro) and I was entranced by the décor, which features in my book as Mario's Masseria della Torre. So, I guess I'm including a huge *grazie* to *la bella Italia* in these acknowledgements: a beautiful country that inspires me to winkle out stories.

Thank you and apologies to my patient husband, Maurice, who never complains about my burnt or undercooked potatoes when I am engrossed in writing; who is always there to listen to me and help untangle plot knots; who reads my scrappy first drafts and offers sensible suggestions and brings me cups of tea or glasses of wine, depending on my writing barometer. You are simply the best.

And last but not least, thank you to my readers. When I sit at my desk, I'm writing for myself in that I have a story inside me that wants to get out. But I'm writing for you too and that is always topmost in my mind.

Made in United States
North Haven, CT
15 September 2023

41591234R10225